Boomerang

Short Stories in a Fictional Life

DICK SNYDER

authorHOUSE®

AuthorHouse™
1663 Liberty Drive
Bloomington, IN 47403
www.authorhouse.com
Phone: 1 (800) 839-8640

Published by AuthorHouse   07/15/2015

ISBN: 978-1-5049-1891-6 (sc)
ISBN: 978-1-5049-1890-9 (e)

Library of Congress Control Number: 2015910091

Print information available on the last page.

Any people depicted in stock imagery provided by Thinkstock are models,
and such images are being used for illustrative purposes only.
Certain stock imagery © Thinkstock.

This book is printed on acid-free paper.

Because of the dynamic nature of the Internet, any web addresses or links contained in
this book may have changed since publication and may no longer be valid. The views
expressed in this work are solely those of the author and do not necessarily reflect the
views of the publisher, and the publisher hereby disclaims any responsibility for them.

Contents

PART FOUR

Introduction

In January 2014, seeking some diversion, I began writing short story fiction to no particular purpose. It pleased me to create narratives drawn from life experience, adding imagination and finding characters that suited a particular account. Once begun, stories tumbled into my mind seemingly of their own accord. Characters surfaced in one story then re-emerged in another. Plot development became a delicate and often delicious imaginative undertaking. Now, in organizing the whole collection, I find that these stories portray significant periods of growth in my own life. In short, they seem to confirm the work of Erik Erikson, and I am surprised that they do.

Erikson created a theory of developmental psychology suggesting that humans evolve in stages throughout their lives, and that one can distinguish these different segments in pursuing both clinical analysis and interpretive history.

Hopes: Trust vs. Mistrust (oral-sensory, birth – 2 years)

Competence: Industry vs. Inferiority (latency, 5–12 years)

Fidelity: Identity vs. Role Confusion (adolescence, 13–19 years)

Love: Intimacy vs. Isolation (young adulthood, 20–24, or 20–39 years)

Care: Generativity vs. Stagnation (middle adulthood, 25–64, or 40–64 years)

Wisdom: Ego Integrity vs. Despair (late adulthood, 65 – death)

Now I discover that my stories, written without any current review of Erickson's work, resonate with his ideas.

So, here I am, serving up for myself and others who might enjoy them, fictional short stories which give me a peek into the progression of my life. When placed in a larger psychological construct, they provide me with an affirmation of a life well-lived, precisely what Erikson says I am most likely to do. Additionally, the stories may provide an interesting read for others who may find cues to an assessment of their own lives. If that occurs then my fiction, in serving them, will have served me well.

I am not alone in this adventure, swiftly joined by characters who surfaced into my imagination as I wrote: Barry Swanson, Peggy, Moe, Sister Mary Agatha, Lauren, Albert, Frick n' Frack, Lori Larken, Doris Dooling, Lilting Song and One Who Sees are among them. Tales of lost love, deceit, human frailty, adolescent behavior, mature commitments, life reflections, university politics and unusual business models also emerged along with a simple story of a day in the life of a homeless man whose only politics was one of self-definition and daily choice.

Over the past year, I have sent about half of these stories out to readers who were kind enough to respond with observation, critical comments, suggestions and encouragement. I have listened to them all, saved their reactions, and examined them in putting together these last drafts. A number of individuals gave my work exceptional time and reflection. Paul Magee invested many hours and thoughtful expertise in reviewing some of the main narratives, gently nudging me to try new forms of expression and suggesting ways to adjust story structures.

Maurine Ratekin, Bill Pemberton, Jim Parker, Lee Smith, Marilyn Reed and Dolly Hei provided me with diverse reader feedback and encouragement. Kent Estabrook, Terry Burke and Murray Johnson found the stories a good read. Tom Lutton first suggested that I publish the collection as a book. Linda Snyder read through every account, quietly offering suggestions for editing, phrasing and points of view. She is a very patient person.

Still, in the end these are my stories, and I bear all responsibility for their construct, tilt, subject matter and tone. I've had a great adventure writing them. I hope that you find them enjoyable.

Walt Farmer, June 2015

If you live long enough, most of your mistakes begin to look a lot like lessons.

Black to Light

At first there was nothingness. In time, there were sensations. It was the gurgling that first appealed to him, a soft washy kind of movement that let his body sway, even as it remained smoothly coated in the liquid around him. Sound resonated through it in powerful, tempered rhythm. Warm and fed, he did nothing to keep his body temperature normal. He flourished in this, the best of places, and when it ended, he wanted nothing more than to return. What else could one really long for? Had it been up to him, his tactile experiences would have remained as they had been, then recorded, repeated and renewed with every month, each passing year.

And yet, there came a day when the gurgling suddenly changed. Pressures around him strengthened and within hours he transitioned from the haven that heaven must surely have meant for him to emerge into a cold, wet space, without attachment, noticing that he needed air to breathe and wishing somehow that his pre-existence could become his default placement.

Of the concept of life, he had none. Of the need to struggle to maintain functions essential to his sense of well-being he was now fully aware. Pain became a new acquaintance, as did hunger, cold, dampness and most amazingly of all, a recognizable need for some person outside his body to care for his new range of senses.

Being fed, dried, cleaned, warmed, touched...all in their time and moment... came as close as he might have hoped to recreating that state of existential satisfaction where the past remained black, the future unimagined, and life unfolded in time fully concealed. Still, there was the loss of that liquid balm, that comforting solution that bathed him, floated him, kept him connected to all that he needed and let him enjoy his occasional twists and turns with passive resistance and gentle support. Wherever that place where he once felt safe, he wanted to return.

His first opportunity came when he learned that he had mobility, that in an odd but effective way he could move his body from place to place. Unsure at first, his curiosity... something he brought with him into the cold...led him to explore crawling, standing, lurching, walking. It worked, and within a brief time he was mobile, on the move looking for newness, wearying, returning to sleep and the embraces that kept him warm, dry and fed.

The automobile stopped and he was set down upon the sand by parental hands. He looked about, saw liquid lapping a dozen paces from his feet and remembered the comfort, warmth and complete satisfaction it provided to him. He walked right in.

A colder liquid than he remembered, but supportive, it lifted his weight, invited him to return to that better place, and he walked until the steps were not there and he floated briefly, but with a new sensation...fear. This liquid denied him air. He splashed for breath, looked for it, could not find it, and then abruptly, far more abruptly than his last departure from liquid life, a hand lifted him gently from the water. It held him and the face imprinted itself. Father saved him. Mother gave him life, but father saved him. To them he made full commitment. If there were a path to the gurgling, a safe way to find security and an open-ended peace, it was through them. He would listen.

The bond that he found in each, father and mother, was an essential, intimate part of his every day, and soon, of his nights. What greater bliss could he have than sleeping between his parents, security on one side, love on the other. It worked for one night and the next, but on the third night, as he passed through the bathroom to their bedroom door, focusing on his natural placement, he found a barrier. A locked door! He turned, went back and circled through the kitchen and living room to the other bedroom entry. Unmovable! He went back to the bathroom door. He pounded and kicked, cried aloud for them to let him in, screamed for them to let him return to the security of their nest, let him become safe, sound, loved and well attended.

No answer. In an inkling he recognized that what he thought he possessed had disappeared. It might be provided from time to time in portions that were reassuring, but would it be there unconditionally? Could he be sure? How often might it need to be reaffirmed? He would never again be without doubt. Life presented itself and launched him into its stream that night just as surely as his journey from the womb seemed to be irreversible. He took note.

Mother, the one who loved him, fed him, taught him, also disciplined him. Red pepper on the tongue for saying a bad word. Slap on the butt for misbehavior. She socialized him with playdates, a kind of trial separation he decided, but one which he grew to enjoy.

3

When something called tonsils had to be removed, she taught him a strategy for crisis. "Listen to me, Walt" she said, "When the doctor puts a mask over your nose, and pours some ether on it, it will smell bad. You will not want to breathe it, but trust me, take deep breathes. If you fight it, you will be more sick after the operation. Accept it and you will find it is not so bad."

He took that breath, committed to her words. He trusted that this invasion of his body would be over soon and that his path to balanced equanimity would resume unaltered. A loose tooth changed the outcome. But then, he thought, new teeth appeared in his mouth regularly. What need had he for one just lost? But where did it go hiding?

Lungs weren't really necessary in that first place where fluids balanced all and he had no need to work at anything. But in this new world, he needed to use them unimpeded by restraint of any kind. There the tooth decided to reside, well outside its natural placement, and so for the first time he felt a new kind of warmth, a temperature that made his head perspire and his body weak, not the buoyant ease of floating, but the ache of muscle crying out for recovery.

Again, his mother counseled. "They are going to put you to sleep, send a tube down into your lung and remove that nasty tooth. Follow what the doctors say. It will not be painful. You will get well." He was learning to accept the inevitable.

Again, he took that leap of faith, and in the middle of the rescue of his lungs, he awoke, tubes in his mouth, just as mother had said, but he could not talk, could not breathe, could not move his arms, found himself bound to a fixed platform from which he had no strength to move. Taught to pray, he prayed for heaven, that place described to him as the buoyant, warm, haven from the world into which he had been placed, a pocket of love and equanimity that would last for eternity. There was nothing else to do.

He missed his journey. The doctors revisited his body, kept it safe and in time the tooth went looking for another home. He learned something. A father's hand could save him from a false journey into the liquid buoyance of lake water. There was security there. A mother's voice could counsel him into courage enough to meet the challenges presented by this world outside the safe fluids of her womb. There was love there. With parents, he believed that he could find his way. Over time, when that secure certainty disappeared and that unconditional love found its limits, he counselled himself that he would just have to find those twin essentials elsewhere... until he returned to that place where all was unknown and he was simply buoyant.

Little Rock

July 31, 1945: The woman sat in the corner of the Greyhound Station with three youngsters in chairs beside her and two suitcases parked in front. Small, dark-haired and slender-boned, her image shrunk even more when measured against the luggage at her knees, and the way her eyes scanned the room told any casual viewer that she was clearly on edge. On a wartime journey with children in hand and her man waiting, she rose to book a bus to Little Rock.

She spoke to the three tykes in their chairs, "I'm going just across the room to buy our tickets. I want you to stay right where you are. Watch me, but don't leave your seat. Do you understand?" Ages seven, six and four, they nodded a vigorous yes, their faces mindful of a brood of chicks listening to every cluck of the hen.

She approached the clerk, asked for tickets to Albuquerque and directions on handling luggage. "Headed for New Mexico, eh?" he asked. "Gonna' be moving there with your family?" he nodded toward the children.

"No," the mother replied, "We're headed for Little Rock, but I was told to get tickets here for Albuquerque then buy passage for the rest of the trip once we got there. Schedules are unpredictable, I guess."

"Good thinking," he commented as he rolled out the thin, orange coupons and stamped them for each destination: Barstow, Flagstaff, Albuquerque. He handed her the string of paper permits, saying, "I can take your luggage now, and get it set up for storage on the bus." She walked to where the children were sitting, then took the two cases, one at a time, back to the clerk.

"Packing light?" he smiled.

"Well," she replied, "This will get us there and then we will see what we need next."

The clerk punched the tickets for the luggage, murmuring, "Right, I wouldn't do it any other way. Lot more humid in the South...don't know what you need 'til you get there. Husband in Little Rock?"

"Yes," she said, "He's in the army at Camp Robinson, an MP, and I just decided that it was time to join him."

The clerk handed her the claim stubs, commenting, "You're doing the right thing...no tellin' how long this war is going to go on. Bus should be leavin' in about 20 minutes."

She returned to the children. They had not uttered a peep and their faces held a bright-eyed silence, a by-product of awe. Their eyes flashed on people of different colors and ages, some in uniform, a few in field clothes, even a man with a tie. They heard unfamiliar conversations, a chatter of Spanish, the terse phrases of the fields, rolling syllables from black people, an occasional white drawl, the quiet murmur of a few educated travelers. They were all taking the bus together: new companions, new personalities, everything new.

Promptly at 6:00 a.m. the Greyhound pulled out of the station and headed for Barstow. As she unfolded her travel map, the mother quietly nodded agreement to what she had been told: "It's a 36 hour trip. No restrooms until you make stops. Kids get antsy. It's a long, long time for them to be on a bus."

She had some ideas about keeping them engaged: crayons, books, cards, a few postcards that had pictures of where they might be traveling. But her best friend was the night when they might be lulled to sleep and she could get some rest.

On the highway the bus gradually found its rhythm. Quiet talk surfaced among the passengers. The oldest boy seemed well absorbed by the scenery. The youngest, a girl, just stayed close to her mother while the other boy spent time watching the strange new faces. They were quiet as fawns following silent instructions. Miles disappeared as the wheels kept rolling.

Dark when the bus stopped in Albuquerque, most passengers disembarked, and the mother roused the children, took them into the depot to use the bathrooms again and bought her second set of tickets. She waited patiently in line while they awakened to yet more strange sounds, new smells and heavy, smoke-filled air. She asked the agent where she might find her luggage and transfer it to the next bus. He pointed over his shoulder to a collection of suitcases. "You'll find yours in that pile."

She reminded the children to keep holding hands and to follow her. She went to the cases, placed them one at a time next to bus #23, destination Little Rock. As she hauled the second case over, the driver noticed her and her tagalongs. She looked tired but resolved, and he knew that she had a long way to go.

He approached and said softly, "Maam, there's usually quite a crowd that goes from Albuquerque to Little Rock. Some get off in Oklahoma City, but most go on through. Seats get scarce when we board. Would you like to board the bus now with the children and be sure that you have seats. I'll put your luggage under the coach, and you'll be set for the rest of the trip."

She looked him in the eye, straightened her weary body and said politely, "That would be very nice. I would appreciate it very much." The brood followed her, and she followed the driver as they quietly left the depot and went to their bus. He stored the luggage under her watchful look, led them on board and found seats for the four of them, two by two on the left side of the aisle.

Twenty minutes later, the crowd boarded. Six people had to wait four hours and the next departure. The driver closed the door, let the engine rev up a bit, put it in gear, slowly pulled out of the depot and hit the open road. In a half hour, the children found their dreams again. At the stop in Amarillo, four people departed and the oldest boy took up some space at the very back of the bus. In the quiet, he lay down.

The engine purred just below his body, and as he maneuvered to rest he smelled the clean, cool scent of outside air leaking into the bus from a small hole just below the window. He relaxed and slept, dreaming that he soared on his own wings in the fresh starlit night above him. When little exclamations awakened him, he took a peak out the window. Lights glittered in Oklahoma City, a bright display after the many hours of darkness, and the boy stared a long time as the bus gradually approached, then immersed itself into the city.

It was a long stop. The mother treated them all to ice cream, and she made sure that the restrooms were clean and usable. Back on board they went on into the night. The sun rose before them and the Greyhound continued toward Little Rock, arriving finally at 3:00 p.m. and after some traffic maneuvers, pulled into the depot.

The woman grew increasingly excited, eyes brightening as they moved through the city. She adjusted her clothing, put on fresh lipstick and spit washed the children's faces. She had not seen her husband for six months, and a lot had happened: tonsillectomy for one boy, eye surgery for the other, a severe bout with chicken pox for the little girl. She could write about it all, and he could tell her how brave she was, and how much he missed her, but pen and paper could not substitute for breath and touch. Their letters rarely languished into the routine words of daily doings at a time of uncertain future.

War in Europe over, his next stop would be in the Pacific invading Japan. He joked that MP's only waded ashore to keep peace among American troops and doubted that he would be dealing with Japs. She was not so sure. At her core, she just felt that she had to be with him, whatever the accommodations, however long it might be, whatever might happen during the rest of the war. For now, they would take what time they could get.

The bus pulled into Little Rock station, and she saw him standing there, smiling, waving, welcoming. In uniform, walking to greet them, delivering security with every step, he pulled his five foot tall wife into his six foot body with arms that held her as might a clamp. Their kisses, full, long and breathless, said how much they were missed, and how intensely they might be resumed. Then, he turned toward the children, picked up the little girl and held her for a long time because she would not let go.

With his other arm he nestled the two boys next to him and made small talk about the trip. What did they like best? Did they meet new people? Did they behave themselves? Mother answered the last question, "They were just wonderful, all the way, all the time. They were so grown up. It was as good a trip as it could be, and we're here!"

11

Father took the family to a local hotel where he had reserved two rooms, one for the children and one for him and her. They spent an hour letting the youngsters unwind, inspecting the bed for ants and finally settling them into the deep sleep of secured passage. They spent the next hour getting reacquainted in their own room.

The next morning his friend, MP Dick Staley, took them to their new home in the country. Staley's wife, Marian chatted with the mother, and the two women forged an immediate bond that lasted years beyond the war.

They stopped at a store to get some groceries, and the children ate a banana for the first time in their lives. Continuing on into the countryside, the car moved down a large paved street and paused to turn in front of a beautiful, large white house. Her new home she thought? Her husband had promised only a clean, comfortable place to live. He hadn't said that it was huge.

It wasn't. Staley turned the car left and drove down a lane running alongside the Big House. A hundred yards later, he turned left again and parked in front of a small, sharecropper's cabin. It had a kitchen, living room, two bedrooms, a wood stove, indoor plumbing and windows to let breezes pass through.

She looked at it hard and assessed her home. The space appeared so small, tiny really, and she had never used a wood stove. How did that work? Five paces and she went from kitchen to bedroom, close quarters indeed she thought.

She walked outside, saw horses roaming a pasture which began five yards from the house, and beyond the horses, cows, lazily grazing, undisturbed by her arrival. Large animals. They would take some getting used to. She walked back into the house. The bedrooms, square with space enough for only sleeping beds appeared clean, bedsheets stacked in a small pile on the foot of the mattress. She could arrange the children's room to suit their needs and she knew their energy would take them outdoors most of the time. Would snakes, ants and bugs become a danger? At least the indoor plumbing worked. It would all work.

The calendar recorded August 1st and for the next week mother and father worked at settling into some kind of routine. She learned that the wood stove had rules of its own, requiring a careful balance between temperatures and wood supply, but to her dismay, the black beast steadily whispered ashes throughout the little house. She hated an unclean home, and the onslaught of summer heat helped her make a decision. Within the week she let the coals die, serving the family dry, canned and refrigerated food.

In the evenings, she and her husband shared cards, drinks and laughter with the Staley's, talking about the Japs, the pace of military life at the camp and whether there would be another depression after the war. Word around the post focused on a shipping out date of December. "Christmas in Hawaii," her husband joked and Staley laughed a lot at that. She wondered if she would remain in Little Rock?

The boys found adventures in the barn, the young one being kicked by a horse to no permanent injury, the other riding a horse all by himself in the company of two older boys from the Big House who rode just like cowboys. The little girl stayed close to her mother, watching her cook, watching her clean, watching her every move so as to be just like her.

As the mother looked around the property that first week, she absorbed an array of green flourishing plants, sturdy trees and the smell of fresh rain. It didn't rain much back home where parched brown lands filled every landscape, accented with tumbleweeds and blots of black oil. Here thunderstorms sometimes flooded the fields and red mud tracked across dark, green grass as might old bloodstains on a dusky tile. High temperatures kept everyone but the children quiet during the day, and she tried to adjust to what Marian called Southern climate.

Erratic winds moved through the fields at night accompanied by distant sheet lightning and rolling thunder, sounds so deep that she thought it might be artillery. High humidity, inescapable and enveloping, forced her into lightweight dresses. Frightened one morning by the sound of a horse grazing outside her window, she insisted her husband fix the pasture fence. Once safe, she grew to enjoy the sounds of the horses, their blowing nostrils and munching jaws. Living in Little Rock seemed more and more a safe haven, an adventure with boundaries, but they would not reach those limits until the army shipped off to fight in the Pacific.

Still, she found herself laughing as she had not laughed for six months, light-hearted about each morning, ready to live an unpredictable day as every day could be, yet finding each one refreshing in its newness, enticing in its ability to impose love on the profession of death. Soldiers moved about the roads with purpose. Sometimes they smiled. Sometimes they appeared lost in thought.

A Sunday visit to Camp Robinson took her and the children through the Mess Hall, sampling food, listening to jokes, sharing the bravado of certainty amidst uncertain futures. She smiled while listening to boasts of invincibility in the face of war's impersonal assault on mortality. Well, "who knew?" she thought, and noted to herself that the popular song, *Sentimental Journey*, said it all: *"Gonna set my heart at ease..."*

Her husband became her nightly companion, and their intimacy seemed laced with a kind of urgency which belied the ten years they had been married. Their whispers, flavored with chuckles and giggles, recalled early courtship memories and the morning never dawned without laughter that all the children could hear and sometimes shared.

As the week passed, they held sober conversations about Japan. Japs didn't quit and conventional wisdom all through the ranks proclaimed an invasion of the home islands. When that happened a lot of people were going to die. He and Staley joked about the fun of vomiting on a troop ship taking them to Hawaii, perhaps Okinawa, to prepare for the big landing. But in the night, he and she whispered their concerns to one another more quietly.

They awakened on August 7, to hear that the Air Force had dropped some kind of bomb on Japan, and that it had caused terrible damage, destruction so severe that many were saying that the war might end immediately. Three days later, they heard the words, "atomic bomb", "Hiroshima" and "Nagasaki".

They marveled that a weapon, a single weapon dropped by a single plane, could burn a city to the ground. The joy of a possible sudden end to the war began to build in their chests and eclipsed entirely any compassion for Japs incinerated or flash-fried into concrete, crushed by exploding buildings or doomed to radiation poisoning. Hiroshima...payback for Pearl Harbor.

The whole army base surged with hope, a growing conviction that the war might end soon, vanishing their nightmares of dying in Tokyo. Still, no word. Tension grew, silencing Camp Robinson as though an invisible force had stealthily robbed every soldier of his voice. Then, the unbelievable, but inescapable news that the war was OVER! Done! The Japanese had surrendered. Camp Robinson would not be sending its soldiers overseas. They would not be vomiting into the Pacific, would not be picking up shrapnel from mortars nor burning in ships hit by kami-kaze planes. They would not be dying on the shores of Japan, nor searching for lost limbs amidst the surging waters that touched the beaches of Honshu.

She and her husband began to make plans for a different kind of future. Before the end of the month, he learned that his unit would be processed for discharge in San Antonio. *"Yahoo, San-An-Tone"* became the new soldier's greeting call, and it echoed around the parade grounds from dawn to dusk.

She decided to take the children back home. On August 31, one month after they had arrived, they climbed aboard a west bound Greyhound bus. Unknown to her, she carried a child, an affirmation of the tender, intimate, fulfilling time that she and her husband shared in the little house down that lane. Could life be that way when they were together again? The future she would trust to her prayers. For now, she felt only joy and took a peek at a better life without war and maybe without economic depression.

When they arrived in Los Angeles, her father picked them up, and she moved into her parent's Ventura home for the few months it would take for the army to release her husband. Then, a new beginning, facing the more gentle challenges of raising their family.

How would it be, she wondered? Life always had its challenges. Things changed. Children grew up, jobs disappeared and life evolved in its own mysterious, unpredictable ways. But, she comforted herself, the entire family had a wartime adventure to remember. Each of them saw new horizons, learned new customs, ate new foods and lived new lives, all accompanied by the uncertainty of unpredictable days. She would never miss that damn wood stove, but it claimed its place in her memories. Little Rock. He and she together. Children safe. Income enough. In later years, she always said that it was the happiest month of their marriage.

Gaming Sister Agatha

I didn't see her coming. Few ever did. Born in Ireland, shipped to America by relatives who did not have a place for her in their homes, she found Christ, and Jesus found her. Her commitment to the Dominican Order allowed her to fashion a life filled with the antics and taunts of children, challenged by the ways of the nunnery and imbued with a sense of justice that previewed the didactic judgments of reality TV judges, whom she lived long enough to see, and whom she always described as "weak".

She greeted me and the other kindergartners with a genuine but thin smile and spoke to us in that slightly higher range voice that carried her through her years, implanting rules and declarations upon hundreds of youngsters looking for guidance, at first, then looking to escape.

There was never an escape. She would have none of it. She didn't advise, didn't offer alternative choices, didn't suggest getaway hatches. She saw right and called it out loud and clear. She saw wrong and her face, carefully framed by the oval in her wimple, twitched a bit as she narrowed her eyes, adjusted her glasses and then fixed her gaze on the offender.

To us youngsters, to be identified by name as a wrong-doer was prelude to being called before the priest, a frightening prospect in our wildly active imaginations, though in the history of St. Mark's no student ever went through the scourging of a priestly reprimand. Sister Agatha's blistering corrections seemed to work just fine in maintaining order, love of God and a commitment to studies.

Yet my history with her had yet to be written. Hustled into kindergarten at age four, because, as my mother said, "You are ready for school," a euphemism that I came to interpret as being, "I am tired of dealing with your daily shenanigans," I nonetheless found myself bound over to the nuns of the Dominican Order and began the daily habit of walking to school.

We assembled in a cavernous room on the first floor of St. Mark's wherein K-2 students found themselves nicely separated by proclaimed rows and seats, cautioned against speaking unless asked and managed by the heroic energies of Sister Agatha. We attended to her every word because our parents told us to. But we also listened to her guidance of first graders who had their own set of lessons and the second graders who seemed to live in an academic world as far from us kindergartners as we might imagine the moon to be from the earth.

In the first days I found myself filled with the curiosity and excitement that every four year old might carry with him into a new social environment. I had been exposed to a few play dates, but nothing like this herd of boys and girls, all full of chat, laughter and smiles, words mixing from time to time with solemn looks, frowns and quiet cries of loneliness. I met Bob, Harry, Fred and Gene and I gazed with interest at girl's faces, all cute and all adorable: Evelyn, Joyce, Paula, Susie. Sister Agatha carefully arranged our seating around two large square tables, one for the boys and one for the girls. There we began learning the letters, counting the numbers and in moments of relaxed creativity, drawing figures, molding clay and coloring in spaces.

For a week all went well, and it was my sense that while we were an important part of the classroom experience, the first and second graders kept Sister Agatha focused and in full control of their energies. Left to our own, we at the square tables tried hard to do our best, trace our lines, print the numbers and letters and in general please our teacher, because after all, she was our teacher.

Still, we had yet to learn the most fundamental part of what a good education was really all about: obeying Sister Agatha. Since she seemed distracted with those older kids, we sometimes had a few minutes to chat among ourselves, imagine special flights of fancy and look forward to recess and play time.

We managed our energies well, had yet to receive reprimand of any kind and bonded ourselves to school and our black and white robed teacher and spiritual leader. That she had special powers, we had no doubt, because she was a nun, she wore a cross, she did not have hair and she carried loops of beads which she rubbed from time to time even as she talked to us. I could almost see the halo around her head.

Ten days into school, increasingly confident with ourselves and the excitement of learning new things, Bob and I took a moment after finishing our numbers to break out some clay and mold it into a few forms, none of them ever to be distinguished as art. Still, we had a creative side, and I said to him, "I wonder if we could put some clay into our ears and then poke a pencil in there and it would stay? Wouldn't that be great!" He agreed and we set to work, never thinking, never worrying that this could be a bad thing because after all, we were just having fun, and we were being quiet, one of Sister Agatha's main maxims.

Leadership surfaces even at early ages, and what Bob and I began to do captured the attention of Harry and Gene who picked up the challenge, even as it horrified the girls, all of whom looked at us as though we were a collective group of trolls. That meant we were succeeding, and we ogled ourselves, made faces, posed our heads in different directions and praised our own work because the pencils weren't flying out of our ears.

I never saw her coming. I felt a presence, as though an angel suddenly hovered over me, felt some body heat emanating from those white layers of clothing, then heard the voice of God coming through the lips of Sister Agatha. "What do you boys think you are doing? Take those pencils out of your ears, clean out the clay!" We did so quickly and quietly. The next order puzzled us, "Now come follow me and line up here in front of the blackboard and face the class."

Now, this was a little more difficult to absorb. This sounded like embarrassment and some kind of penalty. No one had yet to tell us we had limits in anything we did. Being quiet, following orders seemed to be all that was necessary, but now, having shown some initiative, we could sense that Sister Agatha was not pleased. She rattled her beads, adjusted her glasses and walked to her desk as we moved to the front of the class and lined up facing the first and second graders all of whom seemed to have large smiles on their faces.

"Hold out your right hand, palm up!" came the command. We looked at Sister Agatha and like good little ducklings did what she ordered. She went to the far end of our line, stood before Gene, and said to him, and to all of us standing there, "It is wrong to put clay in your ears and dangerous to put pencils in there. God knows that he did not make those things to be ruining your hearing. Now, open your hand, hold it out, and listen for the sound." Then she struck Gene's hand with a flat ruler that she must have kept smuggled into the curtain of cloth about her body. "Wap! Wap!" Twice she flattened that piece of wood down on Gene's open palm, and then she proceeded to do the same to Harry and Bob.

When she got to me, she asked, "Whose idea was this, Walt?" I answered because I was taught to answer and to tell the truth. "It was my idea, Sister. I thought it would just be fun."

Wap! Wap! Wap! "There is an extra one for good measure," Sister Agatha said, "Learn your lesson."

She sent us back to our desks, palms reddened, faces flushed, bodies a little moistened from fear and minds embracing two things just learned. Don't put clay and pencils in your ears. Secondly, even when she was not watching, Sister Agatha was watching.

We four absorbed our public reprimands, told our mothers and were told in return that it was a good thing that she only slapped us twice, or in my case, three times. A half dozen swats might have been even more effective. I had real reservations about the kindness of Sister Agatha after that, but the rest of the school year went well, and I saw her outside on the playground from time to time watching us and smiling. The following year, I entered First Grade, and Sister Agatha was promoted to principal. I should have known then that her magical powers were truly channeling God's will, for there was a decidedly new tone to classroom discipline everywhere in the building. Even Father Eggert was impressed.

Three years later, I found myself again a subject for Sister Agatha's hard-eyed review, but this time I saw her coming. After school kids played as they wanted on the swings and teeter-totters. Gene, Harry and I worked mightily to see if we could match the level of the cross bar at the highest part of our swinging arc. Some girls seemed to watch us, inflating our efforts and we took a good look at them, noting especially our classmate, Evelyn Paulson, an adorable blond with a striking smile and lively eyes. We all thought that she was something really special. After a few efforts to reach the level of the bar, we coasted to a stop and without thinking drifted over to talk to Evelyn.

In the telling of this tale, I must admit what I never admitted to Sister Agatha. On impulse, I just leaned over and kissed Evelyn Paulson, on the lips, with my lips and she didn't scream. Gene and Harry followed and then we all three ran away to hide for fear that someone would see us.

Someone did. Two eighth graders caught our courageous misbehavior and promptly reported us to the icon of order. Even as we three heard the chanting, "You're in trouble, you're in trouble...Sister Agatha is going to get you," we were already heading for shelter. Gene ran home. Harry rode his bike away and I fled to the bathroom. I hid in a stall, tried to figure out how I could escape what was sure to be brutal punishment and worried to myself that this might be the end of my time in school, maybe even on earth itself. When quiet enveloped the school, I slinked away without notice, but even as I entered the safety of my house, I knew that there would be a reckoning.

The next morning when my mother awakened me for school, I told her that I did not feel well, sort of sick to my stomach and felt really funny inside. She looked me over carefully, caught the tone of my voice, and pressed me on my decision. "You look just fine to me, Walt. You have no temperature, and you haven't been sick to your stomach. You'll go to school. Get up and get dressed."

I remained in bed, sickened I thought by the ordeal awaiting me, execution at the hands of Sister Agatha. My only escape was to be sick maybe for the rest of my life, but it was better being stuck in bed than being in front of the nun with the large black cross on her front panel and an irritated hand moving swiftly over those beads, rattling them as though chains to be wrapped around my body. It could get worse. She might turn me into the priest and no one was known to have ever survived being turned over to the pastor of the parish. Sickened by my thoughts, I stayed in bed under the covers.

In a few minutes my mother returned, and I thought to myself that if she knew all the trouble I was in, she would be mad at me too. I had no escape. My life was pretty much over, all because of Evelyn Paulson and those tattle-tale eighth graders. This time my mother seemed gentle, more kind and she took back the covers over my head and asked me, "Walt, you're not sick. Why don't you want to go to school today? What happened? What's wrong?"

I caved. Carefully, putting my best spin on it and emphasizing their leadership in this caper I told her that Harry, Gene and I had kissed Evelyn Paulson on the playground and Sister Agatha was going to punish us. I was afraid, and I did not want to go to school.

"How long do you think you will stay out of school?" my mother asked."

"For a long, long time," I answered.

My mother's voice softened, she placed her head down beside my ear and she said very lovingly, "Walt, no matter how long you stay in bed, you will have to deal with this problem. It will not go away until you face up to it. I'm sure that Sister Agatha will be fair, but you need to learn now that you have to be responsible for your actions. She is not going to shout at you."

"She'll turn me in to the priest!" I countered.

"Very unlikely, Walt. I think she will handle this herself."

What I did not know was that the long arm of Sister Agatha had already reached into the sanctuary of my home, consulted with my mother by phone, explained what had happened and her plan of review. There was no hope of escape.

What I did know was that my mother's word made perfect sense to me. Get the punishment over with and enjoy a free conscience once again. A life lesson learned in the quiet of my bedroom. Huddled under blankets, listening for absolution only to find motherly induced courage, I got up, got dressed, and went to school.

Nothing happened for a while, although I got strange looks from some of the older boys, and none of the girls in my class would talk to me. Evelyn didn't seem upset, though. Maybe she liked the attention.

Then after ten o'clock recess, Gene, Harry and I were called to Sister Agatha's classroom. We entered, stood in front of all of those eighth graders who smiled and whispered visions of great punishment. Mercifully, she led us outside the room into the great hall and stood us before the statue of Mother Mary whose smile seemed ready to offer sweet release from our big worries. But her visage loomed in great contrast to the frown that Sister Agatha presented, and she was alive, standing right there in front of all of us.

She had a way of moving her mouth when she was perturbed, flexing her lips, then pursing them, fingering her beads as she focused her beady eyes on the object of her review. Today we were her target and each one of us found ourselves in a ritual of capitulation.

"I understand that you three were up to something on the playground after school yesterday. Would you tell me what happened?"

Silence. No one wanted to walk into this snare. Sister Agatha tried again, "My information says that you three had some contact with Evelyn Paulson, another third grader. What happened?" She looked slowly at each one of us, her eyes getting smaller, her chin line getting closer, her concealed right hand probably ready to strike.

We surrendered. Gene said that he kissed her near the swings. Harry said that he kissed her near the teeter-totters, and I, thinking quickly and seeking to finesse my conduct, said that as I was running between the swings and the teeter-totters, I had tripped and my lips had accidently touched Evelyn's.

"You kissed her?" Sister Agatha cued me.

"Well, I guess it was sort of a kiss, but it was just an accident. I didn't mean to do it."

I thought then that I had managed to lead my inquisitor into a safe place. Accidents can happen at any time. Kids bump into one another on the playground every day. I had done nothing consciously wrong, and while guilty of something, I didn't think I had actually tried to kiss her.

Would that stick? Would Sister Agatha buy my story? Could I sell her with words on the idea that it was all such an unplanned accident? She looked at me again, the light reflecting off of her glasses, her jaw a little tighter now because she was not getting a full confession. She would dig a little deeper.

"You fell into her, you say, eh?"

"Yes, I did. It was an accident."

"Did you kiss her. Was that your intention?"

"Well, maybe I did, but I didn't mean to."

While this inquisition was proceeding, Harry and Gene just stared at me amazed at my evasions. Gene told me later that he thought that my story was ingenious, but he knew right away that Sister Agatha wasn't buying it. And she didn't.

A few more questions to no particular benefit and there the guilt lay. I did indeed kiss Evelyn, but it was an accident. That was the best Sister could get from me.

She gave me one more hard look, rattled her beads a little more and sentenced all three of us to one hour of kneeling before the statue of Mother Mary, praying for guidance in improving our future behavior.

I went home from school that day with great relief. I told my mother what I had done, and she did not tell me that again she and Sister Agatha had consulted by phone, laughing with some delight as they reviewed the trial and punishment phase of my wrongdoing.

I wondered. Had I managed to finesse my misbehavior? No. Sister Agatha had one more card to play. When report grades came out, Harry and Gene got an A in "Deportment". I received a B. I could not believe it...a B for me and not for them. I asked my mother about this, alleging unfair treatment, and she said to me, "I think Sister Agatha admired them for telling the full truth and she found your story a little fuzzy."

Then, in words that I will always remember, my mother said, "You can't game Sister Agatha."

Feed the Chickens

A hiccup, he thought, a little delay before he could tell the army goodbye, could rejoin his family. Doctors removed a cancer behind his right ear, grafted new skin over the site and kept him under observation for almost a month. Finally cleared for discharge, he rejoined his wife in the valley before Christmas and they bought a small home for $500. In a few months, when his income was more certain, they rented the home to boarders, bought another for $5,240, and settled in to live their lives.

The Great War broke the back of the Great Depression and veterans flowed back to their jobs as easily as they had once left them. He found work in the oil fields, steady income, but he soon realized that it didn't fill the household coffers. In four years, his oldest child would be a teenager with two others to follow shortly, and a new baby was on the way. He looked at the monthly balance sheet that his wife presented to him and wondered if maybe he could do better.

When a loose pipe nipped off the end of one of his fingers, he began to think of new kinds of work. Physical injury, common enough working around drilling rigs, moving cable and motors, could nonetheless impoverish a family. His own dad had suffered a devastating accident when a loose pulley crushed his face, and he remembered the protrusion of fused bone, grafted skin and watery eye which marked his appearance for the rest of his life. He noted to himself that while steel toe boots protected his feet, no glove could protect his hands, nor a steel helmet his face.

He thought again about his experience with the Military Police in Little Rock. He enjoyed the responsibility of keeping order at Camp Robinson. The command structure functioned well compared to his experience with civilian police politics, and he began to look at the California Highway Patrol. It was more professional. It paid better than the oilfields. It might be a life career. He applied.

Still looking for more cash, he took note of Watkins Products. After the war, as women began producing and raising their "boomer babies", door-to-door salesmen for various products brought the marketplace to the front porch. Watkins built a huge distribution network, diversified its product line and built the largest direct-sales company in the world.

He signed on and began making after work and weekend rounds selling the company's spices and extracts. Well known about town, personable, honest and full of entertaining stories, he built a reliable base of customers, and the extra income would tide him over until the CHP acted on his application.

In reflective moments, he noted that working two jobs, looking for another, watching his three children grow and keeping the house in good repair kept him busy enough. Yet, soon there would be another mouth to feed, and he needed to do more. He began raising chickens, putting both eggs and meat on the table, keeping fully tuned to their daily diet and security, enjoying their clucks and plucks and finding them a pleasant part of his daily life. If the children failed to take their turns feeding the flock, he reminded them that hungry hens might not provide their breakfast the next morning. He didn't tell them that a regularly empty nest meant there would be chicken for supper in a day or two.

He remained busy, optimistic, full of fun and easy to be with. He felt well placed at work, held high hopes for the future and had energy enough to balance all of his commitments. An outstanding athlete in high school, he still carried himself with an easy grace, moved with fluidity and power. His laughter seemed to roll in tune with his talk. He had many friends, loved his wife and embraced his family's future. The birth of his fourth child in the spring, a little girl, invigorated him and confirmed his efforts to find a different career. Happy to walk her for hours when she fought a respiratory infection, he remained the rock of the family.

The changes came subtly. It wasn't that he had the flu and needed to take a day off work. It was more a sense of unease, a feeling that some of the buoyancy in his daily doings had begun to settle. He smoked of course, as did everyone, and he thought that cutting back his cigarettes might well change his inclination to sleep more and do less. He still worked his jobs, socialized with friends of long standing, laughed with his siblings and shared beers with them and his father in a local neighborhood bar. But as the winter passed, he noticed that he grew tired more easily and more often.

It became difficult for him to make house calls for Watkins, and his social chatter with the crew in the oil fields grew more listless. His thoughts about the CHP shifted into the category of "maybe", and he noticed that he just didn't have the zip he once had. At first, he wrote it off to short sleep and a bit of aging, but he continued to feel increasingly lethargic. Over three months, he lost weight, began to grow more deeply weary, and found feeding the chickens hard to fit into his days. Finally, he saw a doctor.

A quick exam revealed bulging, badly infected tonsils. They had to come out, and they did. A heavy dose of ether anesthesia almost killed him, but he had done the right thing.

The doc proclaimed his tonsils the worst that he had ever removed, and he expected a quick recovery in just a couple of weeks. No one thought to look at his lungs.

His malaise continued, and in early summer a series of coughing spells left him faint, breathless and frightened. This time he, his wife, and his parents all drove into the city to see a Dr. Fontaine. The doc put him through a complete workup: blood, x-rays, biopsy of a lump near his jaw. Each test piled tension upon fright, left him more worried, gave him dark thoughts of life and his future. He became convinced, with an internal flutter of fear that carries information unseen but inescapable, that he was seriously ill.

When they returned to see Fontaine, the doctor reviewed with them the results of the testing, and he explained to them gently that the skin cancer, removed in San Antonio when he left the service, had spread to his lungs. One of them was completely gone. His lymph nodes had cancer. His tonsils had been obliterated with infection from the cancer and removing them was certainly the right thing to do, but now, there was nothing more Fontaine could offer.

The family returned home devastated, weakened by panic, stunned by news of the disease. He spent days in bed, rolling over and spending the nights there too. It was hot that summer, a "dry heat" as people sometimes praised it, but even in the cool breezes of a swamp cooler, he sweated the sheets to a soak. He struggled to sit up, could not dress himself nor move a chair. His children asked when he was going to be well again, and their mother said, "soon".

A friendly barber, Red Cameron, came to the house to cut his hair and make conversation about town gossip, and they laughed at the stories of the day. His brothers and sisters also tried to rally his spirits, but he grew tired quickly, laughed less heartily, slept too easily. His wife now fed the chickens.

His weakness, his diagnosis, his aimlessness left him silent on matters of life or death, yet she knew that she had to make plans. His dismal prognosis put her and the children at terrible risk. Whatever the disease's progression, their futures were intimately linked to it, and they needed to talk about it.

In the fall, she prompted a good friend, Fred Casey, a local insurance agent as well as an active member of the Veterans of Foreign Wars, to come to the house and see him. "Do you think you are going to survive this?" he asked gently. The father paused, "I don't know. I just don't know."

"Let me offer you a suggestion," Fred spoke softly, "Why don't you check yourself into the VA hospital in Los Angeles. Once you are in its care, you'll have a medical record that leads directly back to the skin cancer that you developed in the service and that can be important for your family."

The husband listened. "I don't want to leave," he said, "L.A. is a long drive from home. Last time I took it, I spent four hours getting there and that two lane road is treacherous." Fred paused, then rephrased his observation, "If you choose the VA hospital and you don't survive, you will fortify a claim for your wife to get special benefits, and for your children to get the GI Bill for education. Think about it."

He did. He thought about it a lot. He didn't want to do it, really didn't want to do it, but he did.

In early January, 1948, he found himself hospitalized in Los Angeles, his health deteriorating, becoming more fragile by the week. New blood tests showed that he had developed leukemia, and he could feel it draining his body every day. Pain from the lung cancer was not adequately controlled, and his youngest brother, Jim, attending USC, made a half dozen trips back home to bring him off-the-grid supplies of liquid codeine. It was an eight hour round trip, but worth it, Jim thought. His brother slammed it down as though it were a soft drink.

Sleep became his closest friend, and his daily naps gradually lengthened. Dr. Barsotti, monitoring him closely, began to administer transfusions to see if they would stem the loss of red blood cells in any long lasting way. They were helpful but temporary, and in early February, Barsotti told the mother that she should bring the children down to see him for one last visit.

To them, this was an adventure, an omen of salvation. They knew their father was sick, but they would see him. He would get better, decide to come home, and they would be a family, together once again. It *was* a long drive to L.A. and they stopped on the Ridge Route to get a bite to eat. The jukebox played, *Bye Bye Blackbird* and its lyric, *"Pack up all my care and woe, here I go, singing low"* sounded more to the oldest boy like a premonition of loss rather than liberation.

The younger boy, recovered from a second eye surgery, wanted his father to see how he looked without glasses. The older girl just missed her daddy. Her longing to see him kept her a shy but active listener to all the adult talk about his health. The youngest, a girl, toddled about with smiles, immune to the weight of the moment.

Los Angeles swirled with people, cars, and buildings. Brother Harry, drove carefully through the traffic, negotiating lights, fending off eccentric drivers, cursing their impetuous maneuvers while the children saw the dance of four tires as a game of narrow escapes. When they walked from the parking lot into the skyscraper hospital, they stayed close to one another and to their mother. They didn't know what to expect, but they knew who they were going to see, and the closer they got to the building the more excited they became.

Instead of walking up stairs, they rode an elevator for the first time and that became another memory. They got off through the automatic opening doors, turned right and walked into a large visiting room where bright lights chased shadows and the scent of antiseptic filled the air. Where was their father? The mother assured them that he was coming, and in a few minutes, he walked into the sun room, opening his arms wide as he greeted them, one by one, giving them all a nice long hug.

He looked GREAT! Smiling, laughing, wearing a pretty, dark blue robe that had his initials on the pocket, he walked into the room clearly in good humor. The oldest boy, the child most aware of his illness, began to think that things were going to be all right. As they visited, his father joked with the mother about being sure that she fed the chickens, and he laughed again as he jokingly showed her and Harry how he could easily cross his legs while sitting, overlap them all the way down to his ankles. He had lost weight and energy, but he felt good because he had received a transfusion that morning.

They talked for a bit, exchanging comments about family, all of whom were praying for him, and the community where his likely return was common conversation on the streets. There were a few jokes about some of the latest doings of the police department and the misbehavior of mutual friends who had made midnight mistakes. The mother reassured him that her new work at the bank was going well. She reported with a smile that she was feeding the chickens, although she did not mention that it was an irregular feeding. She disliked them.

The oldest boy listened to every phrase, seeking nuance in casual remarks, watching eye movements and facial expressions which might reveal comfort or innate sadness. His mother kept one eye on his father, monitoring his stamina, and the other eye on the children. When he held the baby, she worried that the infant's weight might tax him too much, but he felt invigorated by the life in his arms, and he joked about the hours that he had spent walking her the previous winter when she fought pneumonia.

In time, the visit came to a close, and his wife walked him back into his hospital room. He moved more slowly now, and she kept a hand on his shoulder. As she helped him get settled into his bed, the boy noted how weak he had become in the two hours since they arrived.

The father wrote to the mother three days after the visit and spoke of his weariness: *"I feel pretty good today, but I don't think I will ever get over being sleepy so much."* The transfusions might let him come home, if they would just last a little longer. He wrote how good it was to see the kids and hoped that *"someday it will be God's will to let us live together for keeps."* He reported that Barsotti had moved him into a different room, and he didn't like it. *"I guess I am about ready to die and don't know it,"* he wrote, because patients were placed there when they were near death. His last line, *"don't forget to feed the chickens"* conveyed both humor and admonition.

The husband wrote again, March 3, two days after his birthday. Barsotti planned to give him some more transfusions, and he had *"lots of hope in getting home in a week or so."* He was happy to hear that the oldest boy had a paper route, and he thanked the little girl for her letter to him. He told her to tell her brothers that he would write them too, when they wrote to him first. He finished with this comment, *"You're the sweetest, best wife in all this world...and please don't forget to feed the chickens."*

She wrote on March 11 that she hoped to see him on the weekend, even if she had to take a bus. *"Boy, I'll be glad when you're home—this living without you is not interesting. I miss you damn it."* His last letter crossed hers in the mail: *"Honey, this transfusion stuff is just not working. I feel so good for a few hours, and then I get so weak and sleepy I cannot stay awake. I don't think I'm going to make it. I'm getting tired of these ups and downs, I told Barsotti to stop the transfusions."* He wrote in a pencil script that weakened to a scrawl within six lines. He told her he loved her, and that he wanted her to be there.

The mother gathered herself, phoned his brother, Harry, and the two drove to L.A. on Sunday to be with him. He recognized her. She held his hand as he drifted into a deeper sleep marked with slower respiration and easy countenance.

These were transcendent moments as she waited for the next slow, shallow breath, waited for it, seeing his chest move slightly, listening for the air moving into his body. He breathed for hours with the intervals growing longer. Then, without a sound, his chest became still. She sat there for nearly five minutes, and still, no breath. Midnight. The first day of her life without him and no time to grieve. She filled out a few pages of paperwork and left immediately to get home to the children.

When the oldest boy arose that morning, he found his mother crouched over the heating vent on the floor of the living room. He leaned down to her and asked, "Is daddy dead?" She said, "Yes."

Three days later, he approached the casket. His father's eyes were closed, but he was not sleeping. His skin was fair, cheeks lightly rouged. He reclined but he was not relaxed. He did not speak. His mouth seemed falsely closed, aligned with some light glue that left just the faintest line of sealant between his lips. The boy did not know what he was supposed to say, or do, or feel.

He looked at him just briefly, and he knew in an instant that this was not his father. It was a figure of a man, but it was not his father. Mother was, in her own way, as quiet as his father was in his. He looked at the figure in the coffin a last time and quietly turned away, disappointed once again.

In the gathering, from the side of the funeral parlor, there began a series of sobs. They grew louder, longer and higher in pitch until they engulfed the entire room. His grandmother, lamenting the death of her son, the fifth of her ten children now lost, gave voice to a pain that could never be resolved. He was embarrassed. His mother was not crying. Grandma was wailing and the rest of the room seemed to be uncomfortable, waiting for some signal to leave. Finally, his mother gathered the children, walked them out the door and took them home.

The next day, after a ceremonial mass at St. Mark's Church, the family, seated in a very nice car, joined a procession from church to cemetery. He noticed the fine furnishing in the sedan, but apart from that he thought little until the car paused briefly as it turned into the burial grounds. He looked out the left window which gave him a view of the cars behind them, and he noticed that he could not see the end of the line. That impressed him.

They parked, departed the vehicle and lined up at the gravesite. Someone said some words. His mother received a folded American flag, which he dismissed as a poor substitute for his father. When prayers ended, they gathered quietly and left.

His mother kept his father's clothes untouched for two years, but the chickens disappeared within a week. Her conversation about animals focused on the smelly dog pens from the neighbor's hounds, but he developed a fondness for pigeons, took the chicken pen apart and built his birds a roost. His brood seemed to speak to him, relied upon him to provide their food and safety. He protected them, loved them, trusted them to do what nature programmed them to do, even as he wrestled with his deepening suspicions that those to whom he had once been attached could no longer be trusted: priests, nuns, cops, doctors, nurses, even teachers.

For all of their authority, in his eyes the rules they promulgated, the skills they practiced, the wisdoms they offered, and the guidance they provided failed him. Gently, they might counsel acceptance of his loss, but he had yet to embrace it. He did not grieve. He could not discuss it. He flew his birds.

He told a close friend, that he just didn't want anyone to feel sorry for him, and to ensure that, he became a disturbing annoyance in gatherings of friends and family, within school and church. He felt full of fun, but he expressed it aimlessly, and he became a concern for his mother and his teacher, both hoping that he might find purpose.

To their surprise, and his, he found it in scouts, sports and the discipline of the workplace. Tossing newspapers and cleaning up a butcher shop taught him a new code: no work, no money, no excuses. He quickly came to respect the men who paid him, enjoyed their praise and accepted their corrections with resolve to do better. He modeled himself after their focus on work and their views on human behavior. They had much to teach him, as did school, but he listened far more closely to the rules of the purse.

In the fall, he rode his bike to the cemetery, leaned it against a nearby tree and walked to his father's grave. He pondered his bitter, bitter loss, smothered the pain, repressed the tears, left unreconciled. He did not return for fifty years.

Saving Souls

Sister Agatha, she of sharp eye, thin lips, pitched voice, and stealthy presence, became the totem of Walt's time at St. Mark's. For eight years, she either stood directly in front of his classroom or as principal, created a demanding tone of instruction in every grade Walt visited. Each year, she ensured that his teacher, be it Sister Mary Celine, Sister Mary Rose or Sister Mary Angela, taught him and his classmates a clear, concise framework for saving their souls, and he read in the Catholic Catechism the precise way to do it. The Pope and the Church interacted with Jesus Christ, God the Father, the Holy Ghost, Heaven, Hell, Limbo and Purgatory, and sent their divinely ordained formula for salvation directly through Sister Agatha to every nun and every student assembled at St. Mark's.

Walt never heard a nun utter a quote from the Bible in his eight years there, but he learned the Ten Commandments, the Seven Deadly Sins, the Stations of the Cross and the Catechism, a manual of fixed questions and rote answers which stripped clean any thoughts of doubt. It pronounced his time on Earth to be justified by his love for God and reinforced his love for parents, brother, sisters and wider family. He might have asked Sister Agatha or one of her surrogates questions about the nature of the universe and the irreversible nature of death, but he didn't. He tried more fundamental questions.

If he asked, *"Who made the world?"* the answer was *"God made the world."* If he queried, *"Where does God live?"* he learned that *"He is everywhere, sees everything, knows everything and is the guardian to Heaven."* If he asked,

"Why do we pray to saints, he heard, *"Because they have reached Heaven and can talk to God.* If he asked where did God come from, the answer pretty much closed the door on speculations: *"He always was, always is, and always remains the same."* Ritual made thoughtful explorations of powerful topics unnecessary and Walt came to find in it a reassuring certainty about his place in the world and how he could earn his spiritual salvation.

Learning about the purpose of the sacraments, sharing with Jesus the Stations of the Cross, witnessing the miraculous transubstantiation of bread and wine all seemed perfectly structured to help save one's soul. Going to confession, saying his penance, and accepting Holy Communion placed Walt just where the Church wanted him to be, accountable to God through the agency of the priest. While he was never quite sure if the white wafer the priest placed on the tongues of sin-free Catholics was really God's body, he accepted the teaching that it was, and he noted that eligibility for communion fit nicely into the need to go to confession.

It always puzzled him how the wine could become blood and the wafer could become body, but no one who took communion drank any wine. How could a body be a body without blood? Sister Agatha was not pleased to hear these questions and cautioned him not to commit blasphemy. Still, the priest and congregation handled those little white pieces of unleavened bread as though they were intrinsically divine, and he became enamored with the power of prayer and the security of ritual.

Walt learned to serve Mass, assisting in the mystical transformation of bread and wine into the body and blood of Christ, no questions asked. He liked repeating the Latin phrases he learned to utter in response to the priest's Latin declarations. He felt powerful in ringing the bells at the right time and in the right tone order. He knew that when he lit the candles before services, every eye fixed on the flickering flame. When he moved the Big Book from one side of the altar to the other, he basked in the attention he knew church goers must be focusing on him.

He felt privileged to observe just how much water different priests wanted him to pour into the wine when they consecrated it (remarkably little he noted). He even followed carefully the way they held the host, which fingers they extended and how piously they moved when they distributed communion. Clearly, priests were the center of attention for hundreds of churchgoers, and Walt felt that sense of importance lightly touch him as well, made him feel as though he had forged an intimate connection to the miracle of the Mass.

Building confidence in his commitments to Catholic doctrine, he began to model himself after the priestly ways that he observed each Sunday, and as he moved through St. Mark's, gossip of his scandalous kiss of Evelyn Paulson in third grade began to wane. He seemed to become a favorite of Sister Agatha. When she heard from Sister Mary Rose that he and Harry could sing a passable version of *"Buttons and Bows"* and *"Ghost Riders in the Sky"*, she directed them to make the rounds of every classroom to perform their act. A year later, she encouraged him to enter a Catechism contest examining one's knowledge of Catholic doctrine, and she glowed when Walt defeated classmates two grades above him. It was heady stuff, and it both pleased and frightened him that Father Eggert recognized him on sight.

Walt heard his name occasionally mentioned in connection with a "calling" to the priesthood, and while flattering to be thought worthy of such a possible future, he took note of how long one went to school to become a priest. Already, he chafed under adult supervision, and he found it difficult to imagine an entire lifetime regimented by the authority of another priest, worse yet, a bishop. Then too, the requirement that priests live a celibate life became an increasingly suspicious standard. He liked kissing Evelyn Paulson and by the time he was under the direct scrutiny of Sister Agatha again, he had developed a skilled subtlety in keeping a keen eye on every girl in his class. They were changing.

Being in class with Sister Agatha as she worked to put the finishing touches on saving his soul brought him both confusion and confrontation. Buffeted with a growing sense of skepticism about faith, the power of God and the importance of the Church, he found the daily recitations and pronouncements of faith coming from her mouth more and more difficult to hear or to digest.

After his father died, he began to explore issues that a Catechism alone could not answer. His sense of loss, his entrenched disappointment in the failure of the Church, or God, or doctors or anyone else to keep his father safe sent Walt questioning all things connected with Catholicism.

Once begun, the queries did not seem to have a limit.

Submit to God's Will? *Why would he have my father die?*

Heaven? *Prove it. If not, why fear Hell? If so, why fear death?*

Living life rich or poor without complaint? *Yet the Church which made the rules was so rich.*

School rules? *Test them.*

Authority of Nuns? *Suspect.*

There was a lot about life that he didn't know, and a lot about the Church for which he began developing doubt, the enemy of faith. The Disciple Thomas' request for proof seemed more and more reasonable to him, and when he measured what the church offered to him now, he found the dogma, ritual and Sacraments inadequate to his need.

Walt became skeptical of promises. Adults made a lot of promises. Sometimes they delivered. More often, they did not. Catholic doctrine rested on an enormous promise, the belief that only through Church, Pope, Priest and Sacraments could one find a sure path to Heaven. He found himself increasingly testy with religion and those who taught it, becoming more an annoyance than an asset to Sister Agatha's leadership.

Now his overseer, she instructed both seventh and eighth grades and there silence reigned and her voice spoke. Her dominance complete, she held center stage and even with her back turned to the class, she could somehow determine who was inattentive, mischievous, or gossiping. When Walt tripped a student, she knew. When he had a staring contest with a friend, she ended it. When he whispered answers to friends, she disciplined him. Sometimes, she ordered him to write resolute reminders of better behavior. Other times, he might be given extra homework to complete. Most often, Sister Agatha sent him out of the room, into the large hall where he knelt for long periods of time in front of the outstretched arms of the statue of Mother Mary. He tried to pray with sincerity, asking for help in controlling his behavior, but his knees hurt.

Perhaps in desperation, although he never detected any such feeling in her visage, she recruited him and another friend, Tony Burt, to assist the Knights of Columbus evening Bingo fundraiser. They distributed cards, helped find winners and reassured the players of the numbers being called. Toward the very end of the evening, he and Tony decided to invest in a Bingo card for the Jackpot Round. To their amazement, and the dismay of everyone else, they won, splitting the $25 prize, and Walt divided his $12.50, giving half to his brother, George.

They both decided to buy themselves a stamp collecting kit. Walt had heard a lot about how much fun it was to collect stamps, and he thought that the kit would have both a booklet into which to paste stamps and also the stamps that needed pasting. When that proved untrue, he gave his material to George. Going out seeking stamps, peeling them carefully off of envelopes, scurrying about family letters for stamps left Walt stupefied that people would do that. Like many promised excitements, it disappointed.

Still, Sister Agatha continued to work her magic, encouraging appropriate activities and disciplining misbehavior. While she warned everyone against seeing local movies that were on the Legion of Catholic Decency Forbidden List, (*Outlaw* was especially reviled), she liked wholesome film stories and Walt's class began to see them regularly. She would march them, two by two, up to the Church Hall, several blocks away, direct them to set up chairs and prepare the "theatre" for the treat of the day.

Once seated, they felt liberated from the discipline of the classroom and treated both by the movies themselves and the unpredictable surprises that amused them all, as when the 16mm film went "off reel" and spilled hundreds of feet of celluloid over the floor. The lights went on, and students had a special treat...watching the nuns work desperately to save the day...and the movie.

The films reflected Sister Agatha's sense of cultural sharing and Walt found some of them memorable. *The Bells of St. Mary's* with Bing Crosby and Barry Fitzgerald remained a favorite, and any movie with Margaret O'Brien or Deanna Durbin sent little thrills through his spine. Both were pretty, both could sing, and to Walt's surprise, both brought a smile to Sister Agatha. Probably, he thought, she was not thinking the same thoughts he found floating through his head.

Still, he could not confine her to the dark bin of irrelevant adults when she was thoughtful enough to let boys hold hands with girls for the purpose of learning the etiquette of dancing. On two occasions, she led both seventh and eighth grades to the Hall and, calling upon some of the parish women to guide them, she gave a little talk on movement to music. Then, to recorded selections, Walt and the other boys learned how to ask a girl for a dance, how to spend some minutes leading their partners, then thanking them for the treat. He liked that.

Whether it was a brush with entertainment, a competition to see which student knew the most about the Catholic religion, or an artful presentation of a Christmas pageant, the Hall remained one of Sister Agatha's teaching venues. Walt thought of it as a special place---girls and movies alone made it memorable--and he came to think of St. Mark's as an elite school, boasting to public school friends that he was being introduced to Algebra in the eighth grade. He didn't really remember being exposed to science, perhaps for theological reasons, but class time made clear what sin could do to their perfectly pure, innocent lives and for Sister Agatha, the daily grind always focused on her dual purpose of seeing to it that they gained an education and saved their souls.

Still, Walt weakened in his resolve about how to love God the Catholic way. He remembered Sister Agatha asking the entire seventh and eighth grade classes if they knew about the threat of Communism? Would they be willing to die if a Communist government official lined them up and asked them to deny their religion or be shot? Walt thought it a ludicrous question, kept his hand at his side and knew in his heart that he was not willing to die for his faith. He thought later that may have been the beginning of his spiritual departure.

Attending St. Mark's School served him well. Sister Agatha's religious teachings reinforced those of his mother, and embedded rules which pointed him in the direction of living a good life. But he did not embrace the discipline of doing it on the Church's terms and as he learned more about the substantive meanings of Catholic Doctrine, the more he began questioning it. By the time he graduated, he carried around questions that he found both perplexed him and challenged his faith.

For his next four years in high school there was no totem to remind him to rein in his thinking and find God through Catholic rituals. His beliefs weakened, diluted by his immersion in work outside school, undermined by his interest in girls and the ways of the world that others seemed to follow. He remembered Sister Agatha though, found her memory a comfort and placed her robed image into the short lineup of people who made a difference to his youth. Catholic doctrine did not fare as well, and in time he rejected it.

Sorting Things Out

Pity! He could feel it. He hated it. Didn't want it. Words seemed to float all around him, "your dad... great athlete, best ever...wonderful man...funny...committed to his family... great at track and field...shot put record...ran faster than any big man in school history." All those words...wasted. Walt hid from them with noise and pranks, resenting reassurances about his father presented by those who believed they knew him. He deflected, ignored, and slid by those strange faces and well-meant phrases because his Great Truth was that his father was dead...gone. He did not know what he wanted to hear, but shared sorrow felt too much like pity.

For his mother, the challenges facing the family piled up weekly. She needed to keep her job, needed to find child care, needed to grieve, needed to lead the family in its emotional transition. Some things came first, and some, grieving especially, waited a long, long time. For Walt though, she had a plan, pointing him in the direction of the Boy Scouts, hoping its program would absorb his energy and connect him to a man who might give him some guidance.

Already delivering papers after school and Saturdays, Walt felt skeptical about scouting, but he found his first meetings an interesting exposure to new faces from other schools and a scout leader, Cliff Bowden, who seemed especially interested in him, and that felt good. Evening meetings and clearly organized activity appealed to him. Bowden, gently enthusiastic in his talk, encouraged all his scouts to explore the challenges of each rank, pointing out in casual conversation the interesting aspects of different merit badges. He spoke to Walt in a quiet tone of voice, offering encouraging words and quiet enthusiasm, without pressure or didactic direction. Bowden took shape as a surrogate who wore the right kind of clothes.

Scouting, a powerful combination of goals and responsibility, sold itself to him. He liked the color of merit badges, the scent of Scout uniform fabric, the display of the green sash filled with quarter size icons attesting to his new expertise and status. Soon, the allure of new pins to wear on crisply decorated shirts, group recitation of the Pledge of Allegiance, the fun of new faces all gave him a placement providing comfort, and Walt found himself accepted as a member of the "pack".

When summer vacation began, he made three new friends: Rutledge, Litton and Whitey. They spent some time playing pick-up softball together in the company of Whitey's dad Wayne Randall, a tall, angular coach, a little stooped for his age but warm and interested in him and his fielding skills. Walt took to the man, finding his quiet ways inviting and within a week, he bonded with the entire group.

More faces appeared and the lineup began to take form. Billy Raymond, a pitcher with an awesome reputation, baffled batters; Lee Swain anchored third base; Al Dalton roamed shortstop and Whitey caught, with Litton at second and Rutledge in the outfield. Last year, Walt played for St. Mark's, his school's team, but Rutledge told him that they needed another outfielder, and he wanted to be that guy. Would they have him? They would, Mr. Randall said with a twinkle in his eyes and what Walt saw as a silent commitment to him in his heart. He went home to tell his mother.

This news she did not need...her son rejecting St. Mark's for a public school team. But she noted his attachment to Coach Randall, made inquiries, judged the man to be honest and of good values and decided that Walt could play for whomever he wanted. Sister Agatha would just have to accept it. As it turned out, she said nothing, but his siblings, classmates and cousins never stopped criticizing him about his choice. *"Traitor"* entered his vocabulary in a way that he had not appreciated before, and he lived a hard, hard summer.

Still, all the while he dealt with a hostile fan base, he continued to earn merit badges and that brought him into contact with new skills and new adult faces. Visiting with a local smithy, he learned about the furnace, the varying degrees of heat, the characteristics of some metals, and the use of a water pail. He made a chisel. Pounding that hot, red/white metal into a usable form felt good, put him in control of something.

He earned a merit badge for *home repair*, an achievement that won him family fame, for even his cousins and siblings did not see him as the kind of craftsmen who could change folding mesh into taut screening. He noted that sealing the house from flies kept them outside where he could kill them, a favorite activity.

He learned something about water color painting to get an *art* merit badge and forever remembered Miss Baird, the teacher at P.S. 12 who took time to work with him after school. He thought his final project a failure, but she liked the way his sloppily hand painted water-colored images flowed outside the lines, layering colors into a murky darkness portraying his campfire scene.

He hiked seven miles with two friends to establish a campsite and spend the night. Along the way, they stopped briefly to visit Paula Lambert the light in the eyes of every boy in his grade. He had cued a friend to ask her if she liked him and she answered, "No. I don't like his personality." Befuddled, he sought help from the dictionary. "Personality" had something to do with the way one behaved and he thought maybe his loud brand of silliness and energy offended her. Well, not much he could do about that, but he continued to ponder her comment. That she might now see his interest in scouting as the mark of a more responsible admirer invigorated him.

The prospect of seeing Paula made the hike an adventure, but after the visit, he tired quickly, and the drudgery continued for two miles longer than he would have liked. But he finished it, earned another merit badge, progressed in rank, and looked to see what he needed to do next... and then next...and then next. As he accumulated his merit badges, he advanced in rank. Noted as the youngest Life Scout in the county, Walt basked in the praise, took pride in his accomplishment, looked forward to the award ceremony.

It turned out to be a disappointment. A scout leader of some reputation cautioned the audience in general (but Walt felt that he spoke to him in particular), that scouting was an experience, not a contest to see who could get to the highest rank the fastest. Had he done something suspect, something wrong in propelling himself to this rank? It all felt a little tainted now, the same scent of disapproval that he found during his summer softball season.

When they played St. Mark's the first time, the *Tribune* reported that there were 300 loud spectators who had come to cheer on their teams. Mostly, he found, they came to chant "TRAITOR! TRAITOR!" each time he came to bat. The article went on to say that the Great Tom Litton had homered for the "Little Bulldozers", but in the end St. Mark's won, 2-1. He went home in tears, reflecting on the chants in the stands and the painful loss to a team he so deeply wanted to beat.

But, summer wasn't over. The "Dozers" traveled to the coast to play teams in Santa Maria and Ventura, and he came to fit right in with his new buddies. They liked one another, and they wanted to win. Coach Randall seemed especially admiring, encouraging, praising his efforts and his successes in the field. He grew close to his coach, found "siblings" in his teammates, enjoyed the excitement of competition, and wrapped himself around the joy of winning.

In the second half of the summer season, the Dozers went undefeated. Billy Raymond pitched a perfect game against Mesa, and they got even with St. Mark's winning 10-6. Lee Swain homered and again the *Tribune* mentioned that the Great Tom Litton played outstanding defense. He didn't hear any chanting from the stands that night, and it was a deep, personal thrill to send the Saints packing. He loved getting even, and he loved sharing the smiles with his teammates and his coach.

He wasn't crying when mother drove them home that evening, and he felt fully vindicated a few weeks later when they beat Rotary, 2-0 in just 55 minutes to wrap up the summer season. The *Tribune* called it the "best played game of the summer", and he made a catch next to the Natatorium along the left field foul line, thrilling teammates but provoking others who screamed that he had trapped the ball against the wall. He had a sinking feeling that somehow, adults were going to take his catch away from him as they had diminished his Life Scout award.

But Coach Randall shouted the skeptics down, declaring it a catch and putting an end to the outcry. He bonded to his coach in that moment more intensely that at any time throughout the summer. He found safety in Mr. Randall, a man who embraced his skills and his personality and told him that he was not alone. He joined other All-Stars to play in the big ballpark at the edge of the Valley. Great memories. Great security.

He focused on scouting again, discovering that to gain the Eagle Scout Award, he needed a merit badge in bird-watching. Casual observation told him that he was unlikely to find 25 species of birds around town and when he asked where the birds were, he heard the words, "Go to the water works. You'll find a lot of them there."

Well, that was a 10 mile long bike ride, each way. Just how much more energy did he want to devote to scouting only to have some guy in authority criticize him because of his age. It gave him pause. He looked up from the manual, counted his merit badges, speculated on the task before him and began to review his plan.

Life grew complicated. Having a paper route gave him responsibility which he enjoyed, brought him money, graced him with some control over his daily wants, but it took time, weekdays and Saturdays. He had a bike all right, but he didn't need a 20 mile round trip to see and identify species of birds. Moreover, it was about this time that he heard about a new job possibility, cleaning up a butcher shop.

If he got that job he would be busy from 5:30-7:00 each evening and additional hours on Saturday. That made a trip out to the water works an even more challenging time issue, along with a transportation dilemma. He really didn't see how he could meet all of his obligations if he changed jobs, and he quietly told Mr. Bowden that he needed to end scouting. Bowden understood, suggested ways that he could continue to work toward Eagle Scout rank, urged him to think about it some more and reconsider. He did, but not for long. Scouting had worn a bit thin, and the allure of a better job occupied his thoughts, jiggled his pocket book. He felt ready for new adventures.

His decision marked the end to his childhood. As difficult as that might have been to define, he could feel that things were changing. Summertime sports were unorganized for his new age group. He would be moving on to high school, and his time with Mr. Bowden felt like a part of his past. He boxed up his scouting pins and sash, wrapped his All Star jacket in plastic and stored them all in his closet, testimony to summertime fun. Cleaning up a butcher shop? What would that be about? It didn't award merit badges, but it did pay good money. Easy choice.

Manchild and Son

Walt pulled up in front of the small, four room house, it's curb appeal embracing him with green lawns, shadowed porch and the gentle view of a home well-tended. He paused for a few moments, thinking back over his decades with Johnny, smiling at fleeting memories, relaxing at the prospect of seeing him again as he did every few months.

Sighing, he opened his car door and stepped out, a little gingerly because of that balky knee, but he placed it just right, put his weight on it and stood up. As was his habit for many years now, he paused to pretend to adjust his pants while actually letting his knees straighten and his back relax in a standing position. It took only a few moments, then he walked up the sidewalk, rang the doorbell and waited.

Dinah answered the door with that same charm and enthusiasm that he had come to know in the past few years.

"Hey there college boy! How good to see you...so nice of you to come all the way over. Johnny's been looking forward to this all morning. Come on in!"

"Always a treat to take a drive to our hometown, Dinah," he smiled. "You look great," and he walked through the open door and looked quickly around, seeing Johnny rise awkwardly from his chair to a standing position and wait for him to cross the room.

He stepped forward, put out his hand then slid it into a firm grip, cast a direct look into his eyes and barked a warm, "Hi there, Boss."

"You look great, squirt...a little shorter though," he slurred, working to get words out, smiling as he touched Walt's shoulder then sinking gently back down into his seat.

"Well, you're doing pretty damn well too from the look of it. Good strength in your legs and still a lusty look in your eye, is that right Dinah?" he laughed.

"Well, hell yes," she replied, "I knew when I married him that he'd keep me busy, and I ain't been disappointed, but now I can just pop him a gentle shove and put him right back in his chair. He don't bother me less I want him to." Then she laughed her laugh, a musical tone edged with the husky grit of a voice that had aged beautifully.

The two men shared humor in their own style...a chuckle from Johnny providing undertones to his own short, pitched cackle and then Dinah said, "Ah'm gonna leave you two alone for a while...some of those stories that see daylight are more than I want to know, and some of them I've heard more often than I can bear."

She laughed again, headed toward the back TV room and as she turned, hollered, "Let me know if ya'll need anything to drink, Walt, and have Johnny show you his new flavor of liquid food. It ain't whiskey anymore." Again, her lilt filled the room, following along with her as she left them alone to talk and joke about their life together, that time fifty years before Johnny ever met Dinah.

He looked over at the Boss, noting his weariness as they began to jabber about local doings in town. Walt noted on a little drive around a few months ago that the main streets had devolved into glass corridors edged with empty buildings, scratchy shops and meager eateries. He listened

56

now to Johnny's conviction that things weren't going to get any better.

"I remember a time," he began, slurring more when he became excited, "when every damn one of those stores were filled...foot traffic sometimes put people walking around one another. You could smell the burgers, pastries and breakfast foods up and down the street.

He paused, wiped his chin, and went on, "Father said that he was lucky enough to both buy and sell a half dozen buildings before everything went to hell...won't come back."

"You really don't think so?" Walt commented, "Some of those new homes in the Heights are pretty expensive. This little section you live in is clean and modern, and I see new oil wells popping up and old ones being serviced all over the place... most of 'em seem to be operating."

"Nah," Johnny snorted, "There may be oil flowing again, but it doesn't send money into the stores here. Most of it goes to the metro area. Hell, most of the guys in the fields live in the suburbs. Long lines of traffic to and from every day. There's just no interest in staying here...settling in." He paused for breath, took his handkerchief from his little waist pocket and soaked up some saliva. Paused again to get some breath and went on.

"When Periscope Oil left it took the heart and soul of the town with it. Gutted the working class. Wages today won't support Main Street. Too many prisoner's wives and kids; too many poor people. It just ain't the same."

"How about the schools?" Walt asked.

"Oh, they struggle with new faces, brown ones and lots of 'em, drugs and changing times too, but I tell you, if there is any hope for a decent future for kids today, it's the schools."

"Well, that's the way I always remembered it," Walt continued the conversation, "The schools were good...people supported them, expected results and they got 'em."

Johnny paused, grabbed some breath and went on, "Used to be, kid got disciplined at school, went home and got disciplined again. These days, teacher's more likely to be sued...school still the best hope to help those youngsters make it. I didn't like it, but it was there if I wanted it."

"Well, you had a business waiting for you to graduate from high school, and you made it work."

A pause, then Walt went on, "Gosh, we hung out all summer at the Rec, the Natatorium, playing softball, spending time in the school gyms, shooting pool, battling at ping-pong... we were doin' something all the time...too busy to get into too much trouble I guess. Still like that?"

Johnny grabbed some more air, then answered, "Oh, yeah, they still keep 'em busy in the summer...Little League Baseball now, and swimming pools, all kinds of team activities...junior football...I guess skateboarding burns up energy too...good for the kids, even the older ones. Good to see those faces in the paper each week holding trophies instead of posing for a mug shot."

He grabbed his handkerchief again and wiped his lips.

"But...take a look at the Square and you'll see as many drug dealers as cockroaches and there are plenty of them....ugh... damn bugs...hate 'em. Same for South Hills...old homes, junky yards, leaking septic tanks...damn, at least the Oakies and Arkies kept clean homes and tidy yards, but they're disappearing too. More Mexicans now than I can keep count... likely more of them than whites."

Johnny paused, took a breath, then another and went on, "Hell, it's getting hard to find a place to spend your money around here. Shopping...a lot of it...goes to the City. Most of those damn fifty and sixty year old motels are falling apart."

Walt had heard Johnny grousing on brown faces, poorly kept shops, decaying housing and empty stores many times before. Even a casual drive about town revealed some truth in what he said. The best looking institutions were the schools, not businesses on the main street, and for better or for worse, a new mixed ethnic population filled the classrooms in the public school. St. Mark's had to close its doors. A lot of things had changed.

But the Boss didn't go around looking at it anymore. Easier to just ignore it, because as the world outside continued to restructure itself, Johnny found challenges enough right inside his house, deep inside his body.

Too much sitting weakened his legs. Cancer surgeries altered his speech. He could eat, but only through a feeding tube and that left his body distorted as it dealt with a narrow range of nutrients. With great courage he accepted these insults, built model planes, joked of his physical humiliations and followed community news with great interest.

Walt looked at the Boss again, saw him as a young man locked up in the body of an old, sick citizen. What trials he endured, what pains he suffered had until recently been largely payback for his own way of living large. But now time itself worked against him, and his 70 years on earth had blended into decades of memories.

Walt had his own. Every time he visited he remembered the entire sequence of events that brought him into Johnny's world, and as the Boss took a few moments to blot his chin, adjust his feeding tube and arrange his weight in his chair, Walt let his mind wander back to their first meeting.

At age 12, he heard that Johnny Winslow needed help cleaning up his butcher shop, located an easy walk from school. It might pay as much as $9 a week, far more than his 16-18 dollars/month delivering papers six days a week. So, he took himself to the market, went to the back of the store and seeing a figure behind the meat cases he called, "Mr. Winslow". The man turned, saw no one and returned to work.

He called again, and again the man, tall, with dark long hair, very large ears, glasses, sharp eyes and lean body, glanced up. Curious, he came to the counter, looked over it and saw "this squirt" as he remembered it, standing down there. "What do you want?" Johnny asked.

He spoke right up, "My cousin Eugene said you needed someone to clean up the butcher shop at the end of the day. I'd like the job."

Johnny hesitated. "What's your name?

"Walt Farmer!" he almost shouted.

The face asked him, "Do you think you can handle cleaning the large tubs?"

"Yes," he said, "I can." He said it with a certainty he did not feel, but why not. What tub could he not clean?

That brief conversation changed his life! Johnny Winslow ran a business, and he ran it with a hard eye on the bottom line, sharing few characteristics with a scoutmaster, a priest, or a teacher. He didn't ask Walt to earn merit badges, go to church, keep track of his sins, read books, or throw papers. None of that. This man lived to earn a profit. From then on, Walt worked to help him bring in his money and earn his own.

"What's goin' on in that mind of yours, squirt?" The comment brought Walt back to the small room.

I was just thinking about how clever I thought you were, a grown man who knew what life was all about."

"Well, didn't I?" Johnny smiled.

"Hell," Walt commented with a laugh in his voice, "I sure thought so. Took me years to figure out that a 19 year old out of high school and one divorce behind him couldn't have a monopoly on smarts. Right?"

"Well, smart enough to start running a business," Johnny replied with laugh, "and I got smarter." In earlier years that little insult about his first divorce would have brought an edgy, angry retort, but Johnny had been sober now for nine years. It showed. Walt's mind took another timeout and raced through some of those first months with Johnny.

He came to work after school, usually 5:30, and worked for about an hour and a half. He cleaned the meat case windows, swiped down the counters and scales with damp cloths, washed bloody pans, scrubbed out tubs that weighed a fifth of his body weight, scrapped out and washed the cutting saw and the slicer, covered the meat in the case with moist cloths to keep it bright, raked the sawdust and when Johnny could think of nothing else for him to do, he went home. He earned

.40 cents an hour, and after about three months .50 cents an hour.

Walt found Johnny a very watchful, critical, outspoken disciplinarian about his work habits. Although a very poor craftsman in actually cutting things like steaks, pork chops (particularly difficult) and roasts, Walt learned to do it, and he enjoyed making hamburger, slicing lunch meat, waiting on customers and providing Johnny with endless entertainment as he learned more about food products and the ways of the world.

As memories surfaced, Walt commented, "Hey, Boss, do you remember the day that guy came up and asked for some head cheese."

"Christ yes," he began to laugh again causing him to choke on his saliva. The last surgery had damaged his tongue, making it very difficult for him to swallow. He paused, wiped his lips again, and continued, "I thought I would piss my pants. You...about 5' tall, barely able to see over the counter," he laughed again."

"I've forgotten. What the hell *is* head cheese?"

"Oh, it's just a lunchmeat full of brains, pig snouts, kidneys and stuff you'd never heard about. But you tried so hard," Johnny remembered, laughing again.

"What'd I do?" Walt asked.

"You said that you didn't have any head cheese and offered the guy some cheddar cheese. I thought I would have to leave the shop laughing."

"Well," Walt remembered, "I think I was more embarrassed when you convinced me that the military used flexible American cheese during World War II to keep the tires rolling on army trucks."

"Oh, Christ, Walt," Johnny rolled his eyes, "I think I could have sold you a wad of yeast dough and told you it would rise into a carry bag...think I could?"

"No," Walt smiled, "But you could have sold me a sky-hook so we could lift heavy pieces of beef out of the delivery truck."

That brought another round of laughter, some coughing, another pause for saliva control, and then a new light in his eyes, as Johnny delighted in remembering the time he sent Walt up to *Shop Here Grocery* to get a sky-hook, and there, brother Dan sent him on to *A&P* to ask brother Bill if he had a sky-hook Johnny could borrow. Everyone had a laugh at the 14 year old sincerity that Walt brought to his travels... lots of laughter."

"All I would have to do is attach it to a platform in the sky and then lower the cable to hook on to the meat and move it into the locker, right?" Walt asked, and Johnny started to laugh so hard he coughed, choking on the liquid that leaked down his windpipe. "You seemed to know everything, Boss," Walt laughed.

Johnny Winslow became his surrogate father and showed him a dozen different peep shows on how life could be lived. Johnny gave him advice on how to monitor alcohol, though he seemed to ignore his own rules. He told Walt to avoid smoking, laughingly remarking that it would stunt his growth, then sometimes surprised him by starting a slap-box joust in the walk-in cooler. They had races to see who could cut up a chicken fastest, and he learned with embarrassment how a turkey neck could be flung around like a freakish penis.

Walt even heard about women one Saturday night when Johnny set out to explain to him various aspects of sex: using a condom (a "safe" he called it); soliciting women (just ask... one out of three will say yes); satisfying women (Walt had no idea what he was talking about); avoiding commitments because women will take you for your money (no problem there), and an open-door to talk to him about sex and women anytime. Startling peep show.

"Remember when you gave me 'The Talk' about girls, sex and condoms?" Walt asked.

"No. Wha'd I say, something good I hope?"

"It was good advice wasted on an innocent mind, but I did learn that there seemed to be some mysterious world of women that could be in my future. You even told me that being with a woman was never an excuse to be late for work."

"Well," Johnny said, "If you spent the night with a NEW woman, maybe fifteen minutes late..." and he laughed until he choked again.

"Well, that dream never came true for me...what about that time I didn't come back from the school trip on time to go to work. Do you remember what you did?"

For the next five days, when he would call to come to work, Johnny said, "No" and he got the same answer all week until Friday. That was a message. Don't miss work.

Tired, sick, hung over, distracted, lovesick, upset, hungry, angry, offended by others, no matter what, don't miss work.

A few years later, hung over from vodka, he went to work on a Sunday to hose out and clean the meat cases. Johnny gave him tomato juice, laughed at him and watched Walt work. Another peep show.

"Nah, but I'm sure it was smart and effective."

"Hell, you showed me a lot of things I remember, and apart from the three divorces you went through, most of them were pretty helpful," and it was Walt's turn to laugh.

"Well, sometimes a woman doesn't know when she has a man worth keeping," Johnny replied with some reflection, but mostly chagrin. "Now, with Dinah..."

"Your fourth wife, right," he jabbed Johnny, "But she is a winner....knows how to handle you, can stick your ass with a smile and you like it, right?"

"I'm not complaining," Johnny smiled. Then, he excused himself, rose shakily and slowly took himself to the bathroom. While he did his business, Walt began thinking some more about those years in the butcher shop.

Johnny took him to Los Angeles to see a Rams football game and on the way home, let him, age 15, drive the Pontiac Bonneville all the way across the flats. The Boss also allowed him to play high school sports even if he missed an occasional Friday for games. He counseled him on how to spend his money and how to save it. He took him to Las Vegas as a ride-along with his second wife, Lois, and gave him some excellent perspective about going to Vegas. "Don't go", he said, "if you have to count your money." Walt always followed his advice on that.

Then there was a Saturday night when Walt learned something about himself. While he did inventory, Johnny sat on a bench drank beer and bullshitted with Greg Langer who owned the grocery. It took a couple of hours to weigh everything and record it, and when done, Walt reported the results. Langer now gone, Johnny now drunk, he looked at Walt's writing and asked him about his list. It just showed "ham" and X pounds and ounces.

Johnny pointed to the list, "What is this?"
Walt said, "I weighed ham."
"What kind of ham?" Johnny said, getting angry.
Walt didn't know what to say. He repeated, "ham".
Heatedly, now shouting, Johnny pointed out that some ham was butt ham and some was shank ham and they had different values, and then getting angrier, he said to me, "God damn it, Walt, I am going to stay on your ass until you learn how to do things right, or until you quit." He replied instantly, angrily, "I will never quit." Period.

Johnny ran a good shop; he made a profit. A committed businessman, smart and quick with words and ideas, he had an eye for detail, made up excellent weekly newspaper advertisements and knew how to treat customers well. Walt always remembered the Boss' observation about selling groceries to the occasional black person who came through the store. "I don't care what color of skin a customer has so long as he pays in green." For its day, Walt thought to himself now, that view sharply contradicted community values which had for decades quietly rejected black residents or shoppers. Walt could not remember ever saying hello to a black man in public or a black child in school.

Johnny offered other lessons too. He and a friend once drove their motorcycles into a local bar, circled the patrons and left. Cited for trespassing by the police, demoted in rank by the National Guard whom they were serving that day, Johnny characterized it, with chagrin, as "An unusual drill maneuver."

He chased women, and he walked a dangerous line. One husband pulled his motorcycle up alongside Johnny's car at a stop sign, pointed a pistol at his head and asked for a good reason not blow his brains out. In times like that, Johnny counseled Walt, "Say nothing. Just listen. Nod agreement."

Back in his chair Johnny pointed to a model plane on his work table and a ship in a bottle set above the television set, both products of his preoccupation for the last decade. "This B-29 has kept me damn busy with its detail and wing span," he said slowly, still slurring. "Hard to get it just right, but nearly there...something else to hang. I'm thinking of new space in the garage...running out of room."

Speaking of "running out of room," I reminded Johnny, "What about the day your father ran that guy out of the store...the old fart wanted me to cut a ham in a way that would give him most of the center cut. Never forget it...your dad just walked up to that guy and told him to get his ass out and never come back. I couldn't believe he would run off a customer like that. Then he told me, "There are tricks to every trade, Walt, and the butcher trade is all tricks. Can't let customers take away our profit. We take a lot of shit, but we don't have to let anyone rub our noses in it."

"I remember laughing at that," Walt commented, "Never heard those expressions before. He liked me...not sure why."

"Oh, yeah, he liked you a lot. Saw something of himself in you. Ya know when Father was 13, his daddy abandoned the family," Johnny started, "Left him to fend for himself...lived with some relatives in Delano, found work in the packing house processing two beef and four sheep a day, from kill to quarters. All that work...every day...at age 13!"

"Was that legal...working him that way? Weren't there laws or something?"

"Laws don't feed you," Johnny answered. "He did what he needed to do to live. Hell of a job. Skinned, gutted, trimmed them up...every day. That's a hell of a lot of work...jumped at the chance to get into retail meat cutting, and then he learned how easy it was for people to cheat you."

He paused to wipe his mouth. He sighed a bit and Walt could see that he was getting tired. He looked at the Boss closely, really looked, and saw in his softened features, wasted arms, measured breath and fragile legs all the ravages of the cancer, the damage to his lungs, jaw and now Dinah said it had spread again. Still, he was a kinder, gentler man without the alcohol, and Walt remembered that day when he finally freed himself from trying to please an alcoholic, just a mental note to himself that he just wouldn't try anymore...no point to it. But he could embrace a sober Boss as warmly as he had rejected the drunk.

Johnny's passion for making fun of him seemed to know no boundaries. Buy a Corvette, marry a local girl, join the Navy? They all produced raucous laughter and disbelief, predictions of certain disaster. But when Walt, after leaving school and working for a semester in the butcher shop, decided to return to college, Johnny said to him, "That is a great idea. Do it." And he did.

Walt eventually earned his degree in Colorado and one summer, Johnny and his third wife Vera, drove all the way through the Rocky Mountains to see him. Johnny said that he thought he only had to go to Boulder, Nevada and when that turned out to be the wrong state, he just had to keep driving. Hard to tell from the look on his face if he were making that up. He was still drinking and sometimes with a drunk it was hard to tell.

"Boss, I gotta say, it sure is fun visiting when you are sober. Feels like it has been a long time since we could talk without a lot of bullshit criticism and wild talk."

"Well, the devil nearly got me," he said, "but I do a lot better now and I like life a lot better now that Dinah keeps setting me straight and all. But every once in a while, I stray."

"How's that?" Walt asked, knowing that Johnny could not swallow much of anything, much less whiskey, so how could he get into trouble?

"Well," he began, "Sometimes I pour a small airplane bottle of whiskey into my feeding tube. Then, (my, how he grinned when he said this), I put a little on my tongue just to get the taste as I feel the little warm glow from the alcohol."

"Boss, there is no end to it is there."

"No end 'til the end" Johnny replied.

"Well, that's a long ways away," Walt commented.

Johnny was more tired now. Dinah, hearing the weariness in his voice, sashayed back in asking Walt if he heard any truths or just lies.

"I think I heard a lot of lies, but they sounded like truth," he smiled, and they all laughed. It was time.

Walt got up and waited for Johnny to get to his feet. They shook hands again, then hugged, and Walt held him a little longer than usual. He'd be back to see him in a few weeks, but he also knew that time was their enemy. Johnny gave Walt a long look, right in the eyes, measuring something in there to mark the growth of his one-time clean-up boy.

Johnny gave Dinah a friendly hug. He got to the screen door, opened it a bit and turned again to say goodbye. He caught the love in the Boss' eyes, felt it warm him, returned it.

Dinah called two weeks later, crying, wailing, and he knew the words that would follow.

"Johnny collapsed walking to the bedroom, Walt," and her voice broke again as she told him that the doc said he was dead before he hit the floor. She knew that he would want to know. No services planned. He thanked her, hung up the phone and spent many minutes spinning his life with Johnny through his mind one more time.

Dad, friend, critic, mentor, model, antagonist, protagonist, the Boss was all of that to him and Walt felt the pain rising, knew that it would percolate for a long time but finally find its niche among all his other losses. Years crowd into one another, he thought, but death always made its own space.

Looking for Love

There was nothing subtle about the quest. Mother's love, unconditional and unchanging, remained. But Walt wanted more, an emotional connection to a girl whose faith in him emulated that of his mother's, but whose love served a wider spectrum, one that was sexual, modern, and intellectually in tune with the day. He wanted a woman willing to embrace him through an undefined future and to do it fully committed to keeping him as safe in his sense of self as in those early years when he toddled about knowing that nothing could hurt him. He needed a mate.

Looking for a lady to love created adolescent wishes deeply flawed by chronology and an undefined future. Physical security he could provide for himself. Love, the emotional fulfillment of having one's sense of self reflected back through the eyes of another...that he needed to find, and he went looking.

The rituals proved flush with hazards. He was young, too young. The girls were not yet women. Love was a symptom of explorations, not commitments, and yet he kept sorting through his options. Ten, twenty, thirty and more of those smiling faces and attractive bodies paused in his arms. A date was not a date if it did not include solitude, conversation, a kiss or two. That kiss was essential. That wasn't all that might be possible, but that was essential.

He walked into the kitchen of his aunt's home, the small loving home that she opened up to him when he returned to college. He had dragged his body through three sleepless nights, obsessed with the loss of a high school girl friend. He struggled with a reconciliation strategy, an especially difficult task when he was the only one wanting it.

As he looked about the kitchen, he called out for his aunt to see if she were there, but she was not. He walked around the corner and looked into the dining room, stood in the doorway, shaky and confused, and as he looked, the room before him began to move. It wavered, seemed to close down upon him, expanded, twisted a little then tried to resume its previous original shape. It would not remain still. He phoned his mother. That had always worked for him in times of trouble, and it worked again. Within hours, he was on the way home and into a hospital where he spent two days of sedated sleep, a rest which restored his rational mind but not his spirits. Released, he took another three days to assess, accept and address his situation.

The girl he so desperately wanted to save him from hallucinations instead caused them. The love he wanted her to shower on him withheld, he went to the original source of love, mother, let her ease him through the crisis, then resolved that there would never again be nights without sleep, never another emotional investment so deep that its loss could not be managed in plain daylight.

He found himself a little further from that adult womb of security he longed to find, and he began to take risks. Late night adventures mixed with alcohol led to daytime realities and jail. Travelling with friends tripped the boundaries of common sense. Experiments with college led him from one school to another. Wanderlust it might have been. Confused choice it certainly was, and yet, somewhere in it all, he learned about himself, how to focus on worthy goals, how to deal with innate insecurities.

Stepping stones. That was the way across this waterway. Big little steps, risky but a way across nonetheless. He needed a change of scenery...a new school. He needed a change of companions...a new girl...a woman. He needed love to make him feel whole and give him an undistracted pursuit of a future.

Looking for it again in another state, in another college, in another venue with another woman, he learned with each seasonal disappointment how much he would have to adjust his search. Probably no other person would reflect his love of self fully enough to keep him whole. He would have to form himself, be his own security, find happiness in himself, know his own needs and move on in life. Maybe there was no happily ever after.

Linked

Litton hesitated, thought again about his plan, walked away and then stopped. Now? Never? When? He just wanted to ask the big question without getting in trouble. Risky business.

He paused again, turned back toward the Old Man who sat comfortably in his special chair reading the newspaper, sipping a cup of tea. Might as well.

"Hey Pa, I was wondering...?

The newspaper lowered slowly, and the squinty eyes focused on him, looked him up and down and raised the paper once more. Silence.

Litton tried to interpret the look...forbidding talk or inspecting the prospect that he might say something...anything at all.

Well, he might as well try it.

He started again, "Say Pa, I was wondering...I was wondering if I could borrow the car for the Winter Formal...ask a girl to take to the Winter Formal...it's right in town...close to home...I'd be really careful...Winter Formal...big dance of the year...could I...what do you think?

"Eh?" The newspaper stay raised.

Christ, Litton thought, I'm going to have to ask again. The Old Man did have some hearing loss, but more often than not he used it as an excuse to avoid an answer, perhaps to intimidate, certainly to delay indefinitely any response to a question he did not want to hear.

"Eh?" He said it again from behind the newspaper, dismissing the question on the basis of not having heard it.

"Pa, I want to take a date to the Winter Formal. Can I use the car?"

He shook the paper once to get it properly aligned with his eyes, read on for a moment, then slowly lowered it again and looked at his son.

"Is this go'ah be an'ahr Cli' Westwoodie mess?"

Litton did not how to respond. He could say, "No", but that seemed too perfunctory. He needed to reassure the Old Man with some plausible deniability. He let the silence percolate for a few moments while he mentally reviewed the Westwood Caper.

It had begun innocently enough, during a little time out from life with his close friend, Paul "The Toe" Brewster. They drove out into the desert, drank some beer and reassured one another that their ability to make extra points in football games could become part of local folklore. Litton had good hands, liked holding the ball and spinning it to just the right position so that the laces were away from contact. Brewster kicked straight on just like his hero, Lou "The Toe" Groza, famously of the Cleveland Browns. His mantra, "What Lou could do, I can do too," brought a lot of laughter among teammates who more often than not saw an extra point flutter, weaken in mid-flight, sometimes bounce off the sidebar as it made its way through the goalposts. But, it always got over. The Toe took great pleasure in reminding them of that.

Their heroics, part of their beer-flavored conversation, moved on to girls, a favorite subject, and the more they discussed the damsels of their days and the disappointments of their nights, the more they drank. Finally, since Brewster had his dad's car and someone had to drive, he put 'er in gear and carefully took his buddy home. When Litton got out, he wobbled, leaned a hand against the fender and bent over as though to puke. He didn't, but he needed a few minutes to breathe fresh air, get some oxygen to his brain and prepare to get in the house without comment from his mother, Mary by name.

For whatever reason, Litton called her Mary, much like Paul McCartney had written in *"Let It Be"*, and he spoke her name with respect because she had a sharp tongue, a penetrating eye and a flair for short, eviscerating sentences. Migrating from Belfast, Ireland with their three children, Mary joined her husband to raise their family in Oil Country. A tiny woman with ferocious stature, she remembered many things about the Old Country, one of them being her glimpse of the Titanic as it slid out of dry dock for the first time and floated nicely into the ocean. "It was quite a lovely sight," she would sigh.

Still, a fond memory never deterred her from close review of her children's behavior. She raised them to do the right thing, expected nothing less than the best, and, if suspicious, terrorized them with interrogations carried out in razor sharp phrases and unique sentence structure. Hard to avoid Mother Mary.

The Toe watched Litton gather himself, stand up a little, finally straighten. He judged his posture, factored in his alcohol consumption and concluded that he needed help. He got out of the car, walked to his buddy's side and put an arm around his waist. Together they walked carefully to the front door. Brewster decided to get him on to the porch and leave, fearful that Mary might be hovering inside, but he saw Litton's wobble worsen and knew he couldn't make it into the house on his own.

Cautiously, The Toe opened the door, glanced around and saw an empty room. Perfect. He helped his bud across the doorway, left him standing there and turned to leave when a sharp voice stopped him in his tracks. "Eh, what's this! My Tommy looks sick!" Mary looked up, found Brewster in her sight and continued, "Stop where you are you!" and he froze.

She approached her Tommy, looked him over with an experienced, practiced eye and asked the question to the world in general and to the Toe specifically, "WHO GAVE MY SON DRINK?"

A long silence followed. The Toe knew the answer to her question, but he also knew Mary's reputation for launching sharp jabs and firm corporal punishment. His mind, a considerable power in the give and take of teen-age banter, seemed to fail him. How was it that he could conjugate Latin verbs flawlessly, yet find himself without an answer to Mary's question? To say, "I did" might lead to a thrashing so thorough as to destroy his smooth, kicking motion.

In a moment of frightful despair, he uttered words which tasted bad even as they crossed his lips. "It was Clint Westwood," he said.

"CLINT WESTWOODIE! CLINT WESTWOODIE EH?" Mary said the name with a bitter flavor permeating her pronunciation. She didn't know Westwood, the Toe thought, so maybe everyone would find haven from her wrath. On the other hand, if she did find Westwood what would happen? He was known to destroy guys who even glanced at his girlfriend, LuAnn Ford, and his "fist through the fence" antic at Lorena's

Drive-In was the stuff of legend. On the other hand, he might be the only guy in school that Mary could not beat up.

Knowledge of a name seemed to satisfy her for the moment, and she turned her attention to her son. "My God, Tommy, wha'r you thinkin', lett'n a Westwoodie give you drink. To <u>bed</u> with ye! Your dad'll see to it in the mor'en. Sleep on that!"

The Toe slithered out the door before Mary could get her eye back on him, and quickly got himself to a safe place which meant out of her yard.

The next morning, Litton awoke early, way too early, with a bad headache and a nightmare lingering in his head. *Mary found him drinking and threw The Toe out of the house.* Oh no...he struggled with his memory...that was no dream and daylight promised him an audience before the Old Man. His day could not begin worse, and it might end disastrously.

He took his time rising, bathing and grooming then slowly walked into the kitchen to get some breakfast. All the while he kept a wary eye on Mary's Enforcer.

The Old Man sat in his chair without comment. Litton didn't pause, had his breakfast, grabbed his books and kept an eye on the newspaper suspended by those roughened pair of hands. If it came down, he knew his day and many of his nights were going to be very uncomfortable. But the Old Man said nothing...just read his paper.

Now, six weeks later, when he mentioned borrowing the car for an evening, the name surfaced. The Old Man dragged out the Westwood Caper as though it were yesterday. "Is this go'ah be an'ahr Cli' Westwoodie mess?"

Did he have Tommy's attention? Yep. Litton's body language shouted. "Oh My God no," but he said nothing.

The Old Man spoke again, "Is tha' Westwoodie go'an be wi' you?

"Oh, no," Litton responded quickly, "I don't spend time with him anymore. Learned my lesson." *There he had kept the code and protected The Toe.*

He went on, "Never a drink will touch my lips," he began, "The speed limit is my limit. I'll only drive to pick up the girls and Walt Farmer who is double dating with me. We are taking Nice Girls to the dance."

Mary interrupted. "That Toe won't be in the car, Tommy?"

"Oh no... don't know what he is doing, but he's not going with us." *There, used him again.*

The Old Man remained silent, kept the paper in his lap revealing reddened skin covering his shoulders, white lines sometimes showing on the edges of the loops of his cotton t-shirt. What was he thinking?

"Yu'hl be sure...no damage to the car, Tommy...ma' only car...two keys...just one car...ride ta work...only way to get around...yu'hl be sure, eh." It was not a question, but Litton answered.

"Oh, Christ yes. It'll be safe! We'll only be gone a few hours. Most of the time, it'll be parked."

"Du-na take the Lord's name, Tommy," Mary injected, "Haven't I taught you better than that? Eh?"

"I'm sorry Mary," Litton responded, turning to look at his father once more...hoping...hoping.

"All ri' then. *Do right and be right*." It was one of his Old Man's favorite sayings.

Litton fled for fear that either Mary or the Old Man might change their minds, and he told Walt that he had the car!

Their double date to the Winter Formal would be the highlight of their semester. How could it not be? They were taking two of the nicest of the Nice Girls. Both good looking and smart, friends with one another and carrying great reputations, they were glittering diamonds on the social bedrock of the high school.

Litton and Walt knew that just having them in the car was tantamount to being crowned Kings of the Prom. Litton was not sure that anyone had ever kissed Beth, his date. If so, he never heard about it. Her pert hair, pouty smile, quick repartee challenged his own witticisms, and she could dance! For his part, Walt remained entranced with Alaina, his blonde, smiling, popular, dancing girl who carried maturity in her walk and friendliness in her laugh. Used to going to big dances with big-time guys, she nonetheless accepted his invitation. How did he get so lucky?

Winter Formal...amazing! Girl's dressed for it, bought new makeup for it, talked about it in whispers. Parents provided cash, new dresses, flowers, advice, cautions and took many pictures. Guys worried, sweated about their manners, begged for access to the best wheels in the family, bought corsages, practiced compliments and hoped for something exciting to happen...maybe a memorable goodnight kiss.

Saturday night, and Litton scrubbed his body in a nice hot shower, brought out his new suit, shirt and tie, got dressed with plenty of time to spare. He picked up Beth, posed for a couple of pictures and drove over to get Walt, then Alaina and back to Walt's house where his folks brought out the camera and recorded these magic couples for posterity, or at least until the next dance. Memorable night!

Pictures taken, the girls gathered themselves and the guys opened the house door to let them pass safely without damaging artistry or attitudes, admiring their smiles, their formals, their beauty. So delicately turned out, so tidy in their walk, so precise in their entry into Litton's car, they might have been part of the Royal Family. Youth, its effervescent, its innocence, its nervous excitement, filled the air of their chariot, and as they settled into the Old Man's Ford they all remembered Cinderella's fabled magical evening. Winter Formal, Kings Dance...same thing.

Litton turned the key and hit the starter. The engine turned over, then over again. He tapped the accelerator pedal a couple of times, tried it again. RRRRRRRRRRR..... RRRRRRRRRRRR.....RRRRRRRRRRRR. Nothing. Litton looked at the dashboard, pumped the pedal again, then again. He talked to them all in a low confident tone, "Aaaaah... a little car trick...toying with us, eh?"

Walt said nothing. He did not like joking about cars since he knew nothing about what made them run, more to the point, what kept them from running. Still, the situation called for some encouragement. After all, he was a guy. "Give it a moment, Litton," he commented. "Don't rush it."

"It started just fine at home, and over at Alaina's," Litton responded. "It should start," and he hit it again and as the motor turned over he pumped that damn accelerator again... and again. Nothing.

The girls thought this was exciting...a car that didn't start. The guys thought this humiliating...their car would not start. What to do? They sat there a few minutes and consulted about likely problems...the ignition...bad starter...weak battery...hell, they didn't know. Walt went into the house to tell his step-dad Skip about their problem. He knew motors, built them for go-karts, welded parts in his shop, kept his boat motor running. He could get the Ford started, Walt just knew it.

"Well, sure," Skip said, "Let's go out there and see what's happening." They walked out to the car, the girls now quietly giggling and whispering about the excitement of the unpredictable. The guys kept sweating. Skip slipped into the driver's seat, turned the key and the engine turned over nicely, and then...voila'...nothing...nothing. He paused, got out and the guys got out too, as though they were part of the team solution. He raised the hood, poked his head underneath it and took a good whiff of the air.

"You flooded it, Tommy," he said, "It's going to take a while to get it running again...just needs to let gas evaporate and then it'll probably run just fine."

Litten's eyes got a little big. "Is this anything I need to tell my Old Man about. Did I break it?"

"Nope," Skip replied, "It's fine...just going to take some time."

"How much time?" Litten asked.

"Don't know...half an hour, maybe an hour."

"We'll miss half the dance," he murmured as his eyes turned to heaven and Walt catching the drift of the talk just couldn't believe it. How cool would this be? Hanging around his parent's house for an hour, wondering what in the hell to do with themselves while these gorgeous Nice Girls wished they were at the dance. Disaster!

"Well," Skip said, "If you want, I could hook you up to the back of my welding truck. It's only about seven miles to town and I can wire up some flasher tail lights and tow you in. By the time the dance is over, it should be ready to run."

The guys looked at one another...towed to town for the Winter Formal!! Humiliating. Walt couldn't look at the girls. Litten did. He just stuttered a bit and said, "Looks...uh, looks like we can hook up to a welding truck and ease our way into town, eh?"

"Yea!" Beth and Alaina, both tickled by the unpredictable, said it in unison. "Let's do it,!" Beth continued. "Who else has ever gone to a formal being towed by a welding truck.... they'll talk about this for the rest of the year."

"I'm sure they will," Walt commented, knowing that "they" would be everyone they knew and they would be laughing... at him and Litten.

Walt tried humor, "Think we could call Clint Westwood and ask for a ride, Litten? Eh?"

No answer.

"Let's tow it in," Litton finally said. "Better to be on the way than just sitting here hoping." *He remembered the Old Man's warning, 'Do right and be right'.*

He hoped he was doing right.

Skip brought the welding truck around and backed it up to the Ford. He wired up some flasher lights to illuminate the rear end of the Ford, then hauled the rattling chains over the heavy metal bed and latched them into the rear bumper of the welding truck. He lugged them over to the car, got down on the ground and hooked the links on to the front frame of the car. He got out, checked the tension, admired his work and said, "There, she should be good to go."

The guys got into the car, trying to be cool, feeling like eternal losers. The girls, who had never left it, laughed a special giggle, loving the drama. Skip got in his truck and off they went, a chain linked caravan moving at a steady 25 mph, rear lights flashing and the guy's embarrassment leaking out of every seam of the Old Man's Ford. Inside, the girls whispered, giggled, occasionally shouting their ooohs and aaaahs when the chain hit the pavement or when the car got a little too close on a downslope then hit the end of the links as Litton jerkily applied the brakes.

With good will, the two Cinderellas joked for all seven miles about a ride to remember, laughing that their chariot had turned into a pumpkin long before midnight. The boys squirmed and sweated, murmuring little ideas on how to keep the news from the school. When the rig stopped in front of the school, they asked Skip to park it around the far end of the football field where it might never be seen. He did so, stealthily, making sure the auto-train sat parked in dark shadows. Then he unhitched the Ford and left for home cautioning them to call him if they needed any help after the dance. Litton didn't wait. As soon as they entered the gym, he called the Old Man.

"The car's broke."

"Ehhhhh, Tommy. Wha' you say'? Broke?"

"Yep. It won't start."

"Wher's it?"

"Here at the high school. Behind the football field. Walt's dad towed us in with his welding truck. It's broke. It won't run."

Silence.

"Get on ta the dance, Tommy. I'll walk o'er and take a look. G'on ta the dance."

Music floated throughout the gym. Litton hung up the phone, returned to the girls and decided to just do the best he could. How would they take them home? Maybe their pumpkins would change back into a chariot. If not, there was always the chain linked ride that brought them to the dance.

Shortly after midnight, the foursome wandered out past the football field where they had parked the Ford. Still there, it seemed inviting. They got in. Litton turned the key, didn't pump the accelerator, just turned the key. The engine growled as it went through its cycle once, and then it started. A rumbling roar restored the engine and the guy's egos. The girls broke-up again embracing the hilarity of it all, laughing at their unique experience: a welder's truck, rattling chains, flashing lights, the smell of gasoline, an evening of comic relief. No kisses for the boys this night.

Fifty years later, this is the way they told it:

Litton to Beth, "Want to go to the Winter Formal?"

Beth, "Sure."

Walt to Alaina, same question, same answer.

"You do. Great. We'll pick you up in Tommy's Ford."

Alaina, "Oh...sure, guess this means we should call ahead and reserve the welding truck, right?"

Laughter, long and gleeful for the girls...stiff and still uncomfortable for the boys.

The River

He first saw her up close at the River, a narrow ribbon of water that ran fitfully and sometimes not at all across his end of the valley. If left unattended, it would sojourn into an apparent lowland then abruptly turn north and ooze its way up ancient waterways gathering finally to rest in the Tulare Basin. Its flow, perhaps knee deep in early summer, could fill quickly with the emptying of great rain pockets in the mountains to the east, growing strong and dangerous. Receding, it left humid, scented air hanging heavily above its banks, a refuge from the sagebrush and alkaline flavored dirt through which it ran.

On summer nights along a spit of earth at River's edge, high school friends often met, shared gossip and roasted hot dogs to go with their beers. A shadowy place to be sure, but moonlight allowed quick looks at bodies and faces, revealed swift judgments, witnessed suggestive comments. Sometimes romance flourished, blankets disappearing into parked cars cushioning those who cultivated rock n' roll. Memories burned into minds here, sometimes painful ones, but each fall they grew faint as the River gently subsided, disappearing into light brown sands whose meandering path even a quarter moon could illuminate.

Lori Larken's voice carried through dark whisperings, her words nicely rounded with easy tones as she joined in a variety of engaging conversations. She seldom dated, but this night, like the waters along the bank where they all rested, she flowed into their lives, touched hopeful dreams, then left them sorting through gritty, seasonal memories.

Some things all boys agreed upon. Lori's tall, slender body featured attractive hips, classic breasts and ice-blue eyes. Her mouth, generous and beautifully edged with inviting lips, worked in tandem with her eyes to convey false innocence, edgy complaint or thoughtful wonderings. In conversation, she might flutter her lashes two maybe three times, then fix her blue gaze directly on target, make a gentle comment then retreat into silence. No one had a clue as to what went on in her head.

At the moment, she was complaining about how strictly her parents controlled her social life. "They don't want me at rock dances. I can't go to private homes and pool parties, and they absolutely have a fit when I even mention coming out here to the River."

Yet, here she was, hiding in the dark along the banks of warm waters knowing that her parents believed that she would spend the night with her friends, Jean Ann and Paula.

"Gosh," she went on, "I'd like to date more."

"Well then Lori, do." A voice challenged her in a gentle, firm tone.

"What? Who said that?"

The fire faded a bit, darkening the shadows.

"I said it, Lori," Kerry spoke up, "I'm saying that you should see a little bit of our tiny world and make some memories." Tall, muscular and smart, Kerry focused his dark eyes on her and let his words linger in the air. Like many of us, he found her a curiosity. Unlike the rest of us, he broached an overture though he didn't know if he were speaking to an ingenious ingénue or just a tease who wanted a long hello and a short goodbye? Was she a girl literally looking for love in all the wrong places?

Lori fashioned a lovely bright smile, probably her best feature among many, and said, "Kerry, you think I could just go on dates and get away with it? You really think I could manage that? You don't know my parents."

Kerry looked at her for a few, long seconds, "Just do it."

The fire popped, and a smattering of embers floated above the stone ring then gently lifted over the river, blackened and dropped into the flow of water. Silence, and then a new voice.

"You're too worried about your parents, Lori," Kent's low bass tones floated into the conversation. "You only live once. Time for new faces, good times, fun."

Then Walt chimed in, tentatively, softly, "Maybe you're just avoiding people, Lori? Maybe you're just too shy to see the world through the eyes of different guys."

She looked right at him, and kept that look focused longer than he thought he wanted her to. Then she just said, "Well, Walt, maybe you're right, but it's risky business."

The little campfire crackled just a bit more sending some lively embers swirling, this time catching a bit of air and floating down river before they quietly blinked black. Silence. This was a gentle conversation, but not an ordinary one. Lori had a way of setting everyone on edge, and when she started thinking out loud no one wanted to miss a sentence.

Kerry kept at it, "Are you really interested in new doings, Lori, or just posturing a pout from the movies?"

She reacted quietly. "I'm not really sure, Kerry. There are times when I just feel so constricted."

Kent chimed in, "Well, sample life a little," he smiled, "We'll get you home in time to suit your parents."

"Hmm," she paused and thought, "Don't know, Kent; I'm not even sure how to get out of the house?

"Oh, it's easy," Jean Ann commented, "I'll just come by and pick you up like I did tonight, and then turn you over to your date. When you come home, have him drop you off up the block and then you can quietly go into the house."

One could see the possibilities beginning to turn in Lori's mind. She looked around the campfire for a moment, then stood up and walked a few steps into the River. It touched her, mid-calf. Over her shoulder she said with a smile in her voice, and probably one on her face, "Should I date one of you guys and see how it works?"

"Sounds good, don't youse think, guys." Albert spoke for the first time, but he had been following the conversation closely, and his white shirt rippled as he motioned to himself, "Its summer, let's go do something. Let's get outta here."

"I like that idea," Kerry said. He looked at Lori in that quiet, narrow-eyed manner he had when he was serious and said, "So, let's plan to get to know one another better."

Lori turned around, her eyes reflecting the coals in the fire, and met his look. Walt had a thought...she wasn't going to back down. Lori continued to look at Kerry and for just a moment her face did not posture, her mouth remained closed and she was beautiful. Her eyes seemed to narrow just a bit, then relaxed. "O.K.," she said, and as though to anticipate the questions, she followed with, "Why don't I go on a date with all four of you---Eenie, Meenie, Miney, Moe," and as she spoke each name, she pointed to the four of them. Walt was Miney, but he couldn't see clearly who else she chose as she called out the names.

Who? He wanted to know who was who, but she smiled and refused to repeat her identifications, but each guy knew, and now admitted to her dating game, they each had a new focus in life and summer moved along much more quickly. He knew them all. They were experienced, and they knew what they wanted. He was neither, well, he wasn't experienced, but over the remaining two months of summer, Lori dated each of them once and by his close observation she dated no one else.

Kerry invited her to a lecture at the university: *"Gravity, Matter, and Destruction"*. Jean Ann picked her up and dropped her off two blocks away and off they went. Afterwards, to Kerry's surprise, she wanted to talk about Black Holes.

The same parent escape worked two weeks later when Kent took her to a dance at Sunset Gardens. Fats Domino pounded out *Blueberry Hill*, and Kent mixed his moves so smoothly that the dusky crowd didn't hassle them. She could dance. He gave her that.

Albert took her to a midget car race, protected her from flying clay, bought her popcorn, soda and hot dogs, regaling her with stories of his time in Rhode Island. She seemed to find his accent amusing.

Walt bought tickets to the Fox theatre and *Dr. Zhivago*. Omar Sharif seemed to have the right ideas about life and love, he commented, even if his world was being violently yanked out from under him. Lori, he thought, looked as beautiful as Julie Christie.

He wanted to hear about each of the other guy's dates, but their brief remarks told him nothing. She was pleasant to be with, thought more than anticipated, looked as great in full light as in the shadows. Walt agreed, but when he tried to get them to speak more specifically, they each said about the same thing, "It wasn't what I expected, but we got home in time to please her parents." What more could they add to the conversation? From his point of view and his own experience, they had covered it all. Nice evening, nice girl, nice talk, end of story.

By the close of summer, the River had run dry, their dates with Lori a memory. Sports, new faces and classwork sent them all into high school routines, and Lori flowed through the halls, smiling as always, gently curious about daily doings, carrying friendliness in her walk and talk. She flirted quietly with the River Boys, blurting out her sometimes puzzling bits of arcane knowledge yet remaining distant.

In Walt's view she dated not at all and even her good friend Paula had nothing to report on her feelings for any of the guys. When he suggested that they go out again, Lori just smiled nicely and said, "No, not this week." Three other scattered efforts met the same response, so Walt just quit asking. But he kept watching.

The social rivulet set in motion at the River wound its way through the dating game, found its low and settled, unresolved. Still, what did it witness? Had any of the River Boys gotten a privileged look? Were any of them seeing Lori without anyone taking notice? Who was who? Who was Eeenie? Who was Meenie? Moe? They wouldn't say.

Occasional fall rains freshened the air, wet the surface of the River bed and energized one more round of parties. There were a couple of gatherings out there in early October, one celebrating Halloween though no one saw behind Lori's mask, and the guys seemed oddly disconnected from their one-time experiences. Mention her name and they reacted. Mention their dates with her...silence.

Perplexed when she did not return after Christmas vacation, Walt searched for news. The word in the halls was that she needed to spend time with a seriously ill aunt who lived in Wyoming. Winter moved on. High school romances flourished and wilted. Walt waited each week for the latest un-coupling report, wondering who might be a new face he could date, and he filled the season with new faces, fresh kisses and thoughtful memories of Lori. Easter vacation arrived and still no word on when she could return.

Ten days back in school, word raced through the halls. Jean Ann had news from Wyoming. A notice in the Sheridan paper simply said that Lori Larken had given birth to a 9 lb. 6 ounce baby boy. Mother and child were doing well. She named the baby, BRADY LEMM LARKEN.

The news dropped like netting over the entire school. Unwed mothers...rare. Who was the father? Widespread speculation but no answers. The birth date suggested summertime love, but no one knew for sure.

Walt talked to each guy that week. They were edgy and evasive, pleading innocence with real conviction. Lori's pregnancy astounded them all. When? Who? How? Paternity became a constant part of their conversation and even as innocent as Walt knew himself to be, the idea of marriage, child support, end of youth, and the specter of community shame launched little needles of fear through him. The four speculated about what this all meant to any of them.

Finally, Walt offered them a new way to look at the issue.

"I think the baby's middle name can tell us the identity of the father."

"That middle name is spelled weird," Kent said.

Albert just snorted, "Youse guys! She just likes attention. She spelled it that way just to be noticed. She is outta here."

Kerry agreed, but he added, "She can be silly, but she can be pretty serious too, and she has a thoughtful mind." But none of them said anything to help answer the paternity issue.

A week before graduation Walt bribed them with beer. "Meet me at the River Saturday, late afternoon...its running again... it's supposed to be warm. I'll supply the booze." With curious looks, they agreed.

He got there first, hauled the beer cooler to the newly defined water's edge and spent some time just watching the River flow. Its waters gurgled along from spring snowmelt and another round of mountain rainfall and now with generous width, it reflected late afternoon sunlight in the valley. It flowed with force and little curlicues of water spun around loose pieces of winter litter picked up by the rising waterline. Thin edges of dirt which marked its lower flow lines created small pockets of water which under pressure, finally gave way and the water flowed, growing in the force of its release.

He heard the car doors slam, and as they drifted over, he popped a beer into their hands and then asked his questions. "O.K., I'm Miney. Who are Eeenie, Meenie, and Moe? Did *any* of you have sex with her? Were there some follow-up dates I don't know about? Haven't you thought about this? What is she all about, really? We might as well sort it out now where no one can hear us. Have another beer."

Albert finally uttered a comment, "Well, youse guys know her...the way she walks and talks around school, but I found her kind'a surprising. For me, da midget races are fun, but I didn'a think she would take to the noise and crowds... but she did. She screamed along with everyone...louder than most, ya know, and I loved seeing her a bit out of control, yeh? On the other hand, I don't know why I wasted an evening on her. Pleasant enough, but getting close to a kiss was like fielding a bad hop grounder. She always moved at the critical moment, so nuttin' doin there...youse know what I mean... whaddya gonna do?" He smiled with that last phrase.

Albert's remarks seemed to break the ice. Kent chimed in that at Sunset Gardens, she seemed to find her natural element. Black music, loose moves and the chatter of dancers warmed her, and she was a lot more engaging that he had imagined. Still, while Fats may have found his thrill on Blueberry Hill, he wasn't so lucky. She melted a little during some of the slow dances, but that was the best part of the evening. "She's a babe," Kent finished up, "but this ain't my baby."

Kerry, grunted a little, shifted his position, then his soft voice began to speak of her interest in the universe. "She had a real sense of the immensity of space and she understands the effect that gravity has on the planets. I joked that her personality seemed to be attracting a lot of male matter, and wondered if, like a Black Hole she was likely to just absorb it and leave no fragments."

"She laughed at that, and maybe for the first time she spoke directly to me, and we had some fun imagining where we might like to travel if we had our choice of the universe."

"I kidded her that while I was on my trip at the speed of light to Alpha Centauri, she would be settling, literally, on her chosen location, Saturn. When I returned, Einstein's theory said that she would have aged more than I, so I asked her to let me take a good look at her...to remember. She gave me a Hollywood pose, three different looks complete with shoulder turns, and then, she said with a laugh, 'This has been fun, Kerry.' The evening was over, and I just took her home."

Everyone now looked at Walt, and he mimicked Omar Sharif's intense gaze, postured a bit, then said, "I hoped that she might see me in the same way that Julie Christie saw Zhivago, but I think she saw me more like Rod Steiger. She was polite. She let me hold her hand, kept her eye on the screen but held her distance. I had to content myself with enjoying Christie's beautiful, breathless looks. We went home almost immediately, certainly no time for a pause that could have refreshed us. So, no guys, it wasn't me."

There was a long silence. Little mutters floated about, but nothing Walt could understand. Then, he came back to his earlier comment about the baby's name. "What about that middle name?" he asked.

"Huh?" uttered Kent.

"It's a bullshit way to spell that name," Albert chimed in, "It just doesn't look right."

Kerry cleared his throat, then, "Well, maybe the baby's name *is* a clue to the father. Our code names contain three that begin with the letter 'M" but the baby's name has only two. Who is missing: Meenie, Miney or Moe?

Albert commented as he got up to go, "Well, I'm Eenie, so good luck to youse guys...whoever is the new dad. I'm outa here...got to see a man about a beer. I'll tell Red you said hello," he smiled and walked on into the gray dusk. They all began to move out, each step a little hesitant as though wishing there were an answer, but at the same time fearing one.

"Hey, wait!" Walt said, "I know that I am Miney and I know I am not the father. Albert is Eenie. I think that the missing 'M' is the last M in the refrain. So, before we leave, Kerry or Kent let us know. Which one of you is Moe?"

They paused, looked at one another, said nothing, and then just continued to melt away. The River flowed quietly, darker now in the gradual loss of light. Like Lori, it held a lot of secrets and as the guys left its banks they took with them a few of their own.

They all graduated and scattered. None died early and no one won the lottery. In time, Albert sold insurance, developing his independent outlets in two states and three cities. His advertising slogan was simple: "Youse Need Me." Kent moved to St. Louis, bought a franchise for *Pedal Mark* and became rich. You probably see him in the annual, televised, Midwest Cycle Fest where he sets up a booth and floats a huge balloon over the tent. Kerry disappeared into the dark streets of San Francisco amidst rumors that he finally left California. Walt migrated to Colorado, then to Wisconsin and ended up teaching economics in a small college out there.

Time molded their gathering place too. A dam in the mountains and a thousand concrete cuts below it drained the River of its eccentricity. One could not step into the same waterway twice, some said, but the riverbed remained fixed. It held their footprints for a time, its banks framing remnants of their youth and its loose soil covering the secrets of their innocent sexual banter, flirty looks and witty jokes. It remained a discarded landmark, but one which could still be seen, dry and sandy, pitted with smudged depressions of new walkers who crossed from bank to bank, its essence now captured by sentences which began, "Remember when...?"

They had been small town guys living small town lives, and the story of Lori Larken fell into the general gossip which flavored class reunions: "Who was that girl that had a baby in Wyoming? Lori Larken? Did she ever say whose it was?" The answer was always the same: "Eenie, Meenie, Miney, Moe" (loud laughter).

Telling Lori's story refreshed her presence in the various seasons of their lives much as the River used to flow with renewed force each spring. Finally, at their 30th Reunion, all the guys showed up and learned the truth. It was, as Walt had always thought, Moe's story, and they listened carefully as he told it. To their surprise, he provided them a follow-up narrative which deeply piqued, then filled the banks of their curiosity.

"I was sitting reading," Moe began, "when I heard a knock on the door. I answered it and a strange man looked me in the eye and said, "Hello Moe, do you know who I am?"

Speed Trap

Walt was so pissed off! He thought they were his friends, his social connection. They hung around together, laughed and kidded one another, shared dances and gossip while dating back and forth. But not two hours ago, driving home from work, he passed by Beth's house and there he saw them, silhouettes talking in the living room, a group of maybe eight, laughing, sharing gossip by judgment of his quick glimpse, and he wasn't there. Uninvited! Snubbed! He didn't go home.

The land marked by an X seemed safe. North-South, East-West, two roads intersecting land flat in three directions, as level as the eye could see even on a dusty day. To the south about a quarter of a mile sharply defined hills gently lifted homes above the horizon creating a cove of lights, some twinkling, some steady and somber. A thousand feet aloft in a Piper Cub one could view the entire community in one minute, banking to keep lights visible, noting slowly cruising cars flashing headlight reflections off main street window glass as their drivers looked for something to do in the dark. They crawled along slowly, a U-turn and back again. Go more than a mile and there the darkness began. A small town full of edgy wandering youth, many holding unpredictable thoughts on what to do next.

Cars and guys, guys and girls, night and lights, winding roadways and straight line streets, all a part of the heart of this small collection of homes, and in the early morning hours of each weekend, those roads gave the last of the crowd a place to go, to have a run at speed. Drag racing they left for the car clubs, but pushing the speedometer on a solo trip up the western edge of the town tempted many a young driver, and sometimes a crowd of faces parked at Lorena's Drive-In would pause its chatter to listen to what might come whining up the road.

The rules were pretty simple. Put the car in gear somewhere around the oil company encampment at the north end of the two-lane, run it through two shifts of the stick and floor it, let the engine wind...and wind. Near the football field, where exactly depending on one's nerve, the foot came off the pedal and a cool driver hot braked to a smooth stop at the four signs controlling traffic at the X.

The Run drove shouts and hollers out of a laughing, squawking, jostling group of passengers as they felt the speed, the distant possibility of crash, the thrill of surviving manufactured risk. Sometimes the cops hid in the shadows of the local service station on a corner of the X, making The Run all the more risky, all the more a memory to be talked about the next day at school.

Walt *turned his Merc back to town and cruised down the main street at a crawl looking for friends, new girls, new cars, anything to get his mind off those silhouettes. Cooling down finally, he drove over to see his friend, Albert...Albert who had connections, who shared his view of the night and the girls... whose accent charmed the ladies and kept even the tough guys amused. Was he home? Yep, well almost. He caught him just leaving his room in the boarding house, about to slip into his old, red Ford and carouse for the night.*

"Hey, Albert, got a minute?"

"Yea, youse look pretty upset, so I gotta minute."

"I am upset, pissed off actually. Drove by Beth's house and saw them having a party and I found myself on the outside looking in. Why aren't they inviting me to their stuff?"

"Hey, don't ask me; ask dose guys doing the inviting'."

"I'm not asking them."

"Well, what then? Going home? Tomorrow's Sunday, you don't have to work...wanna find Red and have a beer?"

"Yes."

Albert walked away from his Ford, got into Walt's Merc and they headed west toward the X, turned north, headed out into the dusty edges of nowhere looking for Red's signage, a blinking neon blue light that said nothing at all about the owner, offering only the alluring outline of a six pack. A printed metal sign below the flicking light promised "Pabst Packed to Go".

He pulled in and gave Al $5, enough for a couple of six-packs for them to drink away his pain and begin speculating on the good times that were to come some other night.

As was his nature, Albert parted with a caution, "Youse keep eyes peeled for cops. Honk twice. I'll case da joint and make sure I know all da boozers inside."

"Yep...yep," he replied, shut off the lights, and kept his head on a slow swivel scouting for any sign of law enforcement. It all looked clear as Albert entered the door, and it stayed that way.

At Lorena's Drive-In, the crowd grew. Cherry coke's, milkshakes and root beer floats filled car trays hanging from

each driver's window, while the "ladies of the night" hauled food and drink to all, carried away the trash and generally made change with an appreciative look that encouraged tips. A few guys worked parked cars full of girls, chatting about nothing in particular and sometimes commenting on the nothingness of their chatter. Night air, dry and slowly cooling, invigorated life under the neon lights. All in all a quick glance around showed all the flavors of a typical Saturday night.

At Beth's, the evening hours wound down and they decided to go up to Lorena's to see what was happening. In fifteen minutes, they had piled into three cars, in no particular order, and headed west toward the X, turning south at the intersection and cruising slowly into the few openings at the drive-in.

He drove to a dirt road that veered off from the pavement, circled a group of three oil wells and parked at the back side of the middle one. If lights came their way he could leave in either direction. The beer cans, cold and full, filled their hands and they popped the lids, paused, took a couple of deep swallows and settled in for some idle conversation.

"So," Albert asked, "youse shouldda been at da party, eh?"

"Well, yeh. I've dated Beth a couple of times, and same goes for Monica. I play sports with J.D. and Roger...hell, I'm usually the one calling them to go party. Don't know where I stand with them all now."

"Maybe it was a sudden thing; maybe they couldn't get ahold of ya?"

"Everybody knows where I work; they know that I get off kind of late, but I'm always available for Saturday night fun...hell, sometimes they like my ideas on what to do...just

don't understand why they didn't call me, even at work. Store number's not unlisted." He sipped some more beer.

"Well, one thing for sure," Albert began, "Youse ain't in the plans for tonight so better make your own fun...got any ideas? Wadda we gonna do?"

"I'm going to drink another beer and think about it."

"I'm wit ya on that!" and Albert popped another.

Officer Jerry Radford pulled his patrol car up alongside the Fire Department, parking it in the shadows where he could keep an eye on the drive-in, the main street down through town and any unusual traffic on the south fork of the X. It had been a quiet evening, to his relief, and he wondered a bit why this night should be different than other Saturday nights. The bars down on the main street were full enough, but none were spitting fights out in the street and the movie theatre had been out for almost an hour. Still, nothing going on, and he was happy enough about that.

Kids and cars, booze and laughs, cokes and fries, night and lights, shouts and pouts, all were grist for his hourly patrols. The various combinations sometimes amused him in their innocence, but from time to time horrified him in their consequences. His mind wandered back six months when, parked just where he was now, that horrendous crash echoed up his street, and he knew his night would make the next day's newspaper. By the time he got to the X, the one car had small flames coming out of its engine compartment and the other, nearly twenty yards away, sat there upside down, front wheels still turning slowly. He was able to get the driver and passenger out of the flames, both unconscious, both bleeding, both needing doctors and hospitals.

When he went to the other car, he took just one look and vomited. It lay upside down, wheels stilled now but a human head presented itself on the ground, propped up alongside a mound of dirt raised in the crash. At the wheel, a young woman, perhaps 23, nicely dressed at first glance, draped herself over the steering wheel, arms flopped in awkward positions, the driver's side window open half way, blood edged, telling him immediately what had separated her head from her body.

By the time he stopped retching, the ambulance had arrived, as had the Fire Department, and he left them to clean up the mess while he processed the traffic issues and wrote up his sketch of the accident and mapped the layout of the X.

Bad memory.

"Six beers down... I'm ready for more, ay?" Albert burped slightly with his remark.

"Naw, I think I've had enough for now...that other six pack is probably getting a little warm. I'm thinking of maybe going by the drive-in to see whose there, what's going on. You game."

"Oooh, da hangout eh?...you bet...love to see da ladies and talk a little trash with mouthy guys. Sure, let's go."

Walt put the Merc into gear, slipped carefully out around the rigs, and kept his lights off until he got close to the road, the north end of the X. The slow rumble of his pipes told him what his engine was thinking...ready to go...ready to go. But he didn't have purpose, no goal in sight, just a wandering night.

"Don't forget da lights," Albert reminded him, *"Guys don't know ya if they don't see you comin'."*

"Yep, no problem," he replied, switching on the lights as he turned north, brought the Merc up to 55 to avoid any attention...thought about his night, pissed off still, and not much way to express it. What was he going to do on Monday, ask everyone why they didn't invite him to the little party? No, he would have to keep his mouth shut, invent some story of what he did Saturday night and pass it off as a nice weekend.

Even as his thoughts wandered through this little scenario, he felt the Merc picking up speed, asking to be let loose, growling at the restraints, licking its lips for more gas. He let that feeling enter his mind, mix with his disappointments and frustrations, flavor his hurt at rejection, his anger at being ignored. He felt the Merc ask for even more, a little more permission.

He glanced at the speedometer. It reported 60 mph now, and he noted that he was just approaching the old oil company grounds, and he decided he would have some fun and do The Run, see how much he could get out of the Merc, give it what it wanted and plan to stop with hot brakes right at the intersection of the X. He put his foot down toward the floor, felt the car respond immediately, gave it a little more, and said to Albert, "Want to really make The Run noticed?"

"Hell, yes," Albert replied, "Give it da gas and give it all it wants...let's go, turn it loose."

He did and as he floored it, he had another thought and took a long look at the east and west legs of the X. His vision unobstructed, he could see that they were empty, black, no hint of a headlight. The corner gas station well lit up served as a marker, but he saw no cars at the pumps. At this moment and for the next foreseeable moments, the X was clear, and he began to think some more.

"Albert! How about we run the stop sign at 90 mph. I think we can do it if I just let 'er loose. I don't see anything coming. Want to go for it!"

"Damn rights! Let da baby go...that'll give them all something to talk about on Monday. Let 'er go!

Walt flattened the pedal to the metal and the Merc responded full throat, pipes roaring, its rear end settling just a bit, then up on the level and the speedometer began to tell its tale...65...75...and he glanced at the X, both ways, nothing coming, still nothing coming.

Wheels tracked perfectly, no vibration, and he saw the needle hit 80, and took one more look at the X. He either brought it back now, or they were going for it, no second guesses after this. Still no lights, either way, and with some sense of relief he punched it again as though he could ask for more than the Merc was delivering, as though it had been shying away from full commitment. Hurtling toward the stop sign, he looked again both ways knowing that he could never stop, but at least reassuring himself that the path was clear.

At the drive-in, the night cooled and softer small talk calmed youthful energies. Sam Forrester, comfortably parked in his powder blue, leaded Ford had just finished telling Mary Bellemy his thoughts about college when he heard the sound of a revving engine in the distance, closing. Someone was making The Run! He hollered out the news, "There's a car on The Run! Listen for the screech of the brakes...quiet now! Quiet!"

Officer Radford, nearly dozing now, noticed a sudden silence from across the street, and took a look. No fight, no new customers, but people were getting out of their cars and moving toward the west end of the drive-in where they could see him more clearly, to what purpose he did not know.

He noticed that they weren't looking at him, they were looking at the X, and then he heard it, the high-pitched whine of a tightly wound engine heading his way. Someone was making The Run. He waited. They would stop at the sign, brakes screeching no doubt, but what was he to do about that? Just another hot stop. He listened.

Walt glanced at the speedometer and saw the needle hit 88 and hold...damn! He wanted 90 mph and he didn't feel any more acceleration...was there anymore there under the hood? He kept his foot hard on the floor and slowly the needle climbed a bit...89...a little more, then 90, and as it hit the target, he looked up at the X. He hurtled toward it, still nothing showing east or west, a couple of guys in the station standing and looking at him, blurred images awash in a snapshot as the Merc blasted through the intersection at a full 90 mph, immediately slowing as the road began to tilt up toward the hills.

He and Albert began screaming "YES! YES! YES!" their throats hurting, hands pounding the dashboard again and again as the Merc passed Lorena's Drive-In and he began letting it ease itself down to a safe speed...say 65, he thought. THEY HAD DONE IT!

Whoever was at the drive-in would recognize his Merc, would know he had destroyed the idea of The Run, making it now The Ninety Mile an Hour Club, membership of one...him. Who would he invite to attend his party? Let 'em think about that.

Then, he saw the red/blue lights on the patrol car as it lurched into the street, turned toward him with purpose and determination. OH CRAP! It wasn't over...it was just beginning.

"THE COPS, ALBERT!...back there, on us, they're right after us. We're going into the Heights. We gotta' lose 'em." But as he slowed to make that first turn, the cop closed rapidly, not fast enough to get a license plate maybe, but close enough to be unshakable. He turned a hard right at the third street up the hills, drove two blocks, saw the cop turn right to follow him, then remembered to kill his lights. He turned right again, and headed down the hill a block, then another hard right.

"We gotta hide," Albert shouted, "We can't outrun this guy... we gotta hide!"

"Where, where...WHERE?" Walt hollered, his eyes already looking for an alley or another small street where they could disappear.

"Not a'nudder street," Albert hollered, "A driveway, a dark house, a dark yard...we gotta get off the streets right away. He can't find us if we're dark and still."

Walt turned back up into the hills trying to put distance between him and the cop with every turn, but that wasn't working. Then he saw it, black hedges on the right, a home set back from the street, driveway open. He took the gamble, pulled the Merc in, killed the engine and then he and Albert just sat there...waiting...waiting for the cop's lights to come down the street, a searchlight illuminating their driveway, discovery, big tickets, maybe jail. Not good.

Albert rolled down the window, listened for sounds. He opened his too, looked up at the house...anyone awake? All dark up there, no sound. All silence in their driveway. No light rays in the street. He got out of the car, walked softly to the edge of the hedge and peeped around. No cop, no car, no lights. They were safe. They didn't move for an hour.

Officer Radford gave it his best effort. Once he realized what had happened at the X, he wanted an arrest, but as the car blurred by him, he knew it was going to be a challenge. From a dead stop he needed to get close enough for a plate ID at least, maybe a visual on the car itself. Right now, he had only a smeared image of a light color car, sedan, moving fast. It went right into the Heights, and he followed it up the first hill, when suddenly its lights went dark, and then he could only guess. He crisscrossed a four block area for almost 15 minutes, calmed down a little and finally called it a night. When he drove by Lorena's, three cars remained, and he imagined the rest were on the way home full of chatter about the car that ran the X...at what speed he could only guess.

Sam recognized the car, knew the driver, shook his head in a combination of dismay and admiration. It took guts to run that stop sign, guts and nuts. He would never consider it, but he knew who did, and he knew that the word would get around school as fast as fire flamed over a gas stove. He wondered what Beth and Monica's crowd would think, seeing themselves left out of this Great Adventure. Usually that group was inseparable. Bet they would be bitchin' about this all week...wishin' they could have been part of the Ninety Mile an Hour Club.

Walt and Albert relived every second of the night. They talked through the fright, the high, the elation and the fear three times before the adrenaline began to clear, and then they slowly drained the second six pack right there in the darkened driveway. Finally, he backed the Merc on to the street and headed out. He dropped Albert off at about 2:00 a.m., drove carefully along the back roads to his home in the country and crept into his driveway.

He sure didn't want to wake his parents. He smelled of beer and a few critical words could spoil a fantastic evening.

Dangerous run all right, he began to think, but what the hell, if he had been invited to the party, it would have been a different night, probably a lot less risky, but as memorable? He thought not. Wait 'til the word got around school on Monday...he smiled.

As he passed through the kitchen to his bedroom, he noticed under the nightlight a small note propped up with his name at the top.

"Hey, hon...Dad and I decided to spend the rest of the weekend up at the cabin. Monica called, said to come to Beth's when you got home from work...they're having a little party... sounds like fun. Love, Mom

Nice Girls

In Walt Farmer's town, it was a time before tattoos, piercings, braless boobs, pick-pulled hair, scanty panties, and mouthy moaning about injustice. Bette Davis Eyes were gone, Angela Davis Hair undiscovered. Freedom Riders confronted the South, but in Walt's world, racial violence remained a decade away. Women worked inside the home patrolling their children and liking it. Men worked outside the home and if they didn't drink it away, earned enough to raise their families. Cars rolled off assembly lines cheap and unreliable. Seat belts hung unused and gas still flowed freely from oilfield "drips".

Local pharmacies sold the Pill, but that didn't change the dynamics of high school romances, and Vietnam made no headlines. Boys kept their pants around their waistline, though they might slip a little during the day, and they kept their hair full, clean, and trimmed. The musical *Hair* had yet to hit the stage. Daisy Duke was a decade away, and local girls kept hemlines below the knee and ironed formless blouses. They clipped their pony tails and framed their faces with neck-length, gently waved hair, some experimenting with variations on Jackie Kennedy's bouffant. They walked in flats, laughed politely and smiled a lot. Their innocent faces remained in place each day, every day. Hello Pleasantville: white, mainstream, well-oiled.

Boys flirted with various tones of meaning, but few could report intimate touches or remember private moments when a girl's loose clothing and bare skin presented new visions to brighten the night. Nice Girls equipped with friendly smiles, wholesome commentary and unquestionable virtue seemed immune to outlaw fantasies. Date them one might, kiss them perhaps, but however stirred their passions might be, if you were too pushy, the first date would be the last. Sure, there were unwritten storylines of sexy nightscapes, but Walt hadn't found one yet, not one.

Of course, he did not have a car to park at the drive-in theatre until his junior year, and for a long time girls floated through his imagination untouched. Even talking to them outside of school became a complicated ritual. He no longer wanted to meet them at the movie theatre. That seemed pretty childish. He could go to dances, but never take a girl home. That seemed fruitless. He had been deeply humiliated in sampling double-dating, once having the car towed to a dance by a welding truck, another time having witnessed the guy who owned the car kiss *his* girl goodnight.

But once he had the Merc he courted relentlessly, developing his conversational skills, assessing female flirting amidst laughter, wondering if they ever thought about him? Did they talk about boys and their smiles, their looks, their sex appeal? He heard rumors that they did, but nice girls never shared these conversations with boys. Still, he persisted, as might a hummingbird, sampling buds with a buzz and a blur, burning off the energy of youth.

What to do? He flattered them with wit, dazzled them with dance, befriended them with quiet confidences, took them to movies. He kissed them goodnight and still he wandered home, sometimes stirred, but more often confused about what he was doing wrong. There had to be something more to dating than the light embraces he enjoyed. Where were the thrilling mystifying retreats behind closed doors that guys said some nice girls enjoyed?

Walt reconsidered his approach. He had spent time with more than twenty of these lovelies, and while he had enjoyed their kisses, held their hands and admired their figures, he had not yet touched a breast, lifted a skirt nor brushed across concealed skin. Maybe he needed to create the right environment? Maybe sexual experience required a looser setting with a little more warmth to it. Perhaps these maturing woman needed a little more encouragement, a little more access to alcohol, a little more edginess to the night. He needed to find a way to give a nice girl a chance to be bad.

There were two who were especially appealing, both brunets, one tall, one short, one smiling, one observing. Close friends, Beth and Monica had each been in his car, gone to dances with him, kissed him goodnight, but both had been clear about defining when the evening ended, and it was always over before its time. Yet, in conversation around the table in the school library, in witty exchanges at games and talks in the hall, he thought he saw in them a new view of the world. Bob Dylan said that the times were changing. Maybe they were. Maybe some of the nice girls wanted to sample more risky behavior, and if they did, he wanted to be there.

He thought again about his failed dating strategy. Maybe a double-date could do the trick. A more mature smiling girl might feel more confident, free and secure if she shared an evening with a girlfriend. As emerging women maybe they needed an out-of-town adventure where nobody knew their names. If they wanted to press social boundaries a little, maybe a rock n' roll dance at the Armory could be the answer.

He asked his friend Lee if he wanted to double date with Beth and Monica and take them across the River where loud horns and driving rhythms moved bodies in ways more suggestive, more mature than high school dances. They could drink a little vodka on the way over, heightening the girls' response to hot sax and they would be so cool, yet so warm that Beth and Monica would share their inner selves with them. Yes they would.

Lee asked Beth. Walt asked Monica and to their amazement, *both said yes! Yes!!!* They were going to be taking two Nice Girls to a bad-ass dance in another city and if all went well those vodka smiles would welcome their arms and kisses. The girls would drape their bodies all over them, and they could whisper little prayers of thanks for changing times. Then who knew?

Saturday night Lee picked the girls up in town then stopped for Walt on the highway. He climbed in the back seat with Monica, and they set out on their 40 minute drive. As they logged the first five miles he suggested that they all might want to have a drink from a half-pint of vodka that he had purchased from a guy who knew a guy who knew a guy. The girls passed. He did not press the issue, but mentioned that he had it in orange juice if they wanted a sample.

Lee glanced at him over his shoulder, "Uhmm, you know Walt, on the way out here, we got to talking about the dance, and the girls suggested that we might want to go to the movies instead. *Viva Las Vegas* is back in town at the Nile Theatre," he went on, "They really like Elvis, and Ann Margaret is a great dancer. Whaddya think?"

"Whaaaat?" Walt's voice grew tight. "We can watch movies anytime. Smokin' Joe Turner is going to be playing live, for four hours. When he blows 'Shake, Rattle and Roll' and 'Flip, Flop and Fly' people move! I'm not goin' to the big city to see Elvis in a movie. Nope, not gonna do it."

"Gee," said Beth, "Monica and I are really not so sure about that. We really want to see the movie."

"O.K. Look, I'm goin' to the dance. Drop me off, then pick me up at midnight. If you guys really want to see Elvis, just go do it." He had no idea what they would do driving around town for two hours after the movie, but right about then, he didn't care.

He opened his vodka/orange juice container and began to sip it. He offered a taste to Monica who paused, but finally said no. So Beth had led the mutiny, eh? She and Lee chatted away as they drove to the city. He tipped his orange juice again.

He did this for the next 20 miles, and the alcohol coursed through his body, warming his limbs, focusing his mind and preparing his libido for the times to come inside the dance. The Nice Girls were going to see Elvis smile at teen-agers, exchange lame dialogue with Ann Margaret and sing a few songs. He would feel the horn of Smokin' Joe Turner and maybe hold some warm bodies in his arms. Yes he would.

They dropped him off and as he walked to the ticket box, the vodka hit him. His legs wobbled. His eyes became a little unfocused, and he lurched some when he walked. This would take some doing, he thought, and after purchasing his ticket, he gathered himself, walked up to and by the cop stationed at the door. No scent of alcohol. Vodka worked!

Steadying his footsteps, he entered the building, walking right into a wall of rocking, screaming music that made him stumble. Unfocused and unsure he scanned the hall as best he could, looking for a chair, a familiar face, a refuge somewhere and he found one: June McDermott! He remembered that he had once met her at the local theatre when he was about fourteen and they sat together and enjoyed a movie.

He walked up to her, "Hi June...I'm kind of drunk...could you dance some slow steps with me, prop me up 'til I get a little more steady?"

"Sure," she said, and away they went, at a crawl, one step or two at a time, disappearing into the crowd and letting the pounding music find its own beat while they found theirs. She stayed with him for about 20 minutes and then he felt better, and she moved on. He never saw her again.

He did however see girls whose dress, expressions and scent certainly suggested a new way of being good. He liked that. He danced with a few and then saw this petite, blondish cutie wearing a short sleeveless blouse that loosely covered her navel, a pair of cut off Levis that were unbelted leaving room around the waist and a posture that featured delicately enticing breasts.

He asked her to dance. Her name, Peggy. Intelligent, well spoken, she carried an easy sense of self-respect, spoke in intelligent phrases and seemed thoughtful about her future. A Nice Girl and yet so different. He knew within the first half of the first song that he held warm, willing sexuality in his arms and as the music pulsed it became more overt and his dances with her flowed into a subtle mating ritual. She pressed her breasts against him when the music slowed. She looked and taunted him a bit when the tempo increased. He kept his arms around her whole torso when they did the two step and emboldened by her warmth he slid his hand down the back of her Levis and cupped her butt inside her panties. They kissed and danced without an edge of light between them. What she offered he wanted, dazedly determined to have it, but they had nowhere to hide, nowhere to lie.

The witching hour approached. He kissed her again, asked where she lived and said that she would hear from him. He left the Armory, went out to the lamp post, waited for his transport to show up, and when it did, he crawled into an empty back seat waiting just for him. The trip home became a murky blur.

They woke him when Lee stopped in front of his house. Beth and Monica wished him good night with smiles on their faces. He walked to his bedroom, cuddled the blankets, thought of Smokin' Joe Turner and what his sax did to heat up a dance... of the smooth and sexy skin down Peggy's back and butt... of all that might have been, but was not, and then he slept.

At school on Monday, he asked around about her, and the more he asked, the more confused he became. Did she really give him an address? Where did she say she lived? Peggy who? Did she have a last name? He could not remember. He talked to some seniors who dated a couple of girls across the River, but they had never heard of her. It took him a week to realize that she had disappeared in the wavy memory of his alcoholic tide.

More startling was the chatter before school in the library as Lee described Walt's ride home screaming about this "Peggy, Peggy, Peggy!" Smart, sexy and ambitious, she had a future, he hollered, and it might just be with him. Then, he sang at the top of his lousy voice to the music on the radio leaving Lee, Beth and Monica to listen, grimace and laugh for an hour.

It might have been embarrassing, but Walt didn't remember it, and he let the comments enhance a bit of his swagger. All in all, he felt that he had the best of the evening. They chose to waste money on *Viva Las Vegas,* and he discovered a Nice Girl who pressed boundaries, captivated his eye and filled his arms with heat. Where could he find more? Some said you could find them at the River. Maybe, but he preferred to focus his search on rock n' roll. Maybe he would try Sunset Gardens.

Conversation with a Cop

"You'll be back," the cop said with disgust on his face, a red nose flaring and a challenge in his voice. "Punks like you always are." He handed Walt Farmer his watch, wallet and change, muttered another comment about going down the wrong road, and sent him on his way with, "See you again in what, about a month?"

After a long night of restless tension, Farmer was getting out of jail. He was in no mood for insults, and some quick responses floated across his mind, but he said nothing. They might lock him up, and he did not want to be in jail again, not ever.

For the rest of his life, he avoided Sills Corner. It was no place to visit and he didn't want to live there. The only lodging he found was behind bars, and he shared it with a dozen prisoners who were in the slammer for being drunk and disorderly, or for petty robbery and assault. He didn't see himself fitting in with them, but he had more time than he wanted to listen to their chatter, hear their rules and absorb their misdoings.

Cops were a fact of life. His father had been one and in a small town, that meant that he received a certain amount of slack when he brushed up against the law. He knew several of the officers, especially Jerry Radford, a quiet spoken guy full of thought and yet firm on the rules. He would write you a ticket for loud mufflers. Harry Ristow, a veteran of Guadalcanal, patrolled quietly but thoroughly and after 11 p.m., he seemed to be everywhere. Arnold Seal, new to town, but soon the most unpopular cop on the street, enforced traffic rules down to the last roll of the tire or the first peg over the speed limit. Walt had been fortunate enough to avoid Arnie, but on the day after Christmas, there he was knocking on his door.

Without a smile, Arnie looked him up and down for a moment, seemed to find it a painful experience, then asked if he were Walt Farmer. When he heard the word "yes", he arrested him and took him, gently, down to the station to be booked, mugged and printed. Arnie didn't say much. Farmer didn't say anything, but his mind exploded! Arrested! It was one thing to be kicked off the basketball team for joy riding in a university car. That he could understand, but why an arrest?

Before he left the station, he asked Harry, wandering through the office, what was going on? The answer seemed like a series of jabs to his head, chest and gut, "You're being charged with destruction of personal property, abuse of city property, drunk and disorderly, under age consumption of alcohol and malicious mischief." Harry's face didn't offer even a suggestion of a smile and he offered no kindness in his voice.

"My God," Walt said, "we were just having fun. How did that become criminal?"

Harry paused, "Fun is childhood antics. You four crossed that line when you downed your first drink."

Walt commented, "Well, it seems pretty jerky to me for you guys to come to my home to arrest me, especially on the day after Christmas? Why didn't you just ask me to come in?"

"Judgment call," Harry said, "Chief wanted to give you a special present of his own...was going to arrest you on Christmas Day, but I talked him out of it."

Walt thought a minute, then asked another question, "Where are the other guys?"

"On their way," Harry said, "and you had best be on yours. Better see a lawyer."

Farmer mentally ticked off each complaint and knew that he was guilty of every one. He and three others made a nighttime nuisance of themselves following a basketball game. He still wondered why the coach had given them the keys to the car, but he knew that they had abused the favor. They had great fun...at the time...getting served underage, driving a university car about neighborhoods, starting up a city bulldozer, stealing plywood Santa Claus lawn decorations and creeping back into their rooms with no one the wiser

But old people don't sleep well, and even at 2 a.m., one lady heard their voices and saw them each nab a Santa. She wrote down their license plate number and phoned it in. The following Monday the four were called into the university athletic office and quizzed, independently and at length. While they were all quite willing to admit what they had done, they were finding that the laundry list of offenses had grown substantially. Someone had destroyed a crèche in front of City Hall, and had particularly abused the figure of a black child, a black wise man and a black angel.

The police pressed the issue. "We know that there are no black students in your school, no black residents in your hometown, no black athletes on your basketball team. Black images were destroyed on public property. Why don't you just tell us what we think we know and save yourself a lot of additional trouble?"

To Walt, this scenario spelled real danger. Race was not a laughing matter in his hometown, the community that the

Sixties had left behind. True enough, there were no black residents, but they had done nothing to the Sills Corner city hall crèche. Once released, he consulted a lawyer, and was advised, "Plead guilty and ask for probation." Farmer was quite taken with the idea; probation meant freedom, no loss of income, a kind of pardon (wink, wink, nudge, nudge).

So, it began. Travel to the scene of the crime to plead guilty in court cost him wages and travel expense. The lawyer took more money. A second trip for sentencing drained his account again. Then, standing before the judge in the courtroom, as he confidently listened to him intone all that they had confessed, as he grew antsy at the delay of a probation sentence, as he looked about for the closest court exit door, the judge said something that jarred his bones and shrunk his gut.

The robed voice rejected the probation recommendation and instead sentenced them to 19 days in jail, fined them $500 and firmly described his disgust at their nighttime deeds. Then, as Walt and his friends silently absorbed this sentencing disaster, the judge suspended 17 days of jail-time and announced that if they were free of any further criminality for two years, the event would be expunged from their record. That softened the punishment, but it was not an escape, and they were bound over to an officer immediately. This night, they would sleep in jail.

Escorted directly from court, the deputy presented them to the admitting cop and his first words were, "Well, whadda' we got here. Fresh smart-asses, who thought they knew better, is that what we got?"

"We're just caught up in the system," Walt said, "We don't need to hear it from you. We heard it from the judge."

"Oh, yeah?" the uniformed mouth responded, "Well let me see what I can find to accommodate you fine fellows, some lodging that will make you feel real comfortable."

Walt said nothing more and carefully placed his watch, wallet, and change into a plain brown envelope. The jerk with the crisp shirt asked him, sarcastically, "How d'ya spell your name...can you do it?" Walt spelled it, W-A-L-T. "Sure about that?" the cop smiled a nasty smirk. Walt couldn't help himself, "Yes I am. How do you spell yours, J-E-R-K?"

The one with the bulbous nose just looked him, paused, then went on, "Well, you nighttime riders are goin' to have a different kind of layover here. We're puttin' ya into the bullpen with our daily drunks and simple assault, petty criminals."

"Why would we be put there?" Walt asked, "Aren't we supposed to be put in individual cells? Why a drunk-tank?

The dude in blue, paused, looked at him, then resumed, "Some of them been here awhile. They run their own space, so follow their rules." Farmer didn't really think he meant what he said. In jail, cops made the rules. Cops controlled the space. Walt said, "You're kidding, right?" Squinty eyes focused and just looked at him, smiled, commented, "I don't joke with punks," and turned away to other duties. He didn't say another word, but Farmer learned within the hour that if there were one place where cops didn't make the rules it was in a jail cell.

A quiet officer led them down a hall to a large door with bars, rattled his keys, turned the lock and let them into the "bullpen". A dozen residents looked up, reviewed them carefully. Walt could hear their thoughts: white boys, soft boys, little boys, punks. He heard the door close and there they were, in the drunk-tank. The four of them found some empty space against a wall and sat on the floor together. They said nothing. He began watching the inmates, listening particularly to one, clearly the leader. Black, over six feet tall, lengthy and muscular, he had tattoos on both arms and when he spoke, his voice echoed off the walls, set the peeling paint fluttering. His eyes contacted then focused on individuals, and he waved his sharp, flat palms for emphasis.

With volume, he reminded his "clan" about the need to bath daily (an open air shower in front of everyone) or be hauled to the water by his aides. He made other comments directed to some of the inmates and suggested certain changes in their daily conduct. Farmer watched and listened, observing the body language and the glances that were coming his way. He knew now who ran this place, and it was not the cops.

The word, "jail" became a reality which boggled his mind. Overwhelmed by confinement, he felt bound and gagged by the lock-up, and the way that "others" fully controlled his well-being. He had nothing in common with the attitude, talk, humor or discipline floating around him, yet here he was.

Dark emotions, dark space. Jailhouse companions...listless lingerers...energized only through the voice of inmate command. He felt his stomach roil as he came to terms with his capture and heard the word "escape" pounding his mind. ESCAPE! He just wanted to be gone, and that was not going to happen until the next morning. In the meantime, what? Would the four of them sleep in this open space? Did they get fed? Dare they ask about toilets?

They talked quietly about what they were seeing and that attracted some attention from a guy nearby who leaned over to him and slurred, "Whatcha in for?"

What? He couldn't believe what he just heard. Did petty criminals really talk that way, with a line stolen from a movie? He said something about taking some decorations off of a lawn. The guy replied that the local police were really picky about people having a good time and commiserated with him. Walt didn't like the idea that he was a pal to a drunk.

He whispered to the others that they should just be quiet, sleep the night and they would be out quickly after breakfast. That led him to revisit the thought. Where would they be sleeping? Would they spend the night lying alongside one another like a row of matchsticks, turning over on the concrete in concert every half hour or so? Supper clearly was not showing up. When did they decide to just go to sleep? What if the Leader insisted on their having a shower before morning?

They began settling into their cave. Then keys jangled in the door and a guy came in and asked them to follow. He took each one of them to a different cell, a space containing another inmate, and told them that they could spend the night in one of the twin bunks. Walt felt a lot more comfortable and noticed his cellmate on the bottom bunk already asleep or passed out. He focused on getting settled and asleep, awakening in the morning, waiting through breakfast and then getting out of town.

He crawled up on the top bunk, put a light blanket over his body and tried to think quiet, hopeful thoughts. He felt his breathing slow, and a comfortable temperature begin to flow through his body. Sleep approached. And then, slowly, building to crescendo, his cellmate began snoring in deep, chest heaving tones. Walt tried to tune him out. He turned in a different direction, placed the pillow over his head, and hoped for quiet. Nothing changed.

He worked his mind for almost half an hour seeking to find sleep. It wasn't happening. He wanted to get down and wake this guy up, but he wasn't sure what that would mean. What if his cellmate were angry and beat him up? What if he had a concealed weapon? What if he were in a violent half-dream. What if...?

Finally, he crawled down, and very gently, touched his bunk buddy's shoulder, and whispered, "You awake?" Nothing. He tried again, and the lump stirred but did not move or respond. He tried a third time, a little more decisively. The body awoke enough to look at him, and mumble, "Que' quiere"?

Walt had no idea what that meant, so he just did his best and said, softly, "You're snoring, and I can't sleep; can you stay awake for a few minutes?"

"Si, si," he said.

"Bueno" Walt replied and felt as though he had just negotiated a labor contract. He crawled back into his bunk, tried to relax and then, just as he was falling into sleep, heard once again, "zzzzz...ZZZZ" and then...black.

He awakened to the sound of trays, clatter, and voices echoing from down the hall. Some were sleepy, some angry, some wondering where they were. Fresh light leaked into the jailhouse revealing grime on the walls, and he could smell something cooking, its scent carrying images of leftover soup, moldy meat and men's sweat. The four joined the prisoner line and walked through a feeding station where an inmate slopped watered cream of wheat into a tin bowl. He passed it by.

They returned to the bullpen, antsy, humbled, bedraggled and tired. Three hours later, an officer walked them back to processing, recited their obligations under parole and took them, finally, to the guy who had their personal stuff.

"You'll be back," he said, *"punks like you always are."* The cop dismissed him as though he were washing his hands, and Walt, already a lot wiser than he was 24 hours earlier, did not say a word. He just wanted out.

A half hour later he was in his Merc driving down HY 101, thinking of how much money he had spent: lost pay, bail, attorney, two trips to Sills Corner, court fine. He tried to wash away the feelings of failure and deprivation that he carried out of the jail with him, but they stuck to his clothes. The distorted images of dank walls and drunken bodies filled his mind, and his sense of helplessness in the hands of convict control roiled his stomach. The comments of the processing cop infuriated him, and he worked hard to put him out of his life. He just wanted to get home.

Thirty minutes later, he saw red lights in his mirror and pulled to a stop. The CHP officer was polite and succinct. Walt had been speeding. The cop asked for his driver's license, registration and proof of insurance. He asked if Farmer knew how fast he was going (no). He commented on the dirt over the license plate. He checked the windshield washers to see that they were flexible and effective, and then, just when Walt thought that he had passed all of the tests, the officer cited him for going 60 mph in a 45 mph zone.

He thought that maybe he could talk his way out of it, but what would he say, "I just got out of jail, and I wanted to get home right away?" Umm, not a good opening line. He quietly folded and stored the ticket, saying, "Thank you officer."

It wasn't his last conversation with a cop, but he was getting better at it.

The Tijuana Jail

Walt knew the mantra about Tijuana. Stay away. It's a foreign country. Mexican law. Auto collisions not accidents but crimes. Alleys filled with prostitutes. Women diseased and dangerous. Polluted tequila. Stolen cars. People go into the Tijuana jail and don't come out.

Until a junior in high school, those warnings guided Walt's code of conduct. He knew Tijuana as well as he knew New York, which is to say not at all. He hadn't been there and had no intention of visiting. The border offered a barrier to dangerous living. No place to be.

Buzz Newsome, Walt's English teacher, changed all that. Newsome spent a lot of time introducing restless students to various kinds of literature hoping to stir their appetites for fine writing and thoughtful prose. One fine day, he began reading to them passages from Hemingway's *Death in the Afternoon*, a history and assessment of bullfighting. *Death*. The word caught Walt's attention.

For Hemingway, Newsome began, killing bulls according to ritual, tradition, and the principles of geometry demanded courage, knowledge, the grace of a ballet dancer and the reflexes of a boxer. There on bloody sands a three act tragedy transformed a half ton of bulk topped with razor-tipped horns into a pile of fleshy rubble. The transition, completed in minutes, could produce artistic memories that lingered in the mind of an *aficionado* for years. Others saw only the inhumane butchering of a noble animal, rejecting legitimacy to the matador's skillful brush with death.

American tourists typically admired street poetry, a walk on a high wire or the strained notes of sidewalk musicians, Buzz reported, but few appreciated the ability of a matador to estimate angles of a bull's charge, to modulate his speed of attack by simple control of the cape, to create safe passage of the horns...and now his voice escalated in pitch, *"all while standing absolutely still as the bull passed by his body."* A skeptical public, he railed, seldom saw the bravery and skill of the matador, more often viewing that hulk of black moving death as a friendly pet who deserved saving. It was more trick than courage that carried the matador to success, critics claimed, but Buzz let Hemingway educate his readers to the distinctions between skill and hokum.

When he read those passages, Newsome rolled out the words describing the *veronica*; he spoke with some scorn for the work of the *picadors*; he embraced the skilled calculations of men who placed darted sticks, the *banderillas*.

Then Buzz changed his tone to a clipped staccato as he reported the close, dangerous work of the matador with the *muleta*. The *natural* pass, he explained was simply that. Stand at just the right angle to the bull, cite his attention with the small cape and remain perfectly still as he charged the cloth. Within a few minutes the black hulk wore himself down and that led to what Buzz called the moment of greatest risk, the "moment of truth". As he held the *muleta* before the weary bull's lowered horns, the matador had to cite the charge, then expose his full torso to the horns as he went forward to place the sword between toro's shoulders. If done well, Buzz said, it would sever the coronary artery and kill the bull where it stood.

Newsome then noted what Hemingway said. One could talk about an event, discuss its rules, rituals and results, but to truly judge, one needed the experience itself and Walt agreed. He wanted to go to Tijuana.

Four years later, he, his closest friend Albert, his closest cousin Gene, and an old high school friend Terry, found themselves with a need for something to do and a weekend when they were all available to do it.

Albert, working at a gas station, decided to take off work. Gene, at USC nursing a broken jaw fractured in spring football, joined right up. Terry, working as an accountant, had money to spend. Walt, finishing up his spring semester at Fresno State, wanted to celebrate.

They had no shared history of travelling together, but that spring they decided to visit Tijuana and see the bullfight. For reasons unclear at the time, Al drove his car, and one Saturday in May the three of them left town, headed to L.A., picked up Gene and then continued on to the border.

They arrived in San Diego sometime during the night, sprawled and slept in the car, ate some doughnuts for breakfast, and then, because they were young, set out to have their day in Old Mexico.

Violating all that they had been told, Albert drove his car across the border, parked it and paid a young man five dollars to watch over it for them. Then, they headed down the streets, chatting with vendors, bargaining but not buying, stopping into a few bars to enjoy some tequila, ignoring sidewalk pitches to have cheap sex with "young virgins" who awaited them inside an alleyway behind a closed door.

But staying out on the streets did not keep them from admiring other women dressed for Sunday, passing time in shops and enjoying a beer at a sidewalk café. They all, Albert and Terry especially, looked, flirted, and tossed out a series of appreciative compliments in English easily translated by tone and look. At one point, Walt picked up some maracas and kept time with a local street band. They had great fun gradually working their way to the bullring and in time joined in a large crowd filtering into single lines as it passed through the entry gates and into the Plaza de Toro.

Of the four, Terry and Walt had some background in the rituals of a bullfight (*corrida*) and they talked about some of the passes (*quites*) they might see and as they walked, they explained the order of the day's events to Albert and Gene. It would be bloody, but it might also be emotionally stirring, depending upon the bull's bravery and the matador's skills.

Albert, for reasons unclear he said later, found a spiritual resonance in the event, and as they passed by the chapel where matadors prayed before each corrida, he noticed a young man kneeling before a small altar. Taken by the sight, Albert stopped and asked a young woman next to him what the praying meant. Escorted by her parents, she looked at him with dark eyes, a faintly rouged complexion and a generous smile, judged him worthy of her attention and explained that matadors prayed for safety and success in their afternoon confrontation with death. As the young bullfighter left the chapel, she asked if Albert would like to go in and pray. He nodded yes. She took his hand and escorted him into the sanctuary.

Walt, Terry and Gene stopped in their walk to watch Albert's diversion, envious that he had parlayed a conversation with a gorgeous woman into a visit within the inner sanctum of a matador's spiritual search for protection. When they walked out, Albert continued holding her hand and she spoke in Spanish to the matador, now arranging his suit of lights, and told him of Albert's prayers for him. He nodded his appreciation, and then Albert asked for his autograph on the program booklet and he wrote it, "Caesar Briones".

They could see Albert looking to continue conversation with the woman, but she just smiled at him, a smile he never forgot, and moved away with her parents. He lingered in place, intent on absorbing every scent of her being, keeping her memory safe within his thoughts. Then, Terry jarred him back to reality, and they all moved on to their seats.

Gene was pretty quiet. He seemed interested in all that was going on, but he asked few questions, listening carefully to the conversation that Terry and Walt were having about different breeds of fighting bulls and the farms that produced them. After Albert's foray into the chapel, he seemed persuaded that what they were going to see was serious business indeed.

Then, they did just what Hemingway said they should do: "You go to your seat...you buy a cushion from the vender below, sit on it...and look out across the ring to the doorway of the patio you have just left with the three matadors, the sun dancing on the gold of their suits, standing in the doorway." *The cushions were important*. They placed them just so and sat, starring at the large opening from where the matadors would enter and the smaller door from which each of the six bulls, two for each of them, would storm one at a time.

The public address announcer reminded the crowd twice that throwing anything into the bullring, during or after the event, was prohibited,. Violators would be fined $500 and serve 17 days in jail. The voice noted that the previous week, a girl had been hit in the head with a coke bottle and authorities were determined to protect the crowd. That said, the *corrida* began.

The musicians began playing the classic festival music, *Espana Cane',* which heralded the entry of white, prancing horses who carried their riders to the *Presidente* where they asked permission to conduct the event. A soulful Paso Doble, *Bullfighter,* embraced the matadors who entered with serious faces and posture that revealed both courage and a solemn sadness for the risks they would take in the next two hours.

Walt knew that this spectacle played as tragedy, not sport. The bull's death inevitable, the matador needed to dominate the beast with skilled grace, then kill it at the right time as efficiently as possible. The risk of goring, tossing, even dying, accompanied every pass of the bull, but if all went well for the matador, he survived the risks. The bull had but one fate.

Gene asked Walt, "What is there about killing a bull that is artistic or emotional? What happens? Why do people get all excited? Why Olé?" Walt had worked to answer the same questions for himself, and he tried again, "I think," he began, "it comes through the matador's ability to control death, a half ton of flesh, propelling dual projecting horns, thundering toward its target responding only to invisible cue lines connected to strong, sensitive, skillful wrists."

"The bull *is* death. With even a small miscalculation, the matador may find himself within the arc of the horns. They can sever an artery, pierce a bowel, lance the eye and brain or rupture a lung. One miscalculation, just one, can kill a man quickly, and every matador who holds a cape in front of a fighting bull knows this. To control its path, its pace, even its will to charge, and to do it simply with knowledge, posture and cape or *muleta,* is to do what men everywhere wish to do: court great peril and survive. Kill death, and you sample immortality. Do it with style, grace and bravery, and you have earned your olé, and more."

A pause. They ordered a beer from the vendors. More small talk as they watched the crowd shift a bit, then settle, anticipating that emotional rush when the first bull bolted into the arena, his eyes searching the ring, his bulk charging anything that moved, looking to clear the area with horn and hooves.

Six bulls would leave the gates that afternoon, lift horses on their horns, charge capes gracefully kept just out of reach and play their role in the tragedy. Briones would kill two of them, Walt explained. If he did it artfully, with courage and without cheating, and if the bull died quickly, Briones would be cheered and awarded a bull's ear or two as symbols of his great skill and courage.

At the same time, Walt murmured to Albert and Gene, they might simply see butchery. "Keep your eyes on the matador's feet," he commented, "If his legs stay fixed, he has chosen the right angle to let the bull charge the cape and pass him. If his feet are moving, he is making adjustments as the bull charges. Then bad things can happen."

Briones, successful enough in his first appearance, walked around the ring posturing, holding aloft one ear. But with his second bull, he satisfied Walt's ill-defined hunger for art in the midst of risk, his desire to see skill trump charging death. Briones developed a great sense of confidence in his ability to control the bull's charge, turn the horns around his waist and move the beast in what appeared to be a slow motion ballet. For two minutes he guided the hulk so close to his body that blood stained his suit, and he did so without false posturing, with the skill to choose his place and bring the bull around him. Grace, risk, black, red, two legs, four legs, silent mob sometimes gasping, then cheering Briones as he thrilled 25,000 people shouting as though before a single megaphone: OLÉ! OLÉ! GASP...OOHHH... GASP... OLÉ! OLÉ! Whistles, screams and thunderous applause.

Walt had travelled all night to see this. Briones' *veronicas* were slow, classic, complete. His close work with his *muleta*, the small, red cloth draped over the sword, defeated death pass after pass. When ready, he lined up the bull carefully, took that leap of courage and launched himself over the horns, *the moment of truth*, plunged the sword between the shoulder blades to the hilt and saw the bull collapse, dead as he hit the sand. Briones' work unhinged the crowd and the shouts reverberated around the arena for minutes as he paraded two ears and a tail. Art blended intimately with tragedy this day, and the product was a brush with immortality. Probably, Walt thought, this was as good as it was going to get in Tijuana...maybe in Madrid he might see something better, maybe.

As the crowd began to rise in its collective seats, Walt tried to imprint in his thoughts how he felt about the afternoon. Hemingway again came to mind, *"I know only that what is moral is what you feel good after and what is immoral is what you feel bad after and judged by these moral standards, which I do not defend, the bullfight is very moral to me..."*

Walt felt very fine.

He looked around enjoying the enthusiasms of the emptying crowd, satisfied with having finally seen something that had before existed only on paper and picture. Then, to his amazement, a young American jumped into the bullring, picked up a broken lance and began waving it in the air, challenging the crowd to hit him as he became a moving target. Cushions came flying out of the seats, inaccurately spun but whirling with weight well into the center of the bullring. Blonde, collegiate, bare-chested and full of challenge, the whirling dodger moved about blood-soaked sands, shouting insults, deflecting an occasional near miss and catching the full attentions of a happy, slightly drunken crowd.

Albert and Gene had begun to filter down the aisle toward the exits, but Terry and Walt looked at one another then at the crowd and the fusillade of cushions in the air, rolling across the sand, landing but never quite hitting the target. Everyone was doing it!

They had tossed four cushions when they heard a soft voice behind them, *"Un momento."* Walt turned to see a policeman standing there, calm but firm, asking him to remain. Another was instructing Terry with the same order. Walt felt this sudden weakness in his legs and a bit of panic creeping up his chest. He motioned toward the fusillade in the air, and in his best English said to the officers that everyone was doing this. They said nothing. Gene turned and saw them being detained. He walked toward them and asked the cops, "What's the matter?" They detained him too.

Albert, who had been furthest along, turned to see what was keeping the other three and was immediately stopped by two Americans who knew Mexico and knew what was happening. "Your friends are being arrested. You want to stay as far away as possible and get prepared to go to the Tijuana jail and find out what is happening to them. Follow us out, and we will give you information and directions on how to get to the station." Albert followed them, even as Walt, Gene and Terry waved for him to stay away, stay away!

The three, now detained, stood there until the crowd cleared. Then, quietly and without comment, they were escorted down the stairs out of the venue and into a parked van. Inside they sat amidst six others who had also been arrested, for

136

drunkenness, fighting and theft. One of their new sidekicks said to them to be sure to hide their money because once inside, they would be searched by prisoners looking for cash.

Walt, reeling from the sudden conversion of college good-time guys into a gathering of petty criminals, didn't have any money. But no matter. He would be searched as would his cousin Gene, sitting right next to him, big, confident and aggressive. If some inmate tried to search him there was going to be a fight... in the jail...amidst foreigners...without guards to intervene! Moreover, his mind racing to calculate the confinement penalties, they were facing 17 days in jail, probably longer because they had no money to pay the fine. Walt was in misery. He would miss final exams, flunking out of college in his first semester at Fresno State. Who would get them out? Who *could* get them out?

They travelled for about 20 minutes, turning one way then the other. Walt just kept thinking about how he could explain everything if someone at the station would speak English with him. Surely, they would understand that there was no reason to detain them. No one was injured. Everyone was doing it. They were just having fun.

They arrived. One by one, they were led out of the van and kept standing on the sidewalk. Walt asked two different officers if they spoke English? No? Then, the three of them were moved inside the jail entry and told to stand in a spot, which they did, and Walt asked the Sergeant attending them if he spoke English. He said, "Yes".

The words came gushing out of Walt's mouth. He explained his view of the scenario, apologized for breaking the rules, noted that no one had been hurt and that the three of them were all incited by a foolish American, the one in the bull ring. Every syllable he offered carried with it intense fear. He and his friends were about to be placed in the Tijuana Jail, and no one except Albert knew that they were there.

Walt hoped that the Sergeant saw the panic in his eyes, the good will in his gestures, the inherent innocence in all of them, and the need they had to get home, somehow, someway. The policeman did look them over carefully, and then he said, *"un momento,"* turned around and walked to the doorway of a glass enclosed office.

The Sergeant, now their representative, entered and stood before his superior. His back blocked Walt's view, but he could hear the voice explain to the man behind the desk what seemed to be a gentle account of their activities. A question from the Administrator. A pause and then a response. Then, a comment from the Administrator. Our Sergeant took his leave and walked out the door toward us. He looked at Walt, glanced at the others, said quietly, without emotion, "You can go."

They didn't run, but they walked with controlled haste to the door and stepped quickly out in the street even as Walt wondered how in the hell they could find Albert? Albert wondering the same, relying on the directions from the American couple on how to find the jail, carefully drove down what he hoped was the correct street. He saw more cops, hesitated, then he saw his buddies stepping out of a doorway, walking through the uniformed bodies and looking around for their ride. No one chased them, and he called out, "Youse guys, get in the car!"

They pulled open the doors, breathless still in their near panic, piled in the Ford and hollered in jumbled voices, "Get us the hell out of here!" He did. Crossing the U.S. Border seemed like one giant leap from a swamp to a rock. Home at last! Freeway in sight. Jailhouse far, far away! Never before had Walt appreciated what it meant to be in America and they quickly put miles behind the border while mentally adding years to their futures. They never travelled together again but shared memories surfaced in their conversations fifty years later.

In time, Walt returned to Tijuana and the bullfight on three occasions and managed to avoid trouble. Much later in life, he travelled with his sister to Madrid to see corridas in Las Ventas.

Gene went on to finish college and pursue a highly successful career as a coach and high school principal.

Albert took his visions into the insurance business turning his ability to empathize with others into a thriving profession. He still has today the program that Briones autographed.

Terry refused to cross the border ever again.

Tripped Up

Blake called up the stairs, "Farmer, phone!"

"Who's it?" Walt shouted.

"Don't know," Blake cackled, "but its female...you got a date she needs to break?"

A groan, as Walt picked his butt up off of the study chair and walked down two flights of stairs. His roommates ooohd and aaahd a little. "Phone for Walt; phone for Walt," they mimicked Blake, and he ignored them all, grousing to himself that an upstairs home apartment with no phone wasn't much of a place at all.

He picked up, "Hello". Silence.

Again, "Hello".

Then, Peggy spoke, "Hi there, I've got some time, and thought I'd give you a call."

So...Peggy again. In blurred memory, he thought of the occasions that she had called to say "hi" and all of the crappy times that followed. She called to tell him that she was dating other guys during her senior year. She called to break their date to senior prom. She called to tell him that she was going to College of the Rockies, a private women's college sheltered on the far edges of Boulder, Colorado. They quit talking after that, and then she showed up after work one night. He was never sure what that was all about, but she seemed to want to pick up again. She wrote once, and then silence seemed to be the only message she wanted to send. Now, another phone call.

"So, how's it going out there," he answered cautiously. "Classes o.k.? Life in the dorms treating you well?" No way in hell he would ask who she was dating.

"It's just great," she answered, "I like my classes, especially English. Fall is beautiful out here. The trees are full of color and on Saturdays, we all go over to Boulder and watch C.U. football. The crowds just mill by the thousands around Folsom Field. The team doesn't win much, but we have a really good time. I'm thinking of pledging a sorority and moving into it next fall.

That was the kind of report he really didn't want to hear, and he wondered why she called to tell him all of this, her life filling up and his half-empty. This would be a short call, shorter still if he spoke his mind. So, he didn't.

"That's great. Must be a lot of fun to be in a new state, a new school with new friends."

"It is," she replied," but I'm missing you and I'm wondering... would you want to come out and visit? We have a really fun spring party, called Colorado Days. Interested?"

His thoughts flared briefly. Peggy calling, inviting, making overtures, wanting him. She sounded sincere, but was she? Could he trust her?

"Well, sounds like fun, I guess. Are you sure that you want me out there?"

"I'm sure. Can you come? I want to see you." Her words came across the line with an especially warm tone, her words inviting, her phrasing suggestive, and she sounded vulnerable. He loved it. He played the moment out a little longer.

"Are you sure about this. It's a long trip."

"Walt, I know I've been difficult. This whole going off to college thing was largely my parent's idea, and its o.k., but I'm missing you. Come out."

"O.K." he said. He was caving way too early, but what the hell, he wanted to see her, maybe find a way to connect for good. He'd had only one real relationship in his life, and Peggy was it. Who knew what could happen? Who knew?

May was a few months away. He could manage class absence. What he needed were some people to share the costs. Who else at San Jose State had a true love near Boulder. He worked the networks, posted notes on bulletin boards, described the security of his car, the dollar costs, his experience and his interest in a good time road trip.

It took him five months, but he found two other romantics who wanted to share the season of love in Colorado, and they left San Jose in early May, after Thursday morning classes. By noon they were in the mountains.

Bruce Riley, 220 pounds of linebacker muscle, relaxed in the back seat. In the front next to him, Deb Maxwell, slender, quiet, thoughtful, let her eyes carry conversation, chatted little as she tuned the radio and tracked their progress on her map. Bruce's fiancé lived in Denver. Deb's guy went to school in Boulder. Sharing gas and driving, they figured that the trip would cost them each fifty bucks. The rest of their money would be spent on fun.

Climbing Donner Pass, the Merc slipped into standard drive, and rolled through it smoothly without a strain. The trees, pointed old evergreen mixed with the emerging olive of deciduous growth, swayed lightly. Patches of snow remained from a strong series of winter storms, but Walt saw only clear road and light traffic. Engine temperature fine. No scent of exhaust or electrical burning. Tires cool, car tight and quiet.

Through 60,000 miles of work, romance and school the Merc had never let him down. He drove it to and from a jail, parked it in many a dimly lit lane and commuted from home to college, all without a ping from the silent, smooth running V-8. It felt ready for an adventure, as did they all. And what a trip it would be: across three and a half states, two mountain ranges, 1,000 miles, a weekend of parties and back another 1,000 miles to San Jose. All this in five days. For what? For love he thought. For Peggy. Was she worth it? Yes she was.

It began with a quiet hum. He felt it while driving down the east side of the Sierra. It vibrated lightly in the floorboard, but he could feel it in the steering wheel too. A new sound to him, but then, he thought, maybe his car was just going through a transition.

Reno lights welcomed and then wished them safe passage. He felt the transmission engage its overdrive, and they headed east into a black, seamless horizon. Sometime during the night he would turn the helm over to Bruce, now sleeping, and let him drive across western Utah.

Deb spoke little, and Walt filled the silence with radio, a 24 hour station in Salt Lake City alternating between the Tabernacle Choir and soothing songs that eased their travel, so mild they lulled any edginess into a locked box. He sorted through his thoughts in rhythm to the sound of the road and the throb of the mufflers.

He imagined College of the Rockies set amidst the color and crisp air Peggy described in her two letters following the phone call. He felt the cut of the cold waters of Boulder Canyon and saw the soft layered green of moss and grass along river banks. In his mind they lounged on blankets and pillows, and he thought of her warmth as an evening campfire flickered and water splashed white foam from rocks before rejoining the rocky darkness below.

"Woodsies" flavored Colorado Days, she wrote, and went on to describe panty raids, beer busts, co-ed mud wrestling and hot pants. She sent a picture of a group of guys painting fraternity initials on the butts of Levi-covered coeds. She spoke of the swimming reservoir where cases of 3.2 beer created lounging outposts on the sand and some of the girls just went topless. Apparently, he thought, the women at College of the Rockies had an active social life with the guys at the University of Colorado. This was a far cry from Pleasantville, but then, he wasn't looking for small town living. He was looking for life with Peggy.

He let his thoughts roam back to their first meeting, an Armory rock n' roll party. He spent the night dancing with her and wanted more. Drunk at the time, he spent months searching her out and they became an item for a year, but then she went off to college, and he just figured it was over. The phone invitation in November changed things and now, taking the leap, he hoped to put their lives back together, plan a future. It might be a long road to follow, but she would be worth it. Yes she would.

He wondered about the campus. San Jose State merged so intimately with the city that the streets of one entwined with the space of the other. Was College of the Rockies like that? Did all the women live in a dormitory, eat their meals there? How long the walk to classes? Was it really shadowed with mountain edges and green fringes of pine? Did it *...there was something different in the hum now. More rhythmic now, it sounded a little more assertive.*

With some reluctance, he began to focus on its tone. When he accelerated, it grew more intense. When he backed off the throttle, it diminished. *But, it did not go away.* More of a vibration now, it transmitted decisive pulses to his fingertips through the steering wheel.

Well past Winnemucca, Walt decided to make an unscheduled stop in Salt Lake City. He asked Bruce to drive for a few hours while he got some sleep. It was a restless doze, but he stayed in it until the lights of the city started chatter in the front seat. He took the wheel and stopped at the Flying Red Horse where a sign said, "Mechanic Available". He explained the vibration, and the guy said, confidently, that it sounded like an ignition issue. He offered to change the spark plugs.

Twenty-five dollars and 45 minutes later they drove away, and he asked Deb to take a look at the map and find a way to bypass Provo but connect to Vernal. While she struggled with the interior light, he brought the Merc up to cruising speed. When it hit 55 mph, the vibration returned. Spark plugs were not the answer, and his stomach grew a little tighter.

Daylight now, and Deb offered two alternatives. He chose to head due east at Draper and then connect with Vernal via Midway. The road, lightly marked but paved, promised a way to make up the time lost in Salt Lake. Ten miles later pavement crumbled into gravel, and the Merc slowed to 30 mph. Go back? More delay. Go forward? They weren't going to get there at this speed. Maybe 50 mph would work. Twenty minutes more and the right rear tire exploded. He pulled out his only spare, knelt on the hard pebbly surface, changed the flat and thought about their options.

Past midpoint to Midway, their road full of loose stones, gas supply shrinking, he wondered if they should just drive slowly or go for it. But lose another tire...stranded. He saw neither phone boxes nor homes, smelled neither cattle nor horses. No one knew their route and every lurch jabbed their nerves. "Stay calm, Walt," he told himself, yet he could control neither speed nor time, and their weekend plan eroded with every hard traveled mile. He ground his teeth and kept his foot light on the pedal.

The pace slowed. One hour, then on to another, and the gas gauge kept falling. Just how much further was it? The road continued to spit up scratches and occasional thuds as roadbed scattered under the weight of the tires and then, as he reluctantly started thinking about how far they might have to walk, stone changed to asphalt, a sign read "Midway" and he pulled into a one station town with one price for gas. He paid it happily. Then, he checked the tires and headed south. They were all exhausted, running late, without a spare, the vibration constant and growing worse.

Finally back on a good two lane road, he found that when he drove 45 mph, the car ran in silence. If he drove 90 mph, it quieted again. It seemed foolish to go on, but he did not like to quit...anything. He set the needle on 90 mph, and 10 minutes later he saw blue lights flashing behind him. "Well," he thought, "It's out of my hands now."

The officer asked politely if he knew how fast he had clocked them and Walt said, "Yes", and remembering his lessons about talking to cops, quietly explained why. The Trooper looked at them all for quite a while making judgment about their youth, their weariness, their task, and then he said to them, "Why don't you drive a safe 45 mph into town and find out what is wrong with your car." Then he left.

In Vernal, they got the bad news. An empty transmission starved for fluid had been growling its hunger for hours. Walt estimated that the seal probably began leaking somewhere near Reno and its fluid slowly drained away into the flatlands of Nevada and Utah. Take two days to replace it, the mechanic said, and that meant that they were done. They had come so far, fought through hours of nerves, driven so carefully and were now so close to Boulder, so close. He hated to give up.

On Deb's map, Walt noted, they had only about an inch to travel, and he began to wonder aloud if they should go for it. The mechanic looked at him long and hard. He shook his head slightly, and said, "Son, those are the Rocky Mountains you see in that inch. If you leave here now, you won't make it." He heard the words, but they made no sense to him. An inch on the map. Surely, they could get there. He bought another spare tire, paused, asked, "What can you do to keep it running?" The mechanic looked at him, grimaced, then turned and did what he could, pouring a heavy oil into the transmission, repeating politely, "You won't make it." They headed east on US 40.

It was surprising, really, how well the Merc moved. As long as they were on gradually ascending terrain, it rolled along in a nicely controlled manner. The noise, now a low grind, constantly filled their ears, but the miles seemed to disappear and Boulder was still their target, weekend fun their goal.

Two hours he drove. Many miles passed, and then the road began to rise more steeply, the transmission complaining more loudly. Heavy oil leaked through the broken seal, droplets forming for a moment, then blowing along the underside, splattering the road with a black on grey trail. But the Merc kept moving, and he kept his eye on the white line ahead. They were getting closer, by the mile, by the minute.

They would make it to Boulder, he thought, and wondered how he could get the Merc repaired.

As they descended into Craig, a picturesque little community that began and ended within his line of sight, the grinding turned suddenly to silence, and the engine that could take them anywhere surrendered to the transmission that would take them nowhere. As they coasted into town, he picked out a gas station on the left and pulled in just beyond the pumps. Boulder was an inch too far.

He asked about repair and learned that the car could be ready on Monday afternoon. The cost: $125. He signed off on that and asked about a car rental. "Kremmling can have one here in two hours," the mechanic said. "Do it," he told him, and to Deb and Bruce, "I guess we will just relax a bit until the car gets here. But, we're going to get into Boulder tonight."

A new station wagon, it had less than 5,000 miles on it. He rented it for three days and paid $150 up front. They stored their luggage, piled in and headed east. Two hours later, they passed through Kremmling, and he noticed the sun setting behind them, saw the shadows lean into the road, counted miles as the headlights created a path toward their target. They drove through the Front Range, onto state highways, down the canyon into the outskirts of Boulder, a city he had never seen but one which he believed held his future.

A little after 10 pm, they found their way to College of the Rockies, parked in front of Bakkum Hall and looked for a welcoming party. Deb's boyfriend greeted her and Bruce left to meet his fiancé at Tom's, a popular bar in Gunbarrel. Walt sent up a message for Peggy, and she came down, smiling, happy to see him, but apologizing that she had curfew and they couldn't spend time together that night. He really didn't understand that, but it became the opening remark of a sorry, sorry weekend.

The following day, Peggy had to babysit for a local woman, Ariel Swanson, who had one child and one on the way. He didn't see her until the afternoon when they went out to the reservoir to sun and swim. He knew that this was a local hangout for students, a place where beer and babes blended nicely, but still, he was not getting the kind of attention he expected. They swam a bit and while sunning on a raft in the water, she said to him, "You're not going to dump me are you?" That was mystifying. He had just driven across three and one-half states to see her, and he was already thinking of asking her the same question. "No," he said, "I'm not."

Saturday evening was even more puzzling. She wanted them to go with another couple to Denver for supper and "maybe" get back to campus. An overnight rendezvous? His thoughts began to focus on the likelihood that they would get to spend the night together...in a bed. That had never happened. It didn't happen that evening either. Nice meal, nice talk, nice polite visit to a big city.

Sunday was much the same. Then, she suggested that he should transfer to the University of Colorado in Boulder. It's a public university she noted and he could afford that. They would be close to one another. C.O.R. was less than 20 miles from C.U. They could get engaged and finish school. But if that was her best thought, he just wasn't feeling it. The distance she kept between them magnified the distance he had come to see her, and he simply felt the fool.

Deb and Bruce joined him in front of Bakkum Hall early Monday morning, and they headed back to Craig, finding his car fit and ready. Money changed hands. Warm appreciations passed all around and without further small talk, they got into the Merc and headed west. He brought it up to cruising speed and it was quiet, so quiet that they each heard one another gently exhale and settle. Home, a thousand miles away, sounded wonderful.

His $50 budget had ballooned into a $400 payout. That inch on the map left him emotionally exhausted, physically drained and financially broke. Peggy had kept him at arms-length. The Merc had a huge chunk of new, wasted mileage on it, and he, uncertain as to whether he was being loved or used, reflected upon it for a thousand miles. He asked Blake what he thought. After a moment's pause, he replied, "That was a road trip to nowhere, Walt. Forget her and just write the trip off to experience."

It was a thought.

California Leavin'

The letter carried a University of Colorado return address and in that certain way that one knows an uncertain future, Walt opened it, scanned the dozen lines and realized that his time in California was over. He had two days to report for work on the university campus, and without that job, he had no room, no board, no life. He went to his bedroom, grabbed his clothes, his personal items, and his hi-fi, stashed them in his Merc and headed out to Barstow. Just like that.

Working that morning in the butcher shop, leaving that afternoon for a very iffy future, he tried to balance his tumbling emotions. "Go East young man, go East" his spirit told him, even if it meant contradicting Horace Greely. Of course they were going to end up in the same place, Colorado.

The adrenaline began to ease after a few hours on the road, and he pulled into a Barstow motel, slept till morning light, then slid back behind the wheel of the Merc and kept his eye on Route 66. Kingman, Winslow, and Gallup, each sounded like a frontier outpost, and he had plenty of time to sort through his past summer, mull over his feelings, try to find some internal balance to accompany his topsy-turvey world with Peggy and his roll-the-dice feelings about the University of Colorado.

He had spent most of the month of June sorting through his late-semester trip to see her at College of the Rockies. She kept saying how much she wanted to be with him, encouraged him to transfer to CU, spoke of an impending engagement. It all sounded great, but then so had her invitation that took him on that futile 2,000 mile trip. It had given him great pause. Did she? Didn't she? Did he? Didn't he? Were they a couple? Did they really have a future? No clear answers.

But as the summer went on, he found himself focusing less upon her wants and more upon his needs. What was he doing with his life? Maybe a new university in a new state in a new culture would be welcoming because he was certainly not sold on California.

A year at San Jose State convinced him that he still wanted to teach high school, but uninspiring classes, especially those that dealt with education, frayed his commitment. Fraternity initiation rites betrayed his trust, branded his body with permanent scars and left him angry and living with guys whom he never truly befriended. His social life remained frothy, and when he tipped the glass he continued to find unattractive residue.

Peggy spent July and August working at a girl's camp on the coast, a two-hour drive from his home, and she found time for a single half-hour conversation with him. It removed none of the scabs from his trip in May, but he comforted himself with thoughts of their future and tried to be adult about how little he saw of her.

She still attracted him. When she smiled she exuded a warmth and embrace that told him that she felt something honest. Sometimes, somewhere in her words, he thought he heard a commitment. But he began to realize that his attraction to Boulder was as much about wanting to leave California as it was about being with Peggy.

He applied to the University of Colorado for fall admission. If he made it, he would go. Peggy didn't seem particularly impressed, but he was going. He was going. He needed a change in life with her or without her. Boulder? He was ready.

In the outskirts of Albuquerque now, his mind refocused on driving. Eyes weary, he needed to rest a bit. He parked on the city square in front of the jail, hauled himself out of his well-worn seat, locked the doors on the Merc and lay down to doze on the lawn. Cool earth supported the entire length of his body, comforted it really, and Walt could feel in his weariness the little prickles of grass brushing up against his neck, reminding him of the uncertainty that lay at the end of this road. Finishing four years of academic work in six might not sound efficient, but better than no finish at all. Far better than the future likely packed into the lives of those whose voices drifted down from the jail.

Packets of their conversation reached him, sorted themselves into a specialized idiom and lulled his mind. He was reminded of his night in the drunk tank in Sills Corner. Accents and slang cut through the muddle from time to time, and the smell of food told him that lunch had appeared. It became the subject of the moment: "Pass 'on down heah; if t'aint movin', eat it; na' salt again; d'ssert today? (laughter)" They were staying awhile. He was moving on.

What was he leaving? Small town culture, local friends, college roommates, family, hometown work---all comfortable, but known. Why was he leaving? Peggy said that she was waiting, but regardless, and his mind was clear on this now, California had a lot of baggage that he wanted to shed. Too many people, an unsettling tempo of life, too many rules, a social grinder too convoluted to allow him a sense of freedom. One could find any landscape in California, but his had been desert sagebrush and lizards, nighttime raids on gasoline field tanks, fog in the bogs, sprawling colleges, adolescent memories of fools and foolishness, even that night in jail, all best left behind. For him, California crumbled a little with every mile he covered.

It was time. He backed the Merc out and headed up toward Santa Fe then north to Denver. Night driving, radio company, comforting engine, it all settled into his soul and kept him in high spirits. Even another conversation with a cop, near Colorado Springs about 3:00 a.m., did not dim his spirits. When the flashing blue and red lights pulled him over, he responded easily to gentle inquiries as to his wakefulness and sobriety. The troopers welcomed him to Colorado, wished him well, and encouraged a safe trip to Boulder.

Denver's distant lights embraced him as the reflections of a lamp lit bay attract a returning sailor. They lured him, absorbed him, scrubbed him, and in another hour, he went through the toll booth at Broomfield, rose over the last knoll and looked down on Boulder. He'd been there before, and at night, but arriving from the south brought a completely different view than dropping down from the mountains. Dark silhouetted housing threw out an amber glow from windows and dawn's light softly draped the Flatirons in a violet, pink caress.

He drove into the city on Arapahoe, slowly cruised about the downtown, then moving up Broadway passed through the Hill and parked in Chautauqua Park. Morning light now took the Flatirons from a soft yellow orange to their natural deep, brown earth tone. They postured, slabs side by side, their peaks lifting his spirits, their immovable mass comforting in its strength. They became the visual reference of his renewal.

At mid-morning, he went walking among the dorms, found Seward Hall and reported to Student Housing. When he showed the letter demanding his appearance this date to the secretary, she said, "Oh, this didn't mean you. You're assigned work in the meat cutting shop, and it doesn't open for another week."

That news didn't spoil his mood, but arriving in Boulder five days early cost him another $100 that he would have earned back home. He let it pass.

"What should I do?" he asked.

"Oh," she said," You can work in Seward serving meals, and settle into your dorm room. Next week you can report for your regular job."

No problem. He had a place to sleep, food to eat, work to do, and somehow being at the "University of Colorado" sounded a whole lot better than milling about at San Jose State.

"So, where will I be staying?" he asked.

"Baker Hall," she replied.

By sunset, Walt had moved into his room, worked his first serving line and begun fitting into a beautifully defined and architecturally cohesive campus. For a week, he absorbed the atmosphere, played touch football with other early arrivals and acclimated to the mile-high altitude. Then, on silent command, columns of cars began arriving, pouring out first hundreds, then thousands of students.

Once settled, they swarmed throughout the campus filling the dorms, spilling into fraternity and sorority houses above Baseline Avenue, seeking reunion, registration and confirmation. They clogged the sidewalks of The Hill, the seats in Gaylord's eatery and the bars which welcomed them back to the land of thought and drink. Baker Hall resonated with loud voices calling out renewals to friends, checking out new faces and sputtering about the outrageous times they suffered through the summer.

Walt felt himself merging with their spirit. He might have come to CU to be with Peggy, but he found the boys in Baker Hall a more nourishing oasis. They had a sense of place, a shared direction and a friendliness which seem to reach out to everyone, new and old.

His roommate, Jerry, the first black man he had ever engaged in conversation, shared details of his life and the ways of the campus. Soft spoken, shy and introspective, Jerry found his commitment to ROTC as consuming as Walt found his own work in the butcher shop, and they grew confident with one another. If Jerry had a social life, he didn't talk about it, but he knew his way around campus and Walt felt a growing connection to him.

Jerry invited him home to Denver for Thanksgiving and that Wednesday evening took him to a black holiday party in a local dance hall. Walt found himself visually and culturally overwhelmed, a single white face in a new majority, a stick in a circle of loose limbers trying hard not to do the wrong thing. He could not dance their dances, feared to speak to their women, and controlled his tension with a fixed grin. He snacked, sipped soft cola and smiled.

Jerry, kind and attentive to him throughout the evening, kept the night friendly and his family embraced him warmly. It was a nice holiday, but he was happy to get back to Baker. Two weeks later, without elaboration, Jerry said that he was going home for a few days. He never returned and Walt made no inquiries, thinking that he should, wondering why he didn't. Well, he was in the midst of his own metamorphosis.

To be sure, he continued to see Peggy. They got engaged, an almost perfunctory pledge, and his connection to her seemed to weaken every week. College of the Rockies wasn't far away really, but her baby-sitting, her classes, her sorority activities all cut into the small amount of time they could be together. His work cleaning the butcher shop, a daily 4 pm and Saturday morning appointment took energy and time. Like his first work experience at age thirteen, he hosed, scraped and swept the meat-cutting shop each day, a tidy piece of college work that paid his room and board. Still, his schedule didn't mesh much with Peggy's, and he gradually absorbed more fully the culture of his dormitory.

Already there for two years, the Baker Boys had well-established friendships, serious academic business, and an effervescent energy in their declarations that they were God-Damned-Independents. They formed intramural teams in swimming, touch football and softball, spent home-game Saturdays cheering on the Buffalo in Folsom Field, hollered insults and gibes up and down the hall even as they held serious talks late night over a beer. They fashioned panty raids, woodsy campfires, and bar socials with enthusiasm, and they painted on the bottoms of coeds' Levis wittily, they thought, spelling the dorm wing, "KIOWA" with "KI" on one cheek and "WA" on the other, leaving out the 'O" for effect. They liked to have fun.

Diverse in personality, full of banter, arguments, questions and answers, they maintained a united purpose: graduation and a future. Smart, committed, focused, they studied, attended classes, partied and then they studied some more. Walt found himself learning nicknames, joining their teams, and adopting their attention to classes and grades.

Blake, the theoretical physicist who knew classical music, the Constitution and the facts and theories of the universe dazzled everyone with his evenly tempered statements of speculation and truth.

Gordo, the good looking one, combed his hair with artful strokes, carried the swagger of a Hollywood leading man and planned a career in sales.

Kip, tall and friendly, studied engineering. Interested in the arts, the outdoors and the ways of the world, he seemed to gather friends wherever he went, and became one of Walt's favorites.

Teddy, full of humor, acidic wit and a knack for detecting bullshit from every source amused Walt daily, kept them both laughing and focused on what was really important: graduation.

Jimmers, once at MIT, decided that he could live only in Colorado's culture. Walt had no sense that he would later share a season with him in the south stands watching Cookie Gilchrist and the Denver Broncos.

And then there was Cliff. Of them all, Walt thought, Cliff was the one most like himself, but he was a New Jersey guy who spent his youth living life as far from the desert as one could imagine.

About six feet tall, lean, with sharp features, crew cut hair and blue eyes, Cliff was compelling, athletic, moody, short spoken and exuded a body language of purpose, focus and energy. Maybe those features led to him being selected as the Buffalo "Mascot" complete with paper mache head, a tan, loose jump suit, and a tail that he kept twitching with a loose string connected to his hand. Ridiculous to imagine, yet amusing in action, Cliff rallied the fans in the face of certain defeat until the day that "Ralphie", a live buffalo, replaced him.

He admired Cliff, embraced their differences and absorbed a connection to him. Generally upbeat, Walt tried to include everyone in his morning breakfast "Hello". Cliff, if greeted, was more likely to simply say, "Eat shit". Cliff let you take care of yourself, didn't second guess decisions and kept his own compass. Walt found his quirks amusing, recognized the true quality of his character and soon included him in his mental circle of friends. They shared some childhood sports experiences, early work (soda jerk and pin setter for Cliff; paperboy and butcher shop cleanup for Walt), popular heroes such as Johnny Lujack, Whitey Ford, the Lone Ranger and the Green Hornet, yet they had such different childhoods.

While Walt filled his early years exploring the boundaries of the River, shooting rabbits, and fighting pretend wars through oil fields and barbed wire fences, Cliff fished, hunted ducks, slapped pucks, and sledded down an empty piece of land that became The Meadowlands. His life in Lyndhurst, New Jersey reflected his close family ties, deep friendships with schoolmates and endless curiosity and energy.

While Walt rooted for his hometown high school football team, supported Joe Lewis and looked for approval in the laughter of others, Cliff developed an eternal commitment to the New York Giants baseball team, rooted for Billy Conn, and in general measured others against his own standards. At the age of 10, *all by himself,* he attended NIT basketball tournaments at the old Madison Square Garden, cheered the Giants at the Polo Grounds, watched Preacher Roe pitch, and grabbed a ball hit out in batting practice by Dusty Rhodes.

Hearing of events he could only read about from a guy who saw them in person reminded Walt of his own experience in peering into a carnival mirror. A distorted image flashed back at him, recognizable to be sure, but a form with a different set of bulges and curves than the one he knew to be his own.

Willie Mays once handed Cliff a ball that he, Mays, caught in pre-game practice, *handed it to him*. Legend touched life that day.

Cliff carried himself with confidence, quick intelligence and, most impressively to Walt, Cliff refused to tie himself to any woman. When he married, he said, his wife would come to him, and he knew precisely what kind of partner he wanted. He refused to date any girl who did not have blue eyes. His wife would keep his house, cook and feed his family, raise his blue-eyed children and model her life on his cues. It took a while to find her, and Cliff went through a series of relationships sorting and sifting for the woman he wanted. "Why," he might say with a puzzled look on his face, "would I spend time with someone that I no longer liked?" Walt didn't have a good answer for that.

Much like a coastal lighthouse, Cliff both warned and warmed with his revolving beam, focusing on that which interested him, and Walt wondered if he would ever find the woman he wanted. It surely was not his own view of how one fashioned a successful marriage, but then he thought of the distress he had suffered seeking Peggy's approval.

Cliff finally married a blue-eyed coed from New Jersey. She produced four blue-eyed children whom she raised in a motherly way, and when she was forty-five, she divorced him. He was pleased to see her go, so maybe they both got what they wanted.

When Jerry did not return for second semester, Walt asked Cliff if he would be willing to have him as a roommate. His room, double sized, had space and an extra bed. "Yes, on one condition," Cliff replied.

Walt paused, then asked, "What is it?"

"You must make your bed every morning."

Walt moved in that day.

When Peggy continued to treat him with ambivalence, he felt himself picking up Cliff's outlook on life, school and women. Each had its place. Each could be managed. He felt comfortable with that, and he began to sample a mental picture of what his future would be like without Peggy. Still engaged, he hadn't found anyone else, but he began to look.

Then suddenly, impulsively he thought, Peggy asked him if he would like to spend a long weekend together at Steamboat Springs. He didn't think twice. Maybe standing apart a little had motivated her to draw closer. They had a wonderful time. He didn't know much about skiing, nor did she, but they both found themselves floundering and laughing their ways down "bunny" hills, developing a little basic skill. Days were bright, winds calm. Nights were dark, bodies thrashing. He could see a future with her, could feel how it might resonate inside him, but once back in Boulder, she began to fade again, unavailable and when seen, unresponsive, leaving him to sort her out without cues or conversation.

Puzzling that, he found himself with other problems. He had arranged for his co-worker to cover for him at the butcher shop while he and Peggy were in Steamboat. His boss, Fred Algren, criticized him for not reporting to work and told him that he would be fired at the end of the school year. Walt reacted without a thought. "O.K., if I am not coming back in the fall, I will leave now," he said, taking off his work apron and turning to walk out.

"You can't do that," Algren said.

"Yes, I can," Walt said, and he did.

Now responsible for room and board for his final year at CU, Walt faced costs he couldn't control. Working hours off campus seldom matched up well with classroom hours, and he wasn't sure that he really had the energy to manage it. He spent the rest of the semester worrying about work, making grades, and dealing with Peggy.

To Walt, it now seemed as though their time in Steamboat Springs were a single scene spliced into a documentary film titled "Toying With the Boy". He asked her what was wrong. She evaded his questions with comments on the weather, the children she cared for and the business of the sorority.

He tried to draw upon their time on the ski slopes to revitalize their engagement but she ignored him. He could not do more, and soon, he didn't feel like doing anything at all. One cold night, parked in Gunbarrel Greens, she suggested that they see other people, that it was over, and handed him back his ring. Visibly angry at last, his voice took control of his body. He grasped the ring she handed him, shouted at her to "Get out, just get out!" and sent her packing into a cold, cold night. She began making her own path along the frigid mile back to C.O.R., and he shouted as she walked away, "Do me a favor and don't come back to Colorado. It's too small for us!" Film over.

Cliff drove to California with him at the end of the school year. They stopped at Disneyland, and he felt liberated wandering about cartoon characters whose artificial lives posed as reality. Peggy would have fit right in, and he both mulled his loss and embraced his freedom. He liked Goofy.

As they drove over the Grapevine down into the Central Valley, Cliff commented briefly on all of the sagebrush, dirt, irrigated fields of cotton and alfalfa and finally noticed the oil wells. He looked at the clear, cloudless sky and with some alarm said, "You grew up in this?"

"Yep," Walt said.

"What'll the weather be tomorrow?"

"The same."

"Does it rain often?"

"Seldom."

Cliff, rarely at a loss for words, sat silent while they cruised the Maricopa Flats, and then kept going all the way to Taft and beyond. "The landscape doesn't change much," he said.

He spent the weekend visiting Walt's family, plucking grapefruit off trees in the yard and speculating about how long it might be before it rained. On Monday, he said goodbye, walked two blocks out to the highway, and stuck out his thumb. He spent the next five days hitch-hiking back home to Lyndhurst. When he left, Walt mentioned, almost as an afterthought, that if he heard of any work at CU, let him know.

In early August, Cliff rescued him, writing to say that he had talked with Joan Morgan, the head of Dormitory Services, explained Walt's plight, and vouched for his character. Reluctantly, she agreed to hire him as the mailman for three small dorms a block from Baker, and sent him a message. Tell him, she said to Cliff, that "If he misses even a single day of work, I'll fire his ass."

Uncertainty, such a heavy weight all summer, dropped off Walt's shoulders, spoiled up a cloud of dust and rolled down a rabbit hole. He was free!

When he parked his Merc in Boulder that second September, Walt felt that he had come home. Curious about but unencumbered by Peggy, far from the distractions of California living, embraced by the friendships built in Baker Hall and inspired by his impending graduation, he felt as complete as he had at any time in his life.

He checked at College of the Rockies. Peggy wasn't there.

Over the years, he thought from time to time about what happened to them. Something about the whole breakup just left him dissatisfied. He ran different scenarios through his mind, but they all ended in questions, and it took nearly three decades before he had his answer.

Revelations

They met in the 60s at a rock n roll dance back home in the Valley. Shortly after he walked through those doors, drunk, she caught his eye. He grabbed her around the waist and away they went, inseparable for the rest of the evening. A pretty blonde with a light laugh, a quick mind and white teeth, her green eyes hovered above a generous smile. Her legs, presented in cut off Levis, featured warmly tanned calves and thighs that were strong and inviting. Try as he might, he could not remember her last name, and lost track of her for about a year, then ran across her again at Sunset Gardens. They began seeing one another regularly and then exclusively.

Walt began focusing on settling down. She talked of college. He worked six days a week saving money. She made good grades. He talked about raising a family together. She applied to five colleges. He speculated about where in the city they might live. She became silent. When he spoke of their future, she did not warm to his thoughts and he wondered finally just where they were going. When he asked, she told him.

She would be going to a private women's school, College of the Rockies, near Boulder, Colorado, and she thought that they should start seeing other people. Stunned, Walt faced a six day work week which filled his pockets with money but left him now without purpose. He quit the butcher shop, enrolled at FSU and looked to see what Peggy thought. It wasn't a pretty sight. She began enjoying her senior year, dating other guys and sending him a look that asked, "Why are you still coming home on weekends?" When her letter came, he tore it up. Her goodbye. His goodbye.

Summer came, and for three weeks he immersed himself in daily National Guard maneuvers. Sober and awake at night, he followed older guys through bars, listening to their well-oiled passes at women, driving drunken sergeants back to base as dawn quietly slipped through the car windows. He imagined what he might see when camp was over and the dusty, olive hued trucks finally returned to town. Was this his own movie? Would Peggy be waiting for him? She was not.

In late summer he walked out of the store and there she was, as he had imagined that someday she might be. Parked next to the curb, she waved hello. He slipped into her car and they talked. Such a painful, tentative connection, but she had come looking for him. They went to a movie and talked, continued their conversation at a summer play, spoke of a long distance connection. At the end of the month, she said goodbye and left for College of the Rockies. He transferred to San Jose State. She said she would write, and she did. Once.

She was never sure why she parked outside his workplace. Summer was essentially over, and she was leaving. She had dated, looked, searched, wondered and still there was something about him that brought her back. He was in college now. He was thinking about life outside the city, and he had begun dating again. She wasn't really sure that she liked that last part.

She pledged that she would write, and she did once, but college life was too active, the exhilaration of diverse behavior and new personalities was too intoxicating for her to put their relationship on paper and maintain it. Silence seemed to work.

As a lecturer in English literature at a private women's college, Barry Swanson immersed himself in the freedoms and tumult of the Sixties. Social barriers between instructors and students disintegrated as their conversations about war and civil rights played out in public gatherings and intimate retreats. At first, Swanson simply circulated amidst the sexual revolution of The Pill as a single, professional instructor. Eventually he married and soon found himself with a child in the household.

He paused, but found his single habits difficult to ignore. At age 30 his charm, sparkling eyes and deeply confident style, remained strikingly appealing to coeds, opening doors to "mini-affairs" as he liked to call them. Enhancing his textual analysis with a soft southern accent and gentle manners, his lectures thrilled 18 year old women who saw him as a remarkable sentinel for literary awakenings, and he skillfully converted furtive glances into safely secluded intimate adventures.

He always looked forward to fall classes and freshman females agog with their new freedom. He knew that he amazed them with his knowledge, his questions, and his gently supportive reassurances as they searched for his approval. He did so with purpose. As they developed a literary relationship with him they began to regard him as a little more man and a little less teacher. He worked at cultivating their admiration, knowing that when he met his second semester classes he would know who was smitten.

That fall a student, clearly intrigued, caught his eye and answered his questions without hesitation. A blond, she wore her hair with a certain verve and confidence. She sported a generous smile, engaged him intellectually and appreciated his compliments, ones easily given. When he learned that his wife Ariel was pregnant with their second child, he went looking for a babysitter for their three year old and found the blond, Peggy something, sitting front row on the first day of spring classes. As he anticipated, she would love to help Ariel with child care.

In the early weeks of that first semester she missed old friends, and she invited Walt to come out the following spring and spend time with her for Colorado Days. It was a phone call of the moment, and soon her English class become a much higher priority in her life. At first unaware of Professor Swanson's interest in her, within a few weeks it became clear that he was courting her in a subtle, academic way and she absorbed his attention, blushing at her own private thoughts. She made sure that she got into his class for the next semester.

Peggy called, warm and welcoming, inviting him to come out to Boulder in May for Colorado Days, a weekend of party and fun. Good enough. She didn't seem to follow up the invitation with any enthusiasm, but he moved right ahead. He rounded up another guy and a girl to share the expenses of the trip and they drove all night to get to Boulder. It was a hard trip, full of anxiety, mechanical breakdown and exhaustion. They got there in a rented car, but they got there.

God, he was really coming out! It was a casual invitation, well intended, but that was before she began her affair. What was she going to do? Swanson was now everywhere in her life.

His mature reflections, complimentary conversation, and experienced lovemaking introduced her to new romantic standards. She could not be seen with him in public, but local motels gave them privacy and she felt bathed in his wit, admiration and seduction. She saw their relationship as provocative, mature, sophisticated, exciting, but dangerous too. There she was in the house of her lover assisting his wife in the care of his child, and then melting away to meet him in local hideaways.

Now, a high-school boyfriend, at her invitation, was coming out to Boulder for a weekend of partying, and she did not want to see him. It was just too complicated. She would have to spend time with him, a little time anyway. How to balance his interest and Swanson' demands? She decided that she would use her babysitting chores to get her through the weekend. Walt would not like it, but it would reduce risky conflicts with Swanson. No matter what, she wasn't having sex with two different men in one weekend. Once Walt left, she could concentrate on enjoying her affair and assessing Swanson' intentions.

Swanson treasured his trysts with Peggy and while he could sense that she wondered whether they had a future, she did not need promises. In his experience, the first months of his coed affairs flowered freely, without any sense of restriction or limitation, but he could see that she was testing his interest. When she told him that this boyfriend of hers, Walt Farmer, was coming out to visit, he was amused. It was nice of her to entertain a high-school flame, but he knew what he knew. She was in his bed, and she would stay there.

From the moment Walt arrived at the College of the Rockies, Peggy was distant. They spent little time together during the entire weekend, yet she suggested that he transfer to C.U., a public university. They could become engaged. "Don't dump me," she asked.

He pondered. What kind of courtship was this, a three-month renewable relationship? Was this something to build a future upon? It was a mess, but when he tried to think about it objectively, his emotions simply colored his picture with the shades of love that he wanted to believe. It was what it was. She wanted him in Boulder. She said so. Would he then transfer to C.U.? Leave California for yet another college to pursue love and knowledge?

Well, if it were meant to be, it would happen. If not, he still knew the way to San Jose. He applied to C.U., gained acceptance and found a campus job which paid for his room and board. The stars brightened, aligned.

He arrived in the fall ready to be embraced, loved and celebrated in this new commitment and impending engagement. Within a month, a rising sun of reality eliminated starlight. Seldom available, Peggy made dating difficult and intimacy out of the question. Much of her time focused on child care for the wife of an English professor, Barry Swanson, whose wife, Ariel, was now in late pregnancy with their second child. Confused but committed, he proposed to Peggy in late October, and she seemed happy to accept his ring. They flew home to California at Christmas to share the news with their families.

Then, there was that incredibly stupid remark that she made out at the lake. Why would she want him to be on campus? He brought her energy, fun and laughter, but her life would be squeezed in four directions: babysitting, lover, boyfriend, and classes all competing for her time and commitments. How would she manage that? Did she want an engagement with Walt? Maybe it was a way to put Swanson aside? But did she want to shed a professor who enhanced her sense of self so powerfully? If she had no future with Swanson, did she have one with Walt? Did she have to choose? What was he going to do with his life? She wasn't sure that even he knew that answer. She couldn't read his thoughts, but she knew one thing soon after he arrived. She could not continue this balancing act indefinitely. She just couldn't.

Swanson could not have been happier as he moved through the spring semester. His home life was blessed with a healthy pregnancy. Peggy looked after his three year old daughter, and her infatuation with him remained as intense as it had been in January. She still found his witticisms funny, responded intensely to his seductive strategies and bound herself to him in a way that he had not quite seen coming. When she left for the summer, he travelled out to Santa Barbara and spent time with her during one of her work breaks from a girl's camp. The connection was solid, sexually charged, flourishing amidst the freedom of anonymity.

She told him in Santa Barbara that an old high school boyfriend was coming out to CU in the fall. She had encouraged his transfer, and she mentioned in passing that she thought he wanted to marry her. Swanson did not rise to the bait. If Peggy wanted to leave him for youth and a commitment, she could go. She was probably looking for a different kind of reaction, but he knew her place in his life, knew that it was temporary. He could see a little tension building, but her report didn't unsettle him.

In his experience, guilt and time eventually moved a coed out of his life. What made Peggy different was her involvement with his wife, Ariel, and her essential role in the household. In a sense, he and Peggy were living together and he loved the special glances they exchanged, the shaded meanings of their conversation and the allure of the next meeting when they could unleash their feelings.

Still, that ring would mean something to her, and it certainly should mean something to him. Was he really in a position to keep her in his life? This new man coming to be with her seemed to be committed. He would challenge Swanson for her time. He might even learn of the affair. What would that mean for his marriage? Would Ariel's preoccupation with the new baby, and her love for the three year old keep her so absorbed that he could continue to play house with Peggy?

He needed to prepare a new agenda. He was not going to disappear and Peggy's commitment to an engagement felt tenuous. He began to offer occasional hints of their future, knowing that his smile and soft words could keep her on the bubble.

For Walt, Peggy become more distant, virtually disappearing during finals and a brief semester break. His trust eroding, disappointment building, he began to move in new circles of his own, spending more time with friends in the dorm, less time at College of the Rockies. He circulated at parties alone, interested in meeting new people. She must have noticed he thought. In early March, she asked him to take her to Steamboat Springs for a weekend, and suddenly the sex which she had long promised but never delivered, became the memory of the month. Warm, loving, intimate, she bonded with him, and he felt that they had at last found their way.

It was a false read, and their relationship unraveled quickly thereafter. Babysitting became Peggy's first priority once again. She seemed distant, depressed even, and he worried about her. When he pressed her, she murmured only that things were not working out for her. A few weeks more, sitting in his Merc, she finally said what he feared most, "I think that we ought to see other people." He knew where that comment led, and he felt sick when she said it.

All the disappointments, the travel, the required understandings, even the occasional intimacies followed by what seemed planned rejections flowed through his memory, electrified his feelings and shaped his words. He sent her packing through a cold, Colorado night with a shout, "Do me a favor. Don't come back to C.O.R.!" He wondered as he said it whether that was a plea or a threat.

It was impossible to balance her life.

What did she mean to Barry? Did he really plan to divorce and leave Ariel and his children? He had never said he would, but he had intimated that he might. If so, what did her engagement really mean? How did she get out of it? If Barry stayed put, would he still want her? Would she still want him? Was that her future...a mistress? Could she keep Walt on the backburner just in case? That had always worked before. What did she want?

The new baby kept her at the house even more, a dual role that she could barely manage. She admired Ariel, and she loved the two girls. Her betrayal had many sides and they all featured a cutting edge. The pressure became unbearable.

The only thing that she felt she could control was the engagement. She tried to let it end with some sense of grace, suggesting to Walt that they spend a weekend in Steamboat Springs. He jumped at the invitation. For him it seemed to be a shared memory that melted every falling snowflake. But for her, it was a farewell gift and she quietly began to disengage. A few weeks later, she suggested to Walt that maybe they should see other people, and his reaction was so hostile and so edgy that she worried both about his safety, and hers. When he told her to get out of the car that night, she didn't look back, walked the frosty mile from the park back to her sorority house and crawled into bed with a long sigh and enormous relief.

Swanson could understand the difficult position Peggy held. Still, she broke the engagement and while he enjoyed her for the rest of the semester, her life kept falling apart. As she suspected, he had no intention of leaving Ariel and his family. He would move on to someone else when new students arrived in the fall, but until then, Peggy visited his house every day, and his bed as often as he could manage it. His demands escalated. She responded for a time but when final exams approached, she began to withdraw. She was done, and with summer she was gone.

She did not return to College of the Rockies, and in the fall, Walt gave some thought to his long, fruitless courtship of Peggy. Those last few months had twisted them dry, left them groping around one another to hold an unseen connection that slowly grew more and more fragile. When it snapped, scattered debris impaled each of them with tiny fragments of broken memories and flawed futures. He would move on, but he would never again make a full commitment to any woman. He thought of a Bob Dylan quote, "Always keep something back."

She was out of his life. He kept that last look of her walking through the cold nicely placed in his mind. He liked it still.

****

The phone rang, "Hi there....how are you?" Her voice. It shook him, and he quickly counted the years...25...he took a breath and eased into conversation.

He asked, "I'm fine...doing well...where are you?"

"Oregon, just outside Bend. I know you probably don't want to hear from me, but I just got to thinking about you...about us...long time ago, and I know it didn't end well."

"No." He paused, and for a second or three the line remained silent. "It didn't end well at all, and I never quite understood that."

She said nothing.

He started again, "So, what has your life been all about?"

"I married three times, once foolishly, had three children, a girl and two boys," she said. "My second husband was killed in an automobile accident...raised the children myself for a few years then remarried."

Compelling news, but it didn't touch on his main interest. Should he ask the question he had been holding ready for nearly three decades? Would that send her off? Maybe, but why had she called? To what purpose? What the hell...

"What happened to us?" he asked, "There was something going on, but I could never know for sure. What the hell happened to us, Peggy?"

She said, "I'll write you."

"I think I've heard that before."

"I'll write."

It was four pages, front and back, and filled the framework of their difficult relationship with powerful truths. Her affair began shortly into the second semester of her freshman year. Completely immersed in Swanson's world, she found it easy enough to manage Walt during the visit in May, even during the summer when she avoided intimacy with excuses about work at the summer camp.

But Walt's fall arrival complicated her life by multiple levels, and the balancing act became more than she could endure. By springtime, she was emotionally exhausted, and she panicked. "The pressure Swanson put on me to have sex became more than I could endure," she wrote. "You were a casualty as was Ariel, grades and college. I was out of control. I did the only thing I could do. I just left for good."

He read her letter twice, reflected a little on those times and read it again. Her account told him what went on behind closed doors and her honesty satisfied him. He briefly acknowledged to himself a deep enmity toward Swanson, to what purpose he did not yet know, but he found a comforting mindset toward Peggy. Clearly distressed, she seemed relieved to spell out some of the foolishness of her youth.

She rang once again to follow up on the letter. It was a friendly call, and they chatted with a casual intimacy that felt brand new to both of them. She spoke more of her life after leaving Colorado, elaborated on a frivolous marriage, then a better one and finally a third which had worked out well. Remarkable, he thought, how candidly former lovers could speak to one another. He knew that he had dodged a bullet... told her that, and she laughed and agreed. His life had been far, far better without her, she said, and as for hers, well, she was happy enough and she loved her family.

When they hung up, Walt felt a deep sense of peace. He checked his emotional cache and found that he no longer had interest in her...none at all. It was a nice set of calls, a satisfying letter, a concluding conversation 25 years past due. He felt the strength of his relief a bit surprising, but whatever he had been carrying around inside, it was finally over.

Well, it was over for him. Peggy still had another move to make.

Movin' On

And then Walt found what he was looking for, just when he wasn't looking. Nor was she. These two no-lookers radiated attraction, looked one another over and found what they needed, relaxed in their findings, made plans with emotional bindings and set out to make a life together. He found security in her, an emotional resonance that comforted him, kept him washed and safe, enabled him to think about his future, their future, and act to define it. He was not sure what she found in him, but he was more than willing to center himself on her commitment, layer his feelings and focus on a professional career, family in tow, all sharing life as he saw it lived in his youth. In the end, university dating gave birth to real life.

Across the plains, Colorado to Missouri, he traveled to their union, knowing that she was the support base he needed, and in the night of driving to his wedding day, he pondered what future they might make. No thought of children, many thoughts of work, teaching, and income security. Was this the right choice? Was she the partner who would let him be himself, let him explore himself.

In Bellville, Kansas, the road leading ever eastward, his headlights bouncing light in both lanes, he thought about being tired yet exhilarated, about needing coffee. A cup later and back on the road he brought the car up to speed when suddenly, he began losing focus on the asphalt, breath coming in spurts, heart pounding wildly and his sense of controlled consciousness leaking away. He was dying. He knew it. But where to die? Should he stop on the side of the road and expire or keep going and hope to find some kind of help. Was there help to find?

He kept driving hoping that he would not hit another car. A roadside café loomed and he pulled in to find company, human contact which might keep him somehow safe. He sat. He did not die. He walked into the café, did not collapse. He drank coffee and returned to his car. In the August night, dry, warm temperatures comforted him, fresh air floated in and out open windows, and he lay down and slept. He awoke at dawn, started up the car and drove to St. Louis. He tried to ignore his first panic attack. Different from hallucinations, it ignited a completely out of control "hanging on the edge of life" crisis. At first a stranger to him, it became a new companion, returning from time to time for two decades.

When he saw her, her smile, her languid look, her length and classic form, but most of all, her smile, he calmed. She always had strength with the big issues of life, and panic attacks were big issues. Her ways were gentle and soft, comforting and lingering. When frights came and the heart raced, she calmed him with her words and her quiet strength. He knew that, if for no other reason, he had chosen well.

They were married for forty years, and like all things that last a long time, it had its metamorphosis. For a decade, it was an uneven mixture focused on Walt. He had his work at the university. She had her work at home, and her investment in the children. Eventually, he involved himself more with their lives, and together the five of them went through the waterways of competitive pool swimming, leaving it when the young children became young adults. Walt took great comfort in gliding through those waters, swimming a mile a day, sometimes two. The easy breath, the gentle roll, the self-propelled motion, the quiet-- all reminded him of some earlier place where all was liquid and he was safe.

Their transition to a rural home created a life which she loved deeply: horses, animals, space and the challenges of performing with her four-footed friends. Her own artistic interests flourished amidst journalistic writings, painting and sculpture. Twenty years they spent there, until age, injury and weariness sent them packing to neighborhood living once again. There he felt released into the memories of his small-town youth and together they blended into the community as though at one with its founders. When their time together ended, he dropped into a new century with focus only on the old one and for a time without thoughts of even another year.

Breakup

Dear Harvey,

The wind and sun are having a marvelous time laughing and romping outside. Here, in the empty lounge they are as far away as you seem...somehow there, so very close, so very necessary...and yet there are walls which separate us, and I am not able to open the door which would let me leave this solitary room and enter into that happiness outside.

I wish there were some way I could help you to understand how much I want to be able to walk up and open that door... but, you see, it is not in me to do so. Yes, I <u>could </u>say many things and do many things...but unless they can come from inside without hesitation, it is better_(not more pleasant) for all concerned if they remain closed behind that door.

I cannot leave this world and enter yours without knowing that it's what must be...and I would know; (believe me it isn't always "I don't know") but I would know that it <u>must be</u> and would not be worrying about the hows or whys of its being.

To say "no" is something I haven't wanted to do---for many reasons concerning each of us. I kept hoping my silly self would say go on---it's what you want to do and will be right. But it hasn't and by now if it would have ever, I think I should have known.

After this jumble of thoughts I suppose it's ridiculous to say that I do love you---but I do---for the first time that I've ever been able to say those words to anyone that's rather silly, isn't it? But it's not a love which would hold a marriage. I could only love for now and then remember---my but I do sound like one of those stupid musicals. Please forgive me---and while I am at it---and you must listen or quit reading—I want to say "thank you" and if you're feeling that's a formal "polite" gesture in words, please don't. I thank you so very much for being you and letting me share that for a time. I feel terribly selfish to have received so much and given so little.

And now, this student of art must quit this and return to class before Professor Styles comes calling...

Much Love to You, Harvey,

Lauren

Commitment

He first saw her as she ran crying from the shadows of the sorority house, hand across her face hiding embarrassment. Applause echoed off the homecoming sculptures as her sisters complimented her work, praised her art.

This quick wisp of tearful woman, moving from the dark into the lighted security of the brick refuge touched him. He glimpsed her slender torso above her long legs, themselves wrapped in blue jeans graced with a loose top that offered suggestion of breasts nicely placed, well presented. A quick look, his senses caught her essence, and he recorded it in his memory amidst the distractions in his own life.

Four months later, as spring wrested control of winter snows, he saw her again, this time laughing with friends, eyes aglow, body draped in her favorite clothes, again those blue jeans and a loose off-the-shoulder sweat shirt, brown hair to her shoulders, a smile white and generous. Her joy in this moment of conversation piqued his interest. She seemed open, buoyant and full of fun. He filed that look away again, asked a friend for her name, did nothing.

Another month, working hard to escape his failed engagement, still damaged goods, he began looking for something to do. She came to mind, and when he saw her walking from the Hill back to her sorority house one afternoon, he caught up alongside her and introduced himself.

"Hi there, Lauren, you may not know me. I'm Walt Farmer. Wonder if you would like to have coffee sometime?"

She looked at him with a little sparkle in her eyes, as though she were going to laugh, but she did not. He noticed a small little skin tag on the top of her right eyelid as she blinked. He waited to hear words and she broke the silence, "Oh sure, I know who you are...you were seeing Peggy...sure, anytime."

"How about this evening, near eight, at Gaylords?"

"O.K. See you there."

So it began, a courtship founded on coffee, built on conversation and developed with early declarations that neither wanted a serious relationship. She had recently broken up with a guy named Harvey, and she seemed well aware of his failed engagement to Peggy. How aware? Regardless, both subjects served as conversation early in their coffee dates, and Walt learned right away that Lauren could bring sensitive issues right to the surface without judgment or embarrassment but with a deft examination of human behavior.

She had held a real interest in Harvey, but not a compelling one, she laughed, as she remembered that lying in bed with him, she half nude on the verge of her first seduction, she vomited. That set the relationship back a fatal step, and she explained, "My dad told me not to advertise what was not for sale, so I dress casually. He also said to keep my legs together, a crude comment, but he's a hard messenger to ignore, and my mind couldn't put my body to rest. So I had to say goodbye. I really thought that he might be the guy I would marry, but no, he just wasn't right."

He mentioned his broken engagement to Peggy in the most general of terms not really interested in going through that scenario again but simply affirming that he had spent more than one year and one long trip to keep it together, and it just didn't work. Lauren seemed to know all that he might have said.

"Oh, sure, you were in the sorority gossip loop all year. Peggy's in a chapter of ours at C.O.R., my Little Sister last year, and I knew you were coming out for Colorado Days. I've heard about you all year long too, the ups and downs and all," she smiled.

"Good or bad?" he grimaced a little.

"Nothing bad about you. Probably nothing bad about Peggy. Just life I think. She has a lot going on...I think she just decided there wasn't room for you."

Well, honesty he valued, and here she was offering candid assessments about her own behavior and Peggy's and the truth felt good. No wishy-washy here. She knew herself, hell, she apparently knew Peggy and that put her one large step ahead of him.

He wanted good company, laughter, dancing, conversation, no complications, and he found them all. She majored in Fine Arts, painted, sculptured, posed nude for drawing classes, ran around with the theatre crowd, dated no one in particular, valued honesty, rejected pretension. He found her warmly fascinating, wondered about her modeling while honoring her commitment to the arts as being part of who she was and what she brought to any relationship.

Of the theatre crowd, filled with men and women aiming high in the entertainment world, he had some interest though not any particular cultural attraction. Lauren loved their candor, freely shifting morals and respect for individual lifestyles. With them she learned to party and to drink (avoid vodka she told him, it sneaks up on you). She rappelled down the front of the Flatirons when they took her up there and told her there was only one way down, and she admired their willingness to bet their futures on blind faith much as she wagered her life that day on simple reassurances.

She worked backstage creating props, painting scenes, hanging out with those who would be stars, valuing their frank solicitations for sex, warmed by their willing acceptance when she said, "no". Still, among her obligations to classes, plays, sculpting, painting and study, she had time enough for him. Indeed, she seemed to make him a part of her life with an easy smile, a willing response to his overtures and kisses that introduced him to a woman for the first time.

He had no interest in a serious relationship, nor did she, and they affirmed that early and reaffirmed it for the rest of the semester. Yet, increasingly they spent time with no one else, dated no one else, talked seriously to no one else. He found her personality new, mature, direct, adult. He wanted to be with her and even as they repeated to one another that they were just dating, their connection nibbled into their daily doings.

A month after they began having their coffee dates, having seen her only in blue jeans, loose shirts and light sweaters, Walt asked her to go dancing. He arrived at the sorority house early to pick her up, waited in the foyer and then glanced up the steps as she descended slowly with that secret smile on her lips and that one eye of hers half-closed as though it were waiting to surprise. *She wore a dress*. He drew a breath, marked the sight of her in his permanent memory and mentally walked her down the stairs.

That night he did not see a woman in blue jeans. He struggled to absorb every visual inch of a devil in a powder blue sheath. It hugged her body, revealed to him and anyone else just how classic her structure and why she modeled for artists. From that moment, his interest changed. Hers had also, else why that sheath? He learned later that she did not even own a skirt, had borrowed the dress to impress him. Their dating tone evolved more quickly, no more talk about avoiding commitments.

At semester's end, she flew to California to visit with friends in San Francisco. He drove up from the Valley, met her and together they walked the streets, rode cable cars, shared a drink at the Top of the Mark. Miracle little happenings seemed to embrace them every day, and he grew more confident in her, more willing to accept the idea that she offered only that which she meant, and that she asked only honesty in return.

They drove down the valley, past San Jose where he once spent a year, through Sills Corner and its jailhouse memories, crossed the River where he once shared warm, dark evenings with high school classmates, and alighted finally at his home on the outskirts of the city. His mother loved her. His friends brightened visibly when she met them, one confiding to him that he would love to find a woman who looked at him the way she looked at Walt. Without saying the words, they simply began to think of themselves as partners, loving partners pondering longer commitments. When she flew home to St. Louis, he felt for the first time that there was a woman out there who would truly miss him.

They wrote that summer, long letters describing events, giving voice to feelings which emerged with growing strength. They penned the words of love and connection even as the distance between Missouri and California seemed to widen with the increasing discomfort of separation. In the fall, before school started, he travelled to St. Louis to meet her parents.

It was a disaster.

Lauren met him at the train station in a little army jeep which she used to scurry about the city. In that casually reckless way that she had of doing things well, she steered them home as they chattered confident greetings to one another and she promised him how much her family looked forward to meeting him. As they pulled up in front of the solidly built, brick home, he relaxed, feeling that its presence promised him a similar kind of relationship with her parents: traditional, strong, hospitable. Up the steps they walked. She opened the door and he walked in with his suitcase, set it down and turned to greet her mother, Millie.

Instead, he heard a warm welcome from Mabel, their black maid, who said, "Well, here you are, Mr. Farmer, in St. Louis! The Missus is in the backyard. She'll be right around."

He hadn't heard about a maid. He had no sense that Lauren's household supported a servant. Mabel, warm and welcoming, returned to the kitchen where she tended some cooking, releasing a lid letting a little steam escape as she sampled the meat inside. Good enough, Walt thought, hoping that Millie proved to be equally warm.

She wasn't. From the first glance, as she walked in the back door from the porch, he could see and sense that she had to be convinced about him, about the relationship with her daughter, about his fitness to be courting her. False warmth to her greeting, no hugs, no eye contact. All her attention focused on Lauren, cuing her to show him to his room, speaking to him through her daughter, avoiding personal connection.

Well, Walt had a lot of experience with mothers who did not like him. He reflected on it from time to time, reviewing high school and college dates which brought him into a girl's home for a parental review and greeting. Something about him set them back. No prospects? He wondered. Well, here it surfaced again, and he set aside any bruised feelings, resolving that time into the visit would give him an opportunity to get to know Millie a lot better. The more she knew him, they better she would like him, and trust him. He knew it.

He and Lauren took a tour of the backyard, complete with brick barbecue, lawn chairs, a dog and sharply mown grass. Then down they went to the basement, a man's retreat complete with bar, a rack of German beer steins, dartboard, poker table, pipe rack and the scent of rich tobacco whose pungent odor had found a home in the solid wood furniture.

Then Lauren released him to go upstairs and settle in for a few minutes. Plenty of space for him in brother Rod's bedroom. Already at Yale for the year, he left a note on top of some fresh linen on his desk welcoming Walt, and warning him, "I didn't change the sheets." He knew how to do that and relaxed a bit, unpacked a few items and found comfort in his new haven. Then down the stairs again, chatting and absorbing a style of living completely new to him. A little intimidating, but he judged its value dependent more upon the people inside. He knew Lauren. What about the rest of them? Millie didn't sound promising.

They went outside again, sat in the lawn chairs enjoying a late afternoon sun and talked.

"Whew," Walt started, "Your mother seems unhappy to see me."

"Well," Lauren began, "Ma really hasn't decided about you I think. She loves to see me dating people she knows. I think she picked out my future husband a few years ago, a local

189

fellow who has a promising career in medicine. He's nice, but not for me tho...I don't want to settle in my parent's world......I'd like to find one of my own. My dad's sweet, but difficult, really aggressive and dominant. I've learned, being away in Colorado, how nice it is to make my own decisions...I just think......I just don't want to live too close to him."

"Anyway, Ma's going to be looking at you thinking that I am interested in a Catholic guy, and that I will raise a half-dozen kids on a high school teacher's salary and be impoverished all of my life. You can see that she really values Mable...big part of her idea of keeping the house tidy...hire a maid," and Lauren smiled at that and then told a story to illustrate.

"When Ma and Dad first married, they lived with his parents, had an upstairs bedroom and sitting area, bath and dressers. Ma hated living there and despised her housekeeping responsibility. Her job was to vacuum her space upstairs, and she went at it by turning on the vacuum, letting it run in place while she sat and sketched. Guess it sounded all right downstairs...never a comment, but Ma laughed and laughed about her 'hard work'. She never saw herself as a housekeeper; a wife, mother, lover but not a housekeeper."

"Oh my. Well, I don't want many children," Walt smiled. "How do you feel about housekeeping?"

"Oh, some of it's necessary," Lauren laughed.

"Do I need to mention family planning...maybe work it into casual conversation," he kidded.

"Hard to have casual conversation about things like that around here," she smiled.

"Hey," she continued, "Let's go in the house...play some Louis Prima and enjoy a coke."

"Sounds good."

We sipped our soft drinks while Mabel brought supper to a near state of readiness and Millie sipped a martini, all of us awaiting Dad's arrival. Son of a dentist, brother to a dentist, Dad practiced the same profession with a powerful personality that charmed his patients as much as it often confounded his friends. Lauren warned me that he could be critical of most anything, and he spoke with a loud, deep voice...intimidating she thought, but then she opened that lovely smile to Walt and said, "Talk about St. Louis University football. I think he'll like you."

After meeting Millie, he wondered.

The door opened, he glanced at her father as he entered and knew that his football reputation had been honestly earned. He brought a blocky, powerful stature draped with nice clothes into the doorframe and paused as he glanced at the new face. Walt noted through the open door that he drove a recent, but not extravagant Dodge. "Conservative car, conservative man," he thought.

Dad greeted him with a large smile, flashing a gold crown as he assessed Walt with a quick eye and shielded conclusion. His face, marked by a scar that wandered from the center of his forehead down along the edge of his mouth to the point of his chin, still held its youthful structure. He scanned Walt for insight into what kind of man his daughter had brought home. Walt felt the heat of the assessment, thought about Dad's bulk and focused on the scar. It fit the landscape of his face all right, and there had to be a story behind that.

As he entered the living room, shedding his jacket and loosening his tie, Dad said to no one in particular, but clearly including the two of them. "Turn off that damn music. That's terrible noise." They did and in the command volume of his voice and his looming physical presence Walt could well imagine the impressions that Dad made on Lauren as he embedded guides for her moral conduct. Millie didn't carry the weight of parental judgment, Dad did.

Walt went to meet him, shook hands and enjoyed the exchange. They looked each other over a bit, and he sighed that at least he wasn't rejected on first meeting. Dad asked him about the train trip, commented that the rails used to be a lot quicker than they were these days, and looked toward the kitchen with some interest. "How's that food coming along, Mabel?"

"Soon enough, soon enough," she replied with a bit of a laugh. She had long experience in handling his voice and tone of command.

Talk at the dinner table had to do with two new patients and some of Dad's challenges in working with them, and others, who had intense fear of dentists. He had taken up hypnotism as a way of inducing anxious adults into a calmer state so he could work on them without injections. He spoke of football, told stories about his life at St. Louis University, laughed at the decision of one of Lauren's high school friends to become a dentist because he noted that she and her brother often had pork chops for breakfast. Generous in keeping conversation going, he laughed at his own stories, asked Walt general questions and seemed to welcome him to the household. He liked that. He liked Dad. About Millie he was not so sure.

The next day he and Lauren spent the afternoon wheeling around South St. Louis as she showed him her high school, the local park where she formed many of her childhood memories, streets of homes she admired and hamburger joints that she enjoyed. Walt learned more about her brother, Rod, her love for him and how closely she, Millie and her father followed his activities. Valedictorian of his high school class, he had played football, spent a summer hunting seals in the Bering Sea, and now found himself as an oarsman in Yale's crew. The two siblings went through high school together, Lauren being 11 months younger than her brother because she said, "Mom's Catholic doctor would not prescribe a diaphragm for her and Dad wouldn't wait. He is an impatient man," she smiled. No wonder Millie feared Catholic birthing rates, he thought.

That evening Dad took them all to supper at Bevo Mill, one of the really nice restaurants in St. Louis, and one that had been a part of family tradition since Lauren could remember. Indeed, one of her most fond memories focused on the game she and Rod played each Christmas when they went to eat. The contest was counting Christmas trees lit in houses. Each took one side of the street. Whoever counted the most, won the game. Years later, she realized that her brother always took the side of the street filled with houses, leaving her to count businesses unlit with Christmas trees and a cemetery which occupied three entire blocks. She always laughed when she recounted that story, comfortable with Rod's cleverness.

So Bevo remained special in family memories and as a place to judge a new man in Lauren's life. Walt ate comfortably, enjoyed the menu, noted the martinis that flowed into Millie and the bourbon that flavored Dad's meal. Alcohol brightened the food, whetted the appetite too, but it also encouraged Millie to challenge Dad's statements from time to time and that in return lifted the conversation to more intense levels, raised volume and harsh conclusions. Walt remained quiet for the most part, seeking to find his comfort zone, realizing that Lauren in doing the same, had many years of practice at it.

The next day, Saturday, they spent time in Forest Park, attended an evening concert in the amphitheater, and got home in time to watch the moon from the backyard recliners as they chatted about family, future and professions. Lauren mentioned to him that her parents were encouraging her to go to Paris and study art for a year after graduation. He said nothing supportive. Get the girl away from the boy? Was that it?

Sunday, the last day of his visit, Dad decided they would spend the afternoon on his farm, about 20 miles out of the city, and they took a leisurely drive through the country. Walt marveled at the limestone rocks, crumbling in attractive moraines, the heavily leafed greenery of the forests and the open fields still cultivated by local farmers. Their farm property, christened White Oaks, graced rolling fields and mixed woodland and featured an old, two story white home set on a rise overlooking pastures graced by two horses, a flock of Guinea hens, and twin goats who wandered.

Beside the home Dad had built a stone patio and barbecue and in the back he constructed a plexiglass greenhouse where he potted, germinated and raised flowering plants to his heart's desire. In the immediate front plopped a small swimming pool installed with lots of hand work by Dad and family. To Walt this oasis seemed right out of a book that treated the second homes of the affluent. Yet, no one in Dad's family seemed affected by wealth or status except Millie.

That evening, back in St. Louis, as he passed Lauren in the dining room, they paused to talk about travel, what to wear, how to pack, a brief conversation, but somewhere in it he asked her if she still thought that she would have time to iron the white shirt he held in his hand.

"Oh, sure," she said, and she might have said more, but Millie heard his question and Lauren's answer and she jumped as though poked by a red-hot branding iron.

"What! What did you say?" Without waiting for any reply Walt might offer, she went on, "Where is your shirt, give me your damn shirt. I'll iron it myself. She is not ironing shirts!"

Walt surrendered the cloth, felt Millie's anger, knew with certainty that he had not passed the test. Her daughter had become hopelessly entangled with a poverty stricken, Catholic loser and would be ironing shirts, cleaning house and changing diapers all of her life. Millie wanted him gone.

The drive to the train station, quiet, polite and swift, sent him and Lauren back to Boulder and they picked up their courtship in the same tempo as it had begun, but more thoughtfully, more intimately than before. Lauren tried out the idea of Paris again, and he replied simply that she was welcome to go but that he would not be there when she returned. He had plenty of experience with long distance romances. She did not bring the subject up again. When he asked her to marry him, she said "Yes" but asked him to write her father and ask formal permission to marry his daughter.

Walt pondered briefly. He certainly didn't want to cast himself into the net of in-law review every time he and Lauren chose to do something in their lives. At the same time, he had a fundamental affection for her father, hoped to be admitted into the family circle. So, the idea of asking permission to marry Dad's daughter didn't offend him, a small step, he thought, in the direction of a mutual sense of bonding. Father (in-law)...son (in-law).

He wrote the request, received a surprisingly warm, loving response, and felt then and always that the ritual provided him entry into the family in a way that his first visit had not. When they returned to St. Louis for Thanksgiving, Lauren wore her engagement ring. Millie swallowed her anger, along with another martini, and Dad welcomed them with a sincerity that Walt knew as genuine. They were all in this together, Lauren, Millie, Dad and Walt. How it would play out, as always, only time would tell.

They married the following August, in a St. Louis Catholic Church. A reception at the Sunset Country Club embodied all the disappointed dreams that Millie had for her own wedding (she and Dad had been married at City Hall). Champagne flowed, music played, people danced, and as soon as they could gracefully exit, Walt and Millie got out of there, got out of town, got back to Denver out of range of her parents. A thousand miles of road now lay between them and Millie and Dad. It was just enough, and throughout their marriage, they made sure that it never lessened.

Woody's World

Walt walked into the halls of P.S. 105 and felt as though he had just crossed into Mexico. Both slender and weighted brown skinned students flowed as though coagulating blood cells. Edging through the clumps were black dudes and black girls with color swatches in their full heads of hair. Somewhere amidst this container of human crayons, he saw a white face, then another, but by no means did they fill the box. His new school hosted an inverted portrait of the city's demographic.

He tested the social temperature as he walked. What were these teen-age clusters thinking about a young, white face in the halls, and later, in the classroom. He could feel their eyes on him, assessing, sorting, placing his presence somewhere into their own experiences, and as he walked, he listened to their voices, tried to absorb their dress and body languages. Student variants moved in restless motion, small groups forming, morphing into cultural and social units as they walked down the halls registering for classes. He heard easy jabbering, occasional laughter, excited conversations. Clean walls, tan with orange trim, complemented floors squeaking from fresh scrubbing and waxing. He thought to himself, "I like it here."

He found the principal's office, asked to see Woody and waited. Soon, a man in his 50s, short, full-figured, with a smiling face and warm eyes invited Walt into his office with a kindly, gruff voice and asked him to sit down.

"So," he began, "you are fresh out of college and ready for the full-blown teaching experience."

"I am," Walt replied.

Woody paused a moment, as though deciding in that instant exactly what he would say next, but his words were well rehearsed. "I'm going to give you five classes. One will be a delight...great students. Two will be filled with freshmen and sophomores...a challenge. Another will be a new course in Social Economic Systems. We're offering it for the first time, and I don't know what you'll find there."

"What about the fifth one?" he asked.

Woody paused, turned in his chair to look out his window, turned back, "The fifth class is filled with students that no one wants to deal with. None of us are equipped to handle them, nor are you, but I hope you can manage."

Walt just looked at him and said, "I'm looking forward to it."

Young, inexperienced and hungry, he planned to immerse himself in the entire student body. It didn't help that he looked like a vanilla ice-cream bar nestled amidst a basket of Snickers, Licorice and Paydays. The issue, he thought, was whether he would melt.

As promised, Walt's schedule brought him students from all walks of life and all levels of preparation. One class mixed a National Merit Scholar with students who could neither spell a word... "xorlfyz" might mean "glorify"...nor complete a sentence of eight words. Three other assignments were nicely balanced with young people who wanted to learn, and he enjoyed every week with them, gradually being incorporated into their confidence and finding them entering his.

Then, the class of misfits, the ones no one wanted to teach, but offered to him to manage. A dozen friendly faces each judged by testing, experience and classroom performances as "below normal". He quickly found that to be true, although it became apparent that in some cases, performance simply reflected low self-esteem. Appalling home lives strangled academic progress for several, and the eight hour school day sheltered, fed and protected them. In some cases, they just could not perform, but their insight into normality surprised and tickled Walt. He laughed with them and they shared with him. Problem students? No, he thought, they were students with problems.

He decided that he would teach them to read, one phrase at a time, one student at a time and each day, he tried to accomplish something. He grew to know them pretty well, found them to be of good will and good humor. They laughed a lot, talked informally, shared stories of the day. Some of them became special to him, none more so than Tom Grant.

A quiet fellow, although well spoken, Tom kept an eye on the class and on the students. Smart enough to take it all in, he was unmotivated enough to be quite content watching others learn to read and trading occasional jokes and observations. He clearly saw himself as being misplaced, which he was, and on one memorable day, he took leadership.

Alice Goodwin always arrived late because of mobility issues with her legs, and Walt took time at the beginning of class to wait for her to get settled. This particular day, however, she came into class about a third of the way through the period. She lurched through the door, caught herself, moved toward an aisle of desks, bumped into one, careened into another and knocked over a third. She gathered herself and sat down in her place, upon which moment, Tom stood up, pointed at her, and said simply, "Alice...you gotta' go or I do!"

In one brief sentence, Tom recognized Alice's place, dismissed it and expressed his own quietly held conviction that he just didn't belong there. He was right.

There were other memorable parts of Woody's World that Walt discovered in those first few months. Friendly faculty on good terms both with one another and with Woody circulated through classes and found haven in the teacher's lounge. Their life experiences and expectations educated Walt to his new world. Some played bridge. Others smoked and read. A few reported on entertainment in the city and special events they had attended. For years, they had been teaching together and over time they developed easy ways of sharing life and raising hopes. All had routines that comforted them during these respites from the classroom.

Most striking were the comments of a twenty year veteran, Jim Riddle. Walt respected him, a lot, and he heard Jim's weekly complaints about his salary. They always concluded with his declaration that his goal in life was to bring home a check each month of $600 after taxes. Walt's annual salary was $5,000, and it was clear that in Woody's World, after deductions, Riddle's finances would improve very modestly over many years.

Apart from weekly disappointment with the football team, the word in the hall focused on basketball season. It arrived, and led by Ricardo Diaz the squad raised hopes for a championship. Diaz' performances touched on the edge of legend, and his latest move or scoring sequence could easily become hallway conversation for a week. Tensions rose with every win, and his fame expanded the same. On the court, he seemed to move in slow motion through or around defenders all the while keeping his intentions hidden until executed. He passed the ball when defenses tried to tie him up. He rebounded well and his floor leadership kept the team active, intense and focused. His academics were suspect, but the general faculty view was, "Hey, this may be the best moment of Ricardo Diaz' entire life, so let's help him enjoy it." They did, but he could not win a championship.

As the school year progressed, Walt's daily schedule began to imprint itself as his routine: pre-school, bridge; first class, study hall and preparation; classes until lunch when he played bridge; finish classes then play bridge until picked up by his wife, Lauren.

By November, he had before him a view of his teaching life and the word that kept coming to his mind was "boring". He began to see in faculty faces, expressions and comments a glimpse of himself in 20 years, and he did not like the view. The excitement of a new profession, well-worn by January, gave way to thoughts of a different future.

He began to seek some other outlets for his energy, enrolling in night school to take an economic course because he was unhappy with his preparation to teach it. He toyed with creating a monthly Saturday Career Day when he could meet with smart, ambitious students and explore both substantive knowledge and career opportunities. He planned to survey students to help him understand their home life and their future expectations. He asked the basketball coach if he could assist at practices and he poured energy into preparing material for that class in Social Economics, a topic about which he knew very little. He relished teaching geography to an alert group who loved to answer questions about what weather and climate would be like if the earth revolved from east to west.

He was a hit. His students took a liking to him and they were not parading complaints down to Woody's office. Other faculty seemed to like Walt's humor and activity, and he was especially taken with his bridge partners. They combined many years of teaching experience and a thorough knowledge of how to ease through the days...and the months...and the decades.

The year moved on, and likely there would have been many more of them, but for two events. The first was an exam that Walt wrote for his night class on Social Economics. Just sitting in with the permission of the instructor, Bill Pegrowski, Walt asked to write the test as a way to help him learn the material. When Pegrowski returned the exams, he asked Walt to stay behind. That was a little unnerving, but Pegrowski quickly put him at ease.

"Well," he began, "I read your exam and set it aside. I read it again, and it was as I first thought. You are wasting your time teaching high school. You belong in graduate school."

That comment changed Walt's life.

He decided to leave high school teaching, get an M.A. the following year, then teach in a community college. Lauren would continue to work while he completed the degree, and then they would both go looking for other jobs.

Less than a month later, a friend of Lauren's family, Dr. Harry Martz, arrived in Denver for a medical conference. He took them out to supper at the Brown Palace, and hosted them in a gathering of doctors who were enjoying drinks while tossing out $20 bills as though they were quarters. Walking them back to their car, Martz asked about Walt's career, and he explained that he was going to get an M.A. in economics. "Might as well get a PhD," Martz said, and suddenly Walt's horizon expanded a distance beyond any that he could have imagined.

He took a sick day and traveled to Boulder to speak to Carl Oglund, a professor whom he had much admired as an undergraduate. He explained that he was considering coming to graduate school to get his M.A., then teaching in a community college while completing his doctorate.

Oglund looked at Walt and smiled in that crooked little grin that he carried with him, and said, very diplomatically, "It has been my experience that students who leave graduate school before completing their degree never finish. Life gets in the way." Walt understood.

He returned to Woody's World and again looked around. It was a wonderful high school, but he wanted no part of its future. He wanted something more intellectually challenging and at the same time a different academic workplace, one without six classes a day and the after-school commitments that loomed before him.

He and Lauren made a plan and moved back to Boulder in June. She would teach until he finished his degree. Walt committed himself to doing nothing except attending classes, grading papers for money, and completing his PhD in just four years. They found a little basement apartment four blocks from campus and settled in for their crack at a better future.

Six weeks later, Lauren learned that she was pregnant, and the school system fired her. Without monthly income they were dependent upon the salary they had saved (hers), Walt's income from grading papers and whatever money Lauren could find in the community. She spent the year stuffing goose down into booties, coats and tents that she sewed at home. Feathers floated through the bathroom all winter, and while the income varied, it helped them get through the school year. In June, now with a new baby, they went looking for a larger apartment. What they found was a small home whose owner was financially distressed, and for $700 they owned it and began making small monthly payments.

His M.A. in hand, Walt received a teaching assistant appointment, and immersed himself into additional coursework. In their third year, he finished his comprehensive exams and began writing his dissertation. A second son now paired with the first and Lauren took full control of family life as he focused exclusively on finishing graduate school in the four years they had allotted.

He spent valuable time in Washington D.C. learning the rituals of the Library of Congress and the secrets of correspondences written decades before his time. He writhed in emotional pain as his advisor kept him rewriting chapters throughout that last summer, but he ground out revisions week after week knowing that it was just an endurance contest now and that he was going to finish. With a job waiting in Wisconsin, he completed his PhD in August and promptly moved the family to the land of snow and cold, more than doubling his high school salary and opening his life to intellectual challenges and the sense of freedom that comes with being able to manage one's own class schedule.

Life began anew for the family in that Wisconsin fall and the winter that followed. Walt and Lauren learned about seriously cold weather watching the mercury regularly plummet to -10 F. Informed that the boys, now in nursery school, would be playing outdoors every day unless the temperature was below zero, Walt at first thought they were kidding. They weren't. The fireplace in their little country home became a warming unit. New clothing brought new standards: down gloves, feather filled coats, heavy rubber boots, layered clothing for outdoor activity and above all a healthy respect for how quickly one could die in a wind chill of -35 F.

Amidst the clean air, energetic professionals at the university and the social friendliness of his new city, he flourished and within another year, he and Lauren welcomed their last child, a girl, into their household. Living in a rural neighborhood, surrounded by friendly neighbors and fun-loving colleagues, they both found that in many ways life was just beginning. He was as much at ease with university teaching and Democratic party politics as Lauren was with her art, her parenting investment into the children and the social life they built with faculty and community leadership.

Walt heard from Woody, a personal note congratulating him on his success. He joined in conversations with Pegrowski at professional meetings throughout the next decade. Dr. Harry Martz likely never knew of the influence of his few words, but Walt kept track of Ricardo Diaz and learned that he eventually opened a small convenience store. In time, Jim Riddle brought home a paycheck over $600.

Walt thought of P.S. 105 often. Personalities floated into his memory bank and he kept them safe, both to appreciate the lives they experienced and the one that he escaped. Strangely, there was no one that he thought about more over many years than Tom Grant, glancing occasionally at the photo Tom gave him on his last day of the school year. He kept it safe in his album and many years later tracked him down. Tom graduated, did a tour with the U.S. Army, then carved out a successful career as an insurance agent. Maybe he just said to himself one day, "Tom, you gotta go...make something of your life."

Woody's World launched a lot of futures.

A Knock on the Door

Friendships can start in the middle of the night, and they can end there too. This one played out its life span on a small Boulder street which, in the form of a U, wound itself around a gently sloping curve, then emptied into a larger commonly used avenue. Lined with unfenced ticky-tacky houses occupied by middle-class families, its sidewalks held many chalk outlines of children's games. Daily litter included scooters and tricycles and scuff marks made by the twin tracks of twenty pair of skates carrying kids around the curve and down to the intersection. So far, no one had died.

Shielded in late afternoon by the shadows of the Flatirons and within easy walking distance from a small strip mall, the peg-placed homes burned a little in summer and froze a little in winter. The chinook winds which sometimes blew down through the canyons commonly flexed the interior walls of each home and drove entire families down into the basement for safe sleep. Still, so far, no one had died.

One could identify neighbors by their job placement: a policeman, a college professor, a John Birch organizer, an accountant, a publishing cartoonist, a retail merchant, an older retired couple, a realtor, a trucker, and a graduate student... Walt Farmer and his wife, Lauren. Two years into his studies, Walt had a deadline to meet, his pledge to Lauren being that he would finish his Ph.D. in four years, and he was on track to do it. That they could afford to move into a house surprised them both.

Ejected by mutual agreement from a one-bedroom basement apartment, they found this little box on stilts available when a distressed owner asked for a $700 down payment and assumption of the mortgage. She left her furniture and suddenly they had a couch to sit on and their infant son, Rob had his own bedroom. Friendly, personable and approachable, the Farmers were well accepted by their neighbors, and within a few months both felt that they were part of a larger companionable community.

A year later, Lauren gave birth to Buck and now the two boys became linked by birth as one, brothers for life, and he felt good about that. Lauren raised the children, made friends, kept the household on budget and stayed in touch with her desire to paint, draw and sculpture. Walt's studies went well, and he moved on into the writing of his thesis. A year went by, and while the children of the neighborhood grew a little, both in size and number, the families of the U remained in place.

That changed when the cartoonist next door to the Farmer's suffered a heart attack. Again, nobody died, but his wife decided that they would have to move. That sent a twitter coursing through a dozen homes. If someone were leaving, someone would be arriving. A new face! New children? New talk? Curious eyes watched the home empty, then held their gaze on it until a van finally appeared.

New heads popped in and out of the front door. A brunet kept her daughter close while her blonde husband and a couple of friends loaded furnishings into the house for her to direct final placement. Their little dog, properly leashed, moved excitedly about from his fixed station near the edge of their driveway. Clearly they fit the local profile, married with children, and Lauren reported that she overheard chatter between husband and wife revealing a pharmacist. Perfect.

That night, Walt and Lauren continued assessing the new neighbors. Their little girl looked about the same age as their oldest boy, Rob. The wife seemed to be buoyant and fun, smiled a lot and held easy conversation with her husband. He in turn liked to make jokes, moved quickly, spoke in an easy, soft drawl. Energy, wit, and stability now resided next door. They felt lucky.

It may have been a moving day oversight, but by 10 pm that evening the new folks had yet to bring their dog into the house, and as Lauren pointed out, he was tied less than 30 feet away from their bedroom window. Summer breezes cooled the air, and they kept the windows open. They knew his name to be Raja, heard in a snippet of conversation, so they knew that they could call him by name. They had no desire to do so, but within an hour after bedtime, they had no problem uttering his given name along with two or three others which came spitting out of their mouths. Raja barked! He barked because it was dark, barked because he was lonely, barked because he was hungry, and no doubt, he barked because he was good at it.

In that unspoken communication between marrieds which conveys essential messages it became clear to Walt that Lauren, by her sighs and turnings, expected him to resolve Raja's behavior. He was not put off by this, because there were few things that irritated him more than interrupted sleep. Art Linkletter had it all wrong when he wrote that "laughter is the best medicine". Sleep was the best medicine, Walt insisted, and he pronounced laughter to be the best therapy.

By ten o'clock, he found himself still wrestling with the staccato bark of his new neighbor's dog, and he tried talking to Raja through the window screen. No success. His strange voice set off the noise once again. He tried closing the window, but the room quickly grew too warm. He thought of calling his new neighbors, but he had no number and doubted that they yet had a phone. The barking continued. Surely they would want to go to bed and bring in their dog. The barking went on.

O.K. It was time, Walt thought, and he got up and put on his clothes even as Lauren cautioned him to be really nice because they were new and they were neighbors. He walked slowly out of his house, crossed their front yard and went up to their porch. He knocked on the door. No answer. He waited as Raja began barking more frantically and then knocked again much more firmly, and this time he could feel the footfalls inside as someone crossed the floor and finally opened the door.

The living room lamp back-lit her face. "Hi," she said, "You're our new neighbor, right?" He acknowledge the identification with a friendly nod and a smile, "Yep, Walt Farmer... glad to meet you."

He paused, and she looked at him with a question in her eyes, "Why are you here?" He considered how best to say this, and finally, he just tried to be quiet and succinct. "I'm thinking that you may have forgotten to bring your dog, Raja, in for the night. He's barking quite a lot, and I was hoping that he usually spent his nights indoors? Would that be right?"

"Oh, my God, yes!" She turned her head back toward the living room and hollered to her husband, "Dan, we need to bring in Raja!" To Walt, she turned and said, "I'm sorry, I'm Nina Gordon, and we've been distracted all day with moving into the house. I'm really sorry about his barking." As she spoke the side door opened to the driveway, Dan collected Raja and brought him into the house. He quieted immediately.

Shortly thereafter, Dan appeared at the door, introduced himself and pled guilty for not tending his dog. "No problem," Walt replied, "None at all. Sorry we had to meet so late in the day, but my wife, Lauren, and I look forward to getting to know you better...and welcome to the neighborhood." He thanked them again for taking care of the barking Raja and said they would see more of one another, he was sure, and took his leave.

"What are they like?" Lauren asked as soon as he had walked in the door.

"You heard the conversation," he said.

"Yes, but I couldn't see their faces. Are they nice? They sounded nice? Is she as friendly as she sounded?"

"Yep" Walt responded, "I think we're going to like them, and when Raja is secure, he really is a cute thing."

"We should get a dog," Lauren thought aloud. He said nothing, hoping that the idea would float out the window with a bit of breeze and that he would not have to deal with it again.

That month they brought home a St. Bernard/Chow cinnamon colored hunk of loving. Walt didn't need a dog, but Lauren adored *Lundi*, and took care of him from day one. The boys petted him, crawled on him, pulled on his fur, loved to be with him, and *Lundi* just took them gently into his very large circle of love.

The St. Bernard liked Raja and the two frolicked with great energy, the large, sprawling paws of the one plopping and rolling over the body and back of the other, but both had energy for fun, sparring 'til they were panting. Their antics brought the two families into more contact, and they began to arrange playtime for the three year olds, Debbie and Rob. Both quickly became adopted residents of the other's home.

Nina was energetic, full of laughter and pleased to see that the children played together so well. She visited back and forth with Lauren, shared stories of her life in New Mexico where she had become enamored with car racing, following the race circuit for a few months until she met Dan in Albuquerque. She found it stressful being a pharmacist's wife. Dan worked split shifts, his income far less than Lauren had imagined, and he had hopes of one day being able to open a small store of his own, probably in another city. He was quite a tidy guy, Nina reported, and wanted everything in its place, but he liked to laugh and loved a good party.

Lauren shared her own challenges dealing with graduate school income, demanding but loving children, tiresome but essential tasks left to her by Walt's focus on finishing school. All in all, the two women enjoyed their talks and shared their confidences with one another more and more fully. When the children were together, Nina loved to eavesdrop on them, especially tickled when they played house, talked adult talk and in general tried to bond in ways that imitated their parent's behavior. Lauren liked having a girl in the house, and Debbie became an amusing new part of her brood.

The two couples chatted a little in passing from time to time then finally planned an evening together at the Gordon's. New information flowed across the table as they enjoyed an ordinary wine and chatted about neighbors, politics and climate. While the Gordon's were not as conservative as the John Birch organizer across the street, they liked Barry Goldwater. Nina talked at length about her infatuation with the Unser racing family. She had met Bobby once at a casual social, and she was smitten both with his looks and his driving

211

successes. They all commented about the chinooks that blew through the mountains and threatened to collapse interior walls. Dan had a wry sense of humor, enjoyed his wine but revealed little of his general interests.

As they talked, Walt thought that Nina seemed more on edge than usual. She fussed about serving things at precisely the right time and with the right utensils, and just seemed to be more attentive to Dan's little comments than she did in the casual conversations he and Lauren traded with her out in the yard. Tension?

He was particularly interested in her compulsive need, not just in clearing dishes after the meal, but in washing them, drying them, putting them away, then cleaning and scrubbing the stove, and placing the room in perfect order before she would join the rest of them for conversation in the living room. She explained that she just felt a need to have everything in place. Dan liked that, and she laughed, "I know there is a limit to him. I just haven't found it yet."

He asked Lauren about that, and she agreed that it was a little odd, but added that in her own way Nina seemed a little tense about keeping everything in perfect order all of the time. She seemed as neat in her housekeeping as Dan was in his dress. Laughing, Lauren commented, "Maybe it's just that my standards are so lax." She thought nothing of walking about the yard stained with dabs of paint from her work, or smeared with paste from her sculpture. Rob and his brother, Buck, often just drew on large sheets of butcher paper in the basement, and not every mark stayed on the paper. "I'm not sloppy," she would laugh, "but I am casual." She kept a sign in the kitchen, "A tidy house is the sign of a wasted life."

For his part, Walt didn't have much opportunity to talk to Dan, but he felt comfortable with him, and he liked his sense of humor. He also came to appreciate the value of having a pharmacist next door. When Lauren developed a severe cough which counter medicines did not touch, Dan brought her some codeine based liquid, and told her, "Take a teaspoon at bedtime. If it doesn't work, take another and double the dose." The double-dose worked and they slept.

The year moved on, the Gordon's become a little more restrained in their social activity, but on a particular June evening they and a half dozen other couples gathered to enjoy a smattering of snacks, drinks and music at the realtor's house. Right from the start of the evening, Walt noticed, Nina and Dan seemed unusually tense with one another, she more restrained, he more aggressive. Probably the fallout of an unfinished argument in the family, and he could understand that. Daytime stresses often led to nighttime losses. Lauren commented about it too, but figured that it would all pass by morning.

They left the party about 10 pm, paid their baby sitter who walked home across the street. As they climbed into bed, leaving the window open to cool their room, they heard the faint echo of voices and occasional laughter that floated up the street every few minutes.

"Did we leave the party too early?" Walt asked.

"No," Lauren murmured, already slipping into sleep, "They'll be there all night."

A loud pounding on the door, then *Lundi's* barking dragged Walt out of his dark retreat. He heard the frantic call, "HELP! I NEED HELP!"

Dan's voice!

He looked at the clock, 3:00 a.m. He wrestled himself out of bed, muttering, "What in the hell is Dan doing?" He wobbled to the living room and opened the door.

What he saw froze a permanent image in his mind. Nina, slumped in Dan's arms, face white, eyes rolling up and around in their sockets. Dan struggled to keep her on her feet while he maintained his balance. Around her wrists were bloody wraps of cloth, her hands smeared in red which continued to darken as she moved her arms and gravity drew new liquid lines down toward her fingers. Black night, white face, red flow, eyes lost, Dan frantic.

"She slit her wrists!" he said, "I need someone to drive us to emergency while I keep pressure on the cuts." Before I could say anything, Lauren appeared already dressed in pants and shirt. "I'm ready, let's go," and away they went.

He sat down, listened for the boys, and tried to wake up. Then he went next door and picked up Debbie and brought her over to the house. She settled back into sleep on the sofa. It was a hell of a night when the reality was worse than a bad dream. He had never seen a suicidal person in any stage of disintegration, but Nina looked completely gone, in another world. Dan was great: decisive, focused and effective.

It was a terrible sight, but so far no one had died, and he had no trouble staying awake to hear the final report. Lauren returned with Dan in about two hours. Nina was in the hospital, surgical repairs finished. She would survive, but the unspoken message they all heard was that she needed professional therapy. Cutting her wrists, and she cut them deeply, if a cry for help, found a listener. Dan thanked them both for their help. Walt and Lauren talked it all through one more time. They could care for Debbie while Nina recovered and Dan worked, but what caused Nina's decision?

Certainly nothing that they had seen would account for such a desperate choice.

It remained an unknown dynamic over the next few months. Nina recovered quickly from her wounds. She entered therapy and reported that she was doing well, feeling better than she had in years. She seemed stronger too, more decisive about her interests, less fixated on the compulsions of tidiness, more relaxed in her conversations with them and with Dan. It was a good omen, and as they began to focus on finishing the last year of graduate school, their relationship with the Gordon's became more interactive, and they noted a peculiar dynamic.

Each month, as Nina seemed to grow stronger in her emotional tone, Dan began to become more erratic. He quibbled with Nina over issues that seemed meaningless to Walt and Lauren, but then again, they wrote it off to marital dynamics. They also noted that he looked less well rested, more removed from chit-chat, a bit more introspective, and recently more hidden from view. Lauren sounded out Nina, and she put her off with a comment that this was a long time issue with Dan and she didn't want to talk about it. But a month later she came to them both. Dan had begun drinking again.

His alcoholism, she said, was never apparent when they courted. He was fun, pressed the edges of good times, and she loved it. But when Debbie arrived, she wanted more stability and he changed not at all. She found herself covering for him and for her own emotional stress. She simply could not persuade him to stop drinking for any extended period of time and in the last year---she nearly whispered her next comment, "He's started hitting me."

They just stared at her. Neither had ever heard a sound coming from their home, never saw an argument, never smelled a bottle, never felt a tremor in their relationship. Gently, Lauren asked her, "Well, how are you doing now, and is he still drinking?" Nina paused, wanted to speak, wasn't sure, then finally she just said, "He still drinks, but I don't care. I'm just going to worry about myself and Debbie."

And so she did. They could see Dan's demeanor change week by week. His walks in and out of the house became almost furtive. His occasional conversation contained only a few brief words as they cross paths on the sidewalk. He stayed at home more, the car sometimes parked for two or three days at a time. Walt wandered by the pharmacy a couple of times to see how he looked, and didn't like what he saw. Dan's clothing, white but wrinkled, hung on him. He had shaved but his skin was sallow, his hands quivering. He moved behind the counter without a smile, distracted by tasks not immediately in sight.

Within six months, as Walt worked frantically to finish his dissertation, life at the Gordon's continued to disintegrate. Now, Lauren reported, she could hear them fighting during the day, their dog, Raja, joining in with concern over the anger. Less and less often did Dan go to work, and Lauren worried that he might lose his job. In July, she and Nina had a good talk. She spoke, Lauren said, as a free agent. Dan had lost his job. He now drank steadily, no longer loud or angry, just sipping in silence. In two weeks, she planned to take Debbie with her and restart her life in New Mexico.

Two nights later, a scream reverberated around the cul-de-sac. The Gordon's? A fight? Had Dan erupted in violent mayhem? Was Nina safe? The noise came through their screen window as easily as Raja's barking had three years before. Again, a screech and this time out ran Nina. We met her at our door and she screamed "My God! Dan's having some kind of a fit!"

We quick-walked across the two open yards directly into their living room and just stared. Dan lay on the floor across a throw rug, one arm extended, vomit pooling in front of his mouth, his torso moving in spasms that came and went. Not a bottle in sight, but something coursed through his body, still wringing him in contractions. He moaned, but his eyes never opened. He groaned again, his back contracting into an intense, seconds long spasm, then it slowly relaxed, quivering. His arm rolled to flat, twitched once and lay there. His feet turned, toes in heels out, and then...nothing.

That night, somebody died.

Gravity of the Situation

Walt Farmer dreaded seeing his in-laws. He understood that they were not happy with their daughter's choice. He understood that while his mother-in-law Millie adored the three children in a fairy tale kind of way, Dad had little patience with them. He understood that they both drank as a regular part of their evening activity and ended the night tipsy. What he did not understand was why he kept trying to forge some kind of relationship with them. Somewhere, he kept thinking, there had to be a way to connect with them in a meaningful way, especially with Dad.

One lovely summer's evening in August while visiting in Missouri, Walt stumbled upon a social gambit based upon a scientific experiment he had observed in high school. That was long ago, but science kept its rules intact for reasonable periods of time, he thought, and he reached again for a way to have a thoughtful conversation with Dad.

One of Walt's high school delights was physics. In a class of 15, Mr. Shrader interacted with each student personally and Walt responded well to this approach, attentive to Shrader's explanations of the way the universe worked. This particular day, he explained that the formula, $F=MA$, with F being force, M being mass and A being acceleration, could determine how hard a bullet might hit an object. The more a bullet weighed, its acceleration would determine how hard it would strike.

Too, Shrader went on, the higher the perch from which one dropped a one pound weight to the earth, because of the acceleration of gravity, the harder it would punch the ground. The greater the acceleration of a fist to a fighter's jaw, the given mass of his knuckles could hit with greater force. Knockout! Neat.

Shrader worked daily in good humor and contagious curiosity to share his love of physics with his students and Walt liked him. He did not like math, formulas or abstract calculations, but he liked demonstrations and experiments.

He walked into class this one day, with his fingers burning from the successful prank that the Great Tom Litton played on him, heating his key in chemistry lab until it was about 300 degrees and placing it on the hook for him to grasp as he grabbed it and walked to his table. It worked, and his fingers gave off that special scent of seared flesh that somehow smells pretty sweet, almost good, but always feels like a torch has burned a hole in the skin. Between wondering how to get even with Tom and tending to the scorched tissue on his fingers, he was more distracted than usual.

Still, he noticed that Shrader had prepared another demonstration. Attached to the classroom ceiling, was a large magnet holding in the air a metal can about eight inches long and 6 inches in diameter, its circumference being pi x 6. He began class by explaining some of the features of gravity, emphasizing that an object released from a fixed point above the earth, *instantly* assumed an acceleration of 33 ft./sec/ sec (the pull of gravity) which meant that it increased at that same rate every second (assuming an absence of air friction) until hitting something solid like the earth or a floor in a building.

Walt noticed an awkward contraption set up on a table. It had a spring-loaded chamber and a barrel aimed toward the metal can. At the end of the barrel a wire attached itself to a circuit that connected to the can in the ceiling. He began to wonder if he could borrow the thing, aim it at Litton's chemistry beaker and shatter his experimental liquids during a dull moment in lab. Probably not.

Shrader explained what they were about to witness. Gravity, he said, worked with equal force on all objects that they see above the surface of the earth. It works on all matter in the universe too, he said, but he would save that for another day. In class now, if he were to press a switch and turn off the magnet holding the can to the ceiling it would instantly drop at the rate of 33 feet/sec/sec. In one second, it would be accelerating at the rate of 66 feet/per sec, and so on.

He went on to explain that if the barrel of the "rifle" were aimed exactly at the can (and this was the trick of the experiment...getting it aimed precisely at the can), and if the bullet left the barrel at a high velocity, it would hit the can. Target shooting. Farmer understood that just fine.

What would happen, asked Shrader, if the velocity of the bullet was such that when it left the barrel of the rifle it did not hit the can instantly? What if the velocity of the bullet leaving the barrel was strong enough that its arc would only reach 5 feet in height as it passed under the can and the can remained attached to the magnet 10 feet above the floor. What would happen? Well, Walt theorized, it would miss the can still attached to the ceiling. Correct.

But what, said Shrader, what if at the very instant that the bullet left the barrel of the rifle, it broke an electronic link to the can, and the can left the ceiling and began to drop to the ground...at exactly the same moment the bullet left the barrel...what would happen? Well, Farmer thought, the bullet would miss the can because it didn't go to the ceiling.

Nope. Shrader explained very carefully that the bullet would still hit the can because the bullet and the can were both dropping toward the earth at the same rate of acceleration toward the earth, 33 ft./sec/sec. *As long as the barrel were aimed exactly at the can, the bullet, even at different velocities would always hit the can, whether it were attached to the ceiling, half-way to the ground or one foot above the ground.* Of course, if the bullet were too slow, it would not hit the can before the can hit the floor. If it were very fast, it would hit the can before it had dropped more than an inch.

Why? Because both were controlled by gravity and gravity pulled both of them to the earth at the same rate. *Perfect aim, varied velocity of bullet, instantaneous release of the can when the bullet left the end of the barrel, and the bullet would always hit the can.* Gravity.

Farmer did not believe him. Shrader fired several times at different velocities and each time Walt waited for the bullet to miss. It did not. Theory was correct. His supposition was wrong.

It was a lesson he remembered all his life. Gravity required that a rifle on a range had to have the site adjusted to compensate for the distance the bullet would travel, because when the bullet left the barrel it would be falling to the earth at 33 ft./sec/sec. At high velocity it would hit a target 300 yards away before striking earth, but it was always falling at the same rate, 33 ft./sec/sec. Adjust your sights accordingly.

Twenty years later, Farmer decided to use his high school knowledge to forge a new adult relationship with his father-in-law. He, Lauren and children found themselves visiting the family retreat located about 20 miles outside St. Louis. A lovely old renovated farm house set on 200 acres of land, it presented a view overlooking a swimming pool beyond which green pastures dotted with two grazing horses bordered a creek dawdling its way to the Big River at Flat Rock. Walt thought it an idyllic setting for gentle relaxation and easy conversation, a haven for sorting through the events of the world, and yet that kind of talk never quite filled the evening.

Indeed, after supper they usually migrated to the screen porch where Missouri air and the serenade of crickets embraced them all and eased digestion, Dad relaxed in an easy chair, glass in hand sipping *J.W. Dant,* waiting for a conversation to arouse his interest. Millie preferred martinis. Small talk ensued, tentative views surfaced as each offered some insight into public issues or personal piques. Soon, some thought would occur--the power of unions, the corruption of officials, the state of the schools or the hygiene of hill people--and then talk quickly devolved to cursing, condemnations and loud declarations. Dad had to clear the field of any view other than his and so too often the comfort of the night and the nearness of family turned into a gut-wrenching lesson on how to appease a drunk. It wasn't fun.

Walt had noted over the years that Dad had become more irritable, more verbally abusive toward Millie, more critical of Lauren. Still, she insisted on annual visits to see her mother hoping for those few days to provide her with some emotional sanctuary. For his own peace of mind, Walt sought out safe conversational topics that had clear, generally agreed upon conclusions and explored those in a tentative way, sampling Dad's view and whenever possible agreeing with him.

On this particular lovely summer evening, they all sat on the screened porch and in the eroding light of the day, while the cicadas crisply serenaded them, they began to talk about life and the world in general. The topic gradually evolved to education, and the dynamics of schools and their ability to produce well informed students prepared for the real world that awaited them. Dad's view proclaimed that teachers had a soft life and generally failed in their duties.

Walt thought this a perilous conversation. He taught economics. He knew the challenges of high school teaching as well as the intellectual tone of the university. Time to avoid an argument, he thought, excusing himself and finding refuge in the bathroom. While there he sorted through some magazines that he found stored alongside the wall. One of them, *The Readers Digest* (in big print) caught his eye, especially an article: "The Uniformity of Gravity". The *Digest* blurb explained in clear, concise and definitive words the same theory that Mr. Shrader had demonstrated in his physics class. It even described the gun-can link experiment.

Surely, this would be a safe topic to bring up on the porch. If it were published in *Readers Digest*, Dad was sure to believe its authenticity. If Walt brought it into the conversation by way of a casual observation, Dad might view him with a little more respect.

He returned to the porch, and when there was a pause in the conversation, he made reference to the *Digest* article and explained the theory and the experiment it cited. Walt allowed that this was a fascinating way to demonstrate the pervasive effect of gravity.

One would have thought that he had lit a firecracker under Dad's chair. "Stupidest damn thing I have heard in years," he bellowed. "No wonder our students are coming out of college stupid and unprepared; Farmer, (he never called him by his first name), you are so dumb as to believe that sort of bullshit. Stupidest idea I have ever heard." Walt tried to clarify the terms of the experiment, making reference to the impeccable source, *The Readers Digest*. Dad would have none of it, and as his voice raised in a continuing tirade of judgment of Walt's ignorance, the bankruptcy of public education and the idiocy of subjects taught in high schools, Walt reluctantly came to an inescapable and irrevocable conclusion.

His father-in-law could never be engaged in a conversation in which any ideas other than his own could hold command of the discussion. Walt could never bring to him a new idea, could never discuss with him his experiences in the classroom or in graduate school or in collegiate subject matter. Dad was a conversational Black Hole.

Saddened by this, disappointed in more ways than he realized at the time, he mulled it over with Lauren for 700 miles as they returned to Wisconsin. He decided finally that he wasn't going back to see her parents, would not tolerate Millie's martini messages or sip Dad's toxic brew any longer. He just wouldn't do it. Resigned to his decision, sensitive to its validity, Lauren visited her home alone for more than two decades, taking the children with her when they were young, going it alone as they grew too old to be commanded. Walt remained home and missed nothing.

He enjoyed the twenty years of separation. Only Millie's death and Dad's relocation to a small apartment caused Walt's trajectory to cross his path again. Gravity still controlling, he hit the target, and as before, it was noisy and unsatisfactory.

A Swig of Soup

The front door opened and out they came, three tykes in something other than daily wear, Lauren nicely dressed with a working day look on her face. Walt felt a little guilty, not for his hasty praise of how they looked, but for his continued insistence that he would not go see the in-laws. He disliked her father and pitied her mother. In point, he had not seen them for over five years now, and his life seemed none the less for it.

The family gathered near the door of the van and piled in when it slid open. He loaded the suitcases, asked if there were any items forgotten and climbed up into the driver's seat. They were taking the train, and he had the mixed pleasure, a little guilt and a lot of joy, of taking them only as far as the station.

If the Burlington Northern were on time, the family would show up in Chicago four hours later, change to the City of New Orleans and chug right down to St. Louis. By his reckoning, Lauren would spend eight hours on a train with three children under the age of ten and the challenges of bathrooms, snacks, naps, and boredom. She looked more saintly by the moment.

Yet, she knew that their arrival would be the highlight of her mother Millie's month, maybe of her year. Joyously, her eyes would sparkle anew, lighting up her face as the children walked into sight. Reaching out to encircle each of them, her spirits would purify the smoke from her cigarette. She would note the grandchildren's growth, comment on their cleverness, play games with them and delight in their companionship. She would drink less as she and daughter reminisced about earlier days and rekindled the special bond that they held for one another.

It was a mother-daughter connection deepened by their shared mothering experience, and it was a mutual defense pact motivated by a common enemy, his father-in-law, Dad. For a few days Lauren and Millie could circle their wagons and deflect his arrows, jibes and criticisms that had become, over the years, more pointed, more frequent, more demeaning.

But Walt wasn't going. Lauren wasn't driving. They compromised on the train, and he felt relieved, even joyful. His life would be refreshed by a few days of complete control over his daily doings. He could impose rigorous direction on what music he heard, what food he ate, the hours he slept (especially welcome) and the way he dressed.

All this he reviewed as he took the family to the train. A new experience for the children, the boys looked over every corner of the depot, commented on the smelly urinals, and wondered how many snacks they could have before the train got there. It arrived before he ran out of change. They all went outside, stood near the rails and looked down the track, seeking the skittering engine light as the engine moved into focus, slowed and with a steaming sigh, stopped to board passengers. He could hardly wait to offer feigned sorrow and a hasty goodbye to the family, sacrificing any thoughts of their impending discomfort to his excited notions of living alone for a few days.

Lauren, a fatalistic smile on her face, gave him a generous hug, gathered the little girl by the hand, and herded the boys on to the train. Their faces appeared almost instantly at the windows as they waved hello and goodbye, looked at the world from a new height and place and kept their eyes on him until the train pulled out. He watched until he finally saw the last wiggle of the last car.

With some sense of space and power, Walt climbed back into the van and headed home, his mind sorting through the things that he would do. Music! First, music that rocked with artists that appealed to his soul. Loud, loud, raging music! Then, food. What to eat? What to cook, microwave? Finally, time to while away, to stay up late, to see Carson without anyone complaining or calling for a drink of water. Time to scuttle about the house, sleep as needed, take the hours of a new morning and make them part of the last night. He could hardly wait.

The music choice...easy. He hauled out Sergeant Pepper, blew it up and let Billy Shears and friends get their lives underway. While he moved about the rooms with a bit of rock in his step and controlled roll in his shoulders, he began to think of food. Sandwiches were always a comfort, mac n' cheese he would save for supper. Pancakes, good any time of day but maybe a little too filling. They might lull him, dull the edge of his music.

He went to the fridge. What could he find there that would fill his stomach, sooth his hunger and warm his limbs? Soup? Yep, that sounded really good, hot soup, sourdough bread and butter. Simple, filling and tasty. On a shelf, next to the Pepsi, he found a can of vegetable soup, half filled, but still plenty 'cause it was just for him...he savored that idea again... home alone, and he reached for the soup, poured it into a pan and heated it up. He took out the bread, toasted it lightly, buttered it, coated it with honey and waited for the pot to steam, but not boil. Finally, he poured his treat into the bowl, sat at the breakfast bar and sampled his cooking.

Perfect mixture! The sourdough provided his taste buds with an edge of sour milk, yet filled his mouth with the subtle sweetness of well warmed carbs and sweet honey. He spooned his soup slowly, letting the steam settle, and as each mouthful drained down his throat he sighed with a special sense of contentment. For three days he was going to be a man with true control over his life. The music played on, and when Sergeant Pepper went out of style, he switched over to Frank and let him range through his songbook. Next up--Carole King--and he knew he would be dancing solo for much of that. Then maybe he would cue up the Doors and let Morrison rage on. He could join him, with volume up, while his own lousy voice began to sound vibrant, engaged and on key.

As he performed his musical concert, placed himself on center stage with his face lit up by spotlights, and felt the warmth of his unseen audience wash over him, he imagined again the adulation of success, the energy that he found sharing his music with cheering fans, his sweat beading and flowing as he sang song after song. He moved with his mike, postured with his peak notes. He gave a command performance.

He felt a small burp rising in his throat. It surfaced, passed and felt good, the food settling, his energy erupting. While he would miss his wife and children in a day or so, right now he was all the company he needed: good food, great music, controlled environment and energy to embrace it all. What could be better? He burped again.

As Morrison said goodbye to her like he did a thousand times before, he started to think about what could follow. Elton John...now he might be just what he needed...rocking through a full concert and putting huge energy into "Rocket Man". He went looking for the album, and as he sorted through the tapes, he felt some reflux come up into his mouth, and this time it had a taste to it, one that he identified with childhood memories of nausea. Not that he wanted to vomit. There was just a sort of liquid acid edge to the burp, and it partnered with a bit of deep throated gas buried in his lower cavern.

He set Elton John aside, picked up Linda Ronstadt. He needed to settle down and let his body get back in tune with the quiet of the household and truthfully, Ronstadt's voice could calm a concert with a single note at the conclusion of "Blue Bayou". He felt better, walked out the back door, stretched his body, opened his lungs and took a deep breath. *"I'm going back some day, come what may, to Blue Bayou..."* drifted through the window, and he felt better.

Still, as he walked about, his stomach started to let him know it was there. It twitched, even cramped a bit. He walked around the yard some more, determined to let things settle. When he felt a little more in control, he headed back into the house.

He opened the back door as Linda sang, *"time washes clean, love's wounds unseen"* and he began thinking that something hidden was convulsing inside him. He walked about the house some more, and then, Carole King's *"too late, too late now"*, came to mind. The surge was unavoidable, powerful, and he headed for the bathroom with a quick-step that was not a part of his dancing repertoire.

He got to the bowl just as the fluids and chunks of sourdough, soup, acid and bile all erupted through his mouth and burned a path through his nose. "Worshiping the Porcelain God", an expression he had heard some of the college kids use, had a nice imagery. He never thought that he would join the cult, but here he was, emptying all that seemed so good and hoping that he would never taste it again.

Just when he thought that it was safe to rise, another wave gripped him, and fulfilled his fear. He tasted it all over again, then again, until finally there was nothing more to empty. Surely the God was satisfied, but no, now that his stomach was settling powerful waves developed throughout his abdomen. They passed as though a pressure hose were connected to his small intestine and ratcheted up to full power. They pulsed, pushed their way back and forth working lower and lower, and suddenly, he needed to switch ends. He positioned himself at just the right moment, and felt, heard and smelled the product of his own cooking.

He sat there for almost five minutes. Finally, things settled, and he cleaned himself up, brushed his teeth and began to walk out of the bathroom when his visitor returned. This time he rang both the front and the back doorbells at the same time. He couldn't decide which one to answer, and before he could choose, cramps bent him over the God and he heaved an answer to the call even as he leaked an afterthought to the pressure hose. He didn't care about what this meant to cleanliness, household tidiness or bathroom propriety. He just kept heaving and leaking.

And so it went. For the first twelve hours, he walked between bed and bathroom. For the next three days, he slept in segments, tried to drink water and generally failed in any effort he made to feel better. By the beginning of the fifth day, he knew that he was not going to die, and that he needed to drag himself out of bed, somehow, to meet the train that afternoon. He tried to shower, but could not stand. He tried again after a mid-morning nap, and this time, he succeeded. He dressed. He tried to drink carbonated beverage, but that did not settle. He made a cup of tea.

Shakily, he dressed himself, did not worry about shaving or even combing his hair. He just needed to meet the train on time, get home immediately and climb back into bed. He thought briefly that when the kids saw all of the music lined up they were going just toss the tapes aside. He stored them in a cabinet, unsorted but safe.

He paused, resting and collecting some energy and thought about his choice to stay home. His father-in-law was tiresome, but not lethal. Bad soup could be. A visit to the country could have been a pleasant diversion, far better than staring at a porcelain lined pool of water. Being home alone could have been a refreshing interlude, but it turned out to be a week to forget. Even thinking about it dried his mouth.

Still, the thought of Millie's dreamlike comments about her fairy tale world with the children, the old man's nightly complaints about the world's ignorance, bellowed with his bourbon glass in hand...it all still repulsed him. Throw in the jerk's insistence that everyone arise to his lousy music, piped through the house at 7:00 a.m., and he knew that he was better off at home. All in all, he thought, he had made the right choice about the trip, but a terrible choice in soup.

He took himself to the van, carefully backed it out of the driveway, headed for the depot, hoping to beat the train whistle to the platform. It took a lot of energy, but he managed it. Standing there, leaning against the wall when the train pulled in, he stayed put as the children got off and then Lauren stepped down.

She grabbed the luggage, looked at him as though to say, "aren't you going to help me" and came over while the kids began to yammer about what a great time they had riding horses, swimming in the pool, riding in the jeep, having shrimp to eat and watching grandpa get drunk.

She said, above their chatter, "Did you have a good time; we really enjoyed ourselves; I'll bet you liked being at home alone, didn't you?"

"It had its moments," he said, "but I missed you in ways I could not have imagined. Cooking food can be tricky, even heating up soup."

"I hope that you just threw away that can in the fridge. It was old and you can get really sick eating stuff like that."

"Yep," he said, "you can."

As she moved the children to the van, she smiled.

Items to Take Camping

A tent: It would have to be a large one to hold the five of them, but the children would find it a hideout much like the ones they built in the back fields at home. Stakes would have to be driven into firm earth, and he knew that would be his job; couldn't trust that to the kids. The scent of water repellent soaked into the green canvas always pleased him as he sorted through loops and tied off canvas to the pins in the earth. Lauren would help as always, directing and sorting the tools and bedding. The children spent the time touching the lake water and watching, their habit when there was work to be done. In an hour, he was sure, they would have their nest and be ready for exploring, one of their favorite things. His back hurt.

A stove: He could remember when they would cook small meals over an open fire, finishing the night off with SMORES. That didn't appeal anymore, and the children were too impatient anyway. Rob, the oldest, was strong enough to lay a ring of rocks. Buck, with more effort, could do the same but both whined about it. So now Lauren used a Coleman stove, one that matched their Coleman lantern. Fumes smelled strange, sometimes overwhelming, but as the burners hissed, he kept thinking that the food would be worth it. Hot and fast.

Bikes: Sure, they could all take hikes, but the boys dawdled, Elaine hung back with them and Lauren grew weary of their distractions. The bikes freed them all to go where they might. Simple bikes, balloon tires, no gears. Just bikes prepared to carry them through rough road and dirt paths. They never travelled without their bikes.

233

The Van: A big yellow Chevy van with racks on top, front bumper and rear one too. Its sliding door opened widely, let them pack large objects inside. They fashioned it for interior sleeping with a wooden frame Lauren built. Sometimes, during long trips, they slept the night on the floor under it, Rob rolled up on top while Elaine took over the van's middle seat. Buck enjoyed the space between the door and the ends of the seats, padded his niche with blankets, wrapped himself in the sleeping bag and proclaimed it his private cave. The van took them to HOA campgrounds, national parks, county roads, and private driveways. He saw it as their cocoon. He felt in charge driving it. The boys had space enough to move about. Lauren liked the ride and the view from the front seat. When the van grew too old and too small for them all, the boys took it over as their high school wheels. He always saw it as their camping icon.

Fishing Poles: They seldom fished, but on a few occasions, it seemed like the camping ritual required it. He remembered one morning on Colter Bay in the Grand Tetons. For once, fishing went the way the *Saturday Evening Post* would have described it. Bright morning, everyone rested and awake. The boys wanted to fish, and for a change, so did he. Doubtful of success, he broke out the tackle and they hiked a quarter mile to the waters, cold waters, but clear with sparkling stones on the bottom. Cutthroat trout were the supposed catch of the day. For once, the boys fixed their own lures, cast their lines and to his surprise, caught fish. For a half hour they stood reeling in breakfast, gutting the fish, then returning to the campsite. Lauren had the stove cooking in moments, and they enjoyed trout and eggs. He and Lauren liked the boiled coffee.

Toilet Paper: As much as they enjoyed campgrounds, living in a tent or squatting overnight in the van, the daily doings of the toilet could panic any one of them. Toilet paper was a part of modern living that they never wanted to be without. Sometimes it required rationing, but even the boys made sure that their backsides were covered, so to speak.

Drawing Pad/Pencil: There was always a slot in the van set aside for Lauren's drawing supplies. It surprised him every time she sat and sketched. Her favorite pencil drawings caught scenes of their location, a view of one of the boys or Elaine climbing rocks. Others might show discoveries, occasional portraits of any of us at rest, unaware we were being recorded...forever. Her hands moved slowly, gracefully in smooth motions drawing graphite lines that merged into postures or faces that were unmistakably views of the moment. She seemed most at peace when she drew.

A Map: That meant, usually, a map of a state, one that showed parks, rivers, lakes. They never went off the beaten path so far that they needed a county map. He liked counting the small red numbers that added up the miles between locations. It always inspired him, just noting the progress they were making toward their campsite. Lauren liked to use it as a guide, to filter and form information that they could share and quibble over. The children gave no thought to where they were, only where they were going and they didn't care how we got there.

Money: Cash and credit card. For sure, lots of money. He remembered when they paid 42.8 cents a gallon for gas in the Badlands.

Medical Supplies: Lauren really didn't trust those pre-mixed boxes of gauze, tape and creams. They never had what she wanted. Bandages were too big, band-aids too small, antiseptic too scanty. She put together a bag fit for combat: tape, gauzes, ace bandages, iodine, alcohol, ibuprofen, peroxide, more tape, snake bite anti-venom, scissors, sunscreen, antihistamine injections, tweezers, asthma puffer, penicillin pills, even a tourniquet bar and cloth. She assembled a better kit than she used, but so long as he didn't mind punching needles into people it worked fine. He liked wrapping sprains. Lauren stayed calm about injuries, and he liked that. What unnerved her were ticks, and he wasn't fond of them himself so they walked well covered, and when in open skies, well shielded from the sun. Lauren and Rob tanned. He burned as did Buck and Elaine.

An Open Mind: Camping always meant getting away from all of our daily jobs. It promised new views from the open road, small explorations on paved campgrounds, perhaps a small trek on foot but not so much as to get lost. Elaine became transfixed wandering through the cemetery at Custer National Memorial. Rob climbed so high in the badlands that he feared he would fall, needed assurances to get down. Buck found the Elk in Yellowstone fascinating. "They're just eating grass on people's lawns!" he reported. They all fixed their gaze on the bats that left Carlsbad Caverns at dusk. "Do they really bite?" the boys asked. He told them yes, and let their imaginations go to work. We laughed as we traveled the open road, remembering some of the boy's decisions at home to go "on our own" and that meant climbing a hill across the street with a caution to be home for supper. He didn't know how many memories the family stored from camping, but his were safely kept and they were all players on the stage.

Patience: Never a task for children. When the van pulled into the driveway, home from travel, they were off looking for friends. Lauren grew weary of the housekeeping, and for that reason alone, he helped. She vacuumed. He preferred to sort through the pile of goods that they brought back, many trashed, but others replaced, cleaned, tidied and stored for another trip. Maps were the worst. Too valuable to throw away. **Too flimsy to store confidently. Too dirty to clean easily. Too out of date to their purpose. The children all aged quickly. One week, he and Lauren removed the sleeping platform and turned the van into transport for swimming lessons and competitions. Camping days settled below the horizon.**

Splish Splash

A quarter of a century now since Walt last visited his father's grave, and it would be another twenty-five years before he stood over it again. The memories of that loss he buried in a special cave deep within his mind and moved on knowing that the worst event in his life could be confirmed by a gravesite visit at any time. He had yet to grieve, preferring to focus on the future, the next challenge, the next event.

Yet, that death refashioned his life, first through the GI Bill which had passed to him through his father, later by an erratic pursuit of love which took him finally to Colorado. Finding stability there, supplementing those funds with summer and school year work, he completed college, married and finished graduate school.

Armed with a PhD in economics, he began teaching at Saint Clare College, a small private school in Wisconsin. When he earned tenure, he relaxed, took a deep breath and looked around at his family. The children had come along in timely ways, two boys and at last a girl, all active, healthy youngsters. Time to get to know them, he thought. Elaine was a little young, but he took a look, decided that Buck and Rob, now seven and nine, needed to learn something about work, commitment and achievement.

He had memories of his own youth and the excitement of softball. He thought about how much fun he had meeting other kids, getting to know some local adults and building a reputation for skill and competitive fire. He decided that this summer he would become a sports presence in the lives of his sons. He bought them baseball mitts and hats, described what T-Ball was all about and told them how much they were going to like the sport. They didn't have to face a "live" pitch coming from another player. They had only to hit a ball resting on a waist high tee, and then run the bases. When in the field, they could learn to field grounders, catch fly balls and throws from other players, and they could make new friends who could last a lifetime. Twenty-five years after his best softball summer, he still corresponded with guys who were raising families of their own.

He called them in from the cave they were digging, cleaned them up, put loose fitting clothes on them and drove over to the ballpark. Filled with youngsters just the right age and parents looking for a summer release from child care, the scene welcomed them. Three people sat at a small card table just in front of one of the dugouts, and a line stretching around the backstop at home plate jostled itself as adults shifted from foot to foot, muttered a bit to their kids and held their pens in dusty hands. He took his place and chatted as he gradually approached the registration table.

"How old are your boys?" the voice in command asked, and he replied that they were seven and nine. "Have they played T-Ball before? Do they have any injuries that we need to know about? Do they require glasses to play in the field or to hit the ball? Can you get them to practice three times a week? What is your phone number and address? What are their names? Nicknames? O.K. just initial here and they will be good to go."

Walt signed his name and felt a bit of pride that he had enrolled the boys in a program that would nurture them, give them confidence and force them to meet other children. He took them home, making careful note of the schedule of practices and the games for each of the next two weeks. Their coach would be Chester Wilson, and he was told by "old timers" that Chester was one of the best. "He is demanding but fair; loud but not intimidating; quick on his feet, but quicker still in his head. He really knows baseball."

Walt saw his sons entering a passage of their youth, and he told them, "You are going to have some fun here. Don't worry about how well you hit or field the ball. You are learning, and by the end of the summer, you are going to feel good about yourself and your team."

Five days later, after the boys refused to go to any practices, he called them out of their dirt cave and insisted that they get cleaned up for their first game. They had jerseys now and the name "Oaks" spread across their chests. He had been able to cajole them into a game of catch on two separate occasions, but they were a lot more interested in digging a hole in the ground and turning it into their clubhouse. Didn't matter. He was not going to let them spend the summer shoveling in the dirt. Playing T-Ball was going to give them a new interest, new friends and new skills. He knew it.

They arrived at the field in good order and the boys played their first five innings of baseball. They didn't have to field any balls or catch any "flies", and they didn't get to first base when they were at bat. Their faces maintained a frown, their bodies scarcely moved when in the field. They were not having a good time and complained bitterly on the way home that they didn't like T-Ball and they weren't going back.

Time for Plan B, Walt thought. He would not let them go back to the fields and dig caves all summer. He went by the recreational center to target some other activity, and he discovered swim team. His wife Lauren had seen to it that they could survive in the water, and he knew the coach from some incidental contact at the college. It couldn't hurt them to become better swimmers. He went by the pool, talked to the coach, Mike Mason, and learned more about the program. "They'll have early morning training, every day," he said, "Swim meets on Saturday. They'll develop stamina, improve their swimming technique, and learn new strokes." Walt signed them up.

They were not happy. It was an outdoor pool. They didn't really feel like getting wet and cold in the early morning, and besides, they complained, they already knew how to swim. He overruled all of their objections, bought them each a suit, a large towel and took them to practice the following Monday. It was a sunny morning, but an early one. His watch read 8:00 a.m. and they were in the pool. He stayed to watch with a smile on his face.

The younger boy, Buck, was thin, poorly insulated and hugging himself to ward off the cold. Rob, older, larger with more flesh on his bones, quietly took note of the other kids who were on the deck, especially the girls. Walt's smile widened. Swimming competition was divided by age groups, two year intervals, and separate events for girls and boys. The little gathering of human ducks numbered about 24, and there were parents for all of them.

Coach Mike asked the boys to swim one length of the pool so that he could get some idea of their skills. Rob swam steadily enough with a lot of body motion but also a lot of strength. Buck was not willing to swim with his face in the water, so Coach Mike asked him to swim back stroke. He battled through the water bravely and with good stamina. Not long after, all the kids were put into lanes and sent off to swim a workout: one length of the pool 20 times, with a rest interval of one minute between each swim.

While they were going through their work, Coach Mike commented, "You know, Buck just broke the pool record

241

for 7-8 year old competition and Rob fits in very well with the 9-10 year old group. I hope they stay." Walt was both flattered and flustered. Who knew if the boys wanted to swim some more? But if they could be successful while they developed physical conditioning and swimming skills, he decided, maybe the sport would discipline them. He talked with the two of them, and with one eye on the girls, Rob said that he thought he would like to stay on the team. Buck agreed. He seldom strayed from his older brother's side.

The summer went by and the boys continued to swim. They learned, as did he, that competitive swimming offered a marvelous training ground for life itself. One had to work hard to gain muscle and respiratory strength. One had to train regularly to learn new skills and to improve swimming times. The stop-watch was not a debatable referee. When the boys worked, their times improved. When they did not work, they worsened, and in the eyes of their new peer group that was unacceptable. It might not matter whether they won or lost, but it did matter whether their times dropped. They made new friends and brought old ones into the program.

He and Lauren worked the swim meets and enjoyed timing events, handing out ribbons and writing down results. It was a great summer of fun, laughter and competition, and Walt loved seeing how much the boys improved their swimming skills. No longer lunging, splashing, and fighting the water with heads above the waterline, they now swam smoothly, heads leading their body flows through the water, turning briefly to get air and returning to a smooth posture. They learned new strokes: breaststroke and butterfly. They learned to make flip turns, shared places on relay teams and competed with kids from around the area, some an hour's drive away. By the end of the summer they were swimming daily workouts of at least a mile, sometimes more. It was all he could have hoped for, and they came to the final event of the season well-conditioned and hopeful. Eight competitive teams showed up, kind of a regatta without boats, Walt thought. He loved watching the competition.

It was one of those unpredictable afternoons which changed lives. The boys both swam well, but Buck won every event he entered while Rob lost badly in all of his swims. In tears, he asked why he was not as good as his younger brother. Coach Mike told him that he was at the bottom of his age group and that he was swimming against some kids who swam all year round. If he really cared to get better, he could enroll in the YMCA winter swimming competition.

Rob said he wanted to do that. Walt thrilled to his competitive desire to win. There was no need to persuade Buck. He *was* winning. He was better than his brother, gaining reputation and recognized as one of the best swimmers on the team. He was anxious to train in the winter.

And so it began. For the next six years, the family immersed itself in swim team. He and Lauren drove the children to evening practices, transported them to swim meets around the state, and supported their competitions in the region and at the YMCA state championships. The children swam five days a week, 48 weeks of the year, and they became excellent competitors. Buck went on to win Y state championships as an eight, ten and twelve year old. Rob was on a state championship relay team. In time, daughter Elaine took up the sport and won a state championship as an eight year old. Walt and Lauren took up Masters Swimming and rounded into the best condition of their lives. He gave up smoking. She lost ten pounds. Rarely was a family of five so well-conditioned, well-connected, and well-traveled.

Summer fun became a lifestyle which kept them all active, focused and successful. It lasted until the boys entered high school and then things began to change. Lauren longed to have horses. Walt grew tired of his neighbors. They decided to move. It was as simple as that.

They bought a nice piece of timbered land graced with an old farm house which they expanded to fit their numbers. Below it, a cow shed, outdoor well and outhouse testified to the lineage of the property and 28 steeply sloped acres provided a privacy soon shared with Arabian horses. Elaine and her mother bonded more closely as they managed new bridles, blankets and saddles, took trail rides with friends and birthed foals with magical hooves. Walt learned to clean stalls, build fences and transport grain, hay and horses. The smell of chlorine and the splish-splash of swimming competitions drifted away, replaced with the scent of oiled leather, the sweet smell of fresh alfalfa, and the moist odor of fresh sawdust. Over it all hung the quite pleasant welcome of a healthy, active barn.

Sometimes, as he shoveled horse manure, he caught a scent of acrid ammonia, turned away from it sharply and appreciated again the clean edged smell of chlorine in a pool of water. Splish-splash, splish-splash. He missed it.

It's the Horses of Course

It's summer. Sun breaks over the horizon early, but my husband Walt sleeps through it all, as is his nature. I cannot abide sleep when the air is fresh and cool, the house is quiet, and if I travel only a few hundred steps, I can be in the barn where the horses' soft breath reaches out as I pass a stall, fills the air with that earthy, sweet scent of their lungs and lingers in my nose. I love it.

They perk their ears, look bright-eyed at my presence and stir gently in their stalls. I walk up to the grain bin, say hello to Barn Cat, open the lid and begin parceling out a healthy treat to each of my friends. I grab a bale of hay from the stack. It's loosely packed, a sign of local production, and I slide the strings off, making sure to put them in the trash. Too often they become tangled around my feet, worse yet if one of the colts stepped in them.

It's clean hay, carrying a heavy scent of alfalfa, sweet enough to slid a stem in my teeth and taste the flavor. A fleck or two into each stall and the morning feed filled the aisle with the quiet, strong sound of horse's teeth crunching, munching their morning fuel. I never grow tired of it.

Walt would come down later in the morning, late morning I suppose, and then he would clean the stalls, haul away manure in the wheel barrel and rake the sawdust. But well before that, I would have turned them out into the pasture enjoying the morning thrill of seeing the half-dozen of them accelerate up the hill, spread out amidst the grasses and after a snort or two, bury their muzzles in the green growth of spring. The sun, now above the horizon, warmed their backs, tanned my face, connected us again in the secret bond which kept me committed to my mares, colts and stallion.

He paced still in his stall, awaiting his release, but until the others were safely in their places, he would have to wait. Finally, having arranged the gates to keep him safely in his own corral, I released him, and he took off with that high spirited gallop of the Arabian, tail high flagging his body, muzzle in the air searching the wind, a high floating trot getting him to where he wanted to go. I took another look, satisfied that all was well, and returned to the house.

Time to call the children, rouse them from deep sleep and set their breakfasts on the table, hoping that they arrived before it cooled. Usually they did because the bus did not wait for anyone, and it was seven miles to school, a long walk even by the fabled youth of their grandfather, and far more than I would drive them until I was ready and that meant they would be late and that meant troubles for them. In short, they seldom missed the bus.

Walt followed them into the kitchen about an hour later. He had no classes today and he didn't need to be anywhere in particular, and truth be told, he seemed to enjoy a lazy start to the day, a sparse breakfast, then an ambling walk down to the barn where he could start cleaning the stalls. He surprised me with his willingness to shovel those dark lumps, dig out urine puddles, replace sawdust and once finished, spray fly-killer throughout the stalls. When I tried to do that, it made my tongue tingle, but he suffered no ill effects at all.

When I think about it, as I do from time to time, Walt's willingness to haul hay, transport grain, dispose of manure, load hundreds of bales of alfalfa into the top part of the barn...none of it seemed to be the kind of thing he would ordinarily enjoy, but something about the inherent dignity of the horses attracted him. I laughed a lot at his reluctance to actually ride any of them, but he enjoyed watching me train my mounts, puzzled the differences between western and English saddle styles and admired the form I explained to him as I rode.

So my day would evolve. Perhaps some fencing that needed repair. Walt could tend to that. A water tank needed cleaning, a sloppy mess, but in the end refreshing as the cool, pure water poured into it and I finished the job. Then, maybe it would be time for a training session with the stallion to teach him how to present himself to advantage at a show, or maybe ride an hour or two with a couple of mares just for pleasure. The most fun of the day would likely be the treat of teaching a weanling a lesson or two about being haltered and led, or simply exercising a colt at the end of a long strapping line about 25 feet in length allowing those four legs to trot gently in circles. Sometimes the colt surprised me with the way he could float around the barn at the end of that line. He really did have a lift to his movement...beautiful.

I spent my hours in the barn reflecting from time to time upon the love I had held for the horse since my youth. Mom and Dad had invested a few dollars in a partly-broken mare whom I named Lark. I don't remember ever putting a saddle on her, but she and I rode the farm for hours on end, often in an all-out canter which she loved, a scamper which transported me from any worries in my civilized life to the mythical magic of thundering hooves and heavy breathing from my friendly mount, my private companion, my Lark. Some girls I knew spent time talking to dolls and playing house. I spent mine riding, walking Lark into cool springs to drink, letting her roam at leisure as my mind day-dreamed the thoughts of youth and the possibilities of the future.

I really didn't expect to transport my love for Lark to a lifestyle that focused on horses, but twenty years into our marriage, Walt wanted to find more country privacy, and I wanted to reassemble my childhood environment. We found 28 acres of mixed woodland and pasture hidden at the top of a hill, unseen from any other home, but within a few miles of town, school and shops. It sold cheap, which we needed, and we added three rooms to accommodate the kids and give us an open view of the evergreens blanketing the land as it fell away below us.

For twenty years now, we had fashioned a lifestyle that suited our interests, drained our energy in a healthy way and provided a haven from the big city. I learned a lot about my horses, especially my most obstinate Arabian and the first one we bought. Coy, we named her, although she certainly wasn't, and I rode her because no one else would try. I confess that there were times that she brought me to tears at my inability to get her to walk out of the driveway and down the road to a trail ride. She seemed afraid of so many things and her jumps, hops and skips, all with lightning reflexive action, kept me off balance and for a long time, terribly frustrated.

But then, one day as we were walking along the edge of a county road, Coy made another one of her patented jumps and stops. It came with a start when a shadow from a post crossed her path and she jumped sideways, stopped dead still, and started to back away. I calmed her, asked her to approach the shadow again, and at the same time came to a realization: she would do nothing to hurt herself. If she would not hurt herself, all I had to do was stay on her and she would do nothing to hurt me.

I relaxed and my confidence gradually transmitted to Coy. In time she became my favorite mare, in part because she was as obstinate as my first horse, Lark. Lark, who never liked to walk, who demanded to be let run and who I loved to let go, the wind slashing at my eyes, her deep breathing blending rhythmically with her hoof beats. In time, Coy and I raced with the same pace through pastures as green as those of my childhood. Exhilarating!

Horses came into our lives and brought focus, purpose, challenge and a lifestyle that seemed honest, reflected hard work and rewarded us with beauty on four legs. Each had its own personality. Each taught us lessons, sometimes sad ones, but the joy of moments on their backs, leading them at halter, watching them run freely through pastures, that joy fixed itself in our minds. Even Walt came to enjoy some of the light handling work, and fancied himself an amateur vet when it came time to administer vaccines, worming medicine and some of the close clipping required for showing.

We fielded questions from friends in town, even from relatives in far-away places, asking politely but with some puzzlement why we spent so many years in the country, in the privacy, beauty, and quiet views of that small piece of property? There were a lot of reasons I suppose. The school system was excellent. The children seemed to grow up without deep exposure to drugs. Life was of necessity simple and without material excess. But at the end of the day, when age, injury and sensibility took us away from the country and back into the city, I could reflect on our time there amidst the silhouettes of four-legged friends, and say, quietly, "Well, we stayed because of the horses, of course."

A Soft Quiet Morning

He spent the evening as he always spent the evening, bringing in the mares, settling them all in their stalls, feeding out the portions of alfalfa and grain that lured them back inside. He checked the water buckets for each, made sure that the doors were locked and finally, as his last task, walked to the stall with the round, bay, pregnant mare.

She was due to foal, and that meant he had some sleepless nights ahead. Pregnant mares became restless when due, and they could stay that way for a week. Milk might form on their teats, thickening to pearls and promising food for the long-legged arrival, but birth could still be days away. When it arrived, he wanted to be there. Nothing could go wrong more quickly, than the birth of a baby horse. He needed to be there.

Still, it seemed to be a common truth that a mare would not foal when she was being watched. Something in her biological protection told her that she needed to be alone. Once born the baby was helpless for a few hours, and she needed to lick it dry, warm it, nurse it, and protect it while it slept those important first hours on earth.

So, he took his time, walking by the stall shielded from easy view with blankets which provided both privacy as well as improved insulation. A warming light fixed in the ceiling provided wattage for viewing and for temperature control during a cold night. It was early March. Snow could fall again before the frozen clay earth softened into the squishy mud which sucked at the horses ankles, sometimes causing little cuts which could become infected. The vet called the condition "scratches" and it required confinement, penicillin and cleansing. Indoors, the mare would be protected from the mud, and the foal at her side could frolic inside the open area of the barn, skittering with safe footing and plentiful space.

He took a look at her. She was quietly eating her hay, pausing from time to time to take a quick look at her belly as though to suggest that something might be happening back there, but there were no signs of contractions. Every time she lay down, he thought that might be a signal, but no, she would rest, without stress, then stand again, heaving her body and its 40 pound occupant up out of the straw. She would look around a bit, blow some steam and return to nibbling her hay.

He decided to go up to the house and get some coffee, flavor it with milk and sugar and sit a spell. Sipping, he hoped that something good was happening in the barn and that it would play itself out just after his return. It occurred to him that if he had a remote camera in the stall, he could just watch the mare swish her tail, take her rest both standing and lying down, and wait for the signs.

But that technology was for another time. This year, he had spent his money on a stud fee in the hopes that the foal would carry the very best of the parent's genes. If so, it could cavort across both pasture and show ring for years drawing his gasps with its elegant strength and grace. Nine out of 10 colts would become geldings and essentially valueless. But, a really good one could fund his operation for years; a filly could buy feed for a season.

First, though, the birth, marked by the slide of muzzle and legs from the mare and that magical moment when the foal's chest, compressed by passage through the birth canal,

251

suddenly expanded, its eyes popped open and it began to breathe. Then the mare would stand, snapping the umbilical cord, letting the foal finally reach its feet and go immediately to the scent of milk that had splattered between the mare's legs as it leaked from her in the days before birth. He knew watching a new foal find its milk would try his patience, and sometimes he tried to help. Best to just let nature lead the youngster to its first meal.

In a few days, it would jump, leap, turn, run, slide to dead stop and blow steam from tiny nostrils, those air ports which would more than double in size as they matured. Early on, he could tame and train the weanling to follow a lead and to stay calm while his hands roamed over its body, feeling its warmth, noting its muscles and holding it steady.

He would bend his head and breathe into its nostrils, scenting in return that special air that came from deep within its lungs, flooding his senses with purity, innocence and the delightful scent of youth. There was a lot to look forward to with this mare, and he let his mind roam a bit as he sipped his coffee. Then time to check the stall again.

He rinsed the cup, put on his coat, stepped into his large, rubber boots, and slowly made his way from the mud room out into the back path that led to the barn. The light in the mare's stall led him to her without any delay, and as he stepped into the room next to hers, he glanced quickly to see if there were four legs or eight. Still just one resident.

He spent an hour in the barn. The mare's swollen udder told him that sweet milk was ready, packed with colostrum providing vital antibodies to the baby. Without this early milk, the youngster would not last a month, but it was there, ready and in good supply. A quiet still night, he heard the other four horses breathing softly. He dropped the mare another bit of hay, looked everything over and then went back up to the house to rest awhile. He would nap, awaken from time to time and check on her.

For three nights he did this, uncertain during any one of them that there would be a birthing hour. Nature had its ways. The mare seemed calm and his mind roamed from time to time thinking about what this new baby could mean to him. Of one thing, he was certain. The mare was impeccably bred, the daughter of a national champion stallion, and being a bay, she carried commanding color to go with her temperament. In the show ring, her carriage and posturing impressed judges throughout the state.

The sire of that bulk of flesh and bone within her was a national champion himself, and if his genes blended well with the mare, the product could be a show winner. Winning halter competitions...where the foal would be asked to trot on lead, stand and posture with neck extended...even for babies six months of age, could mean a profitable sale indeed. He had hopes.

On the fourth night, in the face of another chapter of idle watching, he gave up the nap routine and decided to bring some additional blankets to the barn, curl himself up in the adjoining stall and just sleep. If she foaled, he would hear her movements and awaken. He need not have worried. It was another quiet night.

During the day, he decided to give the mare some gentle exercise. He haltered her, attached a long lead about 20 feet long and moved her around him in easy circles, wincing a bit as he saw her belly carry its burden, but comfortable in noting that she enjoyed the light exercise. She trotted for about five minutes, showed signs of slowing, and he let her retreat into a walk. He cooled her for another 10 minutes and then brought her to the center of the circle, attached a short lead and took her back to her stall. "Will that do it?" he asked, and although she looked at him, this was not the movies. She did not nicker.

That night, he waited to wrap up in his blankets until a little past midnight. Still comfortable, the mare nibbled at her hay, and he saw no reason to think that she might foal anytime soon.

The soft morning light awakened him. It was a very quiet barn to his ear, more so than usual. He looked toward the mare's stall and did not see her standing. Maybe it was happening! He tossed the blankets aside, and went to the stall door to have a good look.

His knees buckled!

The mare lay on her side. Protruding from her vagina, the head and neck of a dead foal dangled. Unable to exit the womb, its tongue lolled out of its mouth and its eyes remained closed.

Stunned, washed with fright, he stared into the stall trying to absorb what he saw, and a little alarm began to ring in his head, *"The foal is dead, and if you don't do something quickly, the mare will die too."* He went to the barn phone and called his vet, explaining quickly what he was seeing. "I'll be right there," the doc said, "Give me 15 minutes."

Good to his word, he pulled into the long gravel driveway, and went directly to the stall. He said nothing at first, took a look and then barked, "The foal got its legs stuck in delivery. We have to get it out of her right away."

"How?" he whispered.

The vet paused, looked at him directly and said firmly, emphasizing each phrase, "It won't be pretty, but this is what we're gonna do. You encourage the mare to stand. Once she's up, I'll amputate the neck and head of the foal, then shove its body back into her. I'll attach a small chain to its forelegs, pull the legs up into the birth canal and then deliver the rest of its body. I'll pump some antibiotics into the mare and with luck she'll survive."

His gut repulsed by what he was hearing, he wanted to walk away and come back later, but no, the doc went on, "I'm gonna to need you to steady the mare with your voice and carry the amputated head and neck well away from her. Then I'll finish up and we will hope for the best."

"How did its legs get stuck?"

"In normal birthing when the head moves through the birth canal, the legs are positioned just under it. Then, head and legs leave the body together. Last night, the legs were lodged against the pelvis. When she contracted to move the foal through, they remained stuck. She's exhausted and now there's danger of uterine tear and sepsis."

He went on, "The foal never lived because its chest didn't pass through the birth canal. It never had a chance to breath, and just so you know, there was nothin' you could have done about it."

"OK doc, let's try and save her."

He encouraged the mare to rise, and she did. He watched as the vet's knife went cleanly through the neck of the lifeless form dangling from the mare. The vertebrae were the purest of the pure white that he had ever seen. Undisturbed by blood or torn tissue, they were life unknown, a core of strength that the foal never had a need to flex.

The doctor worked quickly. Within five minutes he had the legs positioned for exit, and he pulled his light chain firmly, and the body slipped on out of the mare and fell to the straw. It was a colt. The mare didn't move. The vet told him to place the torso, neck and head of the foal into a sack and put it in the truck. Then he injected the mare with a massive dose of penicillin, looked her over carefully, muttered a few words of light praise and turned to leave.

"Any chance that she can become pregnant again?" he asked.

"Don't know," he said, "She might, but I wouldn't count on it. The question is whether she will live."

She survived. Within a week, she was eating well, chasing around with the rest of the herd and looking as alert and lovely as he had come to remember her. She always led the group across the pasture when they ran for home, and she still did, tail high and flowing, neck arched and extended, two large cavities sleekly placed in the contours of her muzzle, fully dilated, moving air as only an Arabian horse can. He mourned her loss and his. He thought of breeding her again wondering if nature could heal a uterus as well as the vet could empty one.

Throughout the summer, she continued to thrive. In time he began to take her on rides through the near forests and then out into the open fields. At first she winded easily under the load, but by October she carried him five miles easily, with some good portion of the ride in a trot. She healed.

In the particular way in which the horse-breeding business works, his first fee had guaranteed him a "live foal", and when it died, he became entitled to a free breeding. When she cycled at the end of May, he made his calculations and trucked her up to the Cities to be bred.

He wrote his prescription knowing only God could fill it, waited nine months and picked up his package the following spring when she delivered a bay filly with long, long legs. The foal presented with her dished head exactly as she should, stood within 20 minutes, nursed in another half hour. By daybreak she was frolicking about the inside barn unfettered, free and alive with the electricity of new discoveries and the exhilaration of the young. She filled the summer with whickers and ran the pasture full of tricks, curiosity, growth and play. As she grew, her grace and stature once more thrilled him, let his heart rejoice at the beauty his eyes embraced. She healed him, and the nightmare death of her sibling faded bit by bit until one day he could no longer remember the details, just the loss.

Short Circuit

Walt and Lauren spent 20 years on the farm. A new barn replaced the old milk shed. Rocky gravel now filled fields that once sloped 30 degrees, and fencing marked corrals in front of the house and another adjoining the barn below. Even the septic system had been replaced with tiled rocks and a drain system that took the waste far across the fields. Manure piled up by the cubic yard, gradually composting into a rich fertilizer which city folk sometimes took away for their corn and roses, but which for the most simply leveled a sloping bank. Periodically, he hired his farmer neighbor to move it far, far away.

Lauren noticed early on in their visits to evaluate breeding stallions that many farm homes were in disrepair. People chose horses over comfort, sometimes over cleanliness. She never allowed that, but she knew that the boys were always uncomfortable about living in Hicksville, and she saw few of their friends. No matter. They were now teenagers, increasingly out of reach, still mulling the rules of behavior that their mother had placed in their heads, relentlessly reminding them that some mistakes were jail time offenses. Whether they listened she wondered, as all parents wonder, and they had their brushes with the law, but they managed to always find the safe way out. They knew that they had a larger future: college, graduation, careers.

For her, the horses became the center of country life, and as the boys moved into city doings, she and her daughter joined in their great love affair with the spirited, floating, beautiful Arabian horse. Breeding a mare, foaling a new life, riding the trails, showing their favorites in local horse gatherings became the essence of their lives.

When Elaine left for college, the valley echoed only the sounds of Walt and Lauren, a dog and the horses. A decade passed. The dog gave way to another, but their bodies held up for years with the challenges of rural living. The horses improved in quality and Lauren showed her stallion to regional honors, in halter and dressage competitions. Her life was full, much the way she had once dreamed it would be, and Walt's work at the university continued to satisfy him.

Still, they aged. Accidents and injuries which could be accepted as a part of the rural life style they loved, gradually became warning signs limiting their view of the future. A bent finger, acceptable. Rope burns repaired quickly. But a broken leg, two back surgeries, concussions and passing years gave Lauren a message she tried to evade but eventually accepted. They would have to leave the farm.

It took them three years to find a buyer. Three years parceling land to sell separately, culling horses to the minimum, repairing home and barn. Three years of tension, stress and in the last year, financial risk as they finally bought their new home and sold the farm ten months later. When they left, they knew that it was not just another transition. It was their last move.

The children raised, Walt told friends, "If they're not in jail, living at home or dead by age 21, we will have succeeded." Lauren told her friends that she hoped that they left home with financial sense and good ethics. Neither needed to worry. All three completed their college degrees in four years. Each earned a graduate degree. Rob became a criminal defense attorney. Buck emerged a corporate raider. Elaine taught psychology. They lived in three different states pursuing three different professions, and nothing in their lives drew upon the energy or the finances of their parents. So when they sold the farm they left as free agents, much as they had started in Denver such a long time ago. Beaver Creek brought them city water, city sewer, city cable, city garbage collection, city electric and city friends.

Lauren's life blended into the culture of the community: garden clubs, reading clubs, flower beds, socials at the library and walks in Cable Bridge Park crossing a hanging, swaying bridge. That was always fun, every time. Gentle hikes around the lake let her dog Wendy frolic and splash in the water. Her cat, Peter Pan curled softly around her when she read or slept. She enjoyed comfortable living.

Her confidence in herself, her abilities and her life outside the home soared. She made new friends through her work at a local advertising agency and took pride in being the only employee the demanding owner ever fired twice. In her reporting of special events for a regional newspaper, she particularly committed herself to writing a weekly feature on renovated homes. Taken with the eccentric personality of the owners of a local eatery, she sold tickets and designed advertising for their live music productions.

A creative exhibit for residents revived her interest in art, and she spent hours each week in her studio drawing, painting or sculpting. With considerable amusement, she often walked down the stairs to the kitchen with dark lines of charcoal inside her fingers, acrylic smears of reds, greens and yellow on her skin and clothing, and white, sticky paste in wisps of hair curling about her ears.

She found a new, confident voice, no longer shy about expressing her views on public issues. Abortion: *Just call it murder and legalize it.* Careers: *I would like to be like Cher.*

Clinton: *Monica should have just kept her mouth shut, if not the first time, then the second.* On George Bush (either one): *Boo Bush.* Suicide: *I will never just linger and die.* Gay Guys: *They are sensitive to art and they make good money.* Fat Guys: *What a fine figure of a man. (laughing).*

Her reputation in the community became entwined with her reporting, her passion for painting and her love of flowers and animals. She was, perhaps for the first time, recognized for her own strengths and skills and she blossomed with the attention. Her children, returning for visits, noticed the change. "Mom seems different," they would say.

She added a glass enclosed breakfast room to the back of the house, painted the kitchen, installed air conditioning, restored wood flooring, replaced old windows with insulated ones and made their house a home. She boarded her remaining horse at a stable and rode it frequently. They were happy.

Two years after their move, as Walt sat in the large chair enjoying his morning coffee and the newspaper delivered to their door each day, she came up to him, and said quietly, "I'm having trouble...*pause*... speaking. I know what I want to say, but there is a delay between...*pause*...what I think and what I can say." This startled him. Lauren did not complain about much, and he had dismissed her hesitant speech as mid-thought corrections on what was on her mind. But now, something was going on.

They started with their family physician. He examined her and recommended that she see a speech therapist in another branch of the clinic. She did so. He recommended that she see a neurologist, and when he said that, they both grew quiet. She pondered the decision. To see a neurologist meant that something was wrong and she was not sure that she wanted to know what was wrong. She could speak well enough. She felt fine. She was strong and walked easily and long. Still, perhaps there was something the neurologist could tell her that would either ease her mind or address the symptom.

They waited together in the small, quiet room. The doctor entered and asked some questions, looked into her mouth, then did some tests. Then, he turned to them both and said, softly, that she had a motor neuron disease, and that nerve cells that controlled her speech were dying. It was like a short-circuit between her thoughts and her talk he explained.

Before he could offer her a diagnosis, he needed to do two more tests. She asked if there were any specific treatments for this condition, and he said, no, one just learned to use the remaining neurons more efficiently. She paused, remained quiet for a few moments, and then said, "Well, if there is nothing to be done, I don't want any more tests. I will just deal with it as it is."

Surprise crossed the doctor's face, but then he quietly said, "That will be fine. If you want to learn more in the future, just come back to see me and we will take another look."

At first nothing much changed, but over a period of a few months, Walt noticed that Lauren's speech slowed a little more. He began to track the declines noting that every three months her voice slurred more noticeably. She began to choke more easily when she drank or ate. What seemed normal in their lives changed step by step by step. Two years later, Lauren, scarcely understood by anyone other than Walt, decided to seek speech therapy, but the doctor refused to schedule her for an appointment.

Walt pressed him on that refusal, and, finally, with some reluctance, the therapist said, "It is my belief that your wife is suffering from Lou Gehrig's Disease (ALS) and that there is no therapy known that can remedy her condition. You should consult with your neurologist again."

Walt's mind locked. His legs weakened as though disconnected from blood flow. His gut tightened, cramped. For days he balanced the knowledge of this horrific news with his need to keep some kind of control over their lives. He had another neurologist review Lauren's file, discussed with him the symptoms, and got his opinion. Indeed, she did have ALS, so far as the doctor could determine, but he would have to see her to make a final diagnosis. He suggested a return visit to her, but she refused. She would not see any neurologist. Walt then decided to keep the diagnosis from her, working with their personal physician to get medications that addressed the symptoms of her disease's progression.

He did so both because she clearly did not want to hear from any more doctors, and because he feared that if she knew the nature of the disease, she would take her own life far too early. Lauren had always been very candid about death. When animals failed, truly failed, she took them to the vet and had them euthanized. She did the same for horses, two being buried on their property.

For many years, she made it clear to Walt that she would commit suicide rather than remain curled up for years in a fetal position as had her mother. She had subscribed to magazines dealing with techniques of suicide, purchased lethal potions, considered what her best strategy of escape might be. They discussed her thoughts. She selected the method. She told him that she could never slit her wrists the way their Boulder neighbor, Nina Gordon, had done. She would do it in the garage with the car, carbon monoxide poisoning. Until now, it had just been talk.

With ALS, she might be on her back for many months, even years and she would want to die before enduring that indignity. Still, she had to be able to walk to the garage and turn the key in the ignition because he would not assist her. He could walk with her, could kiss her goodbye, but he would not start the car. If she became incapable of walking, her exit strategy disappeared. What to do?

Her form of ALS was not affecting her legs and arms as quickly as it did some patients. She continued to walk as suited her interest. Her pace slowed, but her legs remained strong enough. As long as she could walk, she controlled her decisions and could stay out of nursing homes, but as she weakened, ignorant of the disease itself, she risked her worst fear becoming true...bedridden. Walt told her that if she fell and could not walk, she became vulnerable to health care professionals. Suicide would then be off the table.

By default, she became increasingly isolated. She could not speak. She could write, but whose hand can keep up a flow of conversation? Friends she enjoyed now avoided visiting. A few became closer to her. Even Walt found her speech puzzling, challenging. Increasingly, she found comfort from her dog, Wendy and cat, Peter Pan. Left with her thoughts and the challenges she faced in avoiding loneliness, Lauren wrote, read, and sketched even as her fingers curled, forcing her to hold a pencil between knuckles.

In time, the symptoms grew worse, and both his and her ability to deny a growing reality weakened. In April, he again urged her to see her neurologist. She refused. Walt persisted, and finally she agreed. Because she could no longer speak, she wrote out some hard questions, and he gave her the answers.

"Will I continue to be weak?" she wrote.
"Yes" he answered.
"Will I die?" she wrote again.
"If you have what I think you have," he said softly,
"then yes, this disease will shorten your life."
"Medicine?" she printed this time.
"No", he said, "not one that will stop or cure the disease."
"I don't like this," she wrote and began to cry.

The doctor confirmed the diagnosis and together they cried their fears and sadness. For the next two months, Lauren did all that she could do, walking with Wendy, doing little pushups against the wall, hosting friends who came by to visit.

He found a note. *"It seems that everyone can talk but me; it's not calm in my world, except for my cats and dog; they still understand me. Oh I wish this thing had not happened to me; I feel secluded and abandoned in my Silent World; I do not like it here".*

The song, *"It's a Wonderful World"* brought tears that choked her, sent her coughing uncontrollably until the flow of fluid eased. Her mouth fell open in silent cries, overwhelmed by the loneliness and fright of leaving a world she so deeply embraced.

The disease undermined her health with a progressive assault on her swallowing. When she choked on food or drink, she aspirated food particles and fluids into her lungs essentially obscuring her ability to convert air to oxygenated blood. She lost weight. She refused to consider a feeding tube. In time she fashioned her own daily routine, and their new normal became a horrific distortion of their lives a short two years before.

On Monday, August 20th, a day after their 40th Wedding Anniversary, Lauren told Walt that she was having trouble breathing, and he took her to the hospital where she spent the night. The next morning, they enrolled in hospice and returned home. She wrote him: *"I do not want to die in the hospital; I am getting tired of trying to breathe."*

Lauren became connected to oxygen through a fifty foot plastic hose which gave her slack to walk about the entire house, even walk up the stairs, despite Walt's pleas that she stay on the ground floor. She just smiled and took another step. Still, within two weeks, her mobility slowed, she slept more frequently and for longer periods. The hospice nurse introduced morphine to ease her coughing spasms.

Her time in a haze began to grow, and as her body failed, sleep became a comfort to which she willingly surrendered. Their son Rob, close enough to travel, came to be with them both.

On the morning of September 1, at 7:20 a.m., Walt awoke from the trundle alongside her bed, where he was sleeping with their dog, Wendy. Her cat, Peter Pan, had snuggled between her feet through the night. Now, he touched Lauren's arm, and it felt cool, though not unusually so. He looked for respiration and did not see any. He felt for pulse and did not find one. He touched her neck and it was not cold, and he checked again for pulse and respiration, he did not find any.

She was gone, perhaps having just left, but no longer with him, nor Wendy, nor Peter Pan. In the days that followed, he tried to reconstruct her life, to see how it fit into his own, to identify her abilities, challenges, and successes and define her core accomplishment. Then, in her writings he found that she had answered his question.

"I was *raised when society sent women home to rear their young. I have never quite made the full transition to super woman, beautifully balancing full time job with hearth and home. Bearing my babies and raising them was the one thing I know I did well. In a world full of 'should have done' my now grown men and woman are my one clear 'been there and done that'.*"

He looked at their children, saw how much of her had surfaced in their attitudes, accomplishments, and successes, noted her core values reflected in varying degrees within their personalities and sighed. She was right, he knew, but he remembered her too for her late-in-life emergence as her own person. As artist, journalist, and equestrian, she layered those accomplishments over the growth of their children and brought her innate strength and wisdom to the friction points in their marriage. Her life quilt, a mosaic of panels complementing one another captured the larger full picture of a life so well lived.

Walt retreated into long silences and privacy, wondering exactly how he was supposed to feel, almost curious about what came next. He didn't feel that his world had ended, but rather that his future had become a jig-saw puzzle, and he didn't have a lot of interest in putting it together. He would wait. Just wait and see what happened. God, he would miss her smile.

The Millenium

It arrived as planned by forces larger than himself, and it coincided with changes forged by natural law. Walt saw Lauren leave for the heavens while he continued to muck about the earth. It was a time to reflect, to review all that had been, to address the millennium. That he did was good news in its own way, but emotional pain and loss infused his body in ways that he did not expect, could not have imagined. He survived, scarred by the fragility of life, emboldened by the fact that he awakened each day ready to live that which might come, unable to see even its outline.

He collapsed on the Sixth Hole of a local nine hole golf course, breath suddenly short, heart rate pounding and escalating, legs weak, unable to walk to the clubhouse. Panic Attack? Unlike any others. For 15 minutes he lay on a nearby bench hoping that somehow the heart would stabilize. It slowed, but he was unable to leave. A passerby looked at him, and he motioned him over and asked for a ride back up to his car. From there he drove himself to Urgent Care. Quickly seen, diagnosed with something called Atrial Fibrillation and sent to the hospital, he spent the night, converted to normal rhythm and went home. A calling card?

He recovered, received instruction on how to deal with this syndrome, and set out to live his days in ways that pleased him and let him escape the crumbled sadness of his life. Unwilling to hold responsibility for dogs, cats, family or friends, he began to travel, sampling the European continent, making a great circuit through the Far West and finally, in a thoughtful convulsion, he shed ties to Wisconsin in favor of California. California! A state once rejected, now embraced not for what it offered, but for the person who resided there. In the haphazard world of the internet, he met again a high school classmate, one whom he didn't recall ever speaking to during those four years of adolescence. They married.

He found emotional stability, a new sense of maturity, gently prescribed limits and at the same time economic comfort. He felt free to create, working with professional musicians to set music to his lyrics, sometimes writing his own melodies and then producing two albums which gave him a product that felt good to hold and to play.

Later, when Walt began reflecting on his life, he began to write and found his experiences not far from the norm. He wrote about the same game that everyone plays, *Life,* and he created fictional events and characters that were honest reflections of his time and place on earth, an accounting so to speak, that might provide him with a narrative to hold to the end, and perhaps, in its own way, jog the thoughts of others and their own reviews of life.

He learned that when one starts looking back, making sense, giving meaning to people, events and change that once seemed inchoate, one is doing what almost everyone does. They may not write their review, but they construct one in their mind, fortifying their soul. He reconciled himself to exceptionalism in others by saying that "In most things, I am better than most people, but I am not the best at anything." Walt felt comfortable with that self-assessment.

Years pass in real time and in fictional time. Characters whom we have met and known in varying degrees of intimacy during our lives sometimes show up again, sometimes never reappear. Where, Walt often asked, is Donald Gifford? He would like to see him again. What ever became of June McDermott? Did Tom Grant have a good life?

So it is with fictional personalities, and he could now appreciate a writer's comment that he sometimes wonders where his characters will take him. They go where they want, and one tries to stay with them and keep the reader interested. Barry Swanson and Peggy had strong, lengthy life-spans, and figured prominently in first one story, then another and another. Hard to let them go.

Sensing his own timeline, Walt needed to let his characters slip into their last stages. Did they decline in disaster or become settled with success as they took their final step in life. Bittersweet reality best reflects the truth of a long life, he thought. Most often, but not always, integrity rather than despair, resonates within a last look at self and permits one to conclude that a life, however spent, has been well-lived.

Most of the characters moving through these psychological stages, successfully resolved their challenges. It surprised him how entwined many of their lives remained after decades of misuse, sometimes abuse. A friend once said to him, "Hey, Walt, what if you looked at some of these characters toward the end of their lives. What would you find?" He looked, and this is what he found.

Let's Do Lunch

She was lying. Barry Swanson hoped that he was wrong but no, she was lying. Just another question, "Want to get some lunch?" and the response equally casual, "No, ... I think I'll just work through today."

Rejection didn't give him pause. Her voice did. He detected a slight difference in her usual tone, noted an almost imperceptible hesitancy as she searched for words that should have been flowing. He heard the slightest idiom of distance. This day, he didn't believe her, and he had to be able to trust her...had to.

After his divorce, Swanson spent time trying to reconstruct his core, trying to sort through the women who brought him to this lonely island. Many blurred faces paraded through his mind as he undertook the process of forgetting forgettable women. His restlessness grew, his sexual energy waned and he abandoned the art of cultivating meaningless partners. Without his wife Adair, cut off from his children, he tottered between listlessness and his barely reachable anger toward the police informer who had ruined his life.

Then he found Amanda Kingsley.

He first met her at a local "Share IT" gathering in Boulder, she of average height, brunet hair, but eyes that glittered in humor and a shape obscured by professional dress. Her smile, flashing in conversation, genuinely opened her sense of humor to an observer, and yet kept her one good arms-length away from any jokester, gossip or client. Swanson didn't know quite why he began to circle around her, but she exuded a friendliness that he had missed in his other passing relationships. He began his pursuit. Three months of casual contacts, inadvertent (to her) meetings outside her office building on Pearl Parkway, easy conversation, gently suggestive, kidding, innocent luncheon invitations finally led her to share a meal with him.

She had time for a drive through Burger King, and they chatted, covering life in general while touching on relationships more specifically. Swanson assessed her with all of his knowledge, experience and skill. Was she interested? Two more drive-through chat sessions persuaded him that it was worth a risk.

They sat quietly in a booth at the *Troubadour* and Swanson promised her three things: she would not get pregnant; he would not see any other women; he would feed her well. He asked only one thing, and he made it very, very clear. Apart from her husband, she would see no other man. Rejection he could accept but not betrayal.

Quietly, delicately, thoughtfully, she did not say no, and when he took her back to work, he felt that they were now on a path to that unpredictable abyss that he loved so well. Two decades younger than he, she seemed the most unlikely of any romantic partner he could have imagined. She was professionally correct, socially congenial and focused on her career. Yet, she did not say no.

Did he seduce her or was it the reverse?

She took control and kept it. She rarely spoke of her marriage and controlled their affair with a sophistication which left him intensively attentive. He became assiduous in searching her mood, her inclination, her hints. He wanted never to miss a cue. Even as he noted his own vulnerability, he searched her look, her smile, her words, their tone to see if she would admit him once again. He simply could not stop obsessing about her.

Once allowed into her private world, he found a woman with intense sexual curiosity, deeply honed edges of passion, explosive releases and a way of filling his heart that he had found in no other. Cool, thoughtful, correct, polite, and in public well presented with a gentle sense of humor, in her privacy she melted metal, provoked deep breaths with active hands that breathed life into every naked pore. Her bawdy sense of humor would have startled even close friends. Swanson rejoiced in his fulfillment, embarrassed by his earlier amateurish seduction of young freshman coeds.

He invested his feelings in Amanda so deeply, kept attuned to her moods so closely, pondered her every utterance so thoughtfully that his life became consumed by his constant search for another beguiling smile, another look, another rendezvous. Her guilt surfaced irregularly, sometimes exhausting him, but he never wearied of losing himself in her arms, in her passion. She never offered him anything she did not deliver, and she never realized how bitterly he would punish betrayal.

They stole days and nights during her professional travel. In between, they lunched privately in his car, occasionally at a downtown restaurant, or they took drives up to Estes Park and just absorbed an afternoon. There was no talk of divorce, no future implied nor pictured. Each day they stole an hour provided food for the next. Each week built upon the last, strengthened her grip on his spirit. So far, he had heard only truth.

But today, she had said no, she would just work through lunch, and he did not believe her. Five minutes later, he was in his car, driving six blocks across town and parking where he could see the entry/exit to her office building on the Parkway. He waited.

A small group walked through the doors out into the courtyard. She wasn't there, and he began to relax. Blouses and shirts, white patterns, yellow decorations and blue panels created a small mosaic of motion. A crisp day, he began to enjoy the patterns of muddled clouds promising showers, delivering sunshine. Another group passed, and he began to think how silly this was, and then, out she came.

If she were leaving, she wasn't working through lunch. A few more yards and she went into a nearby sandwich shop, and within five minutes she was out again, with foodstuffs in hand and a direct bead in her stride.

She crossed the street and walked along the edge of a public parking lot paved with asphalt, a hard and today a particularly stark black surface filled with cars. He started his own, went forward slowly, almost dizzy with a sense of lost control. He turned into the lot, saw her with food in hand as she ducked through an already opened door and settled herself beside the driver. Who was this guy she was lying for? When they pulled out of the lot and turned left, he let them clear his sightline and followed.

The car, an old, square Honda with conspicuously drab orange paint and black trim, moved along at a steady pace, cleared three signal lights then headed toward Whipple Park. He followed at a distance, deep and heavy breathing filling his chest in uneven gasps while his hands shook, gripped the steering wheel, clenched it hard. His thoughts ricocheting, he struggled to accept what he now knew as truth. She had betrayed him!

When they parked, he stopped some distance back, left his car on the edge of the green retreat and walked up the road, noting that trees and shrubs, along with the slight elevation of the land, made it possible for him to crouch and creep unseen along the south side of their rendezvous. Challenging work. Stalking taxed his aging muscles, but he stayed low and slow. Was he a lion in the bush or just a voyeur seeking a vantage point? In another minute, he saw the Honda. He crept more deeply along the road, then entered some shrubbery that concealed him from view and on hands and knees gradually made his way forward until he was behind them.

He was too far away to hear their voices. He crept closer, as might the lion, to the next line of shrubs, then to the next. He reflected briefly at how this might look to a biker passing by, an older man on hands and knees moving in concealed foliage in broad daylight. A voyeur? Too bad. He had to know what they were saying.

Finally less than ten yards from the car, its windows open, he could hear every word. Small talk. Easy pauses in conversation. He watched her arm raise and lower, observed their body posture, their gestures, the tilt of their heads. He listened for words, intonation, pauses, smiles, leanings and language. They ate and spoke in ordinary terms. Nothing happening here. It was a first date, but still, she had lied.

Soon, they would be leaving, the circular drive taking them by his parked car. He made his way back and left. Confused, unable to digest what he knew, he turned to the one close person he could talk to about this. Chip Dieterich, his insurance agent, had stood by him throughout his divorce from Adair, offered him counsel and some perspective, kept his spirits intact as he went through police interrogations and finally dismissal from College of the Rockies. Out of pity, he supposed, Chip even fixed him up with a small insurance company where Swanson's language skills seduced clients instead of coeds.

When he first told him about his involvement with Amanda, Chip just said, "You poor bastard. You're going to regret this." Nothing more. Now, Swanson needed more, and Chip, who worked only three miles away, could help.

He saw Swanson's face and knew there was trouble. Jumbled conversation spilled out of both of them.

"Amanda's in Whipple Park with another man!"

Chip smiled, "In broad daylight, having sex?"

"No! She lied to me, said she was working through lunch, and now I find her with this guy."

"She lies to her husband. What makes you so special."

"I trusted her!"

"A mistake. Look, Barry, are you sure she is with another man?"

"Yes, they're eating lunch, chatting...MY GOD! I'm too old for this. She's cheating on me!"

"How do you know this?"

"I followed her."

"Why would you do that?"

"I didn't trust the sound of her voice."

"Really? Have you been lighting up today? How could you know a lie from the sound of her voice?"

"I listen to her words more carefully than a prisoner listening to a judge's sentence, and no, I have not been smoking pot."

"Who is he Barry?"

"Don't know."

"Where are they now?"

"On the way back from Whipple Park. He's going to drop her off in the parking lot."

"Which lot?"

"Next to the pizza house where she works."

"What color is the car?"

"Orange."

"Did you get a license plate?"

"No."

"Stay here, I'll be right back."

Within twenty minutes, Chip returned and he had information: license plate recorded, drop off confirmed, and a reported smile to "him" as she left. Who is he? Chip didn't know but he did know a guy in DMV who could trace the license plate.

Chip sent him home with the comment, "Talk to you tomorrow."

Alone, Swanson worked at controlling his evolving rage. He had warned her...

Chip walked into his office the next day and reported. "I know who he is and where he lives. I know how they met."

All this from a license plate? Well, Chip said, once he had the guy's name from the DMV, he could figure out the rest. The dude worked for her company in IT. There was techie work going on in her office. His home address, public record. He was married.

Swanson, stunned, lurched into his chair, bruising his hip as he dropped around the corner of his desk.

"Who is he?" he asked.

"Name's Carleton Wheeler. Mean anything to you?"

"No," Swanson whispered.

"What do you want to do?" Chip asked.

Acid sloshed through Swanson' arteries. After all their times together, the intimacy, the joy, the deep confidences, cities seen, landscaped vistas...all that and now this. Unacceptable!

"I want to fucking destroy her."

"There is a way," Chip began calmly, "but it would be irrevocable, a total, immediate severance of the relationship. There would be no going back.

"What?" Swanson asked, "Tell her husband?"

"No," Chip explained, "That would probably just get you killed."

"What then?" Swanson asked, and Chip explained slowly and in detail what could be done.

In all the years of his weaving in and out of the lives of women, Swanson had never confronted this dilemma. How could he hurt her enough to satisfy his need for revenge, ease the pain of betrayal and still leave open a path to reconciliation? If he revealed what he had learned and how he had learned it, she might indeed re-pledge herself to him, but would that only be a strategy to ease the danger of his outrage? If she stayed with him, even for a time, out of fear, what did he have to love? How could he bask in the attentions of a woman held hostage? Where was the joy in that?

Chip's solution to his lust for vengeance teased him, resonated with his deep hurt and anger, compelled him to think of life without Amanda knowing that it was she who violated their intimacy, but he who would end any hope of retaining it. Could he abide a reconciliation? Once betrayed, shame on her. Twice betrayed, shame on him. He thought some more, looked at Chip and said, "Do it".

Chip picked up the phone, placed a handkerchief over the speaker, dialed, and when Wheeler picked up, Chip, in a deep base distortion of his voice delivered his message: *"This you need to know: Amanda Kingsley has an STD. I saw you with her yesterday in Whipple Park. I like your wife and I won't place her at risk. If I see you with Amanda again, I will let her know what you are doing. Is this clear?"* There was a pause, and then Wheeler said, "OOOOHHHHHHHHH O.K."

Wheeler was done; Amanda was done. Chip asked, "Are you done?" Swanson paused, "I don't think so...no, I am not." He reflected briefly on the many women he had cheated despite his pledged commitments, and gave passing thought to the recognition that it must have hurt them, maybe more than he knew, and he remembered the old cliché, "Hell hath no fury like a woman scorned." To it, he added his own extension, "... or a man betrayed". Still devastated, he had yet another dose of bitters to administer to Amanda.

Two days later, he appeared at her home just before she left for a Denver work session on computer networking. He told her that he had received a phone call from an anonymous person who reported that she had spent a lunch hour at Whipple Park with a guy from IT. He described the liaison in detail. She looked at him, paused and said, "I'm sorry. I'm really, really sorry."

"Sorry isn't good enough," he responded, and he walked directly out the door.

Her day already scripted, she left shortly after, backing out of the garage, turning slowly and then as though finally decided, moving smartly through the neighborhood.

Swanson, parked down the street, watched her leave. Returning, he took the house key from its nook, went in and walked straight to her bedroom. He opened drawers, found the box, took a handful of condoms and placed them in her husband's office alongside pictures, on the writing surface. When he saw them, Amanda would be far away. Let her explain those, bitch.

Swanson returned to his office saturated with satisfaction. An hour later, he was not so sure. Her husband might not be interested in explanations, only information. A hearty hunter with many a rifle, his inquiries might focus only on finding Swanson. He grew nervous. Finally, he called the workshop and left a message for Amanda to contact him when she checked in. Family emergency he said.

A half hour later, the phone rang.

"What do you want?"

Swanson told her of the condom dispersal, "You probably want to tidy them up before your husband gets home."

"Are you going to do the right thing?"

"What's that?"

Swanson knew what she would ask next, joyous in the dilemma she faced. She always met a professional obligation. Now, she would have to leave one to save her marriage.

"Are you going to go back to the house and clean up the room?"

He paused, then quietly said, "No".

Early the following week, as he returned from lunch, she came walking across the parking lot. He liked that. She smiled. He melted. Without speaking, they returned to his office. Door shut, wordlessly, they began quietly searching one another for reassurance, for a physical release which would somehow close the emotional void between them. Voices on the other side of his office wall told him that it was going to be a very, very quiet reconciliation, or whatever it was that was going on.

When they dressed, she said, "I don't know what this means."

Swanson murmured, "What are you thinking?"

She smiled, paused, as she turned to leave, "I just don't know. Let's do lunch."

He smiled back, took one full, hard look at her face, grabbed a memory of that light scent she always wore and filed it away.

Finally, he answered, "Let's not."

A month later, Swanson moved to Denver.

Three Little Pigs

The first little piggy went to market; the next little piggy stayed home; the last little piggy whined "me, me, me" and cried in its room.

"She did it, Walt, she did it!" Jay blurted the news with a rising tone of excitement and satisfaction.

"Who is she? What did she do?"

"Dooling! She finally confessed to her whole operation...I can't believe it...my God, she actually confessed."

"What about the others?" Walt asked.

"They are done I guess. Smithers and Gong for sure. The only question is whether they'll go to jail or just hide in their homes."

"I'd like to say I'm sad to hear this, Jay," Walt said smiling, "I would really like to say that...but I can't. I'm ecstatic! Tell Billy Bob!" Jay savored the moment, cracked a big smile, smashed his fist into his other hand and they both began laughing... thought about it all with little tidbit reminders...laughed some more. It was quite a morning, and Jay reminded him again that he had it right when everyone else thought he was dreamily paranoid about those three. Boy, did he have it right!

****

285

Jay knew them all, liked two of them. Mostly, they amused him. Properly stated, theirs was a story of academic misbehavior written in the columns of the local newspaper and whispered in the hallways of the university. But who cares about university skeletons except university grave-diggers? Jay did. He found their stories amusing, food for fiction indeed, but in the end, gloriously corrupt.

Carl Smithers, Alice Gong and Doris Dooling entered the Economics Department in the early 90's and each brought a backstory full of warnings, alerts mostly overlooked, and for that the college paid dearly. Smithers, a failed professional baseball player who spent five seasons with the Des Moines Ducks came to the department via a series of failures. He could pitch, but not well enough. He could hit, but not consistently. He teetered back and forth between AA and AAA ball, but he never made it to the majors. His greatest asset was a resilient arm. He never missed a start.

His final appearance was a 5 inning shelling by the Davenport Darts. As he walked into the dugout, his manager, E.Z. Knudson, asked him a question, "Smithers, I hear you are pretty smart, could even go to college. Is that true?" Smithers paused, as he wrapped his glove around his hand and placed it on his hip, "Yep, I guess I could." E.Z. paused, then said in a voice that carried the length of the bench, "Then go."

Smithers found college a lot more welcoming than hitters. In three years, he had a B.A. He needed to try three different graduate schools before he found one that matched his skill set and earned a PhD in short order. His dissertation analyzed the quality of major league bats, recommending oak as much preferred over maple. When he joined the department, he continued his interest in wood. Fascinated with the forests of Wisconsin, he began a study of the correlation between urban development and lumber landings at five Mississippi

River cities. It may have sounded like a needlessly narrow focus, but it kept him busy.

Married, and happily so by all accounts, he seemed respectful of all his senior professors, and they in turn took a liking to him. He played softball, published occasionally, and though quiet, or was it pompous, effectively managed his classroom. Most of all, he showed loyalty. Jay always thought that was the secret to his early success. He voted the right way, and he did it without prompting. His major flaw? He bored students, but then economics *was* boring.

Unexciting but serviceable, in tune with department curriculum and uninterested in challenging anyone anywhere, Carl finally made it through screening for a tenure track appointment and the department recommended him to the dean.

Jay thought that Kimberly Raft, Director of Affirmative Action, would approve Smithers, but no, she asked the department to do another search. Jay always regarded her postures as unreasonable, the sum of the arrhythmia of affirmative action goals favoring the ethnic flavor of the month. Perhaps a black, lesbian, Muslim woman who spoke Hindi and Arabic would have satisfied her, but, for now, it would not be Smithers.

The second member of the emerging troublesome, tiresome trio was Alice Gong. A Quaker and a glowing product of missionary parents (Chinese father and Pennsylvania Quaker mother) she remained an only child, her parent's commitment to China's One Child Policy. Raised in Shanghai, she became a brilliant amalgam of both biological and cultural diversity.

Fluent in five languages, including Mandarin Chinese, French, and Japanese, Alice charmed no one but captured everyone.

Jay never could figure out if she understood politics, but she got by, and the department warmly embraced her. She filled an academic need. Pleasant and married, she had a ready smile, a gentle manner and was as shapely as a Chinese consort.

Her research compared the Caribbean slave trade to the Chinese Opium market. While Westerners had finally become sensitized to the inhumanity of slavery, they were relatively ignorant of the Chinese Opium cloud, and Alice educated her students with the quiet certitude of one who had seen an opium den, smelled its rot, and counted the bodies.

She traced the sale of slaves in the Caribbean to the British and the marketing of opium to the Chinese to the corporate coffers of English institutions such as the India Tea Company and the Shipbuilders of the Quay. She made it clear that Britain defended both trade markets with its navy, and while slavery did not survive the 19th century, the opium business flourished until the time of Mao.

Jay thought her writings illustrated a broad swath of information, corruption, immorality, greed, lust and politics. An Irishman himself, Jay certainly never objected when the British looked corrupt as they did in the context of her research. But Alice didn't worry about appearances, and she tidily sampled, digested and revealed the sins of two centuries. It was good, precise work.

For Kimberly Raft, Alice Gong was a prayer answered. Who could represent diversity better than an Asian in Quaker clothing, and she did it with total conviction. Alice and her husband, King, lived in two different cities, an increasingly modern adaptation to the entry of women into the professions.

They hoped to unite as their careers developed, but there wasn't much opportunity for him in a small college town when his business focused on the delivery of North Carolina ash furniture to a dozen Midwest cities. Jay saw him once when he wandered into the building, but a year later, they were quietly divorced, and Alice, perhaps as a consequence, became a shallow, embittered woman.

Jay never heard King Gong mentioned again. Alice's thin lips began to mirror the line of a closed clam, and her face, rouged circles on each cheek, froze when she walked. It was a tidy, rapid walk--- clickity-click, clickity-click, clickity-click--- but each step echoed anger, suggested hate. In less than a year, she became the student's Inquisitor, and the department's Chinese puzzle. It would have shed her immediately, but Kimberly Raft would not hear of it.

Finally, there was Doris Dooling. Without question, Doris was the Economic Department's third mistake. She had been raised for a few years by Comanche Indians who found her abandoned at the side of a watering hole near Santa Fe, New Mexico. They named her, "Mouth-That-Whines" and at age ten, the tribe dumped her on the Dooling's front porch.

While a white woman, she presented Indian features, excelled at sign language, specialized in mixed messages, and never saw anything someone else had that she did not want to take for herself. A commitment from her was slippery to get and impossible to hold and her appetite for more money seemed insatiable. As an economist, she referred to this hunger as "elastic selection" which could not be priced into the daily marketplace.

The personnel committee, warned that she seemed unusually focused and ambitious, also heard that she was highly unpredictable. But she charmed in person, a peppy little mouth specializing in the mixed flows of Indian trade throughout the Comanche Empire. Unknown to the department, she also conducted research in the social economics of condoms.

This peculiar topic sounded ludicrous to those who idly chatted with her about the subject. But Doris argued that serious, distinctive differences existed in the market appeal of condoms, and that manufacturers could benefit from her research in planning their advertising messages. When asked what these features provided, she spun herself into a long, scratchy throated review of the range of inelasticity in condoms, variations in their color, texture, the grade of lubricants, the depth of reservoir tips, even the ease of ripping open a package designed to facilitate a smooth slide of protection.

How she collected data, no one was quite sure, but Jay found the whole subject fascinating and busied himself from time to time learning how she built her information base. She worked, he told Walt, with three different communities: Hmong, Black and Cuban. She kept consumer preferences on her own internet server.

Still, as Jay learned more about her prickly attitudes toward politics and her smothering protection of her condom research, he also came to recognize that her classroom teaching found an attentive audience among men and women alike, and she quickly eclipsed Carl and Alice by many powers of review. Popular, busy, investigative, she flourished in the eyes of the dean because he knew he could influence her views on political issues important to him. Jay, who essentially protected the department's interests college wide, warned Walt that she could be a problem.

In the mystifying ways that universities operate, both Alice and Doris were hired as tenure-track members, while

Carl continued to linger in his role as an academic staff appointment, vulnerable each year to the swirling winds of politics and change. Finally, the department made a commitment to him, fought Kimberly Raft for six months and won. No one should have been more appreciative of the effort than Carl himself. He wasn't, and Jay, to his own great surprise, saw Smithers' posture rise and his temperament flare.

So, there they were, the three of them, two women and a man, all now tenure track candidates, the future of the economics department, and the core of its young faculty. They were different in so many ways, but in the end, they allied in an effort to destroy those who created them.

In 1996, Walt became chair of the venerable department of sad statistics and took comfort in the academic progress of these three youngsters, the raw material of faculty growth. He noted that while senior members continued to cultivate Smithers-Gong-Dooling, they hired four other new PhDs who were on tenure-track careers of their own. Jay and Walt now looked forward to new times when young scholars could take over governance and lead the department into its future.

Walt served out his term, increasingly weary with the finicky business of finding promotions for the youngsters and appalled at the way deans and other toady's fished for trouble in department business. Finally finished with the heavy lifting, he and the venerable "old guard" of the department decided to let the Millenium bless a new generation of leadership.

They admired the selection of Carl Smithers as the new chair, Then, as Jay liked to remind them, they made the terrible mistake of stepping aside to see how the department would fare. Disastrous!

Within six months, Smithers had bonded with Dooling and his quiet ways resonated with Gong. The three set out to refashion the Economics Department into an elitist collection of esoteric scholars. Smithers believed that the department should narrow its curriculum, curtail its enrollments and concentrate on serious students. To re-orient the curriculum, he needed to prune back faculty positions and refashion the jobs that remained. His targets were the same non-tenured faculty who had helped elect him, and he made it clear that he intended to send them packing.

Without resistance, he leveraged his position with selective favors amidst cries for help that began to surface in the hallways. The elastic clause which had argued in favor of expanding a structure whereby the young governed themselves, contracted as senior professors realized that this permission had produced academic cannibalism. There was little market demand for that.

Jay was the first to see the truth. "Smithers has turned into Ted Bundy and he has two camp followers. We need to do something." Jay asked for a month to make some inquiries, then came back with the perfect marketing plan, a product nicely placed between murder and whining: academic destruction.

While he and Walt went about their business in alerting senior faculty, their friend Billy Bob Pincher worked on the threatened youngsters with the stealth of a B-2 Bomber. The three of them aimed to remove Smithers and pound him, Alice Gong and Doris Dooling into harmless, voiceless colleagues. Billy Bob reassured the non-tenured people that their jobs could be protected. He reaffirmed the freedom of faculty to speak without reprisal. He canvassed the threatened and the tepid and found them pliable even as Jay ignited a fringe fire of criticism about Gong, Dooling, and Smithers within the Faculty Senate.

Walt challenged department meeting agendas and used the votes that Billy Bob gathered to reject Smithers' efforts to re-staff the department, and set their sights on eliminating the influence of those they came to call the Toilet Troika.

Jay quoted an old Chinese saying: "Removing the snake from the garden, does not keep you safe; you must kill the snake." Walt thought that sounded a little extreme, but there was nothing gentle about what followed.

For the chair, Carl Smithers, they attacked his data. He had been tracking Mississippi lumber landings between 1870 and 1895. A midnight search of his office discovered a surprising cache of pictures of Smithers and Alice Gong and left a hard drive irretrievably corrupted. Jay personally delivered the pictures to the local paper with notes about the cross-cultural product of Nixon's visit to China.

Unlike the social tolerance accorded Chancellors who escorted their mistresses to public events, the Carl/Alice link drew deep community gasps. They were seen together, frequently conversing in quiet tones, and were a recognized duo at all major conferences. What Jay didn't know about Smithers and Gong, Billy Bob did, and the gossip grew warmer and more damaging. It surprised even Walt, and he could feel public pressure restructuring the department.

They didn't have to do much with Alice Gong. She pretty much self-destructed. Each week, it seemed, her lips grew tighter still, and at semester break, she took a sudden flight to Chongquing, then extended her absence into a semester's leave. No one seemed to miss her. She returned, but her spirit remained on the Yangtze River, stored in one of the hanging coffins tucked in the cliffs that lined the tempestuous waterway.

Upon her return, anxiety became her bed partner (did she miss King Gong?), and Smithers had to spend more and more time simply calming her down. Jay always snickered when Alice began stomping her foot, shaking her head so that her hair wobbled atop her scalp. Usually, he knew that syndrome would be followed by an uncharacteristic scream, a slammed door and some pounding on furniture. Smithers grew weary. Alice spent more and more time at home, teaching classes then fleeing campus.

For Doris Dooling, Jay had a special observation. "She is ambitious; she seeks promotion; she seeks more money; she is tiresome and whiny; she is untrustworthy." Walt agreed, noting that she said loudly and often that she didn't see why she had to stand in line to get more pay. He explained to her that as she rose in rank, she would increase her salary, but she didn't buy that.

Jay discovered that she had busily filled her bank account with money from her reservoir business, condoms. She began accumulating a large, varied supply in her office, selling them to students and faculty alike, charting consumer reports, adjusting brands to suit the needs of her clients.

Jay leaked anonymous reports to the press that her research involved interactions with three different cultures---Hmong, Black and Cuban---residing in the City, a mere 20 miles away. Doris said that she tried to determine latex use in each population group, and denied intimate involvement of any kind. Moreover, she had data.

Her research showed that Blacks did not use condoms and thus created a widespread pool of genetically varied offspring who had few resources and unknown parentage. This could be helpful in building budgets for welfare mothers, she noted.

Hmong, she reported, were sporting in their use of latex, preferring colors, surface undulations and large tip reservoirs. Their women were insistent on protection, and their population lineage was stable. They had little demand for public health assistance.

Cubans were very clever. They bought condoms in bulk, used what they needed, sold the rest for profit and used the money to improve their collection of clothing, cigars and well-kept women. They looked wonderful in their linen shirts, flowing pants and loose-gaited walks. Self-supporting, they didn't reproduce, and they helped reduce unwanted pregnancies.

Dooling's research yielded four articles with her byline, but Jay's investigation revealed two abortions to her genetic line and documented her privately held company online. She was marketing a new condom, the "Drooling Dooling", and as the department revealed her "back story" her career shrunk dramatically. The dean cut off her travel account. Her hopes for advancement in administration vanished. Her husband left for the Rockies, looking for the remnants of the Comanche tribe who had found her. He kiddingly said that he offered to trade her back in return for three good horses, but they offered only a burro.

The Economics Department, now ready for the election of its chair, became a hallway of rumors, gossip and quiet revolution. As balloting drew close, Smithers began to do some lobbying, and he seemed to gain a positive response. No one alerted him to the impending disaster, and he continued to ply his message of professional leadership, offering wholesale replacement of his colleagues as his policy.

On the eve of the department vote, he received a package in a plain, brown wrapper, postmarked Denver, Colorado. Tipped by an anonymous caller, the local police confiscated and opened it to find a large quantity of marijuana. Smithers had no clue as to its source, but its arrival leveled the *coup de gras* on his career. Jay, never sure why Smithers wanted to destroy himself, happily watched his embarrassed retreat behind a closed door.

The dean counted the ballots three times, amazed but by now relieved, at the results. A sitting chair now stood rejected by a vote of 17-5. The turnover complete, peace settled into the department and Jay brought skill and reputation to his new role as chair of the department. Walt was glad to see it. At his age, he was happy to teach his classes and count his money.

Smithers spent a year trying to blow away clouds of suspicion about his data base and possible black-market pot distribution. He stayed out of jail, barely, lost his wife to divorce and failed at promotion. Finally, as was his style, he left for another job in a different market.

Alice Gong, nearly housebound upon her return from China, developed a severe case of dysentery, became even thinner and angrier until her increasingly frail body began to creak with calcium deficiency. She placed herself under medical care and remained under observation for six months. When she returned, she found new academic worlds to heal her wounds, finally developing a new field of study: *The Economics of Unilateral American Disarmament*. She never smiled again.

Doris Dooling, between abortions in the pursuit of various flaws in her condom selections, cried a lot in her room, pausing only to ask Smithers before he left, "What went wrong?"

"I never could hit a curve ball," he muttered, "and I just didn't see it coming."

She wailed some more as was her wont, and the squeals could be heard throughout the building. Poor Doris. She had no red shoes that she could click and her specialty products were full of the holes of revelation.

Well into the spring, satisfied with their skillful skewering of academic enemies, Walt and Billy Bob sat with Jay on his screen porch, reviewing over sips of wine perhaps their greatest professional victory. Eliminating Smithers and his ilk from power had so many satisfactions it kept them telling stories all afternoon. They wondered if the old bulls of their youth felt the same way about them as they felt about Smithers, Gong and Dooling.

"Maybe so," Billy Bob murmured, "but they seemed to have a knack for shooting themselves in the foot."

"Bang, bang!" Jay chortled, "Let me know when it's time to practice my aim again."

"All in good time, I am sure, all in good time," Walt laughed. They all laughed.

Stain the Earth

Denver had a new citizen, a transplant from Boulder who liked to charm women and dismiss men. He taught English at night for the Air Force, earning a living but not a life, and he was bitter. He cursed the unknown person who tipped his name to the police as a suspect in the Jon Benet Ramsay murder, a false but devastating accusation.

Inquiries cleared him of the crime but convicted him of philandering, and the fallout destroyed his marriage, voided his college lecture appointment and fractured his emotional stability. He became rootless, selling insurance out of a tiny suite located in the alley entrance of a 90 year old building.

Only the attentions of his friend, Chip Dieterich, kept him from disappearing into the streets. Then, an intense affair with Amanda Kingsley gave him that electric thrill essential for his sense of well-being, and when she betrayed him he left Boulder, sinking into a lethargy which saw him put on an extra 20 pounds. For weeks now, he had muddled through many nights of restless sleep trying to learn how he came to be viewed as litter in a city filled with landmarks.

He lived in a four bedroom boarding house, his daily life focused on retribution. Somewhere out there a tipster needed repayment, and he wrestled with strategies to reach out and short-circuit the life that had poisoned his own. His life empty, he welcomed the Millennial New Year with a drink, a prayer and a pledge. He would find the person who had destroyed him and then levy payback. William Gaddis had it wrong when he advised that *"You get justice in the next world."* Barry Swanson didn't intend to wait.

Weekly, he mentally reviewed all the evidence that the Boulder police offered to his defense attorney. The note, anonymously posted from Minneapolis, stumped forensics specialists. Nor could anyone seem to offer a motive for the false lead. Swanson found that the greatest puzzle of all. Why?

Why would someone do this to him? His social habits were common knowledge, and he doubted that they alone could provoke such a vicious attack. Why, given his long sexual history with coeds, did someone choose this moment to destroy him? When he had offended so many, how could he find the one person who actually levied retribution?

He began to sort through his predator past. His coed seductions over the past 30 years, mutually joined, executed with consent and severed with sociability, seldom rippled his life. Young women, away from home for the first time soon developed perspective on what he had to offer and broke off their relationship. He searched for an exception to the pattern, but he had trouble recalling any affair that ended badly.

He continued his mental review, finally making his way into the early 70's, a more distant past, but it had features to it that came easily to mind. Still teaching freshman English to young bodies, he relished his conquests, and while they took him away from his home life, his wife Ariel took no notice as she remained deeply absorbed in balancing pregnancy and childcare.

His mind suddenly paused. That word "childcare" brought him a new line of thought. Childcare and babysitters...he felt a clue.

Babysitters! Ariel needed help at a time when they had one child on her feet and another on the way. He remembered a special moment back then when he seduced a coed whom he had hired to help his wife. He remembered her pretty distinctly. A petite blonde freshman with lively eyes, cropped hair, and generous mouth, he found her smart, not particularly motivated, but smart. He caught her eye, she caught his attention, and the ritual began.

Even now, her memory still thrilled him a bit. He knew her to be captivated with his mind, caught up in a sexual dynamic completely new to her, but young and inexperienced, she carried a load of guilt about their affair. She loved the children, hated deceiving Ariel, and bonded to the rest of his family in a way completely distinct from her infatuation with him. Still, their connection lasted over a year, interrupted by the fallout from her broken engagement to a guy who had transferred from California to be with her.

Swanson paused and thought a bit more about this fellow. He had come a long way to marry his girlfriend, one cheating on him even as he proposed engagement. Swanson laughed a bit as he thought of the guy's innocent integrity. Committed to the blonde, the dupe hung around for almost a year trying to sort through a bramble of love thorns and misguided reassurances. Remarkable persistence.

For a moment, Swanson tried to put himself in the man's place...the embarrassment, anger, betrayal...hmmmm. That kind of emotional tumult could produce retribution, certainly, but the affair ended more than 25 years before the letter to the Boulder police. Who could carry a grudge so long and not act on it earlier? Not sure that the guy ever knew the truth about his girlfriend.

Oooohhhhh!

Maybe he found out. From whom? Only from the coed...that information could come only from the coed. What the hell was her name? He could not remember: Laura? Debbie? Lori? No....LouAnn? No. Something, first letter ...L.M.N.O.P... yes, P...Paula?...no...Peggy. Ah yes, Peggy! What if she had some contact with her fiancé after all these years? Maybe revisiting memories? True confessions might set things right between them, but they might also give her old boyfriend a reason to act. Plausible? Yes.

"Who is this guy?" Clearly, if he were right, Swanson had a target but finding the name would be a real challenge. He had seen him only once, a happenstance meeting at a political caucus some years later. Apparently happily married, in graduate school at CU, the guy appeared to be a little uncomfortable with the way that Swanson had looked at him.

A name? Interested in politics? He could check graduate student rosters for the 70's, see if a name popped out at him, maybe get a lead on where he currently lived...and then he could even the score.

He had a personal contact in C.U. Placement and over the course of the next two months he worked with her to sort through graduate candidates in history, political science and economics. He made a dozen trips to Boulder, fueling his heat for retribution with a personal, daily review of how much he had fallen, how much he had lost. Arrested without cause, his career destroyed, marriage wiped away, he wanted revenge.

Retribution...a modest enough goal, but until he knew this guy's name he could only grind anger against impotence and the resulting frustration sickened him. If he had to work with people who disdained him, he could do it. If his eyes grew watery as he worked through old written records, he would tolerate it. He wanted to find this guy. He had worked his way through four different programs in three departments, and then, suddenly, up popped: *Economics: Walt Farmer, PhD. 1976.*

As soon as he saw the name, he remembered him, and paused to savor his discovery. He now had a target, and the jerk would never see him coming. Records showed that Farmer had interviewed for a faculty position at three different schools. He eliminated Purdue right away, Washington University soon after. He checked faculty rosters for Wisconsin, sorted through various universities until he found him at a private school, Saint Clare College. Imagine that. The twit had managed a career, rose to be the Chair, Department of Economics. Swanson took a deep breath, felt his heart pound with pleasure, exhaled and took his secret home with him wondering what to do with College Boy Farmer.

He could bring him bodily harm. A few broken bones would make the message complete. He could threaten his wife and family, sewing terror in looming violence. He could plant false public rumors and let gossip mills torture Farmer's reputation.

Lots of possibilities. He had a target, and that alone stirred his bile, energized him. He plotted, planned, mentally executed various scenarios to their bitter end, yet even as he sorted through his strategies, he worried. He remembered an old Chinese proverb that his Dean used to quote: *When you seek vengeance, dig two graves.* Hmmmm. Whatever he did he wanted to be thinking clearly when he did it. He liked his freedom.

He rested, reflected, let his mind take some ease. He put Farmer on pause to savor from time to time and began to take another look at his boarding mates: Andy, Ernie and Frank. Curious as to why he knew so little about them when he saw them on a daily basis, he began to mull over their comings and goings. He thought them to be quietly idle fellows with empty minds and flapping pockets, but glances could deceive. He looked a little closer.

First, Andy. He saw him leave after an early boarding house breakfast every morning and return each evening without a crease in his clothes or a smudge on his face. Tall, full of smiles, but taciturn, his brown eyes warmed those around him without ever bringing them fully into view. Clean living seemed to be his controlling mantra. Never hungry, apparently without ambition, he seemed unconnected to regular earnings, and his Apple products seemed quietly out of place with the meagre paycheck he must earn. "How did he do this?" Swanson wondered?

The other two, Frank and Ernie, Frick N' Frack he named them, were identical thirtyish, blue-eyed twins whose conversation with one another seemed intuitive, indistinguishable. Never separated by school or employment, he found them brilliant in mind, bonded both by biology and circumstance, At mealtime, they could jointly spin a flawless narrative, exchanging sentences which never interrupted the subject or the tempo of the tale. They maintained excellent physical conditioning, ran occasional half-marathons and worked quietly through the week. Yet, he knew little about their working lives.

Swanson' days and most nights were free, and he decided to learn more about his housemates. One morning, he quietly tailed Andy's #24 bus in his car and followed it out Colfax to a complex of commercial buildings where Andy got off and entered enter a building advertising, *"Sam's Storage"*. That all seemed fine, but Swanson wondered how a clerk's paycheck supported Andy's techno-toys. Moreover, in a storage facility, how did he keep his clothes so clean. How did he remain so sharply groomed? Questions to be asked.

He then turned his attention to Frank, noting that he usually slept all day and worked somewhere at night, and Ernie just seemed to float in and out of the boarding house from day to day, going nowhere in particular? Losing sleep Swanson finally trailed Frank by car as he jogged an easy six miles to his job, working the night shift in a large, *United Moving* warehouse adjoining...of all places...*Sam's Storage*. Why the proximity? Why a warehouse? Why the graveyard work shift? At least he now knew how Frank trained for his marathons, but Swanson had questions.

What twin brother Ernie did seemed even more curious. His weekly activity took him all about Denver, and Swanson lost a few pounds trying to walk his pace and still stay hidden. Ernie and his backpack would enter a shopping center or a business building, then suddenly disappear. On occasion, he did none of these things and Swanson followed him to his day job. Where? To the same *Sam's Storage* where Andy clerked. Why? Why were both working the same job? Why the subterfuge? What the hell was going on?

Swanson puzzled it more. Clearly the three were connected to some kind of enterprise. Equally intriguing, their consistent efforts to melt into the city were well rehearsed and of long standing. For what? They weren't robbing banks, they weren't funding a fraudulent charity, and they weren't running a printing press. Indeed, they weren't living a very big lifestyle, but they were very careful about how they lived it.

He quit losing sleep following them around, regained 6 pounds from his nicely structured indolence, and sought out a new congeniality with the three of them. It took a few more weeks of gentle "hello, hi, good day, nice evening, good to see you" greetings, and then one day he just asked Andy what he did for a living.

Andy heard the question, paused and told Swanson that he would like to answer, but he needed to think about it. That put Swanson back on his heels...need to think about it? Why the mystery? Three days later, Andy renewed the conversation, "Swanson, what I do is pretty much a part of what Frank and Ernie do, and sharing information implicates you in something you know nothing about. Are you sure you want an answer?"

"Ah do," Swanson replied. A little knowledge can be a dangerous thing, he thought, but what the hell, his life felt pretty tiresome. Excitement might be a welcome change.

Andy paused again, and then began, "We raise pot. Everything we do supports our farming or keeps inquiring minds at bay. We're just local businessmen."

Swanson stammered an O.K. He really didn't know how to respond. Whatever the three were doing, it never entered his mind to think it criminal.

He said the obvious, "That's dangerous, Andy. You're dealing with irrational potheads and a whole lot of nasty people and it's illegal. How do you do it? Why are you doing it?"

"Well," Andy paused, "I could just say, 'we do it indoors', and 'we do it for the money', but if you really want to know the challenges, I can explain them to you. Your choice."

"Well, ah'd like to know it all" Swanson said, slipping into his southern accent a bit, and so Andy gave him a primer on raising pot.

"We grow it indoors," he said, "because it is still illegal and Colorado has a gang of wardens, along with choppers and hikers who can stumble on an outdoor 'grow'. Of course, our business model has problems of its own. It draws a lot of electricity to keep the lights on, so to speak, and it takes a lot of water to keep the plants healthy and productive. Both are usually supplied by public utilities and often, big consumption leads to bothersome inquiries. So, we had to figure out a way to evade utility billings."

"Well," Swanson murmured, "apparently you did it. But *Sam's Storage* just features bins. Where's the 'grow'?"

"So, you know where I work, eh?" Pause.

"I got curious," Swanson said.

Andy just smiled, and went on, "The front row of storage is available for rental. The rest of the 20,000 square feet is hidden behind the false front, and it holds our sunless garden. In it we store soil, nutrients, tools and hang our 'sunlight' lamps. We water our plants by timer, drain the run-off into holding tanks, then empty them by driving off road on some of the trails near Golden. We call it 'staining the earth'. I suspect locals would not like it," Andy laughed.

Swanson just looked at him. Silence. Then, "So, ah'm a little nervous here, Andy...how long have you been in this business, a dangerous business? Why tell me all of this?"

"Three years." Andy replied, "It's risky, but our trucks for *Sam's Storage* transport our product safely into the Boulder/Longmont area. We have a few network connections in Ft. Collins, but we leave Denver/Colorado Springs to really big dealers. So far, they tolerate us, and we don't go looking for trouble."

"The rest of the state is serviced by multiple tiny outdoor 'grows' that blend into forests, meadows and mountain parks. Sometimes those guys lose their gamble and when they do, the press makes it appear that burning a few bales of weed makes the world a safer place. I think life is better when everyone is mellow, stoned and fed, but that's not my call. I just make the pods available; everyone has to choose their own personal medicine," he smiled.

"As for you, we made inquiries long ago and know that you are not the law and that you might have contacts that could add to our Boulder network." Andy paused again, and went on, "We know that you taught there for many years. We also know that you did not leave on good terms with the law, your wife or College of the Rockies. But you did travel in a sophisticated circle of friends. Frank, Ernie and I have been pondering whether you might be able to help us find some investment outlets. You would be able to earn some money... real money."

Andy let the phrase dangle in the air.

"Money?" Swanson echoed that word. It referenced something that he missed a lot: cash, good credit, splurge plus, paper gold, jingle bling, surplus dollars, women, seduction, pleasure. He missed living well above the margin. "What kind of money?" he asked.

"As you can well imagine, Swanson, we have a cash flow problem, which is to say, we have trouble hiding our cash. We need a financial front through which we could invest our money, protect its source and give us a high rate of legitimate return. Sales have grown steadily and Frank and Ernie are having to travel all over Denver opening multiple checking accounts in different banks to ensure that our cash is safe, and unnoticed."

Swanson had questions: "What do you do with your cash besides hide it? Invest it? Spend it...on what?"

Ernie had answers: "Our cash earns a little interest, but nothing like the income it could generate if we could get it into legitimate investments. We need to do that. We think you might help."

"And the consumption of water and electricity? How do you hide it.?"

Well," joked Andy, "we found a pretty cool way to do that. Frank is a highly skilled electrician, and he created a seamless connection to the *United Warehouse* breaker-box. He and Ernie rotate the nightshift. No one notices that they change jobs from time to time...being twins is quite a resource. They see to it that air/humidity controls are lowered to very minimal levels. Then, a daytime draw of juice to run our grow lights is unnoticeable. An aquifer under the storage facility supplies our water."

"And the pot," Swanson continued, "How do you grow it?"

"Typically, Frank sleeps during the day while Ernie, when he isn't running around the city depositing cash, works with me to cultivate the plants. They have to be watered, topped and pinched, and we pull emerging male growths because unfertilized female plants create greater concentrations of THC in their buds. At night, the entire 'grow' sleeps."

Andy paused for breath, then finished his summary, "We market three distinctive strains: Eagle Gold, Lobster Red and Spring Green. There's magic in the 'storage business'," Andy smiled.

Swanson remained silent, absorbing the simplicity of the complex operation. It required trust among the partners, varied skill sets and a resilient business energy. No agricultural undertaking was without risk, but indoor farming...hmmm... really different, and apparently wildly successful.

He didn't know if they were as knowledgeable about his circle of contacts in Boulder as they suggested, but in fact his foraging among freshmen women over the years brought him into contact with a dozen men who traveled in the same circles of fun. Some of them had real money. All of them were hungry for cash. With the market soaring to new highs, they were ready to invest in any number of quick, profitable products. Pot? Profitable. Growth? Quick. Cash flow? Strong. They would be interested. Hell, Swanson was interested.

He asked, "How long does it take you to grow enough pot to take it to market?

"That is the beauty of hydro-farming," Andy explained, "No hail, no drought, no winds, no doubts. The buds mature within 11 weeks of planting, sexing and pinching. From harvest to our distributor in Boulder is just a matter of days, and the cash flow is untraceable, untaxable, and inelastic." With a grin, Andy went on, "When the economy tanks a bit, nothing seems to ease hardship like the soothing soak of a toke."

"Until the day the state legalizes our crop," Andy finished up, "we stain the earth. We aren't greedy. We live modestly. You might like being a part of it."

Swanson sat silently for quite a while, then commented, "You'll need to give me a few weeks to digest all of this, Andy."

Swanson worked through his anxiety in a couple of days and began sorting through his options. His boarding mates were engaged in criminal activity, but he became fascinated with the idea that he might be able to make some of the money they were talking about. Pot was illegal alright, but it was a socially acceptable business.

He mixed the temptation with his memories of the Jon Benet fiasco and his income from teaching English to Air Force personnel. It was dull, dull evening work, did nothing for his love life and kept him on a very tight budget. His conversations with Andy opened a new door for him, led to a new cash flow and re-entry into the seductive world of gullible coeds.

But if he did this, he needed to feel safe. He had to know what social postures he was manipulating and that meant he needed to know more about getting high. He had never smoked pot. Now, he seemed to have crossed a line of inquiry and it led to an open door which featured a great big "STONED" sign. He entered, choosing Spring Green, let Andy load up his toke and spent an hour inhaling and waiting.

Disappointing. Lots of smoke, but no special effects. He finished his first session with only the mildest of mental distortion, clear of sight, acute of mind, and not very hungry as he was told he might be.

A week later, he tried again, smoking Eagle Gold to the Beatles. Without warning, time slowed a little. Andy began to sound like a hilarious comedian. Chips and dips blended into an amazingly delightful mixture, and a mouthful of them led to fistfuls more. A bite of a Brownie seemed to intensify his senses. He learned to enjoy the sound of crunching celery, so hypnotic, so cadenced, so perfect.

The music permeated his body, emotionally enveloping. Lucy soared in his personal high amidst the glitter of her sky. His thoughts overwhelmed him with insight even as his words resonated with wisdom and certainty. Features of the room, especially the tiny woven holes in the doilies under a flower vase, became worthy of extended comment, and his entire persona forgot a troubled Jon Benet history and floated into a gentle kindness. He was stoned.

Deeply soothing, pot gave him a peek into another dimension of his being, introducing him to a person he did not know and...he liked him. It also gave him a new sense of mental acuity, and after a few sessions, he again began to sort through his past seductions. This time, they became intense emotional links. He found his lovers arousing deep expressions of love, passion and timeless embrace. He was in love with them...again. They stirred his soul and he found that Shakespeare said it best, *"Dreaming showed such riches that when he waked he cried to dream again."*

Swanson became stoned a lot in the next couple of weeks. Even the word, "smoke" seemed to calm him as though he could create a cloak of invincibility with a single deep draw. The passage of the clouded drug into his lungs, out through his nose, his mouth, then his embrace of fresh air seemed to unlock his mind, massage his sensibility. His body became an eccentric attachment to thoughts that roamed freely through scents, images and memories, compressing time, enhancing insight. The thought occurred again. What was he going to do about Walt Farmer?

Near midnight, a Saturday night midnight, he and Andy found themselves laughing wildly after an intense conversation about the length of the wing of a fly, when out of a wrapped cocoon in Swanson's mind a thought emerged, one so delicious it were as though liquid candy had been molded into a chocolate covered bon-bon, and he cupped it so firmly it could not escape.

Pot was illegal in Wisconsin and faculty careers could be ruined by association with drugs. Walt Farmer had a payback coming and now Swanson knew how to issue the check. He filled some paper and lit up some more smoky inspiration and toyed with the delicious strategy floating in his mind. A shipment of Lobster Red from Denver addressed to the Chair of the Economics Department, Saint Clare College, could become evidence. He would tip the local police to the plain brown package, and they could take it from there. Farmer would be charged with possession, surely losing his job. For all Swanson knew, it might be the hammer that shattered a marriage. All well and good.

A week later, Andy approached him and asked, "Swanson, we're still thinking that you could help us with our marketing. Waddya think. Interested?"

"Ah am," Swanson replied, "Give me a couple of days to clear my mind and then let's talk."

Three evenings later, Andy made his pitch. "If you could begin to look after the Boulder distribution network and hook us up with an investor who would like to use our cash and pay us dividends, we would guarantee you 25% of the returns." He paused. Swanson did not react, but inside his head he was doing quick calculations and he liked the numbers.

"What kind of money are we talking about, Andy?"

"We'll start with $1,000,000 and if it goes well, we will double it in a year," Andy practically whispered, but Swanson heard every word. His mind began to run the figures. Hedge Fund returns: 20%. Financial regulation by the SEC, none. Annual return on investment, $200,000; his cut, $50,000 per annum for doing nothing more than supplying a name. The pot could grow larger quickly. Twenty-five percent of $500,000 plus in the years to come would give him a very comfortable cash flow, tax free. William Gaddis was right. Money spoke *"in a voice that rustled."*

He paused for effect, looked into the distance as though there were not a wall ten feet away from him, and then said, "My cut would have to be in cash, tax free," he said quietly.

"No problem," Andy replied.

"One other thing," Swanson went on, "I need a free one pound sample of Lobster Red shipped to an address I will give you. Call it a recruitment bonus for me, but you handle it, with gloves, and when you have a receipt to show me for mailing it, I am ready to join up with you."

Again, "No problem," Andy smiled. "Where do I send it?"

Swanson gave him the address, citing the Department Chair of Economics, Saint Clare College as the recipient.

"Consider it done," Andy sealed the deal. "Are you with us?"

"Yes, ah think I can make this happen. Give me two weeks."

"You got it," Andy relied.

That month, Swanson's life took on new energy and focus. Andy showed him the receipts for the shipment of Lobster Red to Saint Clare College. Swanson sent his anonymous tip to the local police, and within a week, *The SC STAR* broke the story: *"Econ Prof Career Up In Smoke"*. He thrilled to the headline until he read on down the article. They had arrested the wrong guy!

A recent faculty election had shifted the chair's office to a toady bureaucrat, Carl Smithers, who had once played baseball for the Des Moines Ducks. Farmer, now clear and free of any entanglements, expressed amazement that Smithers had been dealing in pot, but suggested to police that there might be more personal aspects to the story and Smithers' marriage suffered badly.

This was what Swanson planned to read about Farmer, not this dupe Smithers. He thought about it some more, noted that his own grave was still empty, and finally concluded that Farmer no doubt recognized the dynamic. He had to be unsettled about future deliveries through the mail and maybe that was just fine. Swanson felt like moving on. He had a whole new career to think about now. In time, he might have opportunity to revisit the Farmer issue, but for now, he followed a new scent: money.

He sniffed around Boulder looking for an outlet for Frick N Frack's cash flow, settling finally on Lawrence Belton. In better times, he and Larry had spent a lot of time together on golf courses and public gatherings. Now divorced, Belton concentrated on making his fledging hedge fund, *Cube-It*, one of the most successful in the state.

Belton specialized in huge purchases of common stock issued by corporations with profit hard wired into their operations. He bought when others saw too great a risk, and he sold when the market rallied. Apple was an early success, Amazon a great bet. Railroads grew with the economy and Boeing's future was unlimited. Hell, Belton bought Pfizer well before Viagra hit the market.

In general, he followed a simple maxim. "Buy a company with a moat." Invest in corporations whose high profile and product quality made it hard for customers to escape. A public utility could fit that profile, Entergy for example, but for the most part, Belton traded in about three dozen nationally known entities.

He avoided margin calls, sold on the bounce, bought on the dip and filled his coffers with huge profits for his investors. His strategy, instincts and technical knowledge seemed to let him see the market a month ahead of the Dow's performance, and *Cube-It* lit up statewide financial news as shares rose from $200,000 to $350,000/share. Belton may not have been stealing any customers from major national hedge funds, but he wasn't losing any either.

When Swanson made his pitch, Belton alternated between raising his eyebrows, puffing his cheeks, and holding his breath. He had never dipped into money laundering, but this opportunity he liked. He believed that the tech driven market was about to tank, and he was taking profits, a lot of profits. He didn't really need new cash at hand for now, but later, when the markets reset, he could use pot money to buy back in and grab enormous profits.

There was adventure in what Swanson proposed, but the most persuasive feature of the pitch, in Belton's mind, was the very strong likelihood that in a few years, Colorado would legalize marijuana growth and possession. Having a source of supply and a distribution network ready to serve the public could produce a huge cash flow in a legal market.

Hedge fund managers should be able to make quick decisions, Swanson thought, and Belton made his. "Supply me with that kind of cash, and I'll provide you with that kind of return."

And that was that.

Swanson continued to teach for the Air Force, not wanting to change his habits in any noticeable way. But, Belton's promise about returns on cannabis cash worked out just the way he envisioned. He began receiving monthly distributions of a few thousand dollars, and they grew throughout the year.

Within six months, he had forgotten Walt Farmer and become immersed in the distribution of pot into Boulder. It was a friendly town. Coeds arrived annually. Older men sporting younger women scarcely turned a head. He refashioned himself into a wise, aging former professor now reflecting thoughtfully on the world as seen through a cloud of smoke.

Turned out that was a lot easier than he thought. The more he worked with Frick N' Frack, the more comfortable they were in letting him service the Boulder network, and the more women he met. Staining the earth was just foreplay to the main event...young coeds.

My God, they were healthy! Fit, tanned faces gazed at him with open unshielded eyes, believing that he looked into their souls and knew their hopes and needs. They judged his phrases as unique to the English language. They cycled with tight bodies, ran with resilient pace, ate well-balanced organic foods. They smoked Spring Green, and they were in a near-frantic search for both the meaning of life and their place in it. He could help.

A cold, tingling nerve somewhere in Swanson's body twanged incessantly, begging him to practice the romantic voodoo that he did do so well. Just stir the pot and let the bubbles pop, he thought, and he did. He knew the coed's lines before they uttered them and had three seductive answers ready for every question. Now he added the enrichment of pot to fertilize their imaginations and to bring him the flesh that his body missed. He was fat but they were firm. He was settled, nearly inert. They were pliant and athletic. In the wrap of the smoke he shared with them, languid leisure flooded his body once again, a vacation from life. He thought briefly of Jane Austen, *"It is a truth universally acknowledged, that a single man in possession of a good fortune, must be in want of a wife."*

"Jane," he thought, "you got it wrong," and he kept circulating within the collegiate community, the bars on the Hill and the bistros on Broadway. His romances---varied, transitory, and uncomplicated--- kept him fresh, vital and fully engaged in life.

That changed one Friday evening in the second year of his renewed lifestyle. Strolling along the Mall, he found himself in a flirtation with dark eyes and long, flowing black hair, a tall lithe dark figure lightly draped in soft white linen, accented with turquoise beads, ruby red stones and small wisps of braided feathers. She spoke to him in a voice that seemed to echo the gentle splashes of Boulder Creek.

Lilting Song was from Montana, and her body promised response to every sign language he could invent. Yet, she spoke comfortably of both Shakespeare and Jane Austen, Harper Lee and Kafka, her years at CU well used. They sat for coffee, ate a small snack, enjoyed a glass of wine and talked well into the early evening. They spent the night at the Boulder Hotel, and then they spent a week there.

Swanson found the diversion so intense that it remained even after the smoke of the first night disappeared. Her edges were in her passion. Smooth undulations took her body wherever he placed it and returned favor with favor, flavor with flavor. He smoked more deeply, absorbing her touch, mood and cries in the creases of every memory he held of her.

But while he dallied, Lilting Song composed, placing him in a compelling vision to which she added color, tone and tempo. Deeply affected by his seduction, she spoke of the Sioux tribe from which she came, reported that her father, Chief One Who Sees and her brothers, Waiting Cloud and Lightning Strike would all welcome him into the larger family. Rituals would play out. He could become one with her, with her tribe, with its future.

Swanson heard this and saw only trouble. In time, he knew, he would grow tired of her and move on. He knew how to deal with departure, but had little history of commitment. This bond she forged would last, he thought, but only until he passed his cruel knife of rejection through it.

Lilting Song forged ahead. She sought to know him as a person not just as a lover, and he found that both surprising and flattering. He responded to her confidences, shared more of himself than he thought prudent, but he liked the intimacy. For the moment, all was well. She radiated commitment, and he, surprisingly he thought, absorbed her beyond the immediacy of charm. He expected his feelings to change. It was his nature.

But a year passed and she remained near his touch, immersed herself into his daily life and filled his nights with whatever treats his stoned mind could conjure. He loved her, enjoyed his occasional contact with her brothers, felt no impulse to move on.

Another six months, and now time finally produced its own dose of immunity to her charms. He began to feel a sense of restlessness, and he worked hard to let her down gently, explaining that a series of new demands curtailed his time. He had other responsibilities. He needed to be on site in Denver. There was new travel involved in his sales network. They needed to take a rest from one another.

She would have none of it. She loved him, to be sure, but she also saw him as a highly valued tribal prize: a white, rich man connected to money. His pathways might smooth the troubles of her tribe, the ancient ones of poverty, indolence, cultural abandonment, uncontrolled futures. Where once its wealth could be measured in horses, hides and lands unhemmed by white man lines on a map, fences and highways now constrained them.

Without resources to barter, impoverished by rules and laws made thousands of miles away, the tribe feared reservation life settling into its own special nullity. Lilting Song, her father, One Who Sees, and her brothers, Waiting Cloud and Lighting Strike were at one with a desire to take white man's smoke, that floating, unmanageable, smothering toxin and turn it into Indian power.

When he began to lose interest, she asked her brothers for advice. What to do? Try harder they said. She reported declining interest. Again, she asked, "What should I do?"

Waiting Cloud and Lighting Strike consulted with One Who Sees, and they asked serious questions of Lilting Song. How much money did he have? Did she have access to it? In some sense of desperation, she reported that he marketed pot into the Boulder community. He was not truly rich, but he had, she believed, a very nice cash flow and powerful financial connections.

Her family pondered long, asking more questions. Who were his contacts? How did he access his cash? In the next few weeks, while she struggled to keep Swanson in her life with modest demands and the best rewards her body could offer, the tribe investigated the leads she had given them. Within two months, the brothers had a plan.

They traced Swanson' cash flow from pot sales to the hedge fund, *Cube-It*. They identified him as the principle liaison to Larry Belton, a high-risk entrepreneur who could be a solution to their overriding problem: how to care for the tribe. They explained their plan to Lilting Song. She pondered it for several days, a week in which Swanson remained unreachable, and finally, heartbreaking as it was, she told her brothers that *"If it were to be done, then best it were done quickly,"* nodding to Macbeth and whispering a prayer for Swanson.

Two days more and her brothers sat across from Swanson in Boulder, making it clear, on pain of death, that he needed to introduce them to Belton and *Cube-It*. Once they had that connection, he could keep his Boulder network. They would make their own agreement with Belton.

Swanson did not think long about this. If he could escape now, he would worry about the future later. "Done," he said in a quavering voice. Then, to his own surprise, he asked, "What of Lilting Song?"

"She is out of your life," Waiting Cloud uttered, "Do not seek her out again." Then, as an afterthought, he added, "Tell Ernie, Andy and Frank to expand their storage business and stain more earth. We need the product for the tribe."

The brothers met with Belton and brought him a business proposition. They offered to create a new market for pot in Montana, open their tribal reservation to a casino operation which *Cube-It* could fund and from which it could skim, becoming a cash clearinghouse for pot distribution, casino gambling and equity markets. Was he interested? Absolutely! Belton knew the language of pot. He was about to learn the idiom of penny slots and blackjack.

As the money rolled in, Swanson settled into a lifestyle suitable to his temperament and his temptations. Occasionally, a woman would captivate him, but the flow of money from his share out of *Cube-It* kept him grounded. He circulated through Boulder free of worry, safe from Waiting Cloud, enjoying the treats of his wealthy, smoky life.

Then, one afternoon, as he was trolling downtown in the Mall, his cell phone rang. He didn't recognize the number.

"Hello," he said.

"Is this Barry Swanson, Professor Barry Swanson?" a quiet voice inquired.

"Yeesss? Who is this?"

"This is your son, Trevor," the voice replied.

Swanson' stomach jumped. He didn't have a son.

A Walk in the Park

He coughed, a deep hard cough, then a looser one, cleared his throat, focused his eyes, and continued his walk to his place in the park. Old, wrinkled in hands and face, he moved slowly as dirty clothes, tattered at every edge, showed muddled colors of red, blue and brown. His beard, grey wash water hues, grew everywhere it could, from ear to neck, cheek to cheek, lip to chin. His hair, entwined in his beard, flowed down the back of his head, fell below his shoulders in its own patterns depending upon wind and walk.

If one could have looked into his squinty eyes, they would have been dark brown. They would have reflected a dim light of presence. They would have focused on a spot just beyond where the observer stood, and they would have revealed a wandering gaze in search of a goal. If one looked quite closely, one might have been able to see some of his history, his successes, his setbacks, but one would have to have looked very hard, for those years and those experiences were shrouded in a misty dim memory.

He shuffled, clearly in no hurry but nonetheless a man with his cart fixed on a target. The signal lights stopped him for a minute or two. He jammed his hands into his pockets, both to warm them and to remind himself that he had a little more than two dollars in change and a few folding bills that he remembered as a five and three ones. He sniffled, coughed again, pulled out a rag he found in the last garbage can and wiped his nose. It was a discarded cleaning cloth, marked with the stains of brown polish, filled with the scent of Lemon Pledge, frayed around its edges from the daily doings of a housekeeper.

The light changed. He lowered his cart off the curb, stepped slowly behind it, planted his open-toed shoe on the asphalt and began to cross the road. It was a slow passage, and although he kept an eye out for the waiting traffic, his pace tried the patience of drivers. A muted horn from four cars back let him know his progress was too slow. He ignored it. The cart carried all of his daily needs, and no crossing was ever complete until its wheels found the next sidewalk. He made it before the light changed, and he did so with some small satisfaction. He paused, rested, coughed again, harder this time, and his throat filled with phlegm caught in his windpipe. He spat, caring neither where it landed nor what it might touch on the way to its splatter.

He looked around as the traffic accelerated across the intersection, noting the fixed gazes of passengers, the distracted movements of those texting, and the herd of one-car drivers who filled the lanes in pursuit of their morning tasks. It always seemed to him that the automobile had separated people in far more permanent ways than it had drawn them together. But those were passing thoughts now, and he set off to the end of the next block and the entry to the park.

It was a lovely parcel of green, its sod fertilized monthly, its earth fed by hearty, timely rains and its foliage carefully planned to blossom with the seasons. Mown weekly, it served as a life canvas amidst the asphalt and concrete that framed it and he knew where he would likely find scraps for his daily diet. The first day after a weekend---a good time to rummage about the grasses and the garbage to find things important to him: discarded food, a stray pocket knife, perhaps even a bit of fallen coin. Part of his daily routine, he liked his walk-about particularly well because it was always a path he chose for himself.

He reached the park, placed his cart in some bushes where it would be unseen and began his daily rounds. He went to the playground first, the most likely cache of lost coin, then worked his way through the garbage for little treasures. Finally, he walked the park in a precise pattern which took him to most picnic locations, leading finally to a dark collection of foliage inside which there was a piece of flat empty soil soft enough to support a weary body. And he was weary.

He rested awhile, sitting in the dirt, leaning his head against a tree, dozing in the comfortable early morning temperatures with high heat on the way by noon. Finally, he roused himself, slowly stood and retraced his path back to his cart. He loaded up his new findings, rearranged the placement of goods, wrapped a small tarp over them and slowly rolled his possessions along an asphalt path until he was back to his pad of dirt.

That took a lot out of him. He coughed, paused and then coughed again. His wind was not what it once was, and any strained effort seemed to leave him in quick need of a seat. He sat on dirt, fumbled for one of his cigarette packages, Lucky Strike this time, and quietly lit himself a smoke. He reviewed his findings for the morning, took note that he had enough to eat until supper time, and found himself a niche along the base of the tree and took another nap.

Sometime later, with the sun well past mid-day, he awoke in a sweat, feeling the press of the heat of the day. The mowing crew had done its work and moved on. He reached out to the earth for support and began to ease himself up to a standing position, first kneeling, then propping one hand on a knee to lift himself upright. He brushed off his clothes and scanned the park for better shade, perhaps a breeze. He saw a bench now in shadow, moved his cart to the path and walked with some pace and purpose to the framework of its flat wooden seat and backrest. He parked his cart, padded the bench with an old blanket, arranged his pillow of discarded shirts and lay down to sleep.

The next time he awoke it was late afternoon. The sun had changed positions, and he prepared to move to his night's haven, a large pine, the earth below it graced with many layers of soft needles. When he rose, he coughed again, a hard succession of racking clearing noises as he sought both air and relief from chest pain that kept showing up on a regular basis. Finally calmed, he arranged his goods on his cart, and set off for his retreat. There, he could think his thoughts, review his day, puzzle his past and plan for the morrow which he knew would be much the same as this one. Still, it was his to control, his path to choose. He found his resting place.

By sunset, the park was quiet. The scent of freshly cut grass lingered throughout its boundaries. Families who visited for an after-dinner diversion had traipsed on home. There was still a little light in the sky, but it did not disturb his shadows, and he made a quiet walk again around the picnic tables where he came across some abandoned hot dogs and a sealed container of yogurt. He ate both right on the spot and dumped the trash into the basket nearby. He tried to look up to the first star, but his neck was too bowed to give him good elevation. He looked around instead, found the park quiet, safe and empty. Time to go to bed. He went back to his needle nest, lay down and wrapped himself with some blankets taken from his cart.

The light faded. Shadows began to disappear and as he wrapped himself up into his nighttime cocoon, he felt another cough coming on. He tried to suppress it, but it was going to have its way with him. He sat up, coughed, coughed some more and felt a trickle of spittle on his lips. He wiped it away but not fast enough to avoid a taste of its saltiness, and he knew that its color was red. He coughed again, and his mouth filled with blood. He bent over to empty it, and as he did cramping began in his gut moving up quickly to fill his chest. His legs were logs. His arms weakened, and he had no option but to aim his mouth away from his face and let the blood flow.

"What was this?" he thought. Had he broken a blood vessel in his throat? Scarcely had that image filled his head than he vomited blood through mouth and nose, and his body contorted itself in cramps even as he tried to stretch to relieve the pressure on his chest. Eyes wide open, he looked for a rag to soak the blood. The light was less now. Nighttime loomed, and the quiet in the park seemed the most powerful he had known. His ears heard only a slight ringing and then they too were silent. He breathed lightly, coughed again and dropped his head in his blood. He was aware of his own wet beard. Fixed with pain from the cramps, he felt with some panic that this was not a cough he could end. The night lights in the park came on, suddenly, and he fixed his eyes on one of them. As he lay there, he saw it brighten, then fade gently into a blackness from which he did not return.

Hello Moe

He heard a knock on the door. He got up from his chair, put down his book and walked slowly to the hallway. He debated whether to turn on the porch light in the deepening dusk. Might as well, he thought, and pushed the switch. He looked out the panel window alongside the front door, and paused. He didn't recognize the man. Not surprising. He didn't have many friends, nor visitors. Still, the stranger looked comfortable knocking, and he did so again.

The holiday season was over, winter taking a firm grip on the lakes and lawns, and this figure stood brand new. He looked him over one more time, then gently opened the door. "Yes," he said, "What can I do for you?"

Young, dark haired, probably near 35 or so, this new face sported a gentle smile and a compelling set of blue eyes. He said, "Hello, Moe."

Moe felt his stomach twitch. His face, never particularly expressive, froze, and while his eyes narrowed and focused, he let his mind embrace more than three decades of wonderings about this stranger. He knew exactly what was happening right this moment... a special night on a kind of dare led to this...a young man who was his son...a son whom he had never seen. He waited. Again, "Hello, Moe...do you know who I am?"

Moe listened to the sound of those words softly die in the warm porch light, and then he said, "Yes, I know. Brady. How's your mother, Lori?"

"She's fine," the young man said, then paused, "She said to say hello, Moe."

Jolted a bit by hearing his name again, and realizing that it really was cold outside, Moe welcomed him into the house.

"Come on in, Brady, and get warm. We have a lot to talk about."

Moe took coat and gloves and placed them in his entry closet. They moved quietly down the hallway, turned left into the reading room filled with Moe's books, magazines, and writings, then gently sat down facing one another at an angle that let the fireplace and its flickering light warm them both. They looked one another over, stared at the logs and kept the silence.

"Would you like something to drink, coffee, perhaps some chocolate?" Moe began?

Brady shifted in his chair, paused, "I don't think so, Moe. I'm warm after that nice walk from the train station. It's pretty out there. The oak are bare and their branches framed the street as though in a painting It was a peaceful, sheltered walk. It certainly fueled my imagination. You still writing?"

"Yes," Moe replied, "These days I reflect more than I read, but I still write."

"Well," Brady smiled, "Teaching is a nice venue to share writing projects, personal or professional. Published much?"

"A little," Moe whispered, wondering how much Brady already knew about him. "I've done some work on Wilson and FDR, most of it just plain hard work. I never cared much for research, but I like writing."

"I've read some of it," Brady offered. "When you characterized Wilson as a conniving imperialist using ideology to manipulate the titans of Europe, there were a lot of howls in the reviews. And saddling FDR with the racism inherent in the Japanese relocations of World War II stirred up a lot of buzz in the profession too," Brady paused, then with a smile, "At least you didn't place Pearl Harbor at FDR's feet, and you were kind enough to give Truman credit for bringing MacArthur to heel. Your name is well regarded in conversations about revisionist historians, Moe. How creative is your take on history? Do you really see presidents as villains?"

"Well, Moe replied, "I guess a good writer goes where his sources take him, and adds a bit of imagination. Keep the truth, I think, but put it outside the general reader's comfort zone."

"History with a message, eh?" Brady smiled, "Do you write fiction too?"

"I try my hand at it from time to time," Moe said. "For some reason, I find myself drawing more upon the dark edges of my life than I do the lighter times. My characters start their lives with some equanimity, ambition and love, but murder, mayhem and vengeance eventually seem to undermine their finer instincts. When that happens, when I feel that flowing through my fingertips, I just go with it. I guess I am working through some of my own feelings and frustrations, but it seems to me that the stuff of great stories is both insight and then a kind of courageous, blurted truth."

"So," Brady responded, "When your novel moves in ways that surprise you, do you feel it getting out of control, or do you just see that as part of the flow of life?"

"Well," Moe paused, then spoke softly, "I think that a person, visits many possible character markers in the course of a lifetime. Sometimes we embrace challenge. Sometimes we avoid opportunity, and sometimes we kill the messenger. The outcomes are equally unpredictable. People may sample similar experiences differently. Some hard lessons we just ignore. Some commitments end well. Some destroy us."

Moe took a breath, then finished, "It is a hard thing to go to bed any evening and say that the world seems to be right with itself. There is a lot of personal suffering out there."

"Well," asked Brady, "If that is the stuff of your fiction, I'd be an interested reader. Which sold better, your novels or your histories? I'm guessing your novels," he said with a smile.

"They sold, not well, but well enough to bring in little pots of profit from time to time. On occasion, it was enough to settle a divorce decree," Moe said with a tone of satisfaction, and a smile.

"Well, a little extra money always helps divorce," Brady laughed a little, and went on, "Credit only works so long, and then someone has to settle the bill."

Moe remained silent for a time. Was this it, he wondered? Was the young man after money? Moe asked again, "Are you sure you wouldn't like something to drink?" This time Brady simply said, "Coffee sounds good."

When he got up to go to the kitchen, Moe made sure that he kept an eye on Brady who now rose from his chair and then wandered a bit about the library, looking at titles, glancing at pictures on the tables and gently touching the furnishings. He seemed to be interested in making physical contact with all of his surroundings. The home, a modest bachelor's place, Brady thought, felt clean but untidy.

"You said you divorced?" Brady asked Moe as he returned with a couple of mugs.

"Sugar or cream?" Moe asked, and Brady said, "No, I'm fine with black. Did you marry just the once?"

Moe paused. Just how much information did he want to share with this young man, his son. That he was his son, he had no doubt. His mouth, face and body structure were his own. Those eyes, though, were clearly Lori's, large, blue and intently focused.

"No," Moe said, "I married three times. Good women they were, but I was not a good husband, rather I should say I was not a good provider, and they needed providing. How about you, ever been married?"

There was a pause. Brady warmed his hands on the mug as steam moved up in a slow swirl, and his answer came out of his mouth much the same way.

"I really haven't had the time to marry, Moe. My life has been so focused on education that the idea of sharing a life with a woman remains just an idea."

"College, graduate school, post-grad work...those must have been busy years," Moe observed.

"I guess they really were," said Brady, "Mother kept me well focused and each time I reached a goal, she gently prodded me to a new one. Can't say that it was a bad thing, but I find myself looking around now. My career seems stable, mother has a good professional position, and I see a long road ahead for me. I don't want it to be an empty one and neither does she.

Again, thought Moe, Lori...the presence that fills the room.

"Well, he said, "how is your mother? What has her life been like? For a long time, I've heard nothing."

"She's fine," Brady started, "She invested in me so deeply that she didn't do much for herself until I finished college. Then, she started her own program at the University of Montana, political science. She finished in three years and began to do research into public opinion samplings. When I was in graduate school, she caught on to a couple of campaigns in Montana then got a job with a political pro in Chicago. She's lived there for the past five years or so. We keep in close touch."

There was a pause. Silence began to build its own momentum, and then Brady asked, "Where were you?"

Now, the unavoidable, Moe thought.

He took a few breaths, let the silence continue, thought of how he wanted to phrase his words, gathered some strength and began, "I went to junior college, then transferred to Long Beach State. I was poor, working nights in a mental institution, studying while the inmates slept, and I managed to get my undergraduate degree, then went to UCSF to get a PhD in history. Money was always tight. For a time I worked in a funeral home, dragging in bodies from around the city, studying between funerals so to speak."

"When I finished, I took a job in Nevada, UNLV, then found this position in Wisconsin. I liked the green summers and the snow and icy winters. They are clean, bright features of a new landscape far removed from deathly doings. Life looks pretty good after a summer rain or a winter snowfall, and I guess they have also reminded me of Montana winters and your mother."

"Now, it's your turn," Moe said with a smile, "If you haven't had time to find a wife, what are you doing?"

"Studying genetic medicine," Brady replied. "Somewhere along the end of high school, mom said that she had found some extra financial help, and that I should just plan on going to college. I did, and I just kept on going. Every time it seemed that I was up against a brick wall, she found more resources, and by the time that she was working, the money flow kept us both comfortable."

"So, genetic engineering," Moe said softly, "What does it tell you about the human condition?"

"It provides the final view into the mechanisms that control the body and its repair," Brady replied, his voice rising a bit. "It is the way that medicine is going to be practiced before the end of my life, and we are going to be looking at our health strategies today a lot like the way we look back at practices of Civil War Surgeons: painful, hopeful, but desperately handicapped. It took nearly two centuries for germ theory to move from inoculations for smallpox to vaccinations for polio, but I think that genetic medicine will develop ten times faster."

"So," Moe asked, "What kind of manipulative therapy are you most interested in?"

"Well, I'm well aware of the way that some genetic markers can indicate individual weaknesses to specific diseases. Some arouse suspicions of breast cancer, some can tell a physician whether his patient is vulnerable to suicidal impulses caused by taking some antidepressants."

Moe commented, "That's sort of interesting, Brady. I have two friends who fell victim to that syndrome...started taking antidepressants following loss of jobs and one committed suicide; the other tried it...poor body mechanics I suppose, and he failed." Moe concluded that last phrase with a smile.

"There is going to be a lot of work and publicity 'bout that," Brady smiled, "but what I am interested in is the genetic process of working with the body's own cells to create auto-immune responses to fatal diseases, things like lung cancer, where we can manipulate the body's immune system to attack its own biological enemies. T-cell invigoration I like to call it."

Brady paused. Silence replaced the conversational tone which each had been creating. Perhaps ten seconds passed, with some sense of anticipation hanging in the air. There was a topic as yet untouched, and it needed to surface.

Moe sat quietly, reflecting, breathing slowly, but deeply, and Brady could see his chest rise and fall. There was something stirring in there. Moe finally drew in air and jumped in. "Brady, you know, when your mother had you, I was graduating from high school, without money, and in truth, uncertain about whether I was your father. I finally figured it out, but I had nothing for you except the hope that life would treat you well."

Brady nodded, "I know that now, Moe. Someone helped though...mother seemed to find money for my education every time we really needed it. Heck, I used to think that she might be hooking...even followed her around when she was gone at night, but all I could ever find was her working in a café about four blocks from our apartment. Yet, things always got better when we needed them to."

"Sometimes, timing is everything," Moe suggested, "Did you ever check with Lori's parents. I know that her father was a well-connected executive with Mobile Oil. Were they helping?"

"Mom said that they did, sometimes, and that might account for little treats. Still, when the extra money came, there was always quite a bit more than normal, and it was always badly needed."

"Well, there must have been someone out there looking after you, for whatever reason," Moe mused, "Were they monthly checks or anything like that?"

"No," Brady said, "Always lump sums, and mother used it carefully. In fact there were three times when it just saved us. Once when I started college, once when I was in graduate school and a third time when we were both seeking to find permanent work. Money just showed up."

Moe paused. He rose and took the mugs back into the kitchen, rinsed them, watching the black liquid turn light brown as water flushed out the coffee. He placed them in the drainer and hand-washed a couple of plates.

"I'll use the dish washer in the morning," he muttered.

While the water ran, Brady wandered some more, curious about a series of pictures above a writing desk. He could recognize Moe easily enough, but each frame featured a different woman, two blondes and a brunet. They were pretty, slender, above average in height, and each had a smile that said, "I love you". They all looked the same age, but Moe looked older in each one, and by his reckoning, glancing at Moe right now, the last one was probably taken about eight years ago. Maybe he was ready to marry again.

"Well, Brady," Moe spoke as he returned to the reading room, "I would like to know more about your career. Research in the lab has to be as demanding as research in a library. I didn't care much for the latter, and I am sure I would not do well with science, but I'm interested in how you feel about it."

"The double helix holds a lot of promise, I think," Brady said, "and it can probably help us diagnose and treat illnesses in ways we cannot imagine today. Its secrets runs deep," Brady said. "Once I hooked up with the Medical Center, I became a 'lab rat'. Guess I created an alternative life. I spent most hours of every day and night growing bugs, tiny microscopic ones, studying their DNA and finding out more about its role in medicine. It all takes time. Cells can grow and die while you are out to supper, so you don't go out very often. Some experiments take 16-18 hours to monitor, and of course, whatever the result one needs to repeat the tests to be sure the product is not idiosyncratic."

"So," Moe interrupted, "Do you see a time when DNA can give us a way to treat cancer, or other diseases. Is there a future in moving beyond surgery and transplants?"

"You bet!" Brady responded, "Our ability to sequence the entire human genome means we can take a closer look at the fundamental structure and behavior of our cells, our life. I think there are markers that can indicate cancer potentials, can help diagnose depression variants and can indicate propensity for many diseases. I spend a lot of time in a lab... not your cup of tea I am sure," he said with a smile, "but curiosity can keep a person going for a lifetime, and I think I am a goner. That probably presents a challenge to a successful marriage too, I guess."

Moe, paused a bit, then said, "Marriage is a complicated commitment. I keep thinking that I've learned what it takes to make it work, but time keeps proving me wrong."

"Well, I'm curious about something," Brady said. "I'm guessing that those pictures above your desk are of you and your wives. Is that right?"

"Yep," said Moe, "Each one a beauty. Great women. Each one soon remarried. Alimony relief is a real fact of life," Moe smiled. He went on, "There came a time when it just wasn't working for me. Once I knew that, I cut them loose. It cost me, but it saved me too, I think."

Brady murmured, "Mother always said that a failed marriage took more than the interest earned...it took some of the principle too, so to speak."

"True enough," Moe responded, paused again for a long moment, then asked, "Are you going to be in town long?"

"No," Brady said, still looking at those pictures on the wall, "I leave early in the morning. I have two meetings in Chicago over the weekend, and I want to see her and just enjoy some time in the city."

"Not that I feel anything but good about it, but why did you stop in to see me now?" Moe asked.

"Searching you out was something I have wanted to do for a long time. Mom always said you were a gentle, but skeptical person. I saw that in your writings, and I see it in our conversations, direct and honest. She was right. Hope you felt comfortable with my just showing up like this."

"Count on it," Moe paused a long time, "I've wanted to speak to you for many years." He extended his hand in a gentle wave about the room, "You're welcome to spend the night. I have a guest room, and I make great pancakes."

"Oh, I really do thank you, Moe," Brady said, "but I have a motel room to go to, and I'm pretty happy with our conversation." He rose to his feet. Moe walked him to the hall and helped him with his coat.

As Brady took his gloves, he murmured, "This has been a great visit for me, Moe...all that I was looking for." Moe opened the front door, made sure the light was on, and extended his hand. "Can I ask you, Brady,...if you don't mind, would you call me by my first name, Kerry? I would like that."

Brady met his palm, firmly, looked him in the eye. Then his voice softened and he said, "I think I'll call you 'dad'." There was a pause. Kerry looked at him, hard, kept his hand for an extra moment, then said, "I'd like that even better."

The door closed and he watched Brady as he went down the stairs. When he was out of sight, Kerry turned off the light but kept looking out there for a time. Then, he went slowly back into the reading room and stood before the pictures of his wives. "You were all wonderful," he spoke directly to them, "and you all cost me more than I wanted, less than you needed." He looked at each of them for a long moment, looked about his modest house, thought about his son and reflected on alimony relief and money pots from novels. He always spent it in just the right place. "Tonight was quite a dividend," he murmured.

He walked slowly out of the room and into his bedroom, changed clothes and turned back the covers. He got into bed, lay flat, propped a book up on his chest and began reading. He paused after a few pages, took a deep breath, set the book aside and turned off the light. As he curled up on his pillow, he noted a strange feeling inside of him. The world seemed right for a change.

The Last Cigarette

Outside, the lights flashed *"He's Not Here"* and the cold wiped frost around the edges of the bar's oval window. Inside, Walt Farmer sat wrapped in thought, caught in taut memories that had taken him through the last three decades of his life. He held a nicely packed, white, paper wrapped cigarette cupped within the palm of his hand, the filtered butt rising above and between two fingers. Its smoke filled his hand a bit at a time, then slipped away seeking a nose to fill. He took in a breath as it rose, and threads of the plume drifted toward his face, disappeared into his nostrils and filled his eyes. He blinked, moved the source of the polluted air away from his body.

It was his fifth cigarette, and for a man who did not usually smoke, he handled each one with casual dexterity, knowing how it burned by the feel of the heat at its tip. The opened pack of Pall Mall sat to one side, out of his pocket after years of residence. Today, he wondered if maybe he should change to Marlboro and let his inner cowboy saddle up and just ride away, simply leave his worries in the smoke.

He just could not come to grips with his new truth. Everyone has a past, he knew that well enough, but what he had found over the past several months left him both angry and confused, caught up in an information flow that really didn't need him in the storyline. How could it be, he asked himself, that after all these years a rebellious choice for one night could bring him to this point? Did it all really have to begin with Peggy, with that dance at the Armory? He thought some more, balanced characters, choices and personalities, assessed time and distance and decided that yep, it all began with Peggy.

Sure, he had a great time that night, and so did she. Granted, it took him a year of looking before he finally found her again, this time listening to Fats Domino at Sunset Gardens. Yep, he had travelled a lot in the years after to court her, win her, lose her, rejoin with her and finally to leave her, or rather have her leave him. It was a damn night of pain when he finally sent her packing from his car, and it was a damn cold night too.

Twenty five years later, she jangled his nerves with a single phone call, unannounced and unfiltered. He heard her out, asked for the full accounting and she gave it to him, at first by phone, and then by mail. It all seemed to fit together: innocent teen-ager seduced by smooth, preying professor. He had no interest in reinvesting in Peggy, but he loved hearing the truth from her and in her own voice. Nor did he hold any grudges. She was young then, foolish maybe, but her choices were hers and his own life had moved in a far more rewarding path than any he could have envisioned with her.

Her life, he eventually learned, took her right out of Professor Barry Swanson's world and dumped her at home. Two years later, she found her soul mate, Timothy Tuttle, and they spent hours walking California beaches, imagining life and futures, speculating on moving to Idaho and starting over. Tuttle had little to offer. Two decades older than she, still supporting an ex-wife and two children, he had no education, no job, no money and no prospects. A month after they married, she discovered that he had never obtained a divorce. A bigamist! Walt smiled, wondered how long the annulment took? Peggy didn't mention that.

He had his fun with Swanson, though, pretty much ruining his reputation with that anonymous note to the Boulder police, naming him as Jon Benet Ramsay's killer. The investigation cleared Swanson of murder, but revealed his lengthy pattern of sexual escapades and that caused his divorce, financial ruin and professional destruction. Walt was happy enough with his thoughts that the pompous, portly prof had finally had his balloon pricked. It was done...he thought.

He shuffled through the pack of cigarettes, tapping out one that seemed classically cut with a clean fine edge to the filter, that industry invention which essentially concealed the load of poison it transferred. He picked up the book of matches thinking that if he continued to smoke again, he would have to invest in a nice lighter, something that had both color and flair, and he might have to consider changing his smoking product. What he knew now demanded a new level of relief, a draw from a bud of pot he thought.

He struck the match, watched it flame, saw the quick bright blue transform itself into a hot then mellow yellow. He held the end of the tiny torch away from his face for a moment, feeling the heat consume the cardboard stick much the way that his discovery ate at his years, promising to brand a new truth into all that he knew.

He lit the tobacco, inhaled, saw the orange burn brightly into the brown fibers, felt the heat flow into his mouth, the tar and nicotine floating down into his lungs. He held it, then exhaled slowly letting the smoke wrap its way around his hairline, linger on his chafed cheeks, then float away into the wash of a fan quietly rotating on low. Delicately, he kept the cigarette in an easy grasp between his two fingers, reviewed once again Peggy's recent telephone punch and thought about his sense of place, and purpose.

Her latest call, *just a month ago*, began gently enough. "Hi, there, Walt" she began, "I've heard about Lauren. That is such a sad tragedy...there were times in college when I felt like she was a sister to me, one that I never had. I hope you are handling it well...Pause...Do you have some time to talk?"

He did. Without Lauren, he had all of the free time he could possibly use. Lou Gehrig's Disease was a nasty relentless silent killer, and their journey from her diagnosis to her death pressed them into the most intimate, loving moments of their life together, but it drained his energies, left him wilting in the weeds. Six months after he buried her ashes, he was still looking for his next path. Healthier now, he began to wonder about his future...and then, Peggy...again. Once more her voice surfaced, on the phone, five years after their previous talk. But sure, he had time.

"Yep, I guess so. What's up?" he asked.

She paused, this was unlike her. Usually, her words came freely and in great numbers. Still, she paused.

"You there?' he asked again.

"Yes," she said, "I'm sorry to phone you like this...but I have something I need to tell you, and it is... you have to believe me...it is stunning news to me."

"Oh...well...what is it?"

"Do you remember our last semester together in Boulder, when we took a weekend to go to Steamboat Springs and do some skiing and spend time together?"

"Oh, sure. How could I forget that...best time we ever had."

"Well," Peggy began, paused, then drew a breath, "In my mind, that was a goodbye weekend. I figured I owed you one good time and tell the truth, I really enjoyed it. But we broke up shortly after, and Swanson and I spent a lot of time together for the rest of the semester. I didn't think he was leaving his wife, Ariel, but I did think that with you out of my life, I could manage him a lot more comfortably. I knew within weeks that wouldn't work and that was that. But, Walt, *about a year ago* I found out that there were real consequences from my affair with him, and they have begun to surface in ways I had never imagined."

"Consequences?" he asked, "Is there an outstanding motel bill at accrued interest? Did he fail to tip the doorman?" he joked.

"Walt, dammit, this is serious. I guess I'll take it one step at a time. I need to tell it to you in stages...the whole story."

"O.K., go for it." He smiled to himself as he tried to imagine how anything she could say would be a serious matter to him now.

She paused again, then began with a bit of a rush. "Walt, when you told me that you hoped I didn't come back to school, I heard you loud and clear. I didn't want to come back, but my parents wouldn't hear of it. Then, I missed my period and missed it again. I was pregnant, and that ended any discussion about returning to College of the Rockies."

She had his attention now. Peggy, her story unfolding, was in full stride. "I stayed home until I delivered the baby...it was a boy...and I gave him up for a closed adoption. In my mind, it was the only way that I could deal with the issue. I wasn't ready to raise a child, and until I had the boy placed, I couldn't really move on with my life. I didn't want to know where he went or who his adoptive parents were or where he lived. I just wanted to pretend that he didn't exist. And so, for the past thirty years, I have."

She went on. "A year ago, I received a phone call from a Trevor Reynolds. His voice was hesitant, and I thought it was a wrong number. I was about to hang up, when he said that he believed that I was his birth mother, and he wanted to meet me. Overwhelmed with that mixture of fear and curiosity that a message like this does to you, I chatted a bit more with him, and he sounded like a nice young man. I finally told him that if he could bring me some proof of his claim I would meet him at the local McDonalds and look at the documentation. Then, we could go from there."

"I met him in downtown Bend, and we had a great talk. He is well-spoken, has finished college at the University of Wyoming, and is ready to move on in life. This was one of his first steps, meeting his birth parents. He had all the right paperwork. His adoptive mother and father were Wyoming ranchers, Meg and Lyle Reynolds. He grew up there working cattle from horseback, learning about the business, and seizing all the education that they could give him. He was raised right, Walt, and he is darn good looking...great smile and personality. I think he has my color hair and mouth."

She paused in the telling, and as she did, Walt thought to himself, "Am I ever going to be rid of this maggot, Barry Swanson...now his DNA is infecting Peggy's life, and she's dragging my ass into it...why would she be calling him?

He asked.

"Why are you calling me about this, Peggy? Shouldn't you be telling this to ol' Professor Swanson?"

"Well," she said with a bit of tension, "That's what I did, Walt! I told Trevor that Swanson taught at College of the Rockies, and that he could probably find him through a faculty index. Want to hear more?"

What could he say, "Yep, go on."

"We talked for a long time. I told him about my family and Trevor mentioned that his father, Lyle, had recently died, and that he was finishing up selling the ranch and placing his mother Meg in her own home in Cheyenne. When he was done with that, he was going to go looking for work in public relations. He was a Political Science major. Took him a long time to get through college, finances you know, but he made it. I told him that he might want to visit Boulder and find Swanson before he took a job, and he agreed. We had a nice visit, and I kind of looked forward to hearing from him again."

"A few weeks later, I did. Now, Walt, this was about 11 months ago and the story just continues. It was long phone call...Trevor's voice words just gushed as he told me that he actually went out to Boulder and found Swanson, found his father! Out of teaching, Swanson had taken up work with a storage supply depot in Denver. He spent a lot of time in Boulder overseeing expansion of its storage facilities and generally representing the company.'"

"I asked Trevor where he was now, and he told me that he was still in Boulder. Good things had been happening there. He was gushing."

"Did you believe that?" Walt interjected.

"Well, good things and Barry Swanson don't go together in my opinion, but I was willing to listen. I asked Trevor to name the company because I didn't really think that storage could be such a dynamic business."

"It used to be called, *Sam's Storage*," he said "but now it was a small corporation, *SnakeEyes Inc*. The owners, twin brothers...Frick N' Frack...Swanson called them...and an associate named Andy... amused themselves in naming the company. It sort of appealed to its customer base. In bad times, Swanson told Trevor, people have to store goods and in good times they just buy more and leave their old stuff in warehouses. They were 'snakebit'."

Walt couldn't help himself, chuckled...snakebit he thought... clever. He interrupted again, "You're telling me, Peggy, that Swanson's now a player in the storage business...an English professor?"

"Yes...and there's more. I asked Trevor how Swanson seemed to treat him, and he said that he talked to him like his son and that they spent a lot of time together. He told Trevor why he left the University, something about an anonymous letter linking him to Jon Benet Ramsay's death and the investigation revealing his affairs ruined his marriage and his job at College of the Rockies. He believed that in some mystical way, he was just another casualty of Jon Benet's death."

Walt loved hearing of Swanson's distress about reports connecting him to the Jon Benet homicide, but he wasn't going to clutter up Peggy's account with a story about his own cleverness. "I think I understand that, Peggy. What else did he tell you about Swanson?"

"Well," she began, "He has a soft, southern accent, which I certainly remember, likes to quote literature and drinks sparingly, although he does smoke a lot of pot. He likes younger women, I guess...no change there from what I recall, and he even pointed out to Trevor one of his former lovers, an Indian woman named Lilting Song who happened to be window shopping downtown at the Boulder Mall. Swanson didn't say hello to her, but did mention that they had parted on good terms, and that he continued to have a strong business connection with her brothers and their tribe in Montana."

"Peggy, what seems to be the problem here? Swanson is bonding with his son and Trevor is learning more about his father. That seems normal enough."

"Save your kindness, Walt, there's more. I was curious about these brothers because I know how sensitive Montana is about its Indian reservation relationships. Swanson told Trevor that they were involved in running the Sioux Indian Casino, *Custer's Last Stand*. Apparently, the title struck Montana patrons as amusing, and it was doing a landslide business. He mentioned that he might be able to make a connection with the tribe that could give Trevor some entry into their casino structure."

Walt interjected, "So, as I hear this timeline, Peggy, about a year ago, you hear from Trevor, and a month later, he meets his father and gets inducted into the casino business, the family circle so to speak. So, the good news is that Swanson has accepted his son, is looking out for his future, and wants to bring him into a thriving business in Montana. Heck, Peggy, that is practically in Trevor's backyard. Would be a great opportunity for him, right out of college and all, don't you think?"

"I do not think! There's more. Swanson asked Trevor to swab for a DNA analysis and seemed satisfied because Trevor never heard another word about it, and then Swanson put him up at the Boulder Plaza while he talked to the Sioux brothers about the casino and a place for Trevor."

"Give me a minute, Peggy. This sounds like a story that I need to settle into."

He set his cell phone down, touched the unopened package of cigarettes that he always carried with him, wished that he were smoking again. He went to the fridge and got a diet Pepsi, cold, nearly frozen, the way he liked them, and went back to the table. He picked up the cell, put it on speakerphone, and settled himself into a comfortable chair next to a window where he could keep his eyes busy while he listened to the rest of this sorry tale.

"O.K., what's next Peggy, 'cause so far, it sounds like Swanson is looking out for his son, and there must be something in the story that is going to stink up everything the ol' Professor is doing, eh?"

"Yes...you're right," she said, "and it just gets worse and worse. OOPS! Sorry Walt, my husband just drove into the garage, and he doesn't know that you exist. I'll call you again in a few days. Sorry, got to go."

It was as it always was. She had to go. "O.K., let me hear from you."

He touched "OFF" put his phone in his pocket and then began to think. Peggy probably told the truth. She sure did disappear in a hurry after he last saw her, walking into the cold, her shoulders hunched up against the light wind that put her in a minus five degrees wind chill. He was a little surprised that she didn't come back to school, but now he knew. She was pregnant, and the thought crossed his mind about Swanson and paternity. Peggy was sure. He was sure because he always used condoms. Swanson was sure because he had the results of the DNA test.

So exactly how did this affect him, really? Not his son...not his wife...not his lover...not his problem. Why was he talking to Peggy? Well, he had asked her for the whole story, and she said that he would understand, and there was more to tell. He would just have to wait.

He mulled her call some more. There were a lot of untidy questions. Why _was_ Swanson so receptive to this sudden appearance of a son he never knew he had? What did he mean when he said he could work him into his business? How does one "fit in" to a casino workforce...one day of training and you were a floorwalker or something? What kind of connection did a storage business have to an Indian casino anyway? How did Trevor, a new college graduate, fit into it? He really wanted a cigarette.

Peggy called again, two days later, and picked up as though she had merely taken a deep breath.

"Walt, Swanson is just a disease that infects everything he touches. He put Trevor in contact with Lilting Song's two brothers, and they brought him up into Montana and put him to work dealing at the Casino. He was good at it, and within six weeks, they had him working behind the money counter, and then on the floor."

She took a breath, continued, "They taught him how to analyze gamblers, how to appeal to their greed and how to steer them toward games that offered real long odds and rarely, big payouts. He was a natural. Like his father, he could sell the message and keep the customer happy all the time the mark's money was disappearing."

Peggy went on, "Six months after he started working for the tribe, he met High Note, Lilting Song's sister, and they married. It was then, Trevor told me, that he began to wonder about the whole Casino connection. His brothers-in-law did not seem to respect Swanson, and once he moved to Montana, he seldom heard from his father. Whenever

Trevor visited Boulder, they had a meal together, and over time, as Swanson continued to speak highly of the financial importance of the tribe to the storage business, Trevor began to press him on that question, and one evening, Swanson laid out the entire structure."

"I asked Trevor if I really needed to know about this," Peggy went on, "and he said I did...that nothing made sense unless I had the whole picture."

"And, so what was it?" he asked.

"Really Walt I wasn't prepared for this...none of it."

"Prepared for what?" he asked.

"For this. The storage business is just a front for indoor pot grows! *Cube-It,* a hedge investment company, is the clearing house for their product, and a guy named Larry Belton is the brains behind the money movement. *Cube-It* washes pot money from *SnakeEyes Inc.* and the Sioux pot network in Montana through the tribe's casino, *Custer's Last Stand.* These guys, Frick n' Frack had expanded their original storage depot and now managed a chain in Boulder, Ft. Collins and Cheyenne. They also provide Trevor's new brothers-in-law, Lightning Strike and Waiting Cloud, with pot for their Montana network."

Walt interrupted the story, "Peggy, you telling me that you believe what Trevor is saying...you really believe him?

"Yes, I do," she said. "He was stunned by what Swanson told him and confused by the way he had subtly put him into a criminal network...his own son!"

"Swanson went on to tell him that *SnakeEyes Inc.* was generating more than forty million a year. There were risks, but he liked his odds in avoiding the feds. When Colorado legalized pot, and he was sure that it would, their networks would be ready to deliver product in ways that no one else could match."

"I asked Trevor what made him think that being a part of a pot network would work out well," Peggy's voice was more challenging.

"He said that Swanson told him that freelancers were always just a step away from lethal infighting, but he, the twins and Andy had complete confidence in one another. They laundered their money through *Cube-It,* and while they moved some of it into the Casino, they took out a lot more. Everyone was getting rich as the economy recovered from the .com crash. Of course, Walt, this means that Trevor is now a part of an interstate, illegal gambling and drug operation of huge proportions."

"Trevor told me that he was scared, but it was all working so well. He just didn't want to disturb anything," Peggy went on, "and I told him that he was on the edge of a personal disaster. But, Walt, he just didn't see it that way. He was entranced with Swanson and the entire network scheme. It was just spewing out money...lots and lots of money."

"Swanson played on this," she went on, "He got permission from One Who Sees, the tribal leader, and then hired Trevor to oversee the 15 different "mules" who moved product from *SnakeEyes Inc.* to *Custer's Last Stand* and then returned with casino money to be laundered through *Cube-It.* Swanson convinced Trevor that he was settling into a profession he could use to build a fortune.

"God, it just gets worse and worse, Walt," Peggy went on, "and this is my son. His father is ruining his life. When High Note became pregnant, Trevor found his position in the pot/casino/*Cube-It* connection all the more compelling. It was highly profitable and safe. He really didn't see the risks. He was wrapped up in the tribe's family, and insulated from the risk of actually growing pot. I was *so* angry...and then I just plain got scared."

Peggy said all of this with an edge he had never heard in her before. Guess she had grown up quite a lot over the years, Walt thought, but then, if you live long, maturity sometimes follows.

"Well, Peggy," he began, "It seems to me that Trevor is simply making choices, bad choices maybe, but maybe not. If Colorado legalizes pot, he really is in on the ground floor of a huge industry. His dad may just be looking out for his future, and he really does seem to be well accepted by his father-in-law and the Sioux family. Maybe it is all just for the best."

Peggy exploded, "Nonsense, Walt! That is just horse crap. I called Swanson *last week*. I've never done that once in my life, honestly, Walt, you need to believe that, but I'm glad I did. We had a little awkward small talk, but then I just said it to him outright: 'Barry, you are ruining your son's life. He's *not* the kind of material you need for this dirty, dirty business, and if the wall comes tumbling down, he's going to be in prison. You have got to stop this! I just really can't understand, after all that you have gone through, why you want ruin your son's life.'"

"I thought that I was going to make him back off, Walt, but he didn't and then even through the phone, I could see that conceited smirk he carries when he thinks he is going to surprise you with unique information, "You don't know, do you Peggy?"

"Know what?"

"I guess I should have told you. I think I just wasn't ready. I liked the way things were going."

"Know what?" she repeated.

"Two things," Swanson said in that soft southern accent which now repulsed her, "Trevor is not my son...and he just learned that he is fighting leukemia."

"I couldn't really say anything for a few moments, Walt," Peggy said, "Then I asked him why he would say that. Leukemia was no joke, and he had the DNA results."

"Yes," Swanson said, "I do, and I am not his father. My nominee is Walt Farmer, but only you know who the best candidate is for that honor, Peggy. I was having a great time keeping the truth from Farmer because somehow I know that he ruined me at College of the Rockies. But Trevor is ill now, and I guess Farmer can take responsibility for him. He *is* the father, isn't he, Peggy?"

"I just said, 'yes', and hung up."

"Walt, I wasn't having sex with anyone except you and Swanson, and DNA says Trevor's father is not Swanson. I don't need to know what you did to give Swanson such a motive to hurt you, but I think you have a son who needs you. Want to get a DNA test or do you want to go with me on this?

"I'll get a test. Send me Trevor's DNA profile. You really do know how to change my life, Peggy," Walt commented, and hung up. Even as he said this, he knew it was true. Peggy might deceive, but she did not lie. He sent in a cheek swab, then read about the failure rate on condoms, acknowledging to himself that he may have been a bit hasty using them in Steamboat Springs. Within the month he learned that he was a father...again...a single parent, and his son was dying.

He set down the DNA report, reached into his shirt pocket, took out the long-kept pack of Pall Mall. He opened it, found a matchbox in the junk drawer, struck it, lit the cig and took a long, hard drag. It was like he was smoking for the first time. His brain floated a bit and he relaxed as he exhaled. He remembered the deep, edgy flavor of tobacco, even stale tobacco, and he felt as though he could now control his thoughts.

For the next two days, in the *"He's Not Here"* bar, Walt smoked, sipped some beer and tried to bring his thoughts into alignment with a new reality. Another son, a grown man, a married man with family, a man with leukemia, his son. His usual formula when he dealt with shocking news was to remind himself that in three days, it wouldn't matter. He wasn't sure that strategy was going to work this time. Peggy had set his life in an entirely new direction, and he had not seen her now for 30 years.

"Just when you thought it was over, it wasn't over," he thought, and then asked himself, "Was that a Yogi saying? No," he answered himself. What was that saying he had heard lately? Oh yeah, Silvio in the Sopranos, *"Just when I thought I was out, they pulled me back in."* Yep, she'd done it.

Did he want to meet his son? Did he want to know him? Did he have an obligation to him? Did he feel that he could take on a new responsibility so soon after Lauren's death? What could he do that made sense for Trevor and also satisfy his own cautious desire to help him as best he could? Leukemia! His father had died from leukemia, but that was a long, long time ago. Did modern medicine have something more to offer than the blood transfusions that kept his father living for a crucial few weeks?

He pondered those years since his father's death, took notice of touchstone events, thought about his children with Lauren, wondered what they would think of a new sibling, one who was dying. Did having leukemia mean that you were just a dead man walking or was there some hope for Trevor.

He wondered who he could talk to about all of this, and then with a start, he thought of Moe. Moe, his high school classmate who had regaled them all at their last reunion with his story of Lori Larken and the child he had fathered and come to know a quarter century later. How had Moe handled it?

He looked at the cigarette, noting the way that it burned, the tobacco leaving an irregular pattern in the paper, like life maybe, reminding himself again how bad it smelled when it wasn't your puff to enjoy. He placed it on the edge of the ashtray, ordered another beer, and thought some more about Moe. He seemed to be pleased when he told the story of meeting his son, and he always had a soft tone in his voice when he spoke of Lori. Walt didn't remember the son's name, but that wasn't important now. Talking to Moe was. Where did he live? He could find out from the high school's reunion contact.

The next day, he phoned the high school, got the number he needed and called his class reunion classmate, Sally Monroe. He identified himself and asked for Moe's home address. Sally was really nice about it, and passed Moe's phone number along too. Where was he? Walt found himself looking at a map of Wisconsin, locating Tomah, a small town on the Burlington Northern route less than 90 miles from his own home. He needed to see Moe, wondering whether he should call or write first.

He decided to call him.

The phone rang from the far corner of the living room where Moe had installed it so that it would force him to walk to answer it. Walking was good, he thought, even if it was around the house, and it also let him decide, depending on his mood, whether he wanted to answer a call. These days, he lived with modest energy, level temperament and optimistic thoughts. Writing a new novel, one that tried to encompass some of his life lessons as a child growing up in Oklahoma, gave him purpose. He paused in his scratches, asking himself why he could not compose on a computer, and having no answer, pulled himself out of his chair and walked across the room.

"Hello," he said in that soft, soft voice that he used in social conversation.

"Hello there, Moe, or should I call you Kerry? This is Walt Farmer and I know that we don't talk much...maybe every five years," he said with a laugh, "But you know how life can give you a jolt every once in a while, and I'm dealing with one."

"Hi Walt. Good to hear your voice. I kind of like the name Moe. It holds good memories now and yep, I know about life and surprises all right. What's going on with you?

"Well, the short version is simply this. I apparently fathered a child a long, long time ago, and he has just surfaced into my life. I haven't actually met him, but I'm trying to think about whether I want to, if it would be a good thing for me. He is ill, seriously ill, and I am just not sure that I want to be involved in more death and dying. I know that you have a son with Lori Larken, and I was wondering if you can tell me something about your relationship with him. Are you glad that you have him in your life?"

"It's turned out well," Moe said. "When he found me I thought that he might have been looking for money or something like that, but he wasn't. He just wanted to meet me, and we had a good, warm visit before he left. He teaches and does genetic research at the Medical Center in the Twin Cities and was on his way to Chicago to visit his mother. Lori apparently works for a very high powered public relations firm, and has made quite a career for herself. So, yes, it was a candid meeting and left me feeling pretty good about myself.

"Moe, you just said something that caught my attention. Your son, what's his name, does genetic research?"

"Yep. His name is Brady, Brady Larken, and he is knee deep in something that I don't really understand, but he's getting a bit of a national reputation. Lori and I have begun to talk more regularly too, so there is more of a sense of sharing a son than I have ever had before. It's been a good experience."

"Moe, I don't want to get too assertive here, but my son, Trevor, Trevor Reynolds, was adopted out by his birth mother with whom he recently gained contact. She learned a couple of weeks ago that he is ill with leukemia."

"That's terrible!" Moe said, "I'm really sorry, Walt, and before you ask, let me tell Brady. He might have some ideas about treatment. Come on down and we'll visit with him and see what's what."

Three days later, Walt drove into Moe's driveway and parked alongside a nicely groomed three bedroom home, no doubt full of books, he thought. The arched, sloping, slightly flared roofline suggested the silhouette of the many regional barns he saw on the drive down, and the space inside proved expansive and comfortable to walk about. They had coffee together, caught up on some of the old stories about the River and Lori, and Walt told him about his stubborn decision to attend the Armory dance where he first met Peggy. "I guess first acts are written with an eye on the third," Moe commented. Walt agreed.

They began to talk of Trevor, and Moe said that he had called Brady, explained the health issues that had surfaced in Trevor's life. "He was excited right away," Moe said, "I knew that he had been working on something that he called 'T-cells' and he thinks that some unconventional therapy of that kind might really be helpful."

"How would that work," Walt asked, "Aren't there some kind of regulations about using experimental procedures on people?"

"Oh, yes," Moe answered, "But Brady explained that they were gathering subjects for a FDA approved trial, and just from what I told him...Trevor's age, general health before onset, and current fitness, he thought that he might well be eligible. He asked me to instruct Trevor to send his medical records to the Medical Center and that you should bring him to Brady's office as soon as you can."

Walt paused only briefly, "I guess I am going to have to meet my son." Two days later, he landed in Missoula, warmly greeted by One Who Sees. The chief spoke carefully: "Trevor is a member now, of our family, our tribe. His wife is my daughter. His child will be my child. His life is precious. What can you offer?"

Walt responded with candor and conviction, lightly tinged with emotion, "Trevor is also a member of my family. He is my son and his wife is my daughter and his child will be our child. I want to see if we can find new hope for Trevor and in that way find new life for all of us. Will you help?"

One Who Sees paused and looked at Walt carefully, weighed his words, let the silence linger for a few seconds, then nodded, and said, "Let us begin."

He took Walt by car to the casino headquarters, entered the building from the back entrance, walked a dozen steps and then turned into a hallway that led to a green painted door on the right. They entered, and Walt caught his first glimpse of Trevor Reynolds. He rose quickly, stepped forward and grasped, firmly, cleanly and with strength, the hand that Walt offered to him. They hugged briefly, looked into one another's eyes, and then gently separated and sat down.

"Well," Trevor said, "I've been a long time finding you, and I've gone down a falsely scented path lately, dammit. My birth mother told me of your story, and hers. I know that I'm a surprise with many surfaces, a shine here, an edge there, but I am the complete vessel, Walt. I hope that we're going to travel this passage together, 'cause I have every confidence that it will end well."

As he spoke, Walt could not help but notice that he may have had Peggy's smile and hair color, but his eyes were his own shade of blue, and his square shoulders, long torso and hairline were his. No doubt. No mistake. He also understood why Trevor was so successful in sales and how effective he must be in steering "marks" to ever higher levels of risk. He was genuine.

"Trevor, we have the rest of our lives to get to know one another, but my life has observable limits now, and yours is at risk, so let's get on with it. We need to get to Minneapolis. Right?"

"Right," Trevor replied. "I'm ready, let's go." He offered honor to One Who Sees, stopped at the last door to kiss High Note goodbye for now, and followed Walt out the door to the waiting car. Five hours later, they were in the Cities, checked in for the night. The next day, Moe met them at the Medical Center lobby and introduced them to Brady.

He explained the trial. "I have your medical records, Trevor. You've been diagnosed with acute lymphoblastic leukemia and that poses...a real challenge. We're going to confirm the diagnosis, and then we are going to remove from your blood something called T cells that are failing to produce the immune response that would kill the cancer. We modify them genetically, then infuse them back into your body."

If this works as we believe it will, they will attack cancerous cells. If successful, you will get better in a few weeks, and it will all seem like magic... something like the effects on the first patients who survived infection because of penicillin. We don't know with certainty how long it will last, but our work suggests that it could be effective indefinitely."

"When it doesn't work, there are no side effects. The disease will continue to have it way with you. So, there is no downside, and we think we are on to something. If you're willing to be our guinea pig, so to speak, follow me."

Brady turned, Trevor followed, and Moe and Walt looked at one another and slowly shook their heads. Each knew what the other was thinking: "There they go, our surprise sons, connected in life by confronting death." They went back to their motel. Walt called Peggy and told her that Trevor was in the trial, beginning therapy.

Moe called Lori to tell her that their son was looking well, saving lives and giving them much to be proud and thankful for. He asked if she wanted to come to the Cities for a week to see Brady, maybe stay with him during the first stage of the trial.

To his surprise, she said, "Yes". He hung up the phone, turned to Walt and said, "I'm discovering two things."

"What is that?" Walt murmured.

"I'm going to need a cell phone, and you are going to have to find another room for the week." Moe smiled that broadened grin when something pleased him. He wondered how Lori looked after all of these years, then he asked himself, "Wonder how I look?" Maybe it didn't matter either way.

****

Six months later, Walt again found himself sitting in the *"He's Not Here"* bar, and looked inside his new package of cigarettes. There was one left. He carefully moved the cellophane so that it would drop out softly. He took it in his right hand, moved it about with his fingers, looked at it, and smelled the freshly scented tobacco. Gently, he moved it to his lips, remembering again the old slogan, *Pall Mall: Outstanding, and They Are Mild*. He took a match from the paper folder, the last one it turned out, struck it and lit the stick. He ducked his eyes to avoid the smoke of the match and closed them to escape the plume from his first exhale.

He thought about Peggy, and this intersection of seemingly timeless relationships that people shared. How many directly affected: Trevor, Brady, Lori, Moe, One Note, Swanson, One Who Sees, Peggy and himself. Distribution on the map: Oregon, Illinois, Minnesota, California, Montana, Colorado, Wisconsin. Lives lost: none; Lives saved, Trevor's, at least for a time. Lives changed: all of them.

Trevor brought his wife, One Note, to the Cities where she delivered a boy. Trevor continued his participation in the study and went to work in public relations for a subsidiary of his mother's company, *Sundance Live*. Time was an undefinable commodity. He just didn't know what his equation might conclude, but Brady told him that his chances were good, not guaranteed, but good.

One Who Sees knew that his casino was safe, his family whole and the tribe's investments continued to build new homes and provide employment to a new generation of Sioux. *Cube-It* and *Custer's Last Stand* continued to make millions.

Swanson continued to profit and find new adventure with women who were younger than he, but older than they used to be. Walt knew that he would likely live long and live by his own rules until the day he died.

Lilting Song read of his death, attributed to a heart attack suffered in a suite at the Boulder Regency. Word on the street was that it was an overdose of a twice married and twice divorced graduate student. She smiled softly as she summoned again the image of Swanson's courtly seduction, his unusual commitment to intimacy, his tender treatments.

She still found it sad that he would so often ruminate about the injustice that he suffered when connected to Jon Benet Ramsay's death. Lilting Song could see how his lifestyle made him a soft target for gossip, speculation and eventually a police inquiry that turned his life upside down. Occasionally, he would curse Jon Benet, mention something about a "damn dirt farmer professor who smelled of manure" and then fall into a mood that she combatted with her own body and his supply of Eagle Gold.

Now, she thought, he was gone and only her memories could supply the narrative that led her tribe to become so wealthy. She claimed his body, saw to it that he was buried as he told her he wished to be, in a cardboard box that would dissolve quickly into the earth as would his body. She wept for him, briefly.

She noted that he was but four rows above that of Patsy Ramsay. Strange placement she reflected, as she reviewed again what she knew of him, his past, his passions, and his wasted life. She thought sadly, of Malcom's words in Macbeth, "Nothing in his life became him like the leaving it."

A few years later, when the rains came and the floods poured over the banks, Swanson's remains leaked out of their resting spot, rose to the surface and flowed in an eccentric path down the cemetery hill. Staining the earth as they traveled, they settled into the water-softened pockets of Patsy Ramsay's grave. When the fires came, the organic particles dried, lifted gently and rose into a smoke much like the one that clouded his life.

Brady published his work in the *Journal of Research* and married Sliding Scale, the chief's youngest daughter. She was now pregnant, and Lori was going to be a grandmother, a status that she fully embraced. Moe wrote a piece of fiction about Lori, *Finding Futures Past*, even as he wondered how long she would be in his life.

That left Peggy out there in Oregon, Walt thought, far removed from her son and his life, but content that her commitment to him, once found, had saved his life and led her back to Walt for just one more look. To mutual satisfaction, they both confirmed that what had seemingly ended long ago, was over. Yogi knew.

Walt noted that the cigarette, mostly ash now, burned closer to his finger, but he needed some final thought, some plan of action. He didn't want to live near his children. He would become a burden. He was tired of Wisconsin's cold and snow. Maybe he would find a warm, tax-free state? Maybe he would travel, especially during the winter. Who knew? In this day and age, he might write a blog about his trips and meet someone on line.

He finished the cigarette, ground the butt in the tray so firmly that it squeaked. Only the filter remained. It was his last cigarette, and he went to the counter, bought a pack of Marlboros and placed them carefully in his shirt pocket where they would remain unused. He turned, walked out of *"He's Not Here"* and murmured to himself as his feet hit the sidewalk, "No, he's not."

Boomerang

Where does life go when it decides to take absence without leave. What purpose when the zest leaks out of the bucket and leaves the list behind? Walt felt drained...by Lauren's decline and death, by retirement, by the stillness in the house, the silence in his ears. The business about Peggy and Trevor now comfortably set aside, only his mind seemed active, and what it told him he let flow into a mental reservoir of jumbled phrases and sentences, to percolate until he felt like sorting them into sensibility.

For months, his days passed without purpose or plot. If he felt like walking the dog, he did. If he felt like seeing relatives, he drove long distances, enjoying hours behind the wheel where he could think his thoughts. When he felt like doing nothing, he lolled about the house, listening to Louis Prima, Linda Ronstadt, Joni Mitchell, Pavarotti, The Beatles, Sinatra, discovering Billy Joel. All performed for his four walls and over the weeks he narrowed his preferences until he ended up with the Beatles, Joel, Ronstadt and the Hoboken guy. He played them loud, as loud and as long as he wanted.

When he felt like escaping, getting out of town, something in Frank's gravel edged voice spoke to him. When he felt like courting danger and women, Joel told him the way. When he celebrated life and memories, the Beatles swept him along. When he simply wanted to be lost in the song, Ronstadt embraced him. Searching for love? Joni reigned. But Sinatra's nuanced phrasing, seamless breaths, and cocky certainties eased his spirit, and he listened to Frank's song book over and over again.

Amidst the power of the music, he made three resolutions to guide the next part of his life.

He would never remarry. Permanent partnership demanded compromise, concession, loosely defined but notable boundaries. He just didn't want to invest that energy, did not want the constraints. He mulled that thought a long time and then put a period after it. Nope, he would never marry again.

He would never return to California. Just the thought of mixing with the mob on the freeways, absorbing the enervating heat and dusty air of the Valley, shelling out for taxes, and adjusting to its changing demographics repelled him. He thought with amusement that it may have taken a century and a half, but Mexico seemed to have won the War of 1846.

He would never own a house again. The most stressful moments of his life dealt with real estate, not the purchase of it, but its sale. He thought wryly, one really didn't want to sell a home until one had to sell it, and then all fell into the hands of "the market". God, it was a nightmare. Easy enough to rent. Let someone else worry about maintenance, taxes, insurance, landscaping...all the quarterly worries about keeping a home running. If he felt like moving to another state, another city, he could just do it. Nope, he wasn't going to deal with owning property ever again.

Fortified with principles that filled him with a sense of personal freedom, financial control and geographic rootlessness, he drifted along in his world of music, simple foods, regular exercise and sleep.

There came a time when Walt asked himself whether he wanted to look back into the bucket and pick a slip. He surprised himself. His thoughts took him all the way back to high school, an English class which touched on Hemingway, a trip to Tijuana. He and three friends sampled tourist life across the border, witnessed the bullfight, escaped jail and crawled back home chastened and thankful that their life lesson came without permanent injury.

But, the thought kept occurring. The bullfight, Tijuana. Matadors in Mexico. Could it get better? He remembered that Hemingway suggested that Madrid hosted the finest corrida's in the world, and he decided to go, to see what he had always wanted to see. Why not? He booked his spring flight and on impulse asked his sister Becca to go with him. He wanted to get to know her better, and he suspected she would be a great traveler.

Spain embraced them with its nonchalance, its easy daily tempo, its embrace of the matadors but its more intense absorption of world class soccer. Walt dipped into a cultural warp wherein he neither spoke the language, understood the rituals of socialization, nor liked the dining menus in restaurants and tapas bars that did not open 'til nine pm. But he delighted in the walks he and Becca took, sharing memories, laughing at impulsive choices, walking out of a flamenco performance that both thought unimaginative and loud. Together they enjoyed the Spanish language version of *My Fair Lady*, made fun of themselves eating at McDonalds and generally enlivened one another's days.

She supported every decision he made and on impulse they travelled to Seville, a one day trip on a bullet train that led him to yet another bullring, one where classical matadors fashioned reputations that lasted: Joselito, Manolete, Belmonte. He knew enough to feel the power of the ghosts who lingered near those sands once stained with blood, and in the chapel he reached out and captured a bit of their souls.

Home again, his sister took a little extra time to visit with him in Saint Clare, and then she left for California. He did not envy her life in the Golden State. He left it once, nearly forty years ago, and had yet to feel even a twinge to return. It troubled him a bit that he felt no longing for anything. What exactly did he want in this last segment of life? He asked that question frequently, without answer, and settled in for another Wisconsin winter, thinking about selling his house and taking residence in an apartment.

He spent a little time in local bars, sipping beer for pleasure and flavor, mulling his thoughts, wondering how much of his past might endure into his future. On a whim, he accepted an invitation from the university to visit Swansea, Wales and build good will for student exchange. He took the opportunity to visit London, meeting on the streets another American, from Minnesota, Jonas Kirk. Had to give him a follow-up call sometime...sometime.

Then, a call from Peggy, another voice from a past that he had put away and for a few months, uninvited life controlled him. He found excitement in the emergency of a moment, but in the end, with Trevor safe and Peggy put away, he had yet to answer the question of his own future. Did he care about unmarked time anyway? Maybe aging had to do more with letting life go and simply ignoring its options. Maybe, growing old fit his mood, framed his future. At least he knew what he was not going to do. He just didn't have a hunger for adventure.

His one firm grasp of changing times sat upon his desk in his bedroom: his computer. He liked what it brought to the joys of creative writing, enjoyed some correspondence with email friends and a few relatives, felt complete control over the degree to which anyone made demands upon him. London and Spain had enlivened him a bit, upon reflection, but gathering new energy as he might, he had no thoughts about where to spend it. He still listened to Sinatra almost weekly, still loud, still comforting.

Winter passed. He gave away the cats, made plans to place his dog with a nephew and relocate. He wanted less responsibility, more control, fewer family crisis, more financial stability. He wanted out of Wisconsin winters. Maybe a move to Arizona, maybe Washington State. One had rain, the other did not, but neither levied a state income tax.

Late one night, he opened his email in an effort to postpone yet another day lost to listlessness, and he found a new correspondent. Sender: Sally Monroe. He recognized the name easily enough. Sally had for many years been the correspondent hub for all of his high school reunions and helped him find Moe when he went looking for him. He remembered her look from high school, a lengthy 5' 10" freshman brunet who towered over his 4' 11" frame. She travelled in a circle which abutted his, but while he had dated one of her friends, by the time he grew to height, she was going steady with the man she married. He didn't remember ever exchanging a word with her in high school. Still, nice to hear from her, whatever she had to say, and he clicked "open".

She wrote in the friendly manner that high school acquaintances have: polite, thoughtful, tentative. Learning of his recent travel from a mutual friend, she thought the class might enjoy seeing his adventures through a link she could place on the class website. He thought that a nice thing to do, told her so and asked how life was treating her. Her reply began a series of exchanges. Following her husband's death a few years earlier, she remained living near the River, enjoyed her family, pursued genealogy, loved to quilt, lived a quiet life in a quiet community. That she lost her spouse sparked some interest in Walt because he shared a similar loss, and he wrote about his feelings, asked questions of her thoughts, and their messages began to take on new energy.

He asked if she had thought much about her life, reflected any upon it, and she described her interest in genealogy, a pursuit which confronted her with intrigue, mystery, and imprecision while delivering the satisfaction of putting things together and getting them right. She kept an almost daily journal begun decades before, and she wanted to work on a family history. She mentioned some of the struggles she had raising her family, ones that were outside his experience. He asked whether she could identify a defining moment in her life. She replied, "Yes, the death of my father when I was nine."

In this he joined with her, for as he reflected on his time after Lauren, grieved her loss, he found that those tears never concluded without reaching out and embracing the death of his father. To his surprise, as he emerged from his grieving he found himself able to speak of his dad without breaking down. For the first time in his life, Walt could bring his father's image into his mind, recollect the tone of his voice, play his words into his thoughts, review his presence in his youthful life and do it all without crying but, 50 years and counting, he had yet to revisit his grave.

He identified the many ways that loss had motivated him, embittered him, provoked his search for emotional security, cast a natural skepticism about adults into a bitter suspicion and a dislike of them and their institutions. Powerful fall out from a natural event, he thought, but there it was, written large in his actions, his attitudes and his emotional needs.

To great relief and further curiosity, he explored these feelings with Sally, found her responses open, direct and lengthy. For the first time in a very long time, he found himself interested in someone other than himself. She joked in prose, defined her professional work life carefully and precisely, asked questions of him that he enjoyed answering. He could imagine her laughter being full and hearty. In short, she was a person of interest.

It didn't take much effort to summon the energy to go meet her, once again for the first time, he thought, and as he flew into the Valley he wondered what had changed in the landscape below since he left some 40 years ago. To judge by the brown earth, sagebrush and light white brushes of alkaline soil below, it appeared much the same.

Oil wells, familiar, lower in silhouette but still a productive part of the economy, popped up as though they were tiny metal leeches sucking black liquid from the earth. Where the land turn green, its color had been forced by man in his plantings, an occupation always challenged by draught, heat and soil variances. Nourished by deeply drilled well waters or by canals slashed across the landscape, the plants flourished, as did settlement. All of this in a desert climate, he noted. Life and work in the land of the River remained complicated in what it offered and what it surrendered.

So, not much had changed. His view dropped lower and lower until the familiar bump told him that he had survived a controlled air crash once again. His thoughts turned to meeting Sally Monroe. He knew her better now, her words and her spirit a part of his daily messaging. His question focused now on how he would feel at her door when she opened it.

He relaxed at first glance. He found a smile, a gentle hello, real interest in how he was getting along in life and a relaxed conversation focusing on the high school class website.

He noticed her quilts on the walls, enjoyed the space and placement of furnishings, breathed the air of the home and found it pleasant, embracing. They talked about friends from high school. When a memory brought her to laughter it was as hearty and full, as unrestrained as he had imagined it might be.

He offered supper out. She accepted, and really, from that moment on, he felt connected, and he pondered briefly how quickly could one make a decision about companionship and still trust one's judgment. Her long legs, slender ankles and attractive silhouette filled his eye, pleased his senses, and walking with her alongside let him feel that he was in the right place.

After a nice meal of prime rib, her favorite she said, they ended up at the Crystal Palace, dancing, and as he told Sally later, when he walked her off the dance floor for the first time, he felt a deep sense of connection. Her fingers, long, warm, supple and firm, entwined around his with gentle tones, and he knew that he did not want to lose that special feeling he felt just holding her hand.

When he invited her back to Saint Clare to visit, he saw their links strengthen. Walking through a parking lot outside a restaurant, he told her that he was falling in love with her, to be fairly warned. She smiled a special look, took a glance at him and murmured that she was not afraid.

Things moved quickly after that. Another flight to California, this time feeling as though a personal odyssey would soon come full circle. Another visit from Sally to meet his children, and as they sat across the table from one another, his son, Rob, asked her, "So, did you ever date my dad in high school."

"Oh, no," Sally replied with a moment's pause, "He was way too wild for me."

Walt's jaw dropped, Rob's eyes bugged out, both astounded at the statement but for different reasons. Rob could not imagine his father "being wild" and Walt did not see anything other than "having fun" in his adolescent behavior. He tried to explain to Rob that Sally was a foot taller than he for most of their high school years. His son just smiled. His daughter, Elaine, laughed. In time, as he reported on his youthful adventures to Sally, she simply looked at him, sometimes sighed, and he began to see how she might have thought him a bit wild.

They married three months later, honeymooned in Hawaii, planted their first thin roots in the big city by the River and began to travel. Sally had only one condition. She didn't want to go anywhere Walt had already visited and London and Paris excepted, they didn't.

The countries quickly mounted in number: Canada, Panama, China, Australia, Mexico, Ecuador, Chile, Argentina, Uruguay. Cities such as X'ian, Prague, Rome, and Budapest treated them to visible history, sometimes ruins. They transited the Panama Canal. A river boat cruise from Moscow to St. Petersburg taught them that Russians were dour indeed, but their antiquities were remarkable. He never tired at looking at mosques and their domes set so precisely, marking the four directions E-W-N-S. They found Red Square memorable and Moscow gridlocked in traffic.

Shorter ventures interspersed: Canadian Rockies by train; Alaska by cruise ship to Anchorage, air to Prudhoe Bay and bus down the Dalton Highway; New Orleans, Dallas, Las Vegas and Yellowstone, half of Montana and the Grand Tetons. Sometimes they felt guilty for their late-in-life opportunities.

Most of the time they felt invigorated, treated, thrilled. On occasion they just felt tired.

They decided to cruise the Baltic visiting Estonia, Sweden, Germany, and Finland. A trip to remember, he thought before they left Los Angeles, and he thought the same thing when they returned three weeks later having left his appendix behind in Helsinki. Surprising events kept popping into his life.

He reflected upon those three resolutions he made in the months after Lauren's death: never marry, never live in California, never own real estate. Yet where was he now? A new love in his life which brought him peace, affection and all of the emotional highs that courtship carried with it. He and Sally knew how lucky they were, how much their mature commitments enhanced their loving, provoked creativity, embraced aging.

What more did he find? California living brought relief from Wisconsin winters as well as bad air, good people and gentle living. He found the sudden mixing of ethnicity and colors notable but agreeable. Walled communities and water shortage contrasted sharply with the free form yards of Wisconsin neighborhoods and nearly two feet of annual rainfall. He now navigated heavy traffic to shop, eat, golf or attend theatre, but there was energy everywhere...hard to avoid it.

Then there was his resolve about owning real estate. When he and Sally moved to the East Hills, he invested in the mortgage, shared with her the responsibility of home ownership, one that seemed far easier than he remembered, but maybe there were fewer problems. At least there were no children, no pets.

On the first Memorial Day after they married, they visited family burial sites scattered amidst the carefully aligned grave markers surrounded by the cemetery's flat, green surface. Headstones, illuminated by bright sunlight, bedecked with flowers and small flags fluttering in the occasional whiff of air, presented a mosaic memorial. Walt recalled that a few months after his father's death, he had visited his grave. Never since.

Cautiously, he walked up to the white, weathered stone, stared at its carved data, sat down, let his mind wander, taking time, admitting thoughts and feelings long buried as securely and as deeply as the bones below him. Memories circled, swirled, found a crack and began to leak out of their long locked compartment. His father's essence caught his emotional trigger and surfaced, first in a trickle, then a stream, finally a flood. He began to cry, at first small tears slipping down his face, then as his pain grew, he wept in sobs, gasps, small moans. He let himself go for as long as he wanted, and it was a long time. Eventually the pool emptied leaving a few stifled shudders, and he breathed long rasps of relief, feeling at peace in a way new to both his mind and spirit.

When ready, he stood with a gentle sigh, accepting and now keeping within reach memories of the figure he could never see again. Life felt good somehow, exhaustedly good. Coming home to California, to this burial plot, to his father, released his pain and in making it a conscious part of his life, let him carry it gently forward.

Launched into life by forces he neither saw nor knew, he had for more than 50 years rotated vigorously and noisily, propelling himself across empty space as a boomerang might, framing new perspectives, identifying new geography, swooshing through invisible obstacles and the occasional swarm of insects. His life followed an unpredictable arc as he drained himself reaching for all that he could touch.

Finding his zenith, he flared, paused, reversed in mid-air to seek his point of origin. Floating more, rotations slowing, he found comfort in currents unseen yet essential to his journey. He flattened for his landing as a boomerang floated back to its master, used but not used up, feathering at just the right angle, finding comfort as it landed safely in the soft hands that launched it.

So, there it was. Three years following his pledge on what he would not do, what he wanted his life not to be, Walt found himself invested in all that he had decided to abandon and freed from the anguish of his father's death. A loss, to be sure, but one he could accept, a feeling he could place quietly in his memory and one which now freed him to embrace the years he had left with Sally.

How to account for this sequence of life, love, marriage and health, these intersections of need and deliverance? Good luck? God's wishes? Impulsive correspondence? Freakish fortune? Serendipity?

"Whatever" he thought, the word surfacing out of a current idiom that he always thought amusing in its casual expression, weighty in its existential truth.

Whatever.

Advice for Old Men

Walt stood quietly in front of the urinal, pausing, relaxing his back, extending the wave down to his bladder and waiting for the flow. He shifted his feet a bit, and then went through his routine again. This was not a new procedure. For the past several years, he had noted that emptying his bladder simply took more time. It reminded him of a good friend he knew in college who, even then, was timing the interval that it took him to pee. He thought that eccentric, but then, his friend _was_ eccentric. Today he could appreciate the use of that information. How long was it going to take?

He waited, fiddled with his spigot and tried again. Typically, he could start his dribbles, could go a bit, then pause, start again, and in a series of gentle contractions, he would gain relief. But nothing was happening. He could feel his bladder asking for release, and after a time he tried to push it to empty, without result. He sighed, paused again with some concern and tried one more time. The whole routine...the whole procedure...nothing. Not a drop. No flow. He could not go. "SALLY," he hollered, "I CAN'T PEE!"

A week later, Farmer said hello to his new urologist and opened the conversation by asking, "When you have to sit down to pee, isn't there something wrong?"

The doctor looked at him carefully and said, "If you are a man, yes."

Walt didn't laugh, but he smiled. "So what is it?" he asked, "The prostate has finally enlarged too much?"

"Likely," said this pleasant man with the words M.D. after his name, "but until we do a little examination, I can't be sure."

"What kind of examination? Do I have to bend over or what?" The kindly face said that yes, that would be a part of it, but there would also be a look up the urethra to see what was what. He thought about that, grimaced. He thought about the digital exam he was being promised, and he tensed again. He thought about not being able to pee, and he said, "OK, let's get this done."

Thirty minutes later, Farmer tried to read the doctor's face as he began his explanation of what he had found. His features were kind and neutral, his words shocking. "What I am seeing and feeling is this," he said. "You do not have an enlarged prostate, at least nothing of significance and your recent PSA numbers are very reassuring. Your bladder is in good shape."

Walt held his breath. There was more to come, he could just feel it. The White Coat went on, "However, when I looked up your urethra, I discovered a stricture. Scar tissue near your bladder neck is blocking the flow. You are trying to pee through an opening the size of the tip of a ball point pen."

"Well," Farmer asked in what he thought was his best clinical manner, "Where did that come from and what do we do about it?" The physician's gentle feature responded briskly, "There is no accounting for its cause. A fall on a bicycle bar, teeter-totters in your youth, long bicycle rides on a hard seat, an injury of any kind to the tissue between your legs could have caused it. Fixing it is another question."

He was very anxious to hear the answer to that question, and the voice of all-knowledge went right on, "There are three options, but doing nothing is not one of them. First option, I can go up into the urethra and cut an opening through the stricture and that might work for a while. Second option is I can go in and use a laser and vaporize the stricture, and that might work for a while too." The lab coat paused.

"What do you mean, 'might work for a while'. What is a while?" There was apparently an issue here. No cancer, but still, a real problem.

"Well," the kindly visage spoke softly and clearly, "Neither of those two procedures is likely to solve the problem, long term, and you will likely be getting catheterized periodically to keep the stricture open even as it is in the process of closing."

Farmer did not like the sound of this. He had heard of men who needed to catheterize themselves every day just to pee. Was he about to join the insertion society? If so, how did one do that? Was there a special lubricant, a form of lidocaine, a special type of catheter?

What were the risks? What was the long term prognosis? Would this affect his sex life? Would he have a sex life? Could he practice yoga and learn special relaxation techniques? Was this another step in the final downward spiral?

He had a lot of questions. "Why do you say that it will be in the process of closing?" he asked, "Isn't there a way to solve the problem once and for all. Am I going to have to deal with this the rest of my life? And how long would it be between closing, a week, a month, three months, what? Can I travel for two or three weeks on end? Do I *want* to travel for a month or so? Am I going to 'have catheter, will travel'?"

"Well," his good friend, (the Dr. had been promoted to close companion now that they had shared a kind of intimacy), said, "Management is one option, but there is only one way to really solve a stricture."

"What is that?"

A pause, and then, "We (he guessed that meant the gentle doctor and God) would do a tissue graft. That solves the problem in 90% of the cases."

The voice paused, and there was a silence. The words *tissue graft* moved immediately outside his comfort zone. He could barely utter the words.

"What would you be grafting. From where would it come and how would it work?"

"We take a piece of tissue from the inside of your mouth, scrape all of the fat off of it, sterilize it, and then we make an incision, gain access to the urethra, open it, and insert the new tissue, then close it back up." The voice that fills the room went on, "That makes an enlarged channel, and the scar tissue doesn't grow on the good tissue we put in place. It is a wonderful, simple process and it has excellent results." His new guardian angel was really enthusiastic about this surgical trick.

Silence...

Farmer had nothing to say for a time. Burns and skin grafts, plastic surgery and skin grafts, necrosis and skin grafts. Of all this he was familiar, but urethra and tissue grafts was new to him. Finally, he asked his new protector to describe the incision point, and the professional surgeon explained gently but confidently that the closest access and most bloodless access to the urethra was a dorsal incision.

To Farmer, "dorsal" meant a shark's fin, and that wasn't comforting. He wondered what it meant to God's agent. The gentle hands motioned in explanation. It was a small incision between the anus and the testicles. Walt paused then speculated, "It has to be small doesn't it. Too long and it damages other important features of my dorsal form, right?" he asked.

"Correct," the voice from above responded in a reassuring tone.

"You mentioned that this graft will solve the problem in 90% of the cases; what happens if it fails?" "Well," the smile said, "You will be back where you started. No harm, no foul, and we can try it again."

"This sounds like a pretty technical piece of micro-surgery," he said, noting in his mind the diameter of a urethra. "Oh, yes." the tissue expert replied, "It is done with magnifying glasses and very fine instruments, and while I don't do this surgery often, I am quite familiar with the anatomy and the procedure."

Farmer's ears, which were not the subject of concern here, focused on that last sentence, *"don't do this surgery often"*. "Oh? How often do you do it?"

"I did one last year," the voice replied. This gave Farmer significant pause.

He asked, "You say that this stricture is close to my bladder; is there a possibility of incontinence as a by-product of the operation?" His man of manipulation hesitated, then said carefully and artfully, "Yes, there is that possibility, and for that reason, I would be inclined to refer you to a surgeon at University of California San Francisco with whom I have worked in the past. He once built a man an entirely new urethra."

"An entirely new urethra." That phrase filled the room and stayed there awhile; he pondered. Then, he thanked his surgical figure for the diagnosis and the information, and said, "I'm going to take this home and discuss it with my wife and think long about what to do."

"That is an excellent decision," he reassured Farmer. "When you have decided, get in touch with me. If you want to go ahead with the surgery, I will make an appointment for you with UCSF."

It took the discussion to Sally, and she paused only briefly, then offered her opinion, "Either now or later."

Still it took him a week to decide. The flow remained tricky. The prognosis without treatment not good. A graft, while frightening to think about, looked like the right thing to do. However, as he thought it over, he decided that his local man of knives would not be the one to do it. He asked to go to a specialist in the specialty, and see what he could offer.

Two more weeks, and he was in San Francisco. His new god was young, good looking, quiet spoken, and wonderfully confident. He had replaced the man who built new urethras, but he had also been trained by him. When asked how many of these "mouth to target" grafts he had done, he said, with a smile, "Well, last week I did eight of them." That sealed the deal.

Within a month, Farmer was in surgery, and after an overnight stay in the hospital, he went home to recover, catheter in place, urine flow secure, graft inserted and his mouth sore. For the next three weeks, he learned the acrobatics of showering, drying and hot-air blow drying his incision and surrounding tissues. He healed quickly and well. He protected his surgical site remembering that for the rest of his life, he would sit on his haunches and avoid placing his butt on hard surfaces. An air cushion would accompany him in the golf cart.

Then he was back in San Francisco where Angel Hands removed the catheter, filled his bladder, let him pee and pronounced him good to go, so to speak. The drive back home was a delight, although it required them to stop at intervals to empty his bladder of the many ounces of water that he was drinking. "You will find that the flow will ease even more as the swelling goes down," his graft guy said.

When he got home, he began to see what the new tissue was doing for him. He had full control of all functions; he was able to empty his bladder without effort, and he could shut it down with two, maybe three shakes. A few days more, and Farmer decided to measure the time it took him to complete his duties: 15 seconds. Then, he decided to measure the arc and distance of the stream: four feet. He decided that the world was a better place for him, and he counted the many times in his life that modern medicine had saved his life (four). No wonder people were living longer...and better.

Well, easy come, easy go; easy start, easy flow.

Aim High

He watched the video, trying to digest it upon first effort, realizing that he could not do that. It was going to take a lot of repetitive work to absorb it, but there was a payoff. If he succeeded he could finally soar higher than the rest of the group. Sure, they drank together, joked together, even travelled together sometimes, but at the end of the day, any day, he was going to glide over them; he was going to be looking down on them. It was going to happen someday, and soon.

Each of the guys had real physical strengths, but the way they went about it limited their ability to get their feet properly grounded. Some just lunged, launched themselves without really understanding. Others spent half their moments just thinking about the challenge, knowing that the answers were probably not in their heads, especially if it were taking them a lot of time to grasp the body mechanics they needed to get it into the air.

They reminded him a lot of study groups in college. The subject was before them, their notes beside them, but they spent more time talking than solving. Stories abounded. Jokes flowed. Looks wandered into stares at the women nearby. Subject matter lay before them, just along for the ride, and it didn't get much attention.

He preferred a solitary exploration of the task. He felt the competition to get things together, put them in order and win the pot of money. That being the case, why not just go at it alone? When he was ready, he could float above the others.

So he listened to the tape, imagined how he could follow the instructional cues and spent time trying to reproduce the intellectual process that allowed him to solve the challenge. Sometimes he took to jogging so as to clear his mind and strengthen his legs. Often he carried light weights along with him to strengthen his shoulders and wrists. His stamina grew. Even his balance improved as he ran over uneven ground mixed with grass, dirt and an occasional gopher hole. To misstep was akin to falling down. He learned through all of this the importance of balance, the challenge of timing and the absolutely essential ability to maintain rhythm with every shift of his body. He earned great respect for the whims of the air moving above him. Soaring had many meanings, and to him it led to arduous efforts to make his tool conquer the air currents.

"Get a grip on it", he would sometimes say to himself. He would pause a moment and just get a sense for the challenge. He could imagine its lift-off, its arc, its flight balancing itself against the air, the wind, then its ultimate landing, soft and safe. With those thoughts in mind, he could often duplicate with some regularity the skills that it took to get him close to the answer he needed to find. Find it he would, and he would do it before the rest of the group. That in itself would provide him with the respect he sought and might lead to even wider recognition. He loved problem solving.

Sometimes he talked to the rest of them. They could joke a bit about how "Stella" got her groove back and how the tempo of the music could force the most innocent of turns into a full-fledged attack on the challenge, but even as they laughed at the joke, and at one another, there was that little edge under all the trash talk. Whether in the showers, changing towels, dressing for work or sampling treats on the way to the venue, they had a barb to offer, an edge to keep, a banter that both lifted their spirits and at the same time, lent caution to their every movement. They were quite a foursome, identified by secretaries, approached by admirers, sometimes the subject of local press who found their avocation both a little ludicrous, and at the same time, an accomplishment worth perfecting. What was all of the fuss about?

He thought of how they must look when they took a group outing and tried to pierce the air. Ralph was simply huge. His gut covered his belt and he had a huge head, so large that he had custom made caps to keep his face shielded from hardship as they worked at their challenge. He had a great sense of humor, amused by every frailty known to man, imagined every insult that a woman could offer and kept a ready response at lip's end. While an admirer of the outdoors, he preferred indoor challenges, especially ones that ended in beers paid for by others.

Milt was thin, dressed almost always in an outfit that clashed with the woodlands, slipping into the meadows with a smooth gait that he tried to convert, without success, a method to solve the technology that they were all wrestling with. He had a great sense of humor, both for jokes about his argyle sweaters and his apparent inability to keep an idea in motion for more than about half the time it took to execute it. He was fun to be with.

Gary was a former professional boxer, and when he joined the effort to solve this problem, he brought with it a scientific approach. He knew about angles, deflection, arcs, lift and the product of F=MA. It was not that he was an experimental scientist, but he worked at his task like a lab-rat, quietly concentrating, fully engaged and often nearly successful.

He enjoyed them all whether they were in the bar, the weight room, the classroom, the tape room, the grill or just walking about the great outdoors. They tried to keep score of one another's errors, jokes and failures, and they did so with humor, but with relentless accuracy. Somewhere, sometime, someone was going to float success, and finally, after a year of effort by the group, it happened.

To his intense satisfaction, he was the victor. They had decided to take the challenge one again, and met at 10:00 a.m. to see what they could manage. A favorable wind, perfect temperature and humidity in the air seemed to let their efforts float with ease. They each brought their tools, stretched their limbs, finally beginning their task. They took turns going first so as to keep each of them fresh and lively. Easy enough to get lift with a nice stiff wind in their faces. Still, no one of them seemed to be winning, and then finally it happened.

As they reported it in the clubhouse, Ol' Walt, as he was known, had stepped up and solved the problem on the third hole with five simple words: drive-approach-chip-putt-par. It may not have been for more than $500 bucks, but as the first one of the group, widely known as *Fore For Four*, ever to make par on any hole on the course, he drew out the entire bank. Reputation secure, he made the rest of the round his plaything, balancing bogey with bogey, but finishing the 18th hole with a 45 foot putt for another par that solidified his reputation for years and gave the group a new name: *Par and Pals*.

These things counted in the game of life.

Pitter Pat, Pitter Pat

Walt recalled a variety of comments about aging. Bette Davis famously said that it was not for sissies. The Western artist, Charles Marion Russell, complained about time spent with doctors. At Walt's own social gatherings the topic of conversation from decade to decade had changed from "who's doing what" to "what happened to whom". His peer group all knew that, as a good friend observed to him, "Ain't none of us getting out of this alive." Still, Ol' Jim survived a major heart attack, induced coma, and emotional trauma of major proportions, and that had to be testimony to his determination to linger on a bit, to good effect it appeared.

Some argued, as did his own father-in-law, that one should fight life's exit down to the last remaining breath, echoing the view of Thomas Wolfe that we should go raging into that dark, stormy night. Others counseled that leaving this world could be a gentle journey that we should embrace and experience in the most sensitive, thoughtful reflection we can bring to it. One of Walt's friends, weary and a bit bored, simply cancelled dialysis. A dramatic gesture, no doubt, but then he was an artist who loved a "happening". He got one.

Still, recognition of one truth for all men, death, formed an inevitable part of everyone's self-awareness, and it gave Walt the ability to embrace endless iterations of life itself. He came to acknowledge that what we are born with, self, we die with, and in the passing we live for better or for worse. He himself spent a good amount of time creating his life's story in his own mind, finding that the construct had a happy ending.

Farmer kept track of his physical decline mostly curious about how it expressed itself and how fast it occurred. Slowing movement, sleeping more, longer reflections, travelling less, all of this he believed to be natural functions of aging, and he tried best to capture it by saying that it was not the things he could not do that were so noticeable. Rather, it was recovering from things that he *chose to do* that he tried to note. An active day of walking, golfing, even visiting with friends now no longer followed day after day. Rather, a rest interval came to be a part of the formula for good living.

Walt tried to respond to the demands of his body, even as he wondered what system would begin to fail first, what cues he might detect that he had reached yet another stage of decline. He gave little thought to recovering the zest, energy and frivolous life that he embraced even a few years ago. Still, as alert as he remained, his body had surprised him.

Everyone over the age of 65 needed a cardiologist. Almost all of his friends had one, and they seemed to know what they were doing. He once had one, but when Walt refused to see him as requested, the doc fired him for non-compliance. He didn't miss a heartbeat over that.

Still, curious about what cardiologists said to his friends, he tapped their experiences thinking that he might pick up a tip or two to keep him from having to actually talk to Dr. Whoever. They reported to him the perturbations of their cardiovascular behavior that they brought to their consultations with their specialist. He learned from conversation that cardiologists really do know more about one's heart than the average person wants to know, and they can advise you with wisdom and expertise as to procedures, timing and penalties for ignoring their advice. It was a powerful position they held in life, one not to be used lightly and they seldom did. Still, he did not like them.

His most recent glance at a cardiologist actually occurred because he could not pee. Now, he knew that when one cannot pee, one goes to a urologist, not the heartbeat fellow. However, the problem had to do with a benign stricture in the urethra and that meant that he needed to have a surgery, and that meant that he needed to be hospitalized and that meant that he needed a clearance from...his cardiologist, a gigantic shadow on his wall of life. All paths led to him.

He already knew the cardiologist he would not choose. But who could he turn to? Who might have the warmth and paternal guidance that might see him through this matter-of-fact procedure of being declared ready for surgery. While getting an updated echocardiogram, Walt asked his technician and he recommended a local man who had a warm personality, an easy smile and a real commitment to his patients health. "He doesn't like loose ends," his techie said. Since no other name came to his attention, Walt booked him.

His new cardiologist, short, smiling, round-faced, quick in his movement and his language, spoke with a little accent but he looked Walt right in his eyes, and assessed his sense of anxiety. Consulting Walt about his medical history, Dr. Cardio asked that he get a CAT scan of his coronary arteries, and then they could talk about the A-Fib, a long-standing feature of his heart rhythm, and how it might best be managed for the impending surgery.

Curious, Farmer asked why the CAT scan, and Cardio replied that it was just a base-line test that he administered to people Walt's age. His age? What did his age have to do with anything in his arteries. His problem was that he could not pee. Maybe he really was in the wrong office. But no, Cardio insisted, "we" needed to have that information, and Walt recognizing that he could not get repaired without clearance, introduced himself to radiology and spent some time in the CAT tube.

A week later, they met again in that friendly cautious way that new acquaintances have, and Walt waited for Cardio's perfunctory approval, signed slip and hearty "good luck with your surgery". Instead, he received a sheet of paper, the report from the CAT scan, and a finger pointing him to the appropriate segments of it, and there he read that he had 90% calcium deposits in all of his coronary arteries, and was in danger of a heart attack...maybe. He almost had one on the spot. If he could have peed, he would have.

He gathered himself, "Does this mean that I am at a 90% chance in favor of a heart attack at any time?"

"No," Doc replied and those were the first good words he had heard from him since walking in a few days ago.

The doc went on, "What it means is that you have calcification in your arteries, but we don't know if it is in the lining of the blood vessels, in which case we can ignore it, or if it is emerging and blocking the flow of blood in which case we cannot ignore it."

"Well, how do 'we' know?" Farmer asked in a more collegial, confidential tone.

"I will need to do an angiogram, run some dye up into your arteries, take a look at them with a scope and see what is going on. If there are minor blockages, I can insert a stent or two, but if the passages are too closed off, you will need a by-pass operation, and I can recommend an excellent, skilled surgeon."

The doc said all of this very quickly, as was his natural conversational style, but Walt managed to hear the words "blockages", "stent", and "by-pass" just fine and he became both frightened and pissed off. Well, not really pissed off because that was a part of his problem, but he was angry that he had to deal with this damn heart issue. One small thing just seemed to lead to another, larger thing.

Still, he told himself, angiograms were common, outcomes good and information seemed essential to knowing how to proceed. If it came to a by-pass, he told himself, he could do that. After all, Henry Kissinger survived and flourished following quintuple by-pass surgery more than two decades ago. Kissinger's main concern upon regaining consciousness was whether he had more by-passes than did Al Haig. He did. Hell, if Henry could do it, so could he.

So, he placed himself in Dr. Cardio's hands and off he went to fill out papers, answer questions and visit the hospital early one morning for an angiogram (possible angioplasty), looking forward to a nice easy escape into an anesthesia, and a hope that the examination of his arteries would be helpful, reassuring, transitory.

He noted a new ritual in the O.R. before he escaped into the black night, vocal orders for "time out" to review what the surgery would be, who was the patient on the table (he was) and was everyone ready? They were. And so was he with his last request being, "Let me know before you give me the sleep potion, please." He knew that he might enter that great beyond from which no one returns, but he would do it peacefully as his mother had told him he should when he had his tonsils out. For him, peace meant getting mentally ready before the potion flowed into his veins.

"Just give me a couple of seconds to be ready, O.K.?" he asked, and they did. He saw the lights above turn into a mosaic of colors featuring red, yellow and green, "A new image" he thought, "That's different." Then he didn't think anymore.

Two days later, he was back in his doctor's office to get official confirmation of his status. Dr. Cardio smiled in that warm easy manner he had and reported that the calcification was in the lining of Walt's arteries. No need for stents; no need for by-passes. He was good to go for the pissing surgery and doc signed his waiver which he promptly sent off to his specialist in San Francisco.

Three months later, peeing freely, he visited his compassionate cardiologist again, and learned that his A-Fib was a chronic condition, not to worry (Good!) and he would control it and Walt's blood pressure with medications. Hmmmm, o.k. Pills were easy.

Eighteen months more and Farmer called for a meeting, thinking that his diastolic blood pressure seemed elevated. They met again, Dr. Cardio confirming it as high, but also taking note of his pulse, hovering in the high 30s. "I don't like that," he said, "and I don't like loose ends. Here, see my nurse and get wired with a monitor that will record your pulse for the next 24 hours."

Again, looking for a pill, Walt became instead a pegboard for electronic inserts, more diagnostics, and for a day he walked and slept with a half-dozen wires dangling, tangling, and recording everything going on in his heart. Did Doc really need to know this? Walt did not like the possibilities.

He sat with the friendly face in his white coat in a large office as he went through paper work full of lines, scribbles, waving graphs, close knit symbols and finally, he said to Farmer, "Look at this."

"I don't want to look at that. Just tell me what you are thinking."

"No," he responded with that quick tempo he carried and which always amused, "I want you to look at this." So, Walt, trying to be a thoughtful patient, looked and flipped the pages, thinking that this visual scan would help educate him to whatever it was the doc saw. He did not like that he saw anything. He pointed to some isolated squiggles very tightly bunched and asked, what is this? "Ventricular fibrillation" he heard, a phrase which he knew and associated with sudden death. He looked up, "That's not good is it?"

"Oh, it is just a passing twitch. I can treat it with medication. However, look at your pulse range." So he did. His heart beating at about 38, sometimes 144. "Quite a range," Walt commented, "Why the high number?"

"Precisely. It is the range that I am concerned about," Dr. Cardio began, "When I treat the high number, I will influence the low number and you have nowhere down to go on the low number." He paused, then he took the papers to his counter, flipped some pages, murmured to himself, then said under his breath (those near silent musings that conceal bad news but which eventually become fully uttered words), "I guess we might as well just get to it."

He turned to me, "I think you need a pacemaker."

Farmer's mind raced, though his pulse did not. At least there was no pounding in his head. He paused, asked for time to think about this idea, gave it 10 seconds of reflection and replied, "Why the hell is it that every time I come in here, you want me to do something I don't want to do!"

Quick as words can follow words, doc replied in his soft, but firm voice, "Remember, it is you who called me." Walt shut up and went quietly.

Dr. Cardio smiled. Then he reported that he did not do this kind of surgery, but would refer Walt to a man who was very highly skilled in the procedure. "Pacers are delicate...precise insertions requires great skill. This doc is excellent...best in the area."

Two weeks later, Mike the nurse wheeled him into the cath-lab where he learned that this procedure did not require full anesthesia, but rather "twilight" consciousness.

"You know," Esther, another nurse said, "like when you have a colonoscopy." He remembered that all right. In fact as soon as they got him wired, he would get plumbed again on his regular five year schedule.

"Yep, I know that...twilight eh? Well, when you are ready to give me the juice let me know a few seconds before. I want to get ready."

"No problem," she said.

Then, as he lay there stone cold conscious, technicians began to attach yet more wires to him, a dozen he counted and was amused that they had difficulty in finding the right tab to go with the correct lead.

"I think it is over here, Numbered 4 and black, right?"

"No," the mentor replied, "That will be under here...now where did that wire go...oh, o.k. see, then you just match it up to this other one which is red, check the number and find the patch...now where is it? Oh, here we go."

Farmer glanced at the monitor above his head to see what the wires said, but they were all flat lines and he guessed, hoped really, that this meant they were not connected. Otherwise, the procedure would be a waste of talent and time.

Finally, the wires ready, the nurse with his "twilight juice" said, "O.K., here it comes, take a moment to get ready."

He did, and awaited previous experiences of lights changing, reality falling away really fast, dim, dim, then black. In his more optimistic thinking, he would die, then come back to life.

But, he didn't die. He didn't even get woozy nor slip into twilight. Nothing happened. He asked the nurse. She said give it a minute. Still nothing. Farmer asked for more twilight and she checked with the doctor who had arrived now, and he nodded yes. She gave him another dose. Still, not much happening there.

Perception softened. Then, a cool antiseptic dampened the entire area on his upper chest where the pacemaker incision would be made. It felt good. He told them that, and they swabbed it again. He liked that. Then, they told Walt that they were going to inject the site with lidocaine, and he thought to himself, "Great, now I'll fade into twilight." But he did not.

LOUD MUSIC began to blare from the ceiling. It reverberated throughout the cath lab and it was raucous, heavy metal poundings and Walt heard someone say, "I just love *99 Red*

Balloons". He himself did not see any balloons, but he did ask that they turn down the volume on those raging guitars that stripped him of his hard-won equanimity. He even said it nicely, "Could you turn down the music, please. It is too loud, way too loud."

"No," came this answer from the voice of God. "I like this music and I enjoy listening to it while I do procedures."

He wasn't going to argue with his surgeon, and he asked for more twilight. Done, and he awakened in his room.

So, for a month, he could not drive, could not golf, could not raise his left arm above his shoulder. Comforted to hear that his veins were open, smooth and large, discomforted to learn that meant that his range of motion with the left arm was even more carefully constricted so as not to disturb those wires while they became fixed, enmeshed in scar tissue.

He saw his Red Balloon rocker a week after the implant. Walt was doing well, and RB Doc had a nice way of describing it. "Your heart is healthy, valves are tight. Your veins are smooth and clear, your arteries open It is your electrical system that is deteriorating, and we can always solve that." Comforting.

He mentioned that he had sutured in 100 stiches to hold the device in place, and Walt thought that figured. One stitch for every Red Balloon and one extra just to be sure. Maybe that was why the doc liked that that song so well.

Finally, RB Doc commented that the discoloration was to be expected, the paper stitches which held the surface skin together would disappear in just another few weeks, and he set Farmer's voltage amplitude at 2.5 or 3 (he was never quite sure), commenting that it could be changed as needed.

"Takes one volt to make the heart contract," he said, "and we send at least two, just to be sure." Comforting.

Walt saw his regular cardiologist a month later, expecting compassion and congratulations and he got them. Happy faces all around and the pronouncement that Farmer was good to go for years now. He could remember his youth when he thought of his future in decades. The time frame had changed.

Walt smiled. Having a resting pulse of 70 compared to one of 38 might help. If it improved metabolism, perhaps he would shed some years, maybe some weight. Maybe he would feel younger. Maybe he would lose seven years of age and evolve into a frisky 70 year old again. Who knew?

Pitter-pat. Pitter-pat.

Printed in the United States
by Bookmasters

Printed in the United States
By Bookmasters